PRAISE

A rich, emotionally charged story that will captivate readers who are drawn to complex characters, literary mysteries, and the powerful forces of love, loss, and memory.
— ROD CARLEY, award-winning author of *Ruff*

In *The Lost Queen*, Heidi von Palleske steps back into the haunting, beautiful world she first conjured in *Two White Queens and the One-Eyed Jack*. She writes with a kind of quiet magic — the kind that sneaks up on you, the kind that makes ordinary moments shimmer. Von Palleske sees the world through both a camera lens and a poet's eye, every frame alive, every line rich with feeling. She doesn't just tell a story; she immerses you in one — guiding you through the dark toward something warm, luminous, and deeply human. It's a book to fall into, get lost in, and come out the other side changed.
— THOM ERNST, film critic and author of *The Wild Boy of Waubamik*

In the mesmerizing second novel of her trilogy, von Palleske plunges her extraordinary characters ever deeper into a cauldron of pain, suffering, and unbearable loss, yet always with abundant charm, wit, and abiding tenderness for their hardships and longings. In lesser hands the proceedings risk collapsing under their own weight, but the author's love, admiration, and even awe for her flawed creations is so genuine, and her hopes for their forbearance and transcendence held so dear, that we can't help but take these people into our hearts, hold them tight, share their struggles, and cheer their victories as our own. What a stellar writer. What a moving read. This book ripped my guts out in the very best way.
— JEFFREY HIRSCHFIELD, co-creator and writer of *Lexx*

Heidi von Palleske's *The Lost Queen* is darkly funny, heart-rending, occasionally disturbing, and ultimately uplifting — a novel filled with richly drawn, almost Dickensian characters whom I found myself missing long after the final page.

— PETER HORTON, author of *North*

Heidi von Palleske's long-awaited sequel to *Two White Queens and the One-Eyed Jack* arrives with all the invention, mystery, and emotional charge of the first book — and then some. *The Lost Queen* picks up the threads of her unforgettable characters and the wild, uncanny world she created, carrying them forward with wit, beauty, and a deepening sense of intrigue. Told with energy and soul, the story opens up each character in ways that make whole sections fly by, pulling the reader onward with the irresistible need to know: *Where, oh where, is the lost queen?* A richly imagined, compulsively readable novel. Highly recommended.

— ADRIAN HOUGH, actor (*Assassin's Creed*, *X-Men*)

A haunting meditation on love, loss, and the fierce power of art — *The Lost Queen* illuminates the architecture of longing with rare grace.

— KATI PRESTON, author of *Hidden*

A shimmering odyssey, Heidi von Palleske's novel grabs the reader by the heart and never lets go. A cast of audacious and unforgettable characters, each grappling with a profound loss, joins forces on an epic international search for their beloved lost queen. Exquisitely written, heart-rending, and at times deliciously funny, this story evokes all the senses as it explores what it means to fully love and live.

— BARBARA RADECKI, author of *The Darkhouse*

An operatic ensemble cast, vibrant colours, a mystery to solve and ... cakes. Von Palleske serves a novel like a slice of *apfelkuchen*, layered with sights and scents, twining memory and introspection. Fairytale, modern romance, mythic, sometimes witchy, *The Lost Queen* gives fans of *Two White Queens and The One-Eyed Jack* more to love.
— EMILY A. WEEDON, author of *Autokrator* and *Hemo Sapiens*

At the end of this wonderful book, you will have three thoughts: (1) Wow, I learned a lot; (2) I'm going to miss you, book; and (3) When do I get the third book? A wonderful, deep, touching, beautifully crafted book. Heidi von Palleske is a master storyteller.
— MATT ZIMBEL, filmmaker and host of *Yes We Canada*

PRAISE FOR *TWO WHITE QUEENS AND THE ONE-EYED JACK*

Exquisite writing ... a gorgeous book.
— DANIEL BAIRD, co-founder of *The Brooklyn Rail*

Lush, raw, poetic, and rich. The book uses language to paint a picture. The characters leap off the page. The dialogue is razor-sharp, with both humour and pathos ... This book is original, unlike anything I have ever read, and I am quite sure that I will return to it many times. A brilliant piece of writing!
— EVE CRAWFORD, author of *I Paint Gophers*

This novel weaves worlds together. It is not only full of sensual imagery and pinpoint details, but it is also brave, bold, and necessary.
— LAUREN B. DAVIS, author of *The Grimoire of Kensington Market* and *Even So*

Quirky and meticulous, *Two White Queens and the One-Eyed Jack* is a literary novel of substantial merit.

— *FOREWORD REVIEWS*

I loved it. It captured me and I could not put it down. Great original storytelling!

— JEREMY IRONS, Academy Award–winning actor

A life-changing childhood accident, one that is formative of the adult lives to follow, is a testimony to D.H. Lawrence's view of the novel as "the highest complex of subtle interrelatedness." How the characters in this story are interconnected is a marvel of storytelling. This is a novel about the calamitous changes in history, in both personal and national history.

— JOHN IRVING, acclaimed novelist and Academy Award–winning screenwriter

Such a title promises an out-of-the-ordinary experience, and author Heidi von Palleske delivers ... This is a dense book with a large field of characters and multiple storylines that required Palleske's deft hand to knit it together.

— *THE MIRAMICHI READER*

A brilliant novel with its conceptual expansiveness, its eclectic characters with their quirky attributes, and its erudition and keen observations about so many things. Heidi's writing is a seamless fusion of poetry and prose.

— JEFFREY SIDE, reviewer and editor

THE
LOST
QUEEN

THE LOST QUEEN

HEIDI VON PALLESKE

Copyright © Heidi von Palleske, 2026

All rights reserved. No part of this publication may be reproduced, stored in a retrieval system, or transmitted in any form or by any means, electronic, mechanical, photocopying, recording, or otherwise (except for brief passages for purpose of review) without the prior permission of Dundurn Press. Permission to photocopy should be requested from Access Copyright.

All characters in this work are fictitious. Any resemblance to real persons, living or dead, is purely coincidental.

Publisher and acquiring editor: Meghan Macdonald | Editor: Shannon Whibbs
Cover designer: Laura Boyle
Cover image: 123RF/lisaanfisa

Library and Archives Canada Cataloguing in Publication

Title: The lost queen / Heidi von Palleske.
Names: Palleske, Heidi von, 1960- author.
Identifiers: Canadiana (print) 20250310406 | Canadiana (ebook) 20250315394 | ISBN 9781459756915 (softcover) | ISBN 9781459756908 (EPUB) | ISBN 9781459756892 (PDF)
Subjects: LCGFT: Novels.
Classification: LCC PS8631.A444 l67 2026 | DDC C813/.6—dc23

We acknowledge the support of the Canada Council for the Arts and the Ontario Arts Council for our publishing program. We also acknowledge the financial support of the Government of Ontario, through the Ontario Book Publishing Tax Credit and Ontario Creates, and the Government of Canada.

Care has been taken to trace the ownership of copyright material used in this book. The author and the publisher welcome any information enabling them to rectify any references or credits in subsequent editions.

The publisher is not responsible for websites or their content unless they are owned by the publisher.

Printed and bound in Canada.

Dundurn Press
1382 Queen Street East
Toronto, Ontario, Canada M4L 1C9
dundurn.com, @dundurnpress

For those who have been lost by chance.
For those who have been lost by choice.

Somehow you started and lost your way,
And now there'll be no time for play,
No time for joy, no time for friends,
Not even time to make amends.
— Cheshire Cat, in Lewis Carroll's
Alice in Wonderland (1865)

PROLOGUE

1994 — Cape Town International Airport

POOF! SHE WAS GONE.

Clara was nowhere to be found. At first Blanca assumed that her twin sister might have wandered off, gone to get a coffee or a snack before boarding the flight home to Berlin.

"Where's Clara?" Blanca asked the others.

Panic. The calling of her name. The rushing. The pandemonium. And then, the last and final boarding call.

All Blanca could feel was the pounding of her heart in her ears, like the African drumming they had heard the previous night at the Artscape Theatre; a theatre where they had performed only three days earlier, in celebration of Mandela's election.

"Are you feeling better?" a tall Black woman with kind eyes and a soft smile asked, her voice breaking through the pounding of Blanca's heart. "Do you need to sit down?"

"Better?" Blanca asked back in reply.

"Yes, you fainted. Your husband said it is because you are with child. He carried you out of the washroom."

"My husband?" Blanca's voice was filled with confusion and panic.

"Yes, a big man. Blond. Blue eyes. A very expensive-looking suit."

Blanca grabbed at the woman, wanting answers. What did he look like? Where did he go? The woman became fearful. She backed away as though she were looking at a ghost. Then she started running. Fast. Into the crowd of people. Out of sight. Out of reach. Blanca's only thread of hope, her only connection to her twin, had vanished.

♦ ♦ ♦

Later, Blanca stared at her reflection in the hotel bathroom mirror. The face that stared back could just as easily be her sister looking at her. Same eyes, same mouth with its smear of red. Blanca blinked as the last tear, caught in the heavy fringe of her white lashes, was released, tracing a path over her cheekbone, into the hollow of her cheek, and finally resting at the corner of her downturned mouth. Salty. Very salty. Like the Dead Sea. If she were to fill a tub with her tears, could she float as easily as she once had in the sea? Without any effort at all. Lifted, supported, and as weightless as a spirit out of body and out of time. Could she ever become so buoyant that her body might lift above her sorrows?

Blanca wanted to believe that her mirror image really was her twin, that the face staring at her was not hers but the face that belonged to the other half of her soul. She reached out her hand and placed it on the cool glass of the mirror, touching her reflection.

"I'll find you, Clara. I'll find you."

ONE

2002

THE BEST FUNERALS INCLUDE RAIN. There is something perverse about a sun shining, full of promise, as a casket is lowered into the open earth. Open like a gaping mouth. An old man's mouth. A mouth that has anticipated food and then forgotten all about it once the food's been placed inside it, awaiting mastication.

Iris smiled to herself but lowered her head so no one would see. She thought it was funny how *mastication* and *masturbation* sounded so alike in English. Easy to get them mixed up. *Inappropriate thoughts for the side of a grave.*

She stood quite alone, away from her family. All she really wanted was to be reassured, to belong, and to be loved. Loved like her younger brother was, without expectation. She glanced at little Fritzi, standing directly across the grave from her, nestled into his mother's side, her arm protecting him more from the sadness than from the light rain.

A hand touched Iris on her shoulder. She felt the ceasing of rain on her face and knew that whoever was touching her shoulder must have an umbrella in the other hand. Then she heard words in her own language. They wrapped around her like a childhood blanket that had been lost then miraculously rediscovered at the bottom of a cedar chest.

"*Es hat zu viel Traurigkeit gegeben.* Far too much sadness, little one."

Yes, Iris thought, *Hilda is right. There is too much sadness!* Wise words. How kind of her. How grandmotherly! But the elderly woman was not her grandmother. Her grandmother was at the head of the grave, crying. *Of course*, she was crying, Uncle Tristan was her *son*. The poor woman was burying her child, her first-born. Iris understood the proper order. Parents bring children into the world, and children see their parents out of the world; this funeral was a mockery of the natural order. Iris watched her real grandmother and felt sorry for her but felt no connection to her. She could be any woman grieving. Any poor woman at the head of an open grave. Was it culture or geography that separated her from her real grandmother? Why were there so many miles between them, even as they directly faced each other across the opened earth?

Iris felt a squeeze on her shoulder before the hand released her.

"I have made *Apfelkuchen*. Surely you like that?" Hilda whispered in her ear.

"It's my favourite." Iris smiled up at her.

Iris looked from face to face and tried to read what was in each heart. Sadness and loss, but also a resigned knowing. Her eyes moved to Jack, standing on his own, off to one side. She focused on him, the man whom she called *Uncle Jack*, her father's oldest and dearest friend. She had never seen a portrait of pain quite like that. She had never seen what the loss of love could do. How harsh love was! How cruel! Better, she thought, to never love than to be ripped apart like that.

She felt connected, not to him, but to his grief. She knew that one day she would be the one to give this grieving man another chance. She knew that she would be the one to make it all right. She just didn't yet know how.

♦ ♦ ♦

Iris looked at all the little bottles, the vials, and the droppers. She quickly glanced into the living room. All the adults were eating cake, drinking coffee, and politely consoling one another. A hug, a tear wiped away, and then more strained conversation between people she should know but could not keep straight. Clearly nobody was interested in her, or anything she might do, so she opened the first vial, brought it to her nose, and inhaled deeply. The aroma was so strong that it burned the inside of her nose. She sniffed again, more hesitantly this time. A long, steady inhalation. She could taste the smell at the back of her throat. Yes, she knew what it was! It was the smell of whatever seasoning is put onto a turkey when it is roasting.

A calm came over her body. She no longer felt anxiety about being in a strange house, in a strange land. Even the weeping in the next room seemed to float away from her. Perhaps it was just that the smell made her think of festive meals. There was always something calming about a turkey dinner with all the trimmings. And then there was always that sleepiness that overtook you so you couldn't keep your eyes open, hard as you might try. Another sniff and the memory of previous holidays flooded into her, but in fractured pieces, like bits of a dream that pop into your brain, out of order and unexpected.

Iris put the cap back on and twisted it closed. *Holidays.* When her mother was still in their lives, they had very festive holidays with family, friends, and visitors. The memory of her mother left a hole in her heart, the size of her heart. Iris had been born with a hole in her heart. It was two centimetres across, or so she was told. The other half of her heart compensated and grew twice as big, pressing into her belly so that she could never eat more than a few mouthfuls at a time. She was a grazer, not an eater. Instead of meals there were snacks available to her all day long. Nuts mostly. And chocolate. Iris was fuelled on hazelnuts and chocolate; those were her go-to food groups.

She looked through the other tiny bottles: bergamot, lavender, grapefruit. *Grapefruit, really? Like the bitter but juicy fruit?* One sniff and it was confirmed. Yes, grapefruit, tart and hearty. Then there was rose and eucalyptus, ylang-ylang, mint, and oregano. Between the oregano and the thyme was sage. Then marigold, and lilac.

Not in any order, she thought. It bothered her that the little bottles stood there in mismatched, small vials, hand-labelled and entirely in no order that she could see. What harm would it do if she moved the little bottles, arranged them alphabetically? Surely that would be helpful?

Iris took all the bottles and put them onto the desk in front of her. There had to be over seventy altogether, each holding a smell and an experience of its own. *Little brown bottle soldiers*, she thought. *All lined up and ready to be called upon.*

Then, there it was, amongst the others. A vial of cocoa — liquid, dark, and intense. She looked over her shoulder again, crept to the sofa with the bottle in her hand, and twisted the top off. Then she brought the bottle to her nose. Oh, yes! More intense than any chocolate she had ever ingested. It was pure happiness in a bottle. She knew she could get addicted to this. She brought it close to one nostril, exhaled harshly, so that no air would enter her lungs, just the essence itself. Then slowly, deeply, she breathed in the aroma, filling her nostrils, her lungs, her senses.

"Hey! Go easy on that!"

Iris jumped up and tried to hide the bottle behind her back.

"I was just …"

"Looking?" asked Jack.

"Yes."

"Well, shall we look together, then?"

"Yes," Iris agreed, relieved that Jack was not angry with her.

Jack held out his hand, and Iris reluctantly relinquished the vial. Who knew that comfort, that joy, that escape, could come in such a small bottle?

"I see you are rearranging. You know, my mother once rearranged my darkroom when I was just a bit older than you. The way I had things made no sense to her, so she thought she was helping. It took me forever to find things again after that. Your way is not always the best way for others."

"But I was trying to help. It was with the best of intentions," Iris objected.

"The road to Hell is paved with good intentions," Jack reminded her.

"We both know that isn't true. There is no Hell because if there was a Hell, there would also be a Heaven, and that would mean that there is also a God. And there is no God!"

It was clear that Iris was expecting a reaction. Her arms were crossed over her chest in a defiant manner. Jack shut his eyes and sighed. What to say to her? At twelve, this precocious girl knew loss better than anyone. Her mother gone, disappeared into thin air, when the girl was barely four. No endings, no goodbyes. One moment in her life and the next … poof, she was gone. If there had been a loving God, how could that have happened? And if there was a loving God, why did Tristan have to die? Jack had believed in the concept of fate since he was a child, since he had lost his eye because he had dared to climb too high, but did he ever believe in God? In an omnipresent power who cared about your every move, someone who loved you unconditionally, someone who was a heavenly father? No.

"You're right. There is no God. Oh, and there's no Santa Claus, either."

Hilda was leaning against the doorframe, watching her son as he talked to the precocious little girl. What a wisp of a thing she was! A fairy, really, with messy red hair, so wavy and overwhelming that it seemed to weigh more than the child's whole body. Hilda took note of their reactions as they opened and sniffed various essential oils. The delight, the wincing, and the sheer surprise.

"What about this one?" she overheard Jack ask.

"We had a soap that smelled like that. Is it lilac?" Iris guessed.

"No, lavender."

"Well, close. They both start with an *L*!"

"Not at all!" Jack laughed. "A lilac is a tree. The flowers are high up. Lavender grows in gardens near the ground."

"You seem happier now. Is it because of the smells?" young Iris asked him.

"I only *seem* happier."

"Did you love him? Uncle Tristan?"

"Yes."

"But I thought my dad was your best friend," Iris pressed.

"He is. Your father, Gareth, is my very best friend in the whole world. We've been friends since we were much younger than you. But I loved Tristan in a different way."

"Loved him ... how?"

Jack shook his head. Reached for a bottle labelled YLANG-YLANG. He popped the lid open, took a sniff, and offered the bottle to Iris.

"Try this one," he suggested, changing the topic.

Iris wrinkled her nose and pushed the bottle away.

"Do you think there is life after death?" she asked.

"No idea. Most of the time I cannot figure out life, let alone think about what comes after it."

"I think there is." Iris moved closer to Jack, confiding, "My grandmother visits me all the time. Not her" — she pointed to Gareth's mother, Elaine, grieving in the next room — "the one with the long red hair. Like me!"

"Your dead grandmother visits you? Really? What does she tell you?"

"Not much. She rarely speaks. She just looks and smiles. Sometimes she nods or waves. She likes to collect rocks. Her pockets are full of them! Anyhow, that's how I know my mother is still alive."

"She told you?" Jack asked, careful to keep any concern from his voice. He had secretly searched for her mother, Clara, but after months of looking he'd returned, quite convinced that Clara was dead.

"No," Iris laughed. "But if my grandmother can make the effort to visit from the dead, then my mother would, too. She loved me more than anyone, but she hasn't visited me. Ergo, she is still alive. It's just logic, Uncle Jack!"

Jack stared at the child, wondering if she was simply making up stories in order to make herself seem special or if she believed her stories and had surrendered herself to her imagination.

"And how long has this been going on? These visits from dead people?"

"I think they started just after my mom was stolen."

"Does it frighten you?" he asked her.

"No. Why should it?" The girl laughed. She had a slight gap between her teeth.

"And does your grandmother come to you in dreams or when you are wide awake?" Jack was curious but cautious.

"In between, silly!" Iris laughed again and gave Jack a shove.

"In between? What do you mean?"

"You know. Not awake and not asleep."

Outside the room, Hilda continued to watch the exchange between her grieving son and his best friend's daughter. She watched the comfort they gave each other. The ease they had as they laughed. The hint of joy on a joyless day.

Hilda walked into the study. She took a small bottle from the table. Iris watched, worried that she might be in big trouble for moving the bottles from the shelves.

"Do you want to try something special?"

Iris nodded.

Hilda showed her the bottle of patchouli and slowly opened the top. She waved the bottle under the girl's nose.

"Now take it in — just a little — and tell me what you feel."

Hilda watched closely. She only pretended to be interested in the girl's reaction. What she really wanted was a good look at Iris's eyes. Light grey, darkening to the pupils, with a dark circular ring at the outset of the iris. Light grey with flecks of gold. Eyes that were the same as hers and Jack's. Rare eyes. Central-heterochromia-hazel-grey-coloured eyes.

◆ ◆ ◆

Jack walked from the living room to the kitchen, carrying bits and pieces. Dishes with half-eaten cake and sandwiches. Empty coffee cups and glasses with melted ice cubes. It was like cleaning up after a party. A sad party where the band never showed up and the guests left early.

"Go to bed, Jack, it's been a long day," Hilda said.

"I'm okay. I think I'll have a nightcap. We can clean up in the morning."

"Are you okay?"

"No." Jack gave his mother a weak half smile.

Hilda put her hand to her heart. She felt the world stop for a moment as she watched her only son. Such a handsome man and so accomplished. Working for Reuters and travelling the world, bringing news to everyone. And here he was, when everything should be perfect for him, not well.

"How long have you known?" Hilda asked.

"Known what?"

"That you are ill, too?"

"I'm not ill, Mom. I'm sad."

Hilda started to cry. She wiped her face on a tea towel and shrugged it all off as foolishness. The day had just been too much for her. She had known Tristan since he was a young boy, watched him grow up and strike out in the world. And she had seen her own son fall in love with him.

"What makes me most sad is that we had an argument. I didn't know that he was ill at the time. I was so angry with him. So, I shut him out. I threw myself into work. I travelled. And I went looking for Iris's mom. I became obsessed with finding out what happened to her. By the time I came back, Tristan was in Casey House, stoned out of his mind on morphine. A skeleton. He didn't even know I was there."

"What did you fight about?"

Jack shrugged. What did it matter now? Tristan's opinion, his — none of it mattered. Jack opened the bottom drawer of the hutch and pulled out a single malt. He knew that his mother rarely drank. He motioned to the bottle, and to his surprise, she nodded in agreement.

"Ice?"

"No. Besides, I doubt we have any left," Hilda replied. "Why do you think he got sick and you didn't?"

"Really, Mom? You want specifics?"

Hilda nodded.

"Okay." Jack sighed. "I was never the catcher, always the pitcher."

Hilda sipped her drink. There were things she might never understand and, at her age, she wondered if there was any reason to start understanding them. Still, she couldn't help but ask questions, and more often than not, she found herself in a state of constant amazement.

"But Tristan must have gotten it from someone. If not you, then who?"

Jack shrugged. How could he tell his mother that there had been an understanding? They were loyal when together but had agreed to an open relationship while apart. He knew that Tristan would have preferred a more committed relationship, but Jack just couldn't be tied down. And now it was too late to change any of it.

"It was complicated, Mom. I made mistakes. We both did." Jack leaned back and closed his eyes. He could feel regret coiling around him, its barbs sinking past his flesh into his bones, his muscles, his blood. "And what about you? Don't you get lonely here by yourself, without Siegfried? Weren't you lonely when he died?"

"*Mein Gott*, you sound like your sisters! Always asking if I am lonely. Of course, I am lonely here without him. And you know I tried to live back in Germany, but I was lonely there without him, too. It turns out that loneliness is very good at following a person from place to place."

Jack busied himself, moving dishes from one place on the counter to another. It had always been that way with him, even as a boy. Whenever he wanted to divert a conversation, he found objects to busy himself with, not unlike young Iris with her bottles of essential oils.

"The little girl fell asleep before Gareth and Sabine went home, so I put her in the guest room." Hilda changed the topic to what she thought might be less unsettling.

"Not so little — she's twelve."

"She seems younger."

"Yes. In some ways. Precocious, though."

"It's a difficult time in a girl's life to not have a mother," Hilda persisted.

Jack topped up his drink.

"Sabine is like a mother to her. Loves her like she were her own. She really stepped up to the plate. It surprised me. Sabine was such a party girl back in the day." *Yes*, he thought, *Sabine has really blossomed in motherhood*. But he also wondered if she loved her own son, little Fritzi, just a little more than she loved Iris. She must; she held that child in her belly for nine months. Close to her heart. There must be a difference.

"Doesn't really look much like Gareth, does she?" Hilda pressed.

Jack finished his drink in a final gulp, put his glass down, and looked directly at his mother. "No, I guess she doesn't. But his son is a doppelgänger. Little Fritzi doesn't look much like Sabine. Genetics are a funny thing. I look like you. My sisters look like Dad."

Truths are hidden in silences, in what is not spoken. Words so easily deceive, mislead, seduce, lie. Jack's silence told Hilda everything she needed to know.

"She has your eyes, Jack."

"She can't have my eyes, because I only have one. Remember? I fell from a tree. I lost an eye."

Hilda stood, feeling that too-familiar tightness in her hip. She knew that sooner or later she would have to have it replaced. She was bone-weary. Too much sadness, too much work, and far too many questions. She wrapped her arms around her grieving son and kissed the top of his head. Some things never change. He looked and spoke like a man, quite independent in the world, but he still held the smell of childhood at the top of his head.

"I think I'll go up to bed now," she told him.

◆ ◆ ◆

Finally, in the quiet, Jack could fully feel. The first expressions of sorrow were like the soft cries of a small, injured coyote. Then came a raspy intake of air, filling his lungs with pain, followed by the final sobs that had been waiting patiently in the wings the entire day.

There was only one thing left for him to do. He opened the box that Elaine, Tristan's mother, had given him after the funeral. There was Tristan's first camera. He moved the camera to his good eye, focusing through the viewer, remembering the first time he had done exactly that in Tristan's room so many years before. Under the camera was an envelope with his name on it. Jack opened it and took out a video tape. Written across the tape were the words TRISTAN'S VIDEO DIARY.

Jack pushed the tape into the VCR. After the colour code and a few seconds of black, there was Tristan, looking healthy and handsome — and very much alive.

"Today, I found out that I have AIDS. I will document this final journey to show the world what we are fighting against. So that we will no longer be ignored. This is an epidemic. Every day I will check in to tell you how I am feeling. Every single day, that is, until there are no more days."

◆ ◆ ◆

Siegfried's smell had left the sweater years ago, but Hilda still liked to wrap its worn sleeves around herself. When she first started wearing her dead husband's sweater, she would inhale his smell and then, as she slipped her smaller frame into it, she'd imagine his arms around her in an embrace. There was comfort there, in the imagining, in the remembering. Until the day came when his smell had been entirely inhaled and he was gone.

Once his smell had left, she hung on to every remembered moment, but how could that compare to the instant memory triggered by a scent? So Hilda decided she would try to re-create the smell of her great love. She would create Siegfried's aroma and put it back onto his sweater, the one that she wore in the early hours. The blue hours. The quiet hours, when others were holding on to that last precious bit of sleep but were missing that magic time. The time when the dew was still wet. The time when the fox and the owl were both awake and the larks were just starting their song. The time that was neither night nor morning, when the sun and the moon shared the sky together. It was Hilda's favourite time; she could be with her memories, without the sadness that often comes in the light of day or the dark of night. It was this in-between time when the calm of the world and the calm of her inner being could rest together before the sun's rays shone brightly on the chaos of the day.

Hilda had searched everywhere for Siegfried's smell, sniffing his aftershave, trying to find a trace of him on his feather pillow, or wearing one of his scarves or hats. Then she tried mixing his aftershave with the soap he always used. But no matter what she added to her mixture, it still wasn't quite right. Something was missing. Then she realized that the missing ingredient was her own scent. From the time that he had decided to love her, he wore *her* somehow. He had carried her with him. She had left her mark on him. But what was that scent exactly?

As Hilda was not one for commercial perfume, her scent would have to be a combination of her activities. The time she spent outdoors, the things she grew, the things she cooked. Marigold, basil, plums, and coffee. She mixed that with a few drops of Old Spice and a teaspoon of beer and then left it out in the sunshine. A few hours later, there it was! As close to Siegfried as she could get. And with one inhalation he seemed to live again.

Her longing and missing opened a new path for Hilda; she found herself growing things in her garden as much for their different scents as she did for food. Every flower, every herb, could be eaten or turned into an essence. She boiled things down, used a cold press, and extracted every smell she could. She distinguished between top notes, heart notes, and bottom notes as she made her own concoctions. Now, almost twelve years later, she still put on Siegfried's sweater in the blue hours to go into her garden. To putter about. To talk to her plants. To watch the sky lighten, bit by bit.

When she ventured out to her garden the morning after the funeral, she was surprised to see that she was not the only one up and about. Iris stood amidst the tall yellow flowers, cup flowers that seemed to reach their petals to the sky as they begged for drops of rain. Iris's wavy hair was catching a bit of early-morning light in brilliant red highlights on the top of her head.

How long until she notices me? Hilda wondered. But the child remained unaware. Her eyes were open, yet she seemed in a trance, gazing upward so that she could see the moon and the sun in the sky at the same time.

"Iris?" Hilda said softly.

Nothing. She touched Iris, felt her skin cold in the early morning air. Hilda slipped out of the sweater and felt the cool air blow through her light cotton nightie. Then she wrapped Siegfried's sweater around the trembling child and held her for a moment before gently leading her indoors and back to bed.

◆ ◆ ◆

Gareth awoke with a start, unsure, at first, of his surroundings. Yes, of course, he was back in Canada, in his mother's house, after all those years away. He draped his forearm over his high forehead and pressed his head into the pillows. Not as rich or as dense as what he had become accustomed to. No, these foam pillows were almost as old as he was. Boyhood pillows on a boyhood bed.

He could feel the shape of Sabine's body against his. Every curve rested and fit into his body, as though they had once been carved of the same stone and now, in sleep, they were joined together again. The slight arch of her back fit into the hollow of his chest. The shape of her round bottom spooned into his groin. Her head filled in under his chin. And their legs intertwined. Was it always like this, or had they grown to fit each other? Year by year, their bodies shaped the other's until every inch of flesh touched and rested safely with the other.

Perhaps one's sexual story is written in the first paragraph, Gareth thought. The first lovemaking session sets the tone for all that follows. There had been nothing at stake at first with Sabine. They were both young and up for some meaningless sex. If they pushed the boundaries too far, it was fine because what was there to lose? The sex was pure, without apology.

But then Clara, his teen love, reentered his life and everything changed. He left Sabine with all their sexual adventures, believing that Clara was his true, destined love. His soulmate. Sex was no longer pure because it was all mixed up with caring. Gareth had worried about *what* she thought and *how* she felt. He didn't want her to think he was perverse or too daring or too pushy, and so lovemaking fell into the realm of tender, but never entered the realm of abandonment. The first paragraph in the story of their lovemaking was written with a cautious and tentative pen. The desire for connection trumped the sheer joy of sex, and eventually, Gareth found it harder and harder to satisfy either of them. He loved her, of that he was sure. He would have gladly taken a bullet for her, to protect her. But he had failed miserably. She was gone. Taken.

Sabine moved her body, stretched her back longer. She was always a cat, stretching, purring, self-possessed. Gareth adjusted to her movement, allowing her body to settle and fit back into his. There was comfort in her body, and yet thoughts of Clara haunted him.

Gareth kissed the top of Sabine's head. She stirred the way one does when still clinging to the last vestiges of sleep, rubbing her head into his chest. Yes, he had grown to love her, to depend on her. Perhaps she had always been the one for him and Clara was no more than the desire to fulfill a teenage dream.

"What time is it?" she murmured, her voice thick with sleep.

"I don't know. Five, five thirty, maybe."

"You haven't slept at all, have you?"

"It's okay. It's nice to be cramped in this little bed with you."

Gareth knew that the only way to fully open his heart again was to love. And love was right there, within his grasp.

"Why can't you sleep?" Sabine asked. "Are you too upset about your brother?"

"I'm very sad about Tristan, but that's not why I can't sleep."

"Are you torturing yourself over Clara again?"

Gareth stroked Sabine's cheek. There was no point in admitting to that. Why upset her?

"No. I can't sleep because I have been waiting for you to wake up."

Sabine kissed him, running her tongue over his lips, teasing.

"Very naughty in your childhood bed!" she purred into his ear.

"Forget it, the walls are very thin — you can hear everything."

"Then why did you want me to wake up, if not to fuck me?" she asked.

"Because I want to ask you to marry me."

And with the words of proposal a weight lifted from Gareth, and thoughts of Clara vanished, as she had eight years earlier.

♦ ♦ ♦

Iris seemed to have no memory of her visit to the garden. She bounded down the stairs two at a time, sliding as she hit the landing, then spinning around the corner. She slowed as she approached the kitchen, already smelling of coffee and toast. Iris knew that neither Sabine nor her father would allow her to drink coffee until she turned sixteen, but they weren't there, were they? She could try it on, say that she drank it all the time, and then mimic Hilda with the way she spooned a layer of yellowish heavy cream on top. Whether she liked the coffee or not, she would have to not react in order to keep up the ruse that there was nothing unusual about her drinking it.

"*Guten Morgen.*"

"*Guten Morgen.*"

"Would you like some breakfast? Toast and liverwurst, or do you prefer sweet in the morning?"

"I will just have some coffee for now, please."

Iris was surprised that Hilda just poured, no questions asked. Then she placed a bowl of sugar and a jar of heavy cream in front of the girl.

"I will tell you a little secret. I get the cream from a Dutchman named Karl, just up the road. It is strictly *vorboten* because it is unpasteurized. He just scoops it from the top of the pail when he milks his cows and then puts it into Mason jars for me. I think he likes me!" Hilda winked.

Iris took a tablespoon and carefully, slowly layered an ample amount of heavy cream onto the top of her coffee, trying to copy how Hilda did it.

"I see you are still wearing the sweater," Hilda noted, trying to open a conversation about Iris's sleepwalking.

"Yes, it's nice, I like it."

Iris raised her steaming mug, allowing the combined sweet and bitter smell of coffee with cream to envelop her. Apart from a stolen sip of cold, leftover coffee, Iris had only experienced coffee through scent. At home, early mornings always started with the smell of brewing coffee wafting through the apartment, accompanied by the sound of the first intimate conversations between her father and Sabine. In her sleepy state she would listen to their voices, breathe in the smell of coffee, and curl under her eiderdown, knowing that these were the last few stolen moments before having to get ready for school. Until now, until this moment when she could hold her own mug in her hands, that wonderful smell was only associated with the arrival of her stepmother, Sabine. An arrival that meant Iris would no longer be as lonely. Coffee was the smell of friendship and safety. Of forgetting what, and who, was lost.

Her first sip brought a sudden bitter-burnt taste to her tongue, followed by the sweet, silky finish of the cream. At first it was almost too complicated to understand. The layers, the notes of smell and taste, the contradiction. By the fourth or fifth sip, it all started to make sense. Inhale the smell first, experience the aroma, then sip and let it linger. In time it was not so complicated. Just like the arrival of Sabine.

"Do you often go for walks in the night?" Hilda asked her.

Iris shrugged.

"Do you remember being in the garden last night?"

Iris had a faint memory of her dream. Of hundreds of diminishing stars over her head and the cool night air around her and the smell of herbs — basil, thyme, and sage. And lavender. Surely those smells had made their way into her dream because of the introduction to the bottles of essences in Hilda's study earlier that afternoon.

"That is why you have the sweater. You were cold, and I put it on you," Hilda reminded her.

"No, you didn't. I got it in my dream."

"And did I not give it to you in your dream?" Hilda asked her.

"No. The man who died in the garden gave it to me."

♦ ♦ ♦

Gareth let Sabine sleep in. She had fallen back asleep in his arms. He had to gingerly untangle himself from her resting body before heading downstairs to check on his son, Fritz.

Little Fritzi was being introduced to Froot Loops, something Gareth's mother, Elaine, had bought thinking it would be the very thing her grandson would like. And why not? Gareth was raised on breakfast cereals, Eggo waffles, and Kraft Dinner. The abundance of convenient food was not his mom's fault; she was a working mother, something not so common in those days. She was expected to juggle the demands of motherhood with the demands of work. In those days, if women wanted equality, damn it, they'd have to do it on their own time!

"The milk's in the fridge."

Gareth laughed. "Of course, where else would it be?"

Elaine was still in her pajamas, a sensible blue cotton with the slightest bit of white piping around the collar. It was a variation on the nursing uniforms she had worn over the years: pull-on pants and an oversize button-up top. His mother looked like she hadn't had a minute of sleep. Her eyes were swollen, the puffiness extending from her lacrimal sac to her lacrimal gland. Gareth smiled to himself realizing that, at one time, he would have said that her eyes were swollen from corner to corner, but twenty years of working as an ocularist had made him label the eye very differently.

"Look at him! He is exactly like you!" Elaine exclaimed.

Fritz was sitting on cushions so that he was high enough to be at the table. He looked smug sitting that high, like the king of the castle. His bowl of Froot Loops was overturned and spread out before him. He was busy, his little fingers moving over the many round pieces. He was unaware of his grandmother and his father watching him as he sorted each one according to colour, until there were lines of matching Froot Loops in front of him. When he finished, he looked up proudly.

"*Ich habe Hunger!*" he exclaimed.

"*Iss das!*"

"*Nein. Nein, nein! Das ist kein Essen!*"

"What's the problem?" Elaine asked her son.

"He doesn't think it's food." Gareth shrugged.

Gareth took out some bread to toast. His son must have thought the Froot Loops were a toy, a puzzle to keep him occupied, and not food at all. But now that the puzzle was finished, he wanted his reward, to be fed.

"Sorry, Mom, he doesn't eat cereal. He's never had it ..."

"You know, you should speak to him in English, like you did for Iris."

"She would only have spoken English till school if it hadn't been for Sabine. Clara and I spoke to her entirely in English. But by the time Fritz came along, we all spoke German in the home. Although I did continue with English with Iris, just so that she felt she had something special with me."

Gareth buttered the toast for Fritz, who seemed relieved to finally have some real food. How much more he ate than Iris did at that age. His boy was hearty in his body, like his mother. But his OCD character, his attention to detail, and the angular shape of his face was Gareth all over again.

"And how are you coping?" Elaine asked her son.

"I am broken-hearted over Tristan ..."

"I know. We all are." Elaine paused before continuing with caution, "I meant about Clara. Surely by now you realize that she isn't coming back, and you have two children and a woman who loves you ..."

It seemed that his mother could read his thoughts. Gareth busied himself, feeding his son. If he could think only of the present, of the task at hand, then he might escape the guilt of his past and the uncertainty of his future.

"Mmm, coffee!" Sabine announced as she wandered into the kitchen. She reached for the pot and helped herself to that first cup of the morning, but upon sipping, she wrinkled her nose in obvious disappointment.

"This is the thing I do not understand. You can never have a good cup of coffee here. Even the cheapest coffee in Germany tastes good. I will send you coffee when I get back. You shouldn't have to drink this shit."

Elaine's smile disappeared. She liked Sabine and had secretly hoped that her son would embrace a new life with her, but that bluntness! How did he put up with that?

"You know, I was feeling quite woozy this morning. I think if you go to town today you should get me one of those sticks to piss on." Sabine laughed. "So, maybe the coffee is not as bad as I think. Maybe it just doesn't agree with me."

Gareth stared at her in disbelief. It was the last thing he expected. How could she be so nonchalant, so casual about it? Her last pregnancy had been hell, utter hell. She was sick all the way through the entire nine months. She may have looked healthy and hearty, but the months of gestation were much harder on her than they had been on Clara. Pregnancy had reduced Sabine to a pathetic state. Her knees were bruised from dropping before the toilet many times a day in order to retch and heave. That she would go through such discomfort, such daily hell, to have their child, had filled him with a love he didn't know he held for her. And it was only then that Clara began to fade just a little, even though she had already been missing for over four years.

"Are you serious?"

"*Ja*, I thought you knew. That is why you asked me to marry you, no?"

"No. I asked you because we should get married."

"Should? What do you mean *should*? I think the correct word, in English, is *want*, not *should*! Really, Gareth, this is not a very good proposal."

"Are you sure you want to go through all this again?"

"How can you ask that? Look at our son! We make beautiful children together. The vomiting means nothing when you hold a new baby in your arms."

"But you are forty years old!" Gareth argued.

"There is no need to be mean!" Sabine turned to Elaine. "Didn't you teach him any manners?"

But Elaine was smiling for the first time in months. Even the lines of tension around her eyes seemed to relax. There was nothing like new life to soothe the pain of loss.

"If you have a son, maybe you will call him Tristan?" Elaine offered.

"Oh, no. The name Tristan means 'sadness.' Besides, I want a stronger name if it's another boy. Like Wolfi. And if it is a girl, I am determined to call her Liesl after my mother. I've missed her so much since she passed away."

"Of course, you do, but doesn't Gareth have some say as well? It's his child, too," Elaine suggested.

"No. The child gets his last name, so I decide on the first name. That makes it fair. I chose Fritzi's name." Sabine swallowed another mouthful of coffee and gagged just a little.

"Of course, I have a say! I want Siegfried Mark for a boy and Siegfried Elaine for a girl!" Gareth announced. At first it was meant as a tease, but somehow, the moment he voiced the name *Siegfried*, he felt that it was right. His child should be named after his mentor and after one of his parents.

"Oh no, you can't call a girl Siegfried! That's cruel! It's a boy's name," Elaine protested.

"It's either. But how about Frieda for short?"

"Frieda was my great-grandmother's name. Frieda Elaine! It's settled." Sabine beamed.

Yes, he would marry Sabine. There would be another child. A new beginning. But first he would have to do the unthinkable. He would have to declare Clara dead *in absentia*.

TWO

BLANCA SHOULD HAVE GONE TO Tristan's funeral. She'd had the best of intentions, but the thought of returning to her birth home, without her twin, was just too daunting. Landscapes would only serve to remind her of their shared past. Every breath, every street, every sight, would be a marker for what was her younger life with Clara. She knew that she needed to get on with her life, but she preferred to live a half life. Without Clara, she was a shadow; a shadow who did not know how to express her sorrow except through eruptions of rage.

Yes, she should have flown to Canada, to a past she had left behind. But airports were a trigger for grief. She knew she should have found the courage to support Gareth and Jack, but how could she do that if she could not find the courage to lift herself from her bed?

Blanca was undressed and enjoying the safety of her bed when Martina returned to their upstairs flat. Martina was cross that her lover would waste her life but knew it was an unfair judgment on her part. Mourning takes its own time, adhering to no one's schedule. Not even the discipline of showbiz could nudge mourning to hurry up and get on with it.

"Don't you think that your sister would want to be kept alive through her work?" Martina, the Punk Baroness, asked Blanca.

"No."

"We could remount *Antigone*?"

"No."

"Then all I can say is that you may be twins, but you certainly do not know her!"

Blanca rolled into her pillows, her chalk-white skin looking even more pale against the crimson colour of the sheets. Had she become even paler over the years, more translucent? Sometimes the Punk Baroness looked at her and thought that her skin was wearing thin, like a beautiful fabric. She could see the bluish veins now in Blanca's thighs and arms, and when they made love, there was a vein in her forehead that would pulse with her pleasure. But they hadn't made love for a while. Months. Many months.

Martina knew that a darkness would wrap around Blanca every year as they approached the anniversary of her twin's disappearance. Clara had been gone for eight years, and the all-consuming depression was only increasing. Every year the sorrow seemed compounded, like the interest on her opera company's piling debts. Surely a performance of her sister's greatest work could break the spell that trapped Blanca while also putting them back into the black?

"She never wanted to write that opera. You know it."

"Yes, but once she did, she knew it was a great accomplishment."

"And if I *did* let you put it on, who would play Antigone now that Clara's gone?" Blanca questioned.

"You would. You could dedicate the performance to her. To her memory."

Blanca threw her pillow across the room. "We don't know she's dead!" she yelled.

Martina sat on the edge of the bed, took her lover's hand, and kissed each angry finger.

"You know I would never want to hurt you. But you must also know that your sister would never have left her little girl. She was taken that day, and you will probably never see her again. *But if you love her, you will sing again. You will sing to honour her.*"

"Singing won't bring my sister back."

"No, but what else can you do?"

"Antigone was Clara's role. No one else will ever sing that part!"

The Punk Baroness threw her hands into the air. *Fine! Just fine! Who had been paying the bills all these years? Who had been using all of her savings to keep the company afloat and to put bread on the table? Goddamn it!* She knew Blanca was hurting but come on! Eight years! Wasn't it time to embrace life again? Wasn't it time to look toward passion and purpose again?

There was another question that now began to pop into Martina's head. Wasn't it time for the Baroness to finally move on? At forty-four she was still handsome, aged the way the best German women do. Fit, strong. Still able to wear leather pants and turn heads when she walked down the street. Everyone said that the whistles would stop when she hit forty, but that hadn't been her experience. Her dark hair falling to her shoulders, her astonishing blue eyes, and her big, round bottom on top of her strong legs were things to be admired at any age. Perhaps it took her an extra few years to learn to strut when she passed by a group of people. Perhaps it was a game to turn men's heads because being desired by men, while not having any desire for them in return, gave her a sense of power. It wasn't that she wanted other women, either. The truth was, she really only had eyes for one person, the depressed waif lolling in their bed.

But she never really, fully, had her. Never was she sure of her love. That was the deal you made when you got into bed with a twin. Martina knew she would always be second, always be one degree removed from true intimacy, but she was willing to accept that just to lie, undisturbed, with her head resting on the subtle swell of her lover's belly.

"It would be easier if we knew what happened, I guess. If I knew for certain that she was dead, maybe I could move on. But what if she is out there somewhere?"

Now in her late thirties, Blanca still seemed like a child. Maybe because she was waifish, or maybe because she was trapped in time; Blanca seemed not a day older than that horrible day when Clara was taken. Blanca was like Princess Aurora, frozen in time and preserved in sorrow. Sorrow could be quite beautiful on some. Sorrow was timeless. The Punk Baroness knew that it was stress that aged, not sorrow at all. And Martina had a lot of stress.

"We did everything we could. We stayed there for weeks, called every embassy, and had all the police on it. She disappeared into thin air."

"People do not just disappear into thin air," Blanca responded. "She must be *somewhere*."

"Why don't you go to Hamburg and spend some time with Iris when they get back from Canada? Gareth could use some cheering up now. It is very sad about his brother dying. And young Iris needs you. You are the only connection she has to her mother."

"I don't want to see her."

Blanca knew how difficult it was for both of them. When Iris was just four, she had mistaken Blanca for her lost mother and ran to her, arms open for an embrace, calling out "Mama, Mama!" Blanca, aware more of her own pain than the child's, crossed her arms over her chest, closing herself off, protecting her heart. It took Iris a few minutes to realize the mistake, to realize that it was not her mother but her aunt. Then came a cascade of tears, followed by a fierce tantrum, complete with screaming, punching, and throwing herself, arms and legs flailing, onto the floor. It wasn't that Blanca disliked seeing Iris; she just could not bear to witness the child's disappointment every time Iris realized that Blanca was not Clara.

"Why don't you ever visit her? You know, she is growing up so quickly. Is it because she reminds you of Clara too much?"

Blanca laughed. It was not a friendly sound. More mocking than friendly, and Martina wondered how her great love had become such a stranger.

"You're joking, right? She is *nothing* like Clara. She's my *mother* all over again. Those freckles, that faraway look in her eyes, that touch of madness. I can't bear her. And all that cascading red hair! No good will come of her. Just like my mother!"

There were no more words. Martina had run out of things to say that might appease the woman she loved. She knew Blanca was spiralling into darkness, but no matter how far she might extend her hand, Blanca had no desire to emerge from her shadows.

"After seven years, a missing person can be declared dead *in absentia*. Did you know that?"

"I know," Martina replied as she stood helplessly looking at Blanca.

"Do you think Gareth will marry Sabine now? Now that my sister can be declared officially dead?"

"I don't know. Perhaps we should have a funeral, or a ritual of some kind, so that you can accept that she is gone. So, you can move on with your life. Heal."

Blanca shook her head. "I can't do that. You know I can't do that. She isn't dead."

Martina knew that Blanca was deluded. Almost eight years and nothing. Not a clue, not a trace, not a hint of Clara. But she couldn't argue or reason with Blanca. Hope was the only thing keeping her there.

"Don't you have to work?" Blanca asked.

Martina reached for her tube of MAC Consensual, the darkest, earthiest red-brown with just a touch of gold. Yes, a little gold on her lips would bring her money! She smeared it across her disappointed mouth. Time to go for a walk and turn some heads before tackling the problem of her near-bankrupt company.

"I don't know why you still dress like that. Hasn't anyone told you that punk is dead?" Blanca taunted.

Martina slowly turned and smiled at her lover. "*Nein*, old punkers never die. We just smell that way."

♦ ♦ ♦

Blanca's doctor, five years earlier, had told her that she was suffering from extreme anxiety, possibly even PTSD. He gave her a prescription for Xanax to calm her, but Blanca continued to have flashbacks to the day of the abduction. Next, he prescribed her anti-psychotics, telling her that they would help her sleep. They *did* help her sleep. They also gave her a laser-sharp focus. And with focus a plan is formulated.

Her plan was to make a map of her sorrow on her body. The first cut frightened her. She shook and cried as she placed the razor on her forearm. After two superficial cuts, something else took over her. A delight as the blood rose up in red droplets on her white, translucent skin. The line between pleasure and pain blurred until the physical assault felt less painful than the emotional agony within her. The thought of cutting gave way to the motion of the act; the first few droplets of red became longer tracks along her arm as she moved closer and closer to that point where pleasure and pain meet. Each cut carried her closer to ecstasy. She understood only too well what she must do. Every year, she would mark her sister's absence on her body, like the rings of a tree marking time. Every year she would cut, and bleed. Cut until Clara was returned to her.

Blanca's ritualistic cutting horrified Martina. At first, she could not see beyond the wounds, the blood, and the scars. But then, one day, she caught sight of Blanca just as she was starting her first cut. She saw the look on Blanca's face. An anticipation, a desire she hadn't seen in her for years. Martina felt as though an early frost had tinged her heart. Something beyond the self-harm froze Martina. There was something strangely familiar about it. Where had she seen such longing in a face before? She had never, ever, seen that expression on Blanca's face, but she *knew* that expression well, and it gripped at her. A chilled fist squeezed her heart until it pounded ice into her blood. It was a look of utter escape and yearning combined. It was the look of a junkie, right before the fix.

Yes. She knew the look only too well. She had seen the look in her younger brother's face the time he had left the bathroom door unlocked and Martina, barely twenty years old then, was unaware that the wash-closet was occupied. She caught him, sitting on the toilet seat, fully clothed, one sleeve rolled up, and a needle poised above a vein. She stayed there, quietly watching; he was unaware of her. The needle pierced his skin, then a backwash of blood flooded back into the vial, and her brother, eyes closed with his soul escaping him, pressed the blood mixed with heroin back into his veins. Swoosh. Bliss. That is what he later called it. *Absolute bliss.* But Martina didn't see the bliss, she only saw the loss. Loss that would lurk around every corner, unseen, until the day came when it could pounce. Until the day when all that could be lost *would* be lost. The day that loss itself would win. Yes, that was the same look Blanca had as she held the blade above her pale skin before her first cut. And then, with the second cut, a look that was so much like her brother's when he succumbed to the heroin backwash. Yes, she knew the look. It was loss disguised as bliss.

Martina understood that she was fighting an addiction, a demon that had taken hold in her lover's body. In a few more years Blanca's arm would look like a birch tree, the white bark in rings, peeling away, marking time. Martina removed all the razors from the house. But there were still pencil sharpeners to deconstruct, mirrors to smash, and utility knives to be found. No matter how many things she removed, she knew there would always be *something*. Eventually Martina gave up. Blanca was an adult; she would find a way to make her marks. Every year, on the anniversary of Clara's disappearance, Martina waited, with gripping fear, for the self-harm. Then she patched up her lover, gave her a painkiller, and brought her a cup of tea. What else could she do? She knew that she could never leave Blanca. She was responsible for her grief and so she was also responsible for her life, with all the pain it contained.

◆ ◆ ◆

There was no question about it. When the twin towers were attacked, it was the end of optimism. The thought of a global community, and all the goodwill of the late eighties, was fading. The end of the Cold War, the end of apartheid, and the fall of the Berlin Wall, were merely illusions in a mirror with such a lovely reflection that no one asked if the reflection was real or just imagined.

The Punk Baroness understood the power of reflection, believing that some mirrors held evil spirits and others good. It must be so, because in one mirror she was slim and long and lean, yet in another, she could look quite frumpy and, *Gott* forbid, her age. If an actual mirror could be so deceitful, then imagine what the reflection of the world could be?

What opera, she wondered, could reflect *that*? The hopeful dream of a brand-new world dissipates when the world wakes up to find that nothing had changed after all. Just imagine those one hundred years that Aurora, such a cursed princess, napped away blissfully. She must have been dreaming during that time, imagining another reality, different from the one she'd slipped away from, filled with curses and spells. But when she awoke, the world hadn't changed one bit! Not one iota! It was exactly as it had been before she touched that spindle. All those dreams she may have had, of having dominion over her own being, vanished within a man's kiss. What a tragedy! What an opera! All Martina needed, all she's ever needed, was the right composer. Clara had been a gift, but she was gone. Perhaps, though, she could write it herself.

Blanca would be Aurora. Why not? Hadn't she already checked out from life, sleeping most of the day away? *What alternative life might she be having in her dreams?* Was she imagining a different world, a through-the-looking-glass reality, where her twin still existed? And if so, was there a place for Martina on the other side of that reflection?

Deep down, Martina knew that if a fairy godmother were to suddenly appear, offering Blanca back her sister, she would jump at the offer. But what if Blanca had to sacrifice her bedmate on the altar of love? No question about it, Martina would be sacrificed in the blink of the eye. *Ein Augenblick.* And yet, perhaps if Martina could create a new opera for her lover, it might bring Blanca out of her stupor and back onto the stage where she belonged. Something or someone just had to awaken her.

Who could the one person to break the cursed spell possibly be? Not a prince, that much was clear. No, what was needed was a fairy godmother. Martina knew that there was once a fairy godmother for both the twins. A woman who had pulled them from despair, given them a magical future, and turned their faces to view a larger world beyond their sad beginnings. Martina tried to remember her name. What was it? *Esther.* But where was Esther? And was she even alive?

THREE

BAINBRIDGE AVENUE WAS THE LAST stop on the D-train, but to Esther it was the ends of the earth. A life in Europe, then a life in Southern Ontario, and now here was where it would all likely end. The Bronx.

Esther watched her older sister chewing her toast. Every fourth or fifth chew there was a clack-clacking sound which clearly was only audible to Esther because her sister continued to bite, grind, and swallow without notice. Could Bözsi not feel the bit of butter that was sticking to the corner of her mouth? Did she not remember what a serviette was for? Esther wanted so badly to jump up across the table, napkin in hand, just to wipe the side of her sister's mouth.

Only five years older than Esther, Bözsi seemed to be from another generation. Was Esther deluded? Was she, perhaps, as ancient and as obsolete as her sister? It was hard to believe that this woman was even related to her. Hard to believe that she had once lived a life full of adventure and danger, because now she looked like a skinny old cow mindlessly chewing cud.

Esther couldn't bear it. When she'd first considered moving to New York, she imagined bright lights, Broadway, museums, and culture. Although she would sometimes sneak away to a gallery or a show, she was uncomfortable on her D-train journey, so she mostly stayed in the tired apartment on Bainbridge Avenue, overhearing loud salsa music and arguments (in either Spanish or Yiddish) from other apartments while breathing in the stale smells of cabbage, beans, meat, and reheated rice.

"Perhaps we should go into town. Have lunch, go to a gallery?" Esther suggested.

Still the butter sat there on the top of her sister's lip. The lips were the only place where makeup was still applied on a daily basis. Before anything else, her sister would reach over to her bedside table and, with a shaky hand, apply a layer, without the help of a hand mirror, her hand remembering the approximate outline of her lips. Or rather the outline that was once there, because her lips had thinned and narrowed, and now there was a constant bleed of orange-red that went beyond that thin, top lip in an uneven line.

Esther remembered how envious she had once been of her older sister, with her wavy dark hair, thick eyelashes, and curvy but slim-waisted body. Even as a child, she knew that she would never have those appealing rounded edges, those perky, upright breasts and those long racehorse legs. But it wasn't only her world-class looks that had filled Esther with envy; her sister could sing with a voice that sounded as though she had drunk only the gods' nectar. If there was one of the three sisters earmarked for a life on the boards, it was Bözsi.

When their parents had insisted that Bözsi either get an education or get married, she chose to move in with their married, older sister, Gabby, and her husband, Dov. Esther had always assumed that Bözsi had been rounded up with them and sent to the camps. But no, Gabby had rid herself of her younger sister some time before the roundup because she'd caught Bözsi fellating her husband in their bed. Of course, it had to be all Bözsi's fault; Dov must have been seduced by her! Bözsi had been thrown out and, instead of returning to her parents' home where scowls of disapproval would be her constant company, Bözsi took what little money she had, along with a bit she'd stolen from her sister's secret stash, and chose to survive on the streets instead. Within the week, she'd bedded a transient showman who had a touring company of misfits, and ran off with him and his vaudeville troupe. Her indiscretion had saved her life. At the time, Esther had no idea of these family secrets; she was protected from them by a shield of parental guile. She had once falsely believed that both her older sisters were properly married.

Esther looked at the piano, closed and upright in the corner. When she first moved into Bözsi's overstuffed apartment, Esther would open the cover and play, her fingers remembering the songs of her youth. Her mind would wander as she travelled pathways of memory, resting from time to time on one nostalgic moment or another, always in time with the music and the touch of her fingers. Thoughts of her parents, and how they had doted on her. Thoughts of her husband, and how they met and married and made love. But of all the memories, of all her experiences, joys, and losses, she always went back to the same place. Massey Hall in Toronto, the day the twins, Clara and Blanca, first shared their music with the world. Her heart pounded with the memory of the pride she had felt that night. Her eyes watered with the vindication of that day. How she missed them. Her protegés. Her girls. And yet she had been the one to send them away. Release them into the world.

Then she found her long-lost sister whom she had assumed died along with the rest of her family in the concentration camps. But no! Bözsi had survived everything! She'd had adventures, seen the world, and had enjoyed more lovers than Esther could count on her toes and fingers combined. The story was all there, in pictures, lying amongst the clutter and debris in Bözsi's fourth-floor apartment. Here, in this picture, Bözsi is doing the splits, her long legs bare in front of her, her ruffled show-skirts hiked up well above the knee. Here, Bözsi is posing with a ragtag troupe. A man with a moustache and what must be a gold tooth smiles from his seat beside the piano, a juggler poses, chest out and hands full of pins, and three girls, Bözsi amongst them, have their legs kicked up, their skirts lifted in their hands as though they were doing the cancan. And here, in this prized picture, Bözsi is nestled in the arms of a man, slim, well dressed, wearing a fedora tilted over one eye.

"I was the best cancan dancer, a natural," Bözsi had declared when she caught Esther looking at the photos. "I called myself Lulu, then. No one could pronounce Bözsi. They kept calling me Bossy. Imagine that? Bossy!"

Esther could well imagine her sister as Bossy instead of Bözsi.

"Sometimes I would explain to them. '*Ber-gee*. Imagine if it were spelled this way: *B-E-R-G-I-E*!' But still they called me Bossy. So, I thought, why not go by Lulu? It suited me. You see? I look just like a Lulu in those pictures!"

"Where were these taken?" Esther asked.

"Spain, I think. Before we went to Algeria. I ran a hotel there, of sorts."

It was some time, and many cups of shared tea later, before Esther learned that the *hotel of sorts* was, in fact, a brothel where officers came and went. Sure there were shows, cabarets where Bözsi could sing her repertoire or do a cancan, but that was not the focus of the establishment. After an evening performance, Bözsi would lie down with officers from either side and take their money in whatever currency they offered to pay. Then she would pass their whispered secrets on. She viewed herself as an invisible hero, undecorated but nonetheless responsible for the Allies' victory.

"The French Resistance was very, very small. There was no French Resistance without me. Well, me and Henri; it was all his idea. He's there in that picture. The only one I have of him."

"Henri?"

"Yes. Henri." Bözsi sighed.

And that had been the end of it. After that, the piano was out of bounds, as was the photo — a memory on an instrument no one was allowed to play.

Esther knew that she had been blessed. She was never captured. She had experienced a contented marriage. She had discovered and midwifed talent, and although she had lost her parents and her other sisters, she had found Bözsi in the end. In her twilight years, she had managed to find family and a connection to her youth, reclaiming a bit of a world that had been lost to her. And yet, there was a great sense of missing out. A dark hole that ate at her whenever her sister ate in her presence. She knew that she should be more patient with her sister. And yet, her presence only brought Esther that recurrent sense of loss. Loss of her family. Loss of her dreams. Loss of her identity.

"I think we should go to Ground Zero. Pay our respects. It is a year since it happened." Bözsi picked up her plate and put it into the sink. She did not wash it, though. That had become Esther's job.

"Yes, whatever you wish."

Was this how it all ended? Living in a worn-out tenement block that smelled of sweat, fried beans, and cabbage? Having nothing to look forward to but her sister's *Kaposztás Tészta*? God she was sick of cabbage, and noodles, and sour cream, and caraway seeds. And did everything have to have a thick red layer of paprika? Her days seemed to bleed into one another as she merely pleased her sister's every whim while she waited. Waited for what? Death? But why blame her sister? Wasn't she the one who chose safety at every turn, while her sister had put herself out there and risked her life and, in doing so, lived more fully than Esther ever had?

"Bözsi, there's something I haven't told you."

Bözsi regarded her younger sister with curiosity. She must have some secrets, but hadn't they spent countless hours catching up, sharing the important things? What could she possibly have to say of any importance?

"I have two girls. Twins. But I have lost touch."

"You are joking! Why didn't you tell me?" Bözsi clapped her hands together.

Esther opened her handbag and from her wallet produced two pictures, school pictures that were now creased and worse for wear. She laid them on the table in front of Bözsi, who stared down at them with incredulity. Two white faces stared back up at her. Almost exactly the same, but not quite. Eyes a purplish-pink in the pictures. Hair, long and whiter than bleach-blond. No, it was the colour of the ivories on the piano.

Without thinking, Bözsi inched over to the piano and leaned against it. Her breasts hung loosely in her house dress. Esther thought that perhaps she could do with a new bra. Something to haul those puppies up a bit.

"They are the greatest singers I have ever heard. Opera, but also this other music. Their own music, unlike anything else. They went to Germany to sing opera."

"Well, music runs in our family." Bözsi shrugged. "You are so lucky to have children. I never had another one after my baby boy died. I couldn't bear it. How old are they now?"

"They are in their thirties. Late thirties."

"Late thirties? So maybe not your husband's then? Oh, Esther, you are so full of surprises! Not quite as boring as I thought!" Bözsi was beaming, coming to life. Yes, this was the sister she dreamed of having. Not that perfectly spoiled brat Esther had been. How she had hated her perfectly done tight braids and her pleasing smile when they were children. Her first-place marks at school. For almost five years, Bözsi had the privilege of being the youngest child, and then Esther came along and suddenly all the doting on her changed to expectation, while Esther received the fond looks of approval. There was no way that Bözsi could ever live up to her older sister's perfection or her younger sister's youth. All she could do was rebel.

"Where are they?"

"Berlin, I think. The last I heard they were headliners for a company called Die Punkerie."

"You don't know where they are?" Bözsi was incredulous.

"I lost track of them. But I have missed them every day!"

"Then we will go to Berlin! You must see them."

"We?"

"Yes. I am up for one last adventure. And let's face it, we are bored and boring. So, let's go to Berlin and find these beautiful girls." Bözsi was enthusiastic.

"Really? You really think they are beautiful?"

"Of course, they are. You know, in a weird way. We would have made a killing with girls like that in the cabaret." Bözsi winked at her sister. "Besides, I cannot die without meeting actual albinos. And twins, too!"

"They are not freaks, Bözsi!"

"Of course, they are! We are all freaks in showbiz! I have some money hidden in the piano. We can use that for our *extra-ordinary* excursion!"

"In the piano! Really? Why not at the bank?"

Bözsi nodded knowingly and touched her finger to the side of her nose. "Never trust the banks."

"Bözsi, what do you mean *some* money?"

"Lots. I have lots. Shh. The walls are thin." Bözsi gestured with both arms for her sister to shush.

Esther stared at her sister, who suddenly seemed at least ten years younger, and in the blink of an eye, Esther could imagine the fearless young woman her sister might have been.

"And then, after Berlin, we can take the train to Paris. I have some old friends there I should find. Show people. Resistance people. You know." She winked.

Bözsi opened the piano and reached deep into its body, pulling out fistfuls of cash in every denomination. Esther had no idea how much there was but estimated it was in the tens of thousands.

"For your daughters," she declared. "I don't know why you let so much time go by without seeing them. I would do anything to spend one more day with my child. Don't wait till it's too late, Esther!"

Esther didn't know why she had pretended that the twins were her daughters. Perhaps it was jealousy that Bözsi had better stories. Perhaps she wanted to shock her so that her sister took note of her. Perhaps because, in some way, some small way that was greater than flesh and blood and DNA, Clara and Blanca had always been her girls. Esther ached to be reunited with them. Bözsi was right. Why had she left it so long?

FOUR

IT CAME LIKE A GRIPPING ache somewhere below her belly button, a ripple of pain working its way outward over her small stomach toward her hips, which sat out like two right-angled points from her body. As Iris ran her hand over her lower tummy, she felt a slight swell that had never been there before. Puffy, tender. Then, as she turned to rise from the bed, she felt the ache spread into her back. She had never ridden a horse, never really been in a horse's company, but she imagined that if she did keep the company of horses and one were to kick her in the back, it would feel exactly as she felt at that moment.

She rolled over and brought her knees into her chest. The fetal position. This is how she must have been for months in her mother's stomach. Protected by her mother, her whole being surrounded by the embrace of another body, cushioned. Iris longed to be contained, held safe. She hadn't felt safe for a very long time. She knew that, at any moment, someone could steal her. Steal her and do terrible things. Although she had no idea what the terrible things might be.

When she had first started school, she was given keys to the apartment and was told to be very, very careful with them. To not lose them. Constantly, throughout the day, Iris would put her hand into her pocket to feel for them. Yes, there they were. Safe. But then ten, fifteen minutes later, she would check again just to be sure. Yes, still there. Still safe.

The keys were more than the tool that could unlock the door. Iris knew how to hold them between her middle and pointer finger so that if anyone *untoward* threatened her, she could use them as a weapon. How, exactly, she was never sure. They were not the size of a sword, not as sharp as a steak knife, and they couldn't shoot. Still, she understood that as long as the keys were held that way, between her middle and index fingers, she would be safe. Therefore, keys must have had magical powers.

Do not talk to strangers.

Do not let anyone into the apartment.

Do not tell anyone your address or phone number or last name.

There were many safety rules to remember, which only proved that someone, somewhere, would try to steal her someday. Steal her, as they had stolen her mother.

Five nights now she had slept at Hilda's instead of at her real grandmother's house a mile up the street. Her father had come over every day to check on her and to ask her to sleep with them at the other house, but Iris stubbornly kept refusing because she claimed to be afraid of ghosts and she knew that her uncle Tristan must be lurking about in his old bedroom. How could she possibly sleep there? How could she possibly be safe? But it was a lie. Iris had no fear of those who have passed on. She only had fear of the living.

Iris tried to stretch her back. She lengthened each leg and, although the stretch felt good for her bones, her muscles gripped and pinched. She could just cry. What was wrong with her?

"Breakfast, Iris! Are you going to sleep all day?"

Iris got up and everything went a bit woozy. It was then that she felt a trickle down the inside of her upper thigh. Panicked, she raised her hand up under her nightie to wipe away the drops, and then, with a look at her fingers, she saw the first drops of blood.

"Coming!" she called back.

She put on her underwear, went to the bathroom and put some rolled-up toilet paper into the crotch of her panties, and then stared at herself in the mirror.

"Do I look any different?" she asked her reflection.

A pale, sad version of herself silently stared back.

♦ ♦ ♦

Hilda knew the moment she saw her. That wan look, that paleness of skin, that darkness under the eyes, could only be one thing. Where was Sabine to speak with the girl? It had been so many years since she had to have that kind of talk with a young lady. Was it possible that it was almost thirty years since her own daughters had passed that milestone? Thirty years, gone in *einem Augenblick*.

"You look so pale. I have something to relax you. It will help a little."

Hilda did not pour her the usual contraband cup of coffee, suggesting a chamomile tea instead. She had harvested and dried a bunch of the tiny, perfect yellow flowers herself. Some boiling water, a tea strainer, and a little time to steep was all that was needed. That, and a hearty teaspoon of honey, because Hilda knew that the girl had a bit of a sweet tooth.

"Your tea will take a few minutes. Just try and relax while I make you a special treat."

Hilda then went to her makeshift laboratory to get a vial of essential lavender. She carefully measured ten drops of the lavender oil and added it to a small container of shea butter. She couldn't decide between the eucalyptus, mint, and cedarwood for the heart note, but after a sniff of each, and a quick look at the frailness of

Iris, she chose the cedarwood. The other two scents could be very effective but also overwhelming at times, especially as she was going to choose grapefruit, a mere six drops of it, as the top note. Base, heart, and top, melded together as one scent but each acting independently of one another. As one aroma presented itself, then exited, the next would make itself known. The cedarwood would take care of the cramps, the lavender would relax her and lift her spirits, and the brightness of the grapefruit would feel clean as it cleared away the puffiness and water retention. All she had to do was gently rub it on her stomach, then lie back and relax, letting the magic of the scent do its work.

"Take your tea up to your room, and I will bring you up a few good books to read today. Here is a special rub I made especially for you. It will help with your sore back and tummy."

Iris took her tea and carefully balanced the cup on the saucer as she headed up the stairs, back to her comfy room. She had so many things she wanted to ask but was afraid to start the conversation. All she hoped was that Hilda would come upstairs, sit at the edge of her bed, and tell her that it was all normal. That everything would be fine, just fine.

◆ ◆ ◆

Hilda pounded the veal down until each piece was a paper-thin strip. She grabbed a loaf of her homemade sourdough bread, now slightly stale and hard, and made the bread crumbs for the coating. A fresh egg from one of her hens, and then the usual salt and pepper. Crispy edges, almost burnt, giving way to tender, succulent meat, all wrapped in her special bread crumbs. Each schnitzel large enough to cover an entire plate. Side plates would be for the beet salad and mashed potatoes. A simple but festive meal.

"Smells good. Schnitzel?" Jack asked as he entered the kitchen.

"Where have you been all morning?"

"Seeing Elaine and Mark. We looked at pictures of Tristan. But there is news …"

"*Ja*? Well there is news here, too. This meal is special for Iris. I wish you could be here. Can't you cancel on your father?"

"Hardly. I never see him. Haven't spoken to him or my sisters since Tristan died. Not that they bothered to come to the funeral. They are in such denial. My gayness is just a phase, apparently."

"That is too bad. I'd like you to be here. You should cancel." Hilda laughed. "But don't tell your father I said that."

Jack looked at his mother, his expression inquisitive.

"She has started her monthly times. So, tonight, we celebrate her and her passage into womanhood."

"Oh no."

"Oh no, what?" Hilda questioned.

"Sabine is pregnant. I think she was going to announce that tonight."

"Well, she will also be pregnant tomorrow and the next day. But a girl only has her first period once. Sabine will have to save her news." Hilda was as adamant as ever.

"I'll call her and give her the heads-up."

Hilda poured a little olive oil into her skillet and added butter to it. Mustn't ever just use butter alone because it would quickly burn, but with a bit of oil as well, the butter would heat without burning. Yes, these were the things Hilda learned from her own mother and remembered throughout her life. She taught her daughters all the old cooking tricks. But who would teach Iris? Especially now that another baby was coming?

"Did you talk to her about, you know, things?"

Hilda nodded. "We had a talk."

Jack helped himself to a coffee. He had just had one at Elaine's house, but it had tasted like doughnut-shop coffee, the kind that was only tolerable with double cream and sugar. No wonder *double-double* had made it into the Canadian dictionary. Still, Jack preferred his coffee black. He took two fast sips, his custom.

"How are Mark and Elaine coping?"

"They're sad but Gareth and Fritz cheer them. They seem to be coping better than I am. Ah fuck, Mom. AIDS is such a bitch."

Hilda took off her apron and wrapped her arms around her son. He was so tall, had been for years, but it always seemed a surprise to Hilda because when he was away, it was the little boy she thought she missed.

"Yes, it is a such a bitch."

"It broke my fucking heart to see all those AIDS orphans. I covered AIDS in Africa. Spent a year there, taking pictures and documenting how it was eating the whole continent. And the whole time, I had no idea that it was so close to home, that my lover was dying because of it. I saw so many people dying there …"

Jack's voice caught in his throat. Words wrapped around his Adam's apple, trapped by the swell of his loss. He broke from his mother's embrace. Gulped down more coffee.

"It is okay to cry, you know. To mourn. Only if you mourn death can you live."

"I just … I just cannot bear to watch Tristan's tape. To watch him die. Every time I watch it, he gets thinner and thinner. And where was I when he needed me most?"

"You didn't know."

"What am I going to do now, Mom? How did you do it? How did you live after Siegfried died?"

Jack seemed like the same boy who so often came home, upset that the other children teased him about his glass eye. The same boy who cried himself to sleep the night she told him that she and his father, John, were divorcing. And now her youngest child was at a loss again. Too young to be mourning the death of a lover.

"After Siegfried died, I thought I'd start again somehow. So, I went back to Germany, but that just made me miss him more. Then I realized that I carried him with me. And, of course, the land pulled me back here. So, I created a life right here, but without him."

"How do you do it day in and day out?"

"You just do. Sometimes it feels like a half life. Sometimes it feels like a life in the shadows. But then something or someone comes along and reminds you how much in life there is to love."

Hilda knew that she always had nature and her relationship with the land. But what did Jack have to heal him?

◆ ◆ ◆

"Why are you sad?" Iris pushed herself up onto Hilda's countertop, her feet dangling in the air.

Hilda wanted to shoo her off, to tell her it wasn't proper to sit on the counter when she was cooking and there was food. She would have told her own children exactly that years ago, although none of them would have dared to sit on her counter in the first place. And yet this scrawny child had Hilda wrapped around her little finger.

"I am sad because you are leaving soon, and this will be our last special dinner."

Iris dunked her finger into Hilda's freshly whipped cream, wrote her initials across the top, then lifted the finger to her mouth. It was only when she went in for a second taste that Hilda stopped her.

"You cannot put your fingers in your mouth, then back in the whipped cream. You'll get your spit in the cream and ruin it for everyone else!"

Iris shrugged. She was neither ashamed nor upset. Any correction rolled off her slender back like the lake's morning fog.

"Anyhow, you shouldn't be too sad about me going."

"Oh?" Hilda asked. "Why is that?"

Iris smiled, her lips gently curling up, whipped cream still smeared at the corners.

"Well," she confided, "I'll be coming back here. And I'll stay way longer."

"Is that so?"

Iris nodded.

"First for just the summers, then full-time when I go on to college." She put her finger to her lips. "But it's a secret."

Hilda felt a breeze across her cheek. She looked at the window, but it was closed. She felt an eerie sense that the child might be right. What an odd little creature! Hilda lifted her off the counter and picked up the whipped cream and two spoons.

"What do you say we just eat this ourselves? You've ruined it anyhow. Then you can help me whip up some more for the guests."

Iris smiled at Hilda, traces of whipped cream between her teeth.

"Now, let's get a wiggle on. The guests will be here soon."

"Will Uncle Jack be here, too?"

"No, just your dad and Sabine and Fritz. Jack has to have dinner with his father and Jean."

"Who's Jean?"

Hilda paused. She couldn't say to the child that Jean had been the younger woman who had lured her husband away. She couldn't say that Jean was her replacement. Jean the usurper. No, that story was just too long and sordid.

"You know, curiosity killed the cat!"

"What cat?"

"It's a saying."

Iris shrugged. She'd never heard the old saying. At least Hilda didn't have to explain the complications of a divorce to her.

"Sabine always says we could get a cat whenever I say I want a pet, but I'd rather have a dog. She says a dog would take up too much space. Also, she says she wouldn't want anyone seeing her picking up dog poo on the streets when she walks the dog. I always tell her that I'd walk it, but she thinks I would get bored of it and that she would have to do it. But I still want a dog."

"Dogs are good. They are our friends and they protect us."

Yes, a dog! Iris thought to herself. A dog for protection was just what was needed. A dog would stop her from being stolen like her mother.

♦ ♦ ♦

It would be Iris's last sleepwalk in the garden. She drifted down the stairs, as though suspended in air, above the wood. Her feet touched the cool planks on the deck, but the hint of the coming autumn chill did not wake her. Her dreaming mind held her in its grasp and motivated her to continue, across the grass, beyond the trellises, to where the earth was turned and rich, planted with uneven rows of basil, ripened tomatoes, and herbs and vegetables of every kind.

"Ah, you have come to say goodbye."

Even in her between state of walking yet still sleeping, of dreaming with eyes open, Iris could not help but wonder if he was made-up or real.

"Yes. I leave tomorrow," she said.

"I will miss you. As will Hilda."

"I feel bad. She's all alone in that big house."

"She's not alone. I'm here with her."

Iris was surprised. She thought she was the only one aware of the man in the garden.

"Does she ever talk to you?" she asked him.

"All the time! Sometimes so much! I couldn't get a word in even if she could hear me!" He laughed. "Now, do you know why she plants these lovely marigolds all around the garden on the outside?"

"They're pretty. I like their colours. They don't smell that good, though!"

"To keep the aphids from eating her veggies. She lets the rabbits eat what they want, but she doesn't like the bugs!"

"I don't like bugs, either. And I'm afraid of spiders."

The old man laughed. Then he pointed across the garden. "Look. There's a little rascal now!"

In her short stay, Iris had seen the rabbits sneaking into Hilda's garden to nibble anything leafy and green.

"You know you have to leave the sweater here, for Hilda. She is very attached to it."

Iris hugged the long sleeves of the sweater around her body. She didn't want to leave it behind. She wanted to take it with her to remember her weeks at the farm. She had planned to ask Hilda in the morning if she could have it, but now she knew that she couldn't do that.

"Now, I must tell you something. Listen carefully and do not forget this. You may have some rough waves ahead. But then it will be smooth sailing to take you home."

Iris stood for a long time, hugging her arms in the sweater, feeling the wind on her upturned face, while she breathed in every smell the garden, the orchard, and the lake could offer. She stayed that way, for a moment and an eternity, until she felt herself lifted from the ground and transported back to the comfort of her bed.

Hilda placed the child on the bed, knowing that if she did visit the following year, she would be too heavy for her to carry up the stairs, knowing that this would be the last time she would so easily lift her and carry in her arms.

FIVE

THE ENVELOPE STOOD OUT FROM the other mail, partly because of its size and partly because of its stamps. Martina turned it over in her hands, felt the weight of it. She was always one to take her time; guessing was more important than just tearing into an envelope to see what was inside. What sweetness there was to those few minutes of imagining! An unexpected grant with all the needed paperwork attached. A magazine filled with opera history, photos, and playbills. A singer or dancer or musician, wanting a job and sending her press clippings, resumés, and photos.

Martina took the package to her desk. Even though the rehearsal quarters were sparse, dusty, and dilapidated, the Punk Baroness had a certain level of opulence to her work quarters. Her desk was baroque, with gold inlay along the carved wooden corners. There were lion heads for drawer handles, and her large chair was a dark oak with a generously padded seat, upholstered in burgundy leather. Martina leaned back in her chair, opened her drawer, and removed a sterling silver letter opener, the edge recently sharpened. The initials, however, were not hers. They were those of her father, a man who would have enjoyed life as an aristocrat, if it hadn't been for the war. But still, there was wealth left, hidden away for the future. It did allow her a certain lifestyle and it kept her punk opera company going, even when ticket sales were down.

Now, what could possibly be in the large envelope? Certainly, it seemed to be paper inside. She felt the edge of her envelope opener, sharp and exact. She pierced the glue on one end with its point, righted the blade, and then in one deft action, she pulled up on the blade so that it sliced through the top.

She eased her hand inside and pulled out the papers. Handwritten — a title page with no return address and no authorship. She turned over the first page and looked at the rows and rows of music, carefully written out by hand, with lyrics printed in blue ink underneath. Simple, clear, and rudimentary. Martina took the music to her piano, stretched her fingers near the keys, and began to pull the sound off the page, something she didn't really have to do as she could have just as easily heard the music in her head.

The chord progression, the quick change from major to minor, the keening high notes. It all seemed to hearken to music she knew only too well. Her hands froze, her heart began to pound hard in her chest, she could feel a change in her blood pressure. How could it be possible? Was it possible? The music was like a walking ghost.

She flipped through a few more pages till she found words from a language she had never heard. Martina had studied languages in school, but this language had not one familiar word. And then the notation "click, click, click," scattered throughout. Seeming random but, when she played the music, were totally in keeping with the rhythm of the piece.

Here were characters brought to life, Clytemnestra and Helena, Hermione and Hecuba. Martina closed the opera manuscript and stared at the title.

The Lost Queen: The True Abduction of Helen

Martina could barely breathe beyond the shallowest small gasps. This envelope, this piece of music, somehow held the clues to Clara's disappearance. She knew it. Should she tell Blanca, renew her hope? Or should she bide her time, just a little longer, until she could figure it all out, piece the clues together? Wait until she had some answers? *Despair will never kill you, but hope will get you every time.* Yes, she would wait. But not for too long.

♦ ♦ ♦

Of course, Bözsi had often thought of her parents and her sisters. Of course, she had missed them terribly, even though they had never approved of her. Her talk was too loose, her hair was too loose, her morals were too loose. Yes, everything about her was too, too loose.

The passage across to Gibraltar, those many years ago, had been choppy. The waves both rocking and churning at the same time, but to Bözsi it didn't matter that she was seasick. What was it to be sick? Alive! That was what sick was! As long as she was retching, she was breathing. As long as she was breathing, she was living.

"If you go up top on the deck, you will feel better."

Bözsi had heard the French accent before she even took in his appearance. Handsome. Tall, for a Frenchman. Bright blue eyes and a full, petulant mouth. She had noted the fitted and tailored pants and shirt, his manicured nails. Yes, this was a man of breeding and money — two irresistible things in a gentleman.

"I do not think I could bear to look at the water, though," Bözsi had replied.

"That is the trick of it. If you look at the thing you fear, then you conquer it. Come." Then he had offered his arm to her, and Bözsi knew from the moment she took it that he would change her fate forever.

"Now, what brings you to North Africa? Surely you cannot stay in Gibraltar. The population has been mostly evacuated," the Frenchman had informed her.

"I am part of a performing troupe. We are going there to perform."

"And what do you do?"

"I dance. The cancan. And I sing."

The man had squeezed her arm. Bözsi felt the firmness of his grasp, his fingers leaving an imprint on the memory of her skin. Later she would squeeze her arm, in the exact same place, attempting to re-create the sensation.

"May I suggest, perhaps, that you stay in Africa? You're Jewish, yes?"

"Yes."

"No place in Europe is safe. I will find you lodgings. It's in a house with other women. There, you will be safe. I have an apartment nearby." He smiled.

"Where, exactly?"

"Algiers," he replied. "It is French there. You'll be fine."

And at that moment Bözsi's life took a new and exciting course. What times those were! All a game to young Bözsi! All terribly romantic! Her Frenchman became her lover, confidant, and co-conspirator. Bözsi imagined them as glamorous and mysterious as characters in a film. They were both just actors, performing! All fun and games until the day when the news came that her lover, Henri, had been captured, tortured, and killed. All Bözsi could do was to wait for them to come for her as well. Who cared what they might do to her? Her family was dead. Her lover was dead. She had no zest to continue the fight. Who was there left to fight for? Evil had taken over the world, and she could either hide out or die. She chose to hide and wait for the inevitable. But no one came for her. Either Henri had taken the torture and didn't betray her or, worse, she just wasn't important enough.

Six weeks later, the war ended. Bözsi sat in an armchair at the brothel and wondered what purpose her life held. Not a life of adventure anymore. Not a life of grand romance. And not a life to be shared with her family. So she did what had been expected of her in the first place. Found a nice Jewish man, one who ran a jewellery shop, settled down, and had a baby. She did all of those things, only to have her husband leave her and her son die from meningitis. It seemed that loneliness was all she had to look forward to.

And then Esther, her annoying younger sister, showed up. Esther, who had behaved impeccably throughout the war, and yet still managed to survive by riding it out as a governess in Switzerland. Esther. Steadfast Esther. What did she know of moral sacrifice?

Esther slept beside Bözsi on the train. Her mouth was a little open and there was a faint snoring sound, like purring. Of course! Wasn't she nicknamed *Kiscica* when she was small? Kitten. Yes. And even as an old woman she was still a kitten. Small paws for hands. Dainty little feet. Large, greenish-brown eyes. A bit of whisker on the top lip. Here they were, two old women, the only link left to their shared childhood.

Bözsi wondered if Esther had ever experienced passion as she had. Had she ever waited for a man, counting the days and hours and minutes of his arrival? Had she ever thought that it didn't matter if she died, as long as she could be in her lover's arms one more time? Bözsi remembered how she would tremble on the days she knew Henri was coming. How she came to life on those days. He had been Bözsi's greatest love. Had he lived, how old would he be now? Around eighty! An old, old man.

Bözsi had tried to prepare herself for aging. All those years of caring for the flesh with creams and salts and exercise, only to have her muscles, skin, and joints betray her. Maybe Henri was the lucky one. Taken before the body could betray him. Taken while he was still full of life and passion. Taken, and not worn away, day by day, by the mundane.

Any idiot can survive a crisis, it is the day-to-day living that wears one down ...

Esther stirred. "Where are we?"

"On the train."

"Yes, I know we are on the train, you silly goose. But where are we?"

Right. Bözsi had been the "silly goose" and Esther had been the "kitten." No wonder she resented Esther. No wonder she'd run away. Well, the disapproval of her parents combined with the affair she had with her sister's husband had left her no choice. How old was she at the time? Not quite sixteen. And he was, what, twenty-eight? So, who should have really known better? Ah well, no point in holding a grudge. Their lack of compassion had saved her life.

"I think when we get to Paris, I will see if Henri's wife is alive. I will tell her how I loved her husband as well. And I will tell her about our affair."

"Do you think it is wise?" Esther asked hesitantly.

"Probably not. But I feel it must be done."

Esther stared at her older sister. All those years and she hadn't really changed.

"Do you think that this woman will be better off for meeting you? She must be almost eighty by now. Why upset her?"

"Oh please, what is there to upset? She's probably remarried. Henri has been dead for over fifty years. Water under the bridge."

"If it is all water under the bridge, perhaps you should let sleeping dogs lie."

"Dogs do not lie under bridges, do they?" Bözsi's tone was dismissive. "Bridges join two solitary islands. She is an island, and I am an island, and that bridge that joins us is our experience of

Henri. I need to talk about him with someone who knew him. And I bet you that she needs to talk about him as well."

"I bet she doesn't!" Esther crossed her arms.

"Oh please, they are French. It is not such a big deal, a mistress. You are so bourgeois. We should have been called Bözsi and Bourgeoisie!" She laughed at her little joke in that annoying carefree manner she had managed to maintain over the years. A laugh that still held the coyness of youth. It seemed to Esther that only her outer trappings had aged, but that part of her that was selfish in love, that part of her that demanded male attention, that part of her that was more flirtatious than anyone Esther had ever known, was still youthful. Close your eyes, and she was any age, eternal. Open them, and an eccentric old woman stared back dementedly.

"Let it go on record that I do not support this."

"Oh, Esther, when have I ever needed *your* approval? When have I ever needed anyone's approval? Some are ruled by the head and some by the heart. You are the former, and I the latter."

No, Esther thought. *Untrue.* The entire trip was an act of love and something she would have preferred to do on her own, but Bözsi had the power because Bözsi held the purse full of questionable cash.

"Oh look! Ours is the next stop. You should put on some lipstick, Esther. Make yourself a little more presentable."

Esther cringed as Bözsi applied an orange-red smear across her mouth before handing her the worn-down tube.

♦ ♦ ♦

Martina was unprepared for the call. First there was the envelope, and now this! Der Deutsche Oper National on the phone asking her about the twins and if they were still in her employ.

When Clara had suddenly disappeared, Martina made a choice to keep it quiet. At first, the hush-hush was because she had hoped, beyond reason, that Clara would return and that all would be well. Then she chose silence because she didn't want the publicity to hurt her lover. Of course there were rumours, but eventually they all stopped. The public gaze refocused; punk was dead, grunge had come and gone, and her opera company was struggling.

"There are two mature ladies here looking for them. The mother and the aunt," the voice on the phone informed.

"They are imposters. The mother of the twins is dead. She died over twenty-five years ago."

Martina slammed the phone down. How dare they pretend to be the twins' relatives! Likely some gossip rag. Mature ladies, *mein Gott*!

She looked over at the mysterious envelope. The only clue she could grasp was there. The stamp was *La Poste*. From Paris. France was so close. A mere train ride away. Surely Clara wasn't in France? No, someone else must have taken the envelope and mailed it for her. But who? And why? And why was there only the music and no note?

Martina imagined that Clara must have shoved her music into someone's hands and that person carried it to France to be mailed. Or perhaps Clara was dead and gone, and someone found the music. Perhaps the address was already on the envelope. Martina looked at the writing on the manila envelope. Not Clara's writing at all. She always used lettering that looked half like printing and half like writing, but this was cursive in fluid strokes. Flowery. Feminine. If writing could have a gender.

There was always the possibility that Clara hadn't written it at all. But still! *The Lost Queen: The True Abduction of Helen* ... who else would write such a thing?

Martina slid the music manuscript from the envelope. She could hear the music play in her mind, but she was more interested in the text. Here is the start of the story — Clytemnestra and Helen are twins, hatched from the same egg. Their mother has laid eggs because she has had adulterous sex with a giant, beautiful swan. Not just any swan, mind you, but a swan who was actually the great god Zeus himself. Martina was well aware of the myth, knew that in each egg there was one twin who was mortal and one who was divine, a demigod. Same twins, same mother, different fathers — one a king and one a god.

Martina placed the music on the piano. She looked at the strange rhythms in the musical interludes and saw that the composer intended there to be dance within the opera, with pounding of feet, between the scenes. Helen is gone, abducted and now married to Paris, a prince of Troy, and the tribesmen of Troy are dancing. *Yes*, Martina thought. *This is a clue.* Clara might still be where people dance.

Martina played what she read, building to a climactic crescendo. Helen does not die like so many of the other Trojans. Nor is she taken as a slave, as are the other Trojan women. Helen returns home, to a husband she did not love as much as she had loved Paris. She lives, in spite of everything. She lives to tell the tale. She is immortal. What was the opera trying to tell her? Where was Clara? And how would Helen have reacted if she thought that Menelaus had moved on, gotten over Helen, and had new children with a new princess? Someone earthier and mortal. Someone named Sabine, perhaps. A Germanic slave? How would the story have ended if Helen had been replaced by a Sabine-of-sorts?

Martina stopped playing so that she could wipe the tears from her cheeks. She was torn, her heart shards of glass, cutting through her chest. Martina was not only overwhelmed with the thought that Clara might still live; she was also overwhelmed by the otherworldliness of music. Music she knew she would never be able to write. Not in a hundred years. Her plan to write a modern *Sleeping*

Beauty would be put aside. Aurora would have to sleep another century. This would be her next opera. *The Lost Queen: The True Abduction of Helen.*

A voice startled her. Then another. Martina wiped her tear-stained cheeks and jumped up, only to be confronted by two old ladies, each carrying a small suitcase in one hand and an old-fashioned handbag in the other.

"Excuse us, the nice man at the opera house gave us this address. Are you Martina?"

Martina stared at the old women who had addressed her in German. German with a heavy Hungarian accent.

"The Punk Baroness, correct?" asked the other. The younger of the two.

Two old ladies. One with a smear of bright lipstick, the other with bright, clear eyes.

"I am Martina, the Punk Baroness, yes."

"I am Bözsi, but that is of no consequence. May I introduce you to Esther? She is looking for her girls."

Martina stared, her face a map of surprise and shock. Had she conjured her and now, *voilà*! It had to be her, the Esther of Blanca and Clara. Martina had seen a photograph once — Blanca and Clara, awkward teen girls, exuberant at having won a singing competition and a much younger-looking Esther embracing them with all the familiarity and pride of a birth mother. Sure, the woman looked older now, but who didn't? This had to be her! The fairy godmother she asked for in the flesh! The woman who might get Blanca to sing again.

"I can bring you to Blanca, but I have shocking news, so prepare yourself. Clara is missing. She has been missing for eight years."

Silence. Esther just stared at the Punk Baroness.

"Did you hear what I just said? Clara is missing. For eight years now."

Esther swayed on her feet. For a moment she looked like she was going to go down. Then she steadied herself.

"Missing? What do you mean missing?" Her voice was a raspy whisper.

"Vanished. One minute there and the next minute gone. Lost to us all. To Me. To Blanca. And to her dear daughter, Iris. I was there when she was taken in an airport in South Africa."

"Eight years?"

"Yes. Eight years ago." Martina tried to sound calm.

"Eight years. That is a very long time," Esther whispered, as if a full voice would only make the news more real.

Bözsi cleared her throat and shook her head. She had not come all this way to give up!

"Eight years is no time. I lost you for over fifty years, Esther, and we found each other. No one has looked hard enough. Or deep enough. Sometimes it is right under your nose." Bözsi touched her forefinger to her nose and nodded.

Martina hesitated. Should she show these women the music, the envelope with its French postmark? Should they see it before Blanca did? Could she trust these two old ladies? She wasn't sure; all she knew was that she could never solve the riddle of the manuscript on her own, so she was willing to take the chance. As risky at that might be.

"Tell me what you know," Bözsi pressed. "Leave out no detail. And I must warn you that I worked as a spy for the French Resistance, so there is no point in withholding anything."

The Punk Baroness handed Bözsi the envelope.

"What is this?" Esther asked.

"It arrived a few weeks ago. There is music inside."

"Oh look! France. It just so happens that we are going to France!" Bözsi exclaimed as she studied the postmark on the envelope.

Esther looked at her sister. *How perfect*, she thought. No matter what happened, Bözsi would always get her way. Land on her feet, survive any fall, and end up the better for it.

◆ ◆ ◆

Blanca believed she was seeing a ghost. How was it possible that Esther could be there, in their apartment, after all those years? Seeing her, she reverted back to a teen, awkwardly vying for approval. She rolled her sleeves over her forearms, hid her scars, and stammered an explanation as to why she wasn't singing anymore. But Esther waved her off, sat on the edge of her bed, and kissed her forehead and cheeks.

"You do not sing because you do not wish to live. Your voice gives you life, and you reject it."

"I'm nothing without Clara," Blanca asserted.

"You are everything, with and without her. You were always a strong girl. The one who thought things through."

Blanca shook her head. Wasn't it Clara who wrote the music? Wasn't it Clara who was the poet? It was Clara who always believed that music would bring colour into their pigment-less lives. That was why Blanca puffed herself up like the stronger twin. It was her job to protect the flame.

"I am old now, Blanca. But I have two purposes. To make you sing and to find your sister, because, like you, I believe she is still alive."

"Why? Why would you think that? And why would you say that and give me false hope?"

"Because if she were dead, you would sing. In heaven, we sing. In hell, we sing. The only place where there is no song is purgatory. There is no music for those condemned to wait."

SIX

HILDA'S DAUGHTERS WERE GANGING UP on her. Again. If only Jack were home. He would quiet them down. But Jack was off somewhere, chasing down a story.

"Your father is older than I am. Why don't you fret over him instead?" she asked them.

"Because Dad doesn't live alone. He has Jean, whereas you are all alone in this big house, Mom. We worry. We shouldn't have to worry."

This time it was Elizabeth speaking. The sensible one. Elizabeth was solid, in nature and in stature. Where did she get that stockiness? Her legs were shorter than her siblings', her waist was wider, and her fingers were short and stubby. Neither Hilda nor her ex-husband, John, were stocky. Then Hilda remembered John's mother, a tank of a woman with thinning hair and downturned lips. She had always bulldozed her way into every family event, and everything always revolved around her. Hilda had never been quite good enough for her son John, at least not until the day he'd left her for Jean. Only then did John's mother become an ally, because if Hilda wasn't good enough, then Jean was no more than a home-wrecking little tart, a seductress sent to ruin her son's reputation.

Hilda couldn't help but wonder which of her daughters was happier in her marriage. Neither would ever say if things weren't working out. Hilda understood that there was a competition with her, that her daughters would hold on to their marriages, happy or not. Such was the way of children from broken homes. They marry and, as much as they make a commitment to their new spouse, they make a greater commitment to themselves. *"Oh, I will never get a divorce the way my parents did. I will never do to my children what my parents did to me."* Such is the resentment bred of a broken home.

"Why," Hilda asked, "is it that neither of you, nor your father, went to Tristan's funeral? It would have meant so much to Jack."

"Tristan wasn't exactly *our* friend growing up. The boys were so much younger ..." This from sensible Elizabeth.

"But Jack loved him," Hilda reminded them.

Margaret slowly sighed. Hilda stared at the freckles on her daughter's face, straining to be seen through the heavy foundation her daughter used to cover them. Hilda had always loved the freckles on her daughters' faces and had spent hours counting them, touching their noses and cheeks as she went along. The freckles were the sun's kisses, she had once whispered to them, but in time, they came to care about the sun's kisses as little as they cared about *her* kisses.

"Mom, come on! That is just Jack being a drama queen. Yes, he lost his friend. But to make it more than that is just plain crazy. It wasn't a relationship, it was, you know, friends with benefits?" Margaret's words were far harsher than the tone she chose to use.

"He loved Tristan. That is all there is to it." Hilda went to the kitchen counter and started to grind some coffee. The whirring sound was a roadblock in the conversation.

She took a large Mason jar of yellowish thick cream from her fridge, pried open the lid, and poured most of it into a cooled stainless-steel bowl. She never used an electric mixer or a blender; to Hilda that was just plain ludicrous. Her daughters could see, as she vigorously beat the cream, spinning her old whisk quickly, that her muscles in her working arm came to life, all sinewy and defined. Hilda was considered a senior, but she had the arms of a young woman. Much nicer arms than either of the girls, and although they resented it, neither would give up the comfort of a blender to achieve arms like their mother's.

"Aren't you lonely, Mom?" Margaret asked. "Wouldn't you be happier around other people? People your age. You know, movie nights, playing cards …"

"I'm happy. And I hate playing games. Besides, I am friends with Karl."

"Karl?" Margaret asked. "Who the hell is Karl?"

"*Ja*, Karl. You know. The farmer up the road. He gives me my milk."

"Unpasteurized milk!"

"Okay," she finally said, "I give up. This is a loose-loose situation. I am not going to enjoy this visit with you if you keep nagging me."

"I think you meant to say lose-lose, Mom." Margaret couldn't help but correct her; she was a primary school teacher after all. Just like Jean.

Hilda started to clean up, putting away the coffee mugs she had just taken out, replacing the cake plates before firmly shutting the cupboard door.

"But, but what about the cake? I thought we were going to have your cake and coffee?" Elizabeth protested.

"No. Get used to it. If I go into one of those senior apartments you are so fond of, I won't be able to pick plums and make cake anymore. So, you can go now, without even a bite! Think about that!"

The two grown daughters laughed, thinking that Hilda wasn't serious. Hilda held her ground. Not a bite, not a single bite they would have. Go into a senior apartment! Ridiculous!

"I am fine. I am healthy. I will likely live to a hundred. Probably outlive you!"

"Siegfried thought he was fine, too," Margaret whispered to Elizabeth, just loud enough for her mother to hear.

"Siegfried loved this house! This was his home. He didn't ever want me to sell it to strangers. I would hope that maybe one day my grandchildren would want to keep hold of it. A family house to pass down the generations."

"Your grandchildren don't want a big old house in the country! They have dreams of their own," Margaret reasoned.

"We just think you should unburden yourself of all the work and trouble. You could travel then," Elizabeth coaxed, her tone as smooth as the whipped cream Hilda had just beaten.

"You want me to go into an old-age home?" Hilda questioned her daughter. "You know, I can always get another dog."

"We are not talking about an old-age home, Mom. Of course not. A senior's *apartment*. It's totally different. And there are lots in town, so you could see the grandchildren more. It would be good for everyone." Again, Elizabeth used her sensible tone.

Hilda took out the large pan of *Zwetschgenkuchen*, the plums heavily spread over the cake's crust. She quickly cut the cake evenly in two and wrapped each slab in wax paper.

"Here, for the children. Take it." Then she added, pointedly, "Not for you, for the children. You both look too fat." Even as she spoke the words, Hilda knew that Elizabeth would be picking at the sugary plums off the top of her slab of cake before they had even pulled out of her driveway.

Hilda watched as their car pulled away, then closed the front door. How quiet the walls were. How silent was the floor, and what secrets were kept in the stairs leading up to the second floor. The house held within its structure all their stories and dreams. It was home, a monument to her story. Here was the door jamb where every year the children's heights were recorded, and Jack, being six and eight years younger than his sisters, was always the lowest one until the year he was thirteen. Although his sisters had left for university, his height marks started to soar high above theirs. That was the summer he had sprouted up, growing almost five inches in three months. How his legs ached with the growing pains. Her daughters never had growing pains. They both grew in methodical ways, half an inch a year — year in, year out. It was all there, as proof, mapped out on the door jamb.

Here was the big wooden table that Siegfried had bought them for Thanksgiving. Here was the makeshift darkroom that Jack had once made in the mudroom. Here were the walls filled with photographs, all those faces through the ages staring out openly. And the wonderful windows! Windows that looked onto her garden. A garden she had created and re-created, year after year. A garden that provided beauty and food, and later, the source of her aromatic concoctions. A garden that always gave more than it took. Except for the day when the love of her life had died there.

She'd wanted to bury him in her garden. She'd asked the town authorities if she could but was refused. Instead, she had him cremated, then scattered his ashes in a corner of her garden. There she planted forget-me-nots and told him that she would be there one day, too. That he should wait for her. How could she ever sell the house if Siegfried was waiting for her in the garden?

Hilda poured a fresh cup of coffee then stepped into the late autumn air. She could smell the earth with its mossy, damp aroma. Beyond the garden, toward her neighbour's fields, there were the last rows of corn, reaching their tall heads toward a diminishing sun. The days would get shorter and shorter now, while the shadows got longer. Then winter would be upon the land, and Hilda would hibernate, cloistered in her office, creating new concoctions of smells. She could feel the first cool chill of the change of the seasons. Hilda lifted her coffee mug to her face, breathed in the rich bitterness, then drank it down in measured sips.

◆ ◆ ◆

The scents Hilda chose for Iris were very specific. For her top note, Hilda chose basil. It was one of Hilda's favourite scents. It wafted on the breeze of the morning air, from early summer to the fall. She always planted a lot of basil, making sure that she snapped off the seeding tops regularly to encourage the prolonged growth of the basil plants. Hilda wanted to use as many ingredients from her garden as she could. The basil as the top note would be the first aroma her nose would smell.

The next bottle she created was the essence of rose. Rose was perhaps the dearest of all essential oils, but Hilda had wanted something special for Iris. A tiny drop requires the petals of many, many roses. Hilda had been growing wild roses, mostly in a light-pink shade, for over a decade. There were trellises of roses up the exterior walls of the farmhouse, and roses grew and covered the arbors. Rose opens the heart to love, which is why it is considered a flower of love and passion. Love, like the rose, is fierce. Thus, the thorns. But it is not the beauty of the bud, but the smell of the petals that evoke feelings of love. Hilda took the petals from almost a hundred roses to make one vial of rose essence. Young Iris would never know how dear the gift actually was, but perhaps the scent would make her feel more loved.

The lavender, mint, and chamomile were staples, although chamomile was another of Hilda's favourites. A German plant, daisy-like and small, it grew close to the ground, and although the flowers were white to yellow, once extracted the distilled essence was blue.

Finally, thyme and sage for the base notes. The more savoury scents would help to ground Iris. While some of the scents would open her philosophical mind, encourage spirituality and imagination, it was important to include the scents that would give her resilience and keep her feet rooted on earth. Hilda took a chance with the thyme because she knew that it could open a channel to the angels, and not only did she want angels to protect Iris, but she also wanted to encourage Iris's second sight. The sage was the final protective element. It would keep any evil away from the gentle girl. No one would steal her away against her will — as had been the fate of Iris's mother.

SEVEN

IRIS SLIPPED HER HAND INTO her coat pocket, expecting the usual relief. *Ah yes, there they are. The keys. Now I'll be safe. All is fine.* But today, the ritual found no keys in the left pocket of her coat. She shoved her other hand into the right pocket. Again, no keys. Panic.

Iris raced back into the classroom. She got onto her hands and knees and crawled along the cloakroom floor, hoping they had simply slipped from her pocket, but she knew there was no hope as there was no hole in her coat pocket. Iris could never wear a coat with a hole, let alone a loose seam. How could she possibly manage to get through an entire day knowing that her coat was in need of repair? If there were ever a hole in her coat pocket, that would be all she would be able to think about during class. That hole would call to her, draw her back to the cloakroom, where she would slip her coat on, quickly, just so that she could put her hand into the pocket and stick one finger into that hole. *Yes, there it is, there is that hole!* But within an hour of returning to her desk, that hole would call out to her again, and she would try to push it from her mind until the compulsion to revisit the hole would be too overwhelming. Every night before bed, she made sure that there were no holes in her pockets just so that she could be prepared for the following day of school.

At first it was much like that with her keys, but Iris developed a ritual that helped her cope. After the satchel was hung on her hook, she would remove all other outdoor clothing. Then she would feel for her keys and tap them three times, *tap, tap, tap*, with her index finger. As soon as she sat at her desk, she would repeat the *tap, tap, tap*, on the wood of her desk, making sure that her classmates did not see her. The keys were safe in her pocket because their essence was with her at the desk. But today, the daily ritual hadn't worked. The keys were gone, and now her knees were quite dirty from crawling along the cloakroom floor.

Iris stood and tried to appear composed. Again, she felt in her pockets, knowing they wouldn't be there, but hoping, just the same, for a miracle.

It wasn't that there would be no one at home. Sabine would be at the apartment, playing with Fritz, or cooking some food, or looking at magazines filled with wedding dresses. Of course, she would not be in trouble, and no one would scold her for this — after all, the missing keys were not her fault. She had tapped them. *Three times*. No, that wasn't the problem at all. It was the fact that, if she did not have her keys, her *magical* keys, then someone could steal her. Some bad person could kidnap her and do nasty things to her. All she could think of now was why her mother hadn't taken her keys with her, to protect her, when she was in such a dangerous place as an airport?

"Iris? *Warum bist du noch hier?* School has been finished for half an hour!"

Her teacher looked down at her with concern.

"*Ich kann meine Schlüssel nicht finden.* I looked everywhere. My keys have disappeared!"

Disappeared, like her mother.

"Is there no one at home?"

Iris shook her head. "My stepmother is home. I'm sure of it."

"Are you afraid that she'll be angry with you?"

Again, Iris shook her head. Frau Bergen reached her hand out, helped her up.

"I am going that way. I will walk along with you."

Should she tell her? Confide in her that the keys were more than a tool for unlocking doors? That it wasn't about entry into their apartment but about protection from bad men with evil intent. Although some part of Iris knew that it was just a superstition, she also knew she would need a new set of keys before she could possibly ever walk home alone again.

♦ ♦ ♦

The flame licked the side of the glass as Gareth turned the stem, holding the eye evenly, slowly, in the small fire. There were few left who could forge artificial eyes from fire and sand, doing the work of an alchemist. He knew he could easily paint eyes, work in acrylics, like his contemporaries in North America. But did he want to? Only when he was there, working in the oculary, did he realize how much he was at home.

He touched the centre of the hot orb, pushed gently into the pliable glass with his metal instrument, until a dark centre emerged. The pupil rarely differs except, perhaps, in size. Perhaps one may be a little less round, a little more oval, but the darkness remains the same. Except with albino eyes. A touch of red is required with albino eyes. Gareth knew this, although he had never made an albino an eye.

Clara. Was she really dead? How could she not be? Eight years and not a word. He knew that Clara had loved Iris above everyone else. He believed that she loved their daughter more than any mother had ever loved her child. Gareth had heard her whisper, more than once, into the baby's ear, "I'll never leave you. Never." And yet, she had.

Gareth tried to push the invasive thoughts from his head, to focus on the creation before him. He touched the centre of the pupil again, but he was too quick, too firm, and the black of the pupil lifted away on the metal, leaving an accusatory hole in the middle of the eye. Gareth stared at the empty space. A small abyss that threatened to grow, widening large enough to swallow him up, away from troubles, away from memory, away from guilt. How much easier it would be if the truth could burst forth from the emptiness, telling him what had truly happened to his first great love.

Of course Clara was dead. All the wondering and the imagining was only hurting Iris. It was getting worse yearly. Iris was developing more quirks, more rituals, to get through the day. Gareth needed to give them all a fresh start, a start filled with possibilities.

Gareth turned the glass eye once again with a steady, unwavering hand, touching the centre, and a perfect pupil emerged, shy at first and then bold, and deeply knowing. He gently put the vulnerable orb onto the cooling rack. It will harden in time. *We all do*, he thought.

Gareth wasn't ready to return home. It was still early, and he knew how Sabine liked a little late-afternoon time alone with the children. There was nothing more he could do with the eye he was creating, and the idea of taking out a canvas to paint only saddened him. Painting had been abandoned; he hadn't finished a piece since Clara went missing. It was a strange penance. If Clara wasn't singing somewhere, then he would not paint.

Gareth took out sand and colour sticks to begin something new. He wanted to make small glass orbs in a range of bright colours, encompassing the entire spectrum so that a rainbow of wishes would shine in the glossy but transparent glass. Each orb, a world unto itself. One world would balance the next, in both colour and weight. And they would hang, suspended, above the expected baby's head. A mobile, in movement, offering the newborn all the dreams of a future life.

♦ ♦ ♦

The package sat out on the table, wrapped in brown paper, and addressed to Iris in a smooth blue ink. To Iris, it seemed exotic. She had never received a package by airmail before. From Canada. *Kanada*. She thought how odd it was that the word was pronounced exactly the same and yet, in Germany, they spelled the country with a *K* and not with a *C*. Nevertheless, there it was, a package from Canada — with a *C*.

"May I open it now?" she asked Sabine.

"Why not? It doesn't say that you have to wait for Christmas. Besides, that is over a month away. So, go right ahead!"

"What do you think is inside?" Iris asked.

"Only one way to find out!" Sabine handed her the brown package.

Iris stared at the writing. Hilda's name and address were clearly written on the top left-hand corner. Iris could feel herself filling with joy. She couldn't tear at the paper quickly enough. Inside the paper was a box. Small, wooden, not cardboard. She lifted the lid. There, amongst the wood shavings, were eight small bottles, each labelled with the same blue ink. From Hilda's fountain pen, no doubt. And at the bottom was a handmade book and a letter. Iris glanced at Sabine.

"Go on. You can go into your room if you want privacy. It is a moment between you and Hilda. If you want to share with me later, you can, but this is something just for you, I think."

Iris wanted to experience each scent before she read the enclosed booklet. She wanted to know if what she really felt was what Hilda thought she would feel. Lavender, rose, mint, thyme, sage, basil, and chamomile. These were all scents that came right from Hilda's garden. Iris knew that Hilda had harvested and extracted the scents herself. And then she had made a special package just for her.

Iris also knew that, somehow, she could combine the smells herself to create a scent that would protect her. Make her strong and keep her safe. Then she would never have to worry about losing her keys again.

♦ ♦ ♦

It was late when Gareth returned home. What had started as tinkering had captured him, and he'd worked creating magical orbs of blown glass for far longer than he had intended. He couldn't wait to show Sabine the mobile he created for their child. The thought of a new baby inspired him. How long it had been since creation had consumed him!

Sabine was asleep on the couch, Fritzi curled up beside her, his chubby hand resting on the swell of his mother's belly. Perhaps she had felt the baby kick and she had laid her son's hand onto her stomach so that he could feel the life moving inside of her. Hadn't she done that with Iris while she was carrying Fritz? And Iris's eyes had gotten big when she felt him kick. Then she had moved her mouth closer to Sabine's belly and had told the baby to stop kicking. To be quiet. Told him that it was mean and rude to kick.

Gareth kissed the top of Sabine's head. She stirred with a deep inhalation, and a fluttering of her eyes. Even after knowing her all these years, Gareth still found himself startled by the disarming blue-green of her eyes, a contrast to the dark of her hair. She really was beautiful in an unsettling way. She had an athletic body, but a delicate neck and small wrists. Her thighs were muscular, but her ankles were like a racehorse's — narrow and tapered. Her hair was dark, her skin easily tanned, but her eyes looked as though they were floating on water. And those lips of hers, lips that he had kissed so many times, were full and puffy, but so pale that it was hard to know where the lips ended and the skin began. She had been his friend and his bedmate for so long that when he did step back on those rare occasions, like when she was just waking from sleep, or lost in a book she was reading, Gareth could suddenly see her as he would a beautiful stranger. In those rare times he would think, *If I didn't know you, I would* want *to know you.* Only when he forgot how familiar they were did he appreciate her all over again. Yes, he appreciated how she helped with Iris in the beginning. He appreciated her friendship and support. He appreciated sharing a bed with her and how she made him feel as a man. But that was not the same as seeing her with fresh eyes. When what he saw in her was the eternal woman.

"You fell asleep on the sofa again. You must feel all stiff."

"I was telling Fritz a story, hoping he would go to sleep. I tried to make it as boring as possible, but I think I bored myself to sleep first!"

Gareth had seen it so many times. Fritz would be close to sleep and then something of interest would happen in Sabine's made-up stories that would spark his interest — the changeling turns a corner, the dwarf finds a magic flower, the wizard reads from his spell book — and Fritz would become alert one again. Thus "the list" was devised. The list always worked. Sabine would send the changeling on a quest over and over again, but first the changeling would have to pack a sack full of supplies. Sabine would just list all kinds of stuff that would be packed, and eventually Fritz would get bored and fall asleep. Evidently the list even bored Sabine, transporting her to dreamland as well.

"So, I wanted to tell you, the amnio results came back. Perfectly healthy!"

"Yes, and …?" Gareth asked because the other question was always what sex the baby was. Health was the first concern, but whether the baby was a girl or a boy was the next curiosity. Gareth had no interest in having a gender-reveal party, but he did have an interest in knowing. Then he could imagine a son or a daughter, staring up at the mobile, transfixed.

"And …" Sabine slapped her thighs in a drumroll. "It's a girl!"

Gareth lifted Fritz from his mother. Carried him to his little bed that was so near the floor that even if he fell from it no harm could be done.

"A girl," he beamed. "Fantastic!"

"I thought a boy would be better. Two boys close to the same age. They could be friends. Play with each other." Sabine winced as she stood. She wasn't throwing up as often, but now there was heartburn and stiffness. The miracle of pregnancy certainly came with its drawbacks.

"Fritz can be her big brother. Her protector."

When Gareth put his son down, he was suddenly filled with gratitude. He took Sabine's hand, weaving his fingers between hers. Then he gently squeezed, as if to reassure himself that this was indeed real and would not vanish.

"I smell roses," he suddenly said. "Do you have an admirer? Did someone send you roses and you've hidden them from me?"

"It is a very strong scent, isn't it?" Sabine responded.

Gareth followed the scent to Iris's room, to that section partitioned off from Fritz's half. There she was, sound asleep with little brown bottles on her bedside table. Gareth went and tightened all the lids, but when he came to the one marked ROSE, he saw that it was half empty, and his daughter reeked with the overpowering scent of the reduced and distilled flower.

♦ ♦ ♦

When Iris was very young, she could not tell the difference between her mother and her aunt. The fact that Blanca was an inch taller than her mother did not tip her off. They both dressed all in white, same eyes, same lashes, and same lips smeared in red. There was only one difference that Iris learned to discern. This difference was only evident when very close to either Blanca or Clara, when her sight did not distract her from the truth. The great difference was that they *smelled* different. And that was why it wasn't until Iris was clamouring to be in her aunt's arms that she realized that it was her aunt who had returned from South Africa, and not her mother.

What was the difference in their smells? Clara had a fresh smell. Floral and springlike and, yes, there was a middle note, a heart note, of rose in her aroma. Blanca, on the other hand, smelled of earth and salt with undertones of sweet vanilla. Although she applied her perfume sparingly, there was a heavier quality to Blanca's aroma. Iris wasn't sure if her aunt wore her scent behind her ears or on her throat because Blanca stopped hugging her after her mother had disappeared.

When she closed her eyes and imagined her mother, she had a memory of a scent somewhere around her neck. A neck that she would nuzzle into as a toddler. She had a faint memory of whispering secrets into her mother's ear. She did that because the smell that meant *mother* was somewhere between her mother's neck and ears. Iris was old enough now to know that the unimportant secrets she had once told her mother were no more than an excuse to smell her. To convince her that her mother and her aunt had not switched places.

And then the thought, that constant, intrusive thought, came to mind. What if they had? What if Blanca and Clara *had* switched places and it was Blanca who was really missing? And to secure the lie, they had also traded their perfumes. Perhaps there was no abduction at all. They were simply bored with their lives and their partners, so Blanca disappeared and Clara assumed her role, just close enough to watch Iris grow up, but not so close that she would be hampered by her.

She was clearly unwanted. And to make matters even worse, she knew that the arrival of a new baby would bring great excitement into the home. But she felt left out of it all. It was only Fritz who marvelled every time the baby moved. Only Fritz who clapped his small hands with joy.

The only balm for Iris was the scent of rose. Essential rose oil. When she dabbed on a bit, she could feel her heart open. But still, there was not enough love to fill the hole in her heart. She was born with a small hole in her heart, but hadn't that hole been successfully closed when she was five? Then why did she feel that the hole was back and that love was leaking out of it? She knew that another dab would help close that hole in her heart. And another, and another, until she was swimming in the scent of rose. It was all too much, too heady. She didn't know what it meant to feel high, but that was what it was. She was carried away on the scent of roses, floating on petals, embraced by love.

Later, when Gareth went into his daughter's room, he looked at his sleeping daughter. Then he put the brown bottles away, opened the window, and invited in the cool November air.

EIGHT

WHEN ESTHER FIRST SAW IRIS, she wanted to cry. Her throat seemed to close around her heart, which had surely leapt up from her chest. She tried to compose herself; she didn't want to frighten the girl with overwhelming emotion. She put her hand out, gesturing for a polite handshake. But there was a tremor in the gesture. Iris looked at the outreached hand, not sure what to do with it.

"*Vörös kutya, vörös ló, vörös nő,*" Bözsi laughed heartily as she stepped forward and regarded the girl.

Red dog, red horse, red woman was an old Hungarian expression. The second part of the expression was never voiced but always understood. *Red dog, red horse, red woman should all be beaten.* Why were the Hungarians so suspicious of red hair that they even had a saying for it? *Well,* Esther thought, *it wasn't just red hair, was it?* It was the Jews and the Roma, too. Anyone different. Maybe that had changed, though. Maybe Hungary was like anywhere else now and no longer the Hungary of her youth. Esther had not been back to her birthplace since she escaped being rounded up for the camps in 1944. Perhaps if she returned for a visit, she would see a new country. Perhaps her own nightmares would go away. Perhaps, perhaps, perhaps ... but she would never go back; she did not want to keep the company of ghosts. Her past and her sorrows were all compartmentalized and put away like gift boxes you intend to take down and reuse but never do.

"I hate that expression," Esther whispered to her older sister.

"Oh, Esther, do stop with the formal handshake. Can't you see you are frightening the girl? Give her a hug. She's *family*!"

Iris allowed the woman to take her into her arms and squeeze her, unsure of whom she was exactly. If she was family, why didn't she know her?

"You are so like your mother," the old woman, Esther, whispered in her ear.

Iris looked over to the kitchen where her Aunt Blanca was speaking with Gareth and Jack. Why would this woman think that she was like her mother when her mother's identical twin was standing right over there? *She* was the one who was like her mother. An exact copy. Not her. For a moment, Iris wished that she had been born albino.

Iris wondered if her mother would have aged the way her aunt had. If her mother would have become more angular with time. She thought that her aunt was very beautiful with her white downy lashes and pale pinkish eyes, all the more noticeable because of the contrast with her red-stained lips. *Yes*, Iris thought, *that is exactly how my mother would look now. But a bit shorter and a lot softer.*

Iris wondered why her father had wandered off, leaving her alone with the doting older ladies in the Punkarie rehearsal space. As soon as she could break away from their grasp, she settled herself awkwardly on a dark blue velvet divan. Blue had never been her favourite colour; she preferred to be surrounded by greens and purples, believing that red hair would stand out against those colours. But this blue was different. Richer than most blues. And the velvet was soft and aged, with a little of the fabric worn away by the armrest. Iris couldn't help but rub her hand across the worn bit, aware that there was a certain beauty with age. And then she thought of Hilda, whom she regarded as very beautiful, with her curious and wise face and her long, strong back and upright posture. She was like an oak tree, solid and formidable, unlike the two old ladies across from her who seemed more like doddering old aunts straight out of an Agatha Christie novel. Perhaps it was their height that made them comical. Or rather *lack* of height. They were acorns compared to Hilda's oak tree. Iris squeezed her eyes closed and willed herself to grow. *Please*, she thought, *do not let me be one of those little women. Make me tall and beautiful and* — she searched for the word — *statuesque*. With that, she swung her legs up onto the divan and leaned into the reclining back. She arranged her black skirt so that it fell over the edges of the royal-blue velvet and remarked how well the blue and the black looked together. Black and blue. *Like a bruise*, she thought. *Like my bruised heart. My bruised heart with the hole in it.*

If it was true, if her mother were truly dead, then surely she would be there, in the room, watching this celebration of her life. If she were really dead, she would be looking down at Iris, seeing her arranged across the divan, aware of her startling beauty. A pre-Raphaelite knockoff of the twenty-first century.

"Ach! I see you have the best seat in the house, Iris!" The Punk Baroness always made an entrance, and usually with something she had baked in her hands. This time it was a platter of *Vanillekipferln*, moon-shaped cookies made of hazelnuts and covered in a blanket of vanilla sugar. Iris loved them because she thought that they were the shape of a bow. With each and every bite, she would imagine that she was paying homage to the goddess Artemis, every cookie a symbol of the silver bow the goddess always carried. Yes, she would grow up to be just like Artemis. Tall, strong, and independent. She would never marry; she would be the huntress. Love would never mess up her life!

"I don't want you to move, you look perfect! Let me bring the princess one of my creations. I will not know if they pass or not until I have your approval!" Martina carried the heaping plate across the room to Iris. She was dressed from head to toe in soft, black leather. Not the hard, stiff leather they use in shoes and boots, but a leather that fell over her curves, hugging her like a lover. Even the pants draped softly around her, except for where her large ass pressed against the cut of the pants in two impressive cheek orbs. Iris suddenly felt quite girlish and plain compared to the sophisticated Punk Baroness. Every time Iris saw her, she seemed to have an exotic air about her, and Iris couldn't help but wonder if she baked the cookies dressed like that, all in black, with perhaps a frilly, protective apron over the leather.

The thing about *Vanillekipferln* is that the vanilla sugar is a very light and powdery coating. One breath onto the cookie and the sugar flies off, leaving incriminating proof on your face or clothes that you have succumbed to its pleasure. Iris knew this and held her breath as she took that first bite, only exhaling once her mouth was full of the nutty, sweet concoction.

Blanca was watching the gathering safely from the kitchen. All those shiny faces atop a sea of black clothing. She had refused to wear black, believing that if she did it would authenticate the ridiculous pantomime of her sister's celebration of life. In retaliation, Blanca wore all white. High-waisted linen pants that only made her look longer and leggier. A man-styled oxford shirt, with a subtle collar and two buttons undone to emphasize her swan neck. Blanca rolled her sleeves down on her white cotton shirt, covering the map of her freshly scarred arms.

"Why do you do that?" Jack asked her.

"Do what?"

"Cut yourself. You have scars up and down your arms! It must hurt when you do it. So why? Does it soothe you somehow?"

"It is a representation of my interior well-being. Or rather, non-well-being," Blanca answered him.

"Is your interior pain so great that you need some physical pain to equal it? I mean, I don't mean to pry, but I do want to understand it. To understand you," Jack prodded.

Blanca smiled at her old friend, seeming to hold a long-ago expression Jack had all but forgotten. They were all so innocent once. So filled with those lofty dreams that seemed to be immortal. But dreams do not pop like bubbles; they erode away in such small increments that you don't even realize the distance travelled from them, until a gesture or a smile brings you back to what you once hoped and desired. You turn around. You look at your younger self and wonder when you became a stranger to the person you once were.

"Our bodies are marked by all the love and sorrow of our lives. Some get tattooed, some make their own maps with a razor or a knife, and some, like you, are marked by metaphor."

Jack tapped his glass eye and seemed to look right through her.

"I think this is a bit more than a metaphor, Blanca."

It was said in a whisper so that Gareth could not quite hear him. Gareth was preoccupied anyhow, looking over words on a piece of paper. Likely a speech about Clara. Jack knew that his sorrow for his lover, Tristan, could be contained and understood, but how could Gareth deal with the loss of Clara? With not knowing the truth of her absence?

"I think the last time we were all together in this space was the night the Berlin Wall came down," Blanca mentioned.

"You were very naughty that night!" Jack whispered in her ear.

"What do you mean?"

"Well, you know. Sneaking into my room. Of course, we were all very high from the excitement. Not to mention the champagne and the pot!"

Blanca glanced at Gareth, who was still looking over his speech. She quickly and conspicuously shook her head, her eyes wide in warning as she looked pointedly at Jack.

For Jack it was the confirmation of something he had suspected and feared. He looked past his best friend and past Blanca to the precocious princess sprawled across the divan, her mouth full of *Vanillekipferln*, her black clothes covered in a white sprinkling of powdery sugar.

◆ ◆ ◆

When Blanca recited "A Boat Beneath a Sunny Sky" from *Through the Looking-Glass*, she changed the name Alice to Clara.

> "Still she haunts me, phantomwise,
> Clara moving under skies
> Never seen by waking eyes."

Martina knew that it was far more than a eulogy for Clara; Blanca was making a defiant statement. Blanca's sister was on the other side of a mirror, and Blanca felt her presence, in an unworldly dream that no one else had access to. Perhaps Clara did still haunt Blanca *phantom-wise*. Whether Clara was dead or not, the reality was the same. Her ghost sat uncomfortably between them. *A gooseberry in the middle!*

Martina still had not shown Blanca the mysterious music, and she had sworn the two crazy old Hungarians to secrecy. Why had she even told them? She could have simply hidden the music from everyone, pretended it didn't exist, then the acceptance of Clara's death would have been easier. And now she could, just by looking at the bargain-basement rip-offs of Eva and Zsa Zsa Gabor, see that they didn't believe that Clara was gone either. Not gone for good.

When Blanca finished the recitation of the poem, Martina wrapped her arms around her. Told her that it was perfect. She could smell the light perspiration on her skin. *Yes, this is my lover, my life, and somehow, I must turn her from the looking glass so that she may once again face the world beyond the trap of the reflection.*

Together they watched Bözsi and Esther at the piano, singing a refrain from a Hungarian operetta. One Martina didn't recognize. Perhaps it was something they had made up together. But Esther seemed to know the music, and as she played with focused concentration, Bözsi increased the vigor of her singing, lifting her skirt above her knees and kicking her legs into the air. Suddenly her old body seemed to possess the memory of a much younger dancer.

Gareth and Jack were cleaning up, washing glasses and putting away food. Their voices were low, and neither Blanca nor Martina could make out what they were saying above the singing and the piano-playing. But from time to time, they saw Jack look over to where young Iris slept on the blue velvet divan.

Perhaps, Martina thought, *perhaps she* is *the true Princess Aurora, escaping a world that had dealt her a bad hand.* Perhaps it wasn't yet time to tell her story. And Martina wondered if, like Blanca, the girl might be dreaming of Clara and the imagined day when her mother might return.

♦ ♦ ♦

Once everyone had gone home to bed, Jack sat alone in the rehearsal space of Punkarie Opera. The high ceilings ensured that his every step, his every move, echoed through the space. He pulled out his video, found the VCR, and inserted the tape. He hadn't visited it for almost a month. The viewings were becoming increasingly difficult. The image of Tristan was starting to show signs of the disease. His face had a lean look, with cheekbones that seemed to press out beyond his translucent skin. His eyes were larger and sunken. But he still managed a smile, though more difficult than at the start of the tape.

"Hello, my love," Tristan's image said to him, staring straight into the camera. "If you are still watching, you're pretty brave. Are you still there?"

"I am," Jack whispered. "I'm still here."

Tristan seemed to smile, as if knowing from the grave that Jack would not be able to turn away.

"Probably just as well you weren't here for this part. I suppose it's not much longer now. I hurt, Jack. I hurt so much, every day ..."

Jack paused the video. He froze the frame so that Tristan looked still, quiet, listening.

"There's something I never told you, Tristan. Something I kind of knew, but didn't know for sure. Not till today. But you have to keep it a secret." Here, Jack paused so that he was as quiet and as frozen as Tristan's image. "You see, Trist, you see, I'm a father. I mean, by the time she was three, she looked a lot like me. But it was a secret. And then, you know, Clara went missing. And I went to find her because ... because I didn't want my daughter not to have a mother. I went away to find her, and I left you. I left you, and you were dying. I never told you why I left. And I am so, so sorry. And now you are gone and so is Clara." Jack could feel his throat tighten. "If there is anything on the other side, I just hope that you can forgive me."

Jack pressed Play and Tristan sprang back to life, sort of.

"Of course, I can't be angry with you. We both had our secrets. I never really told you everything, did I?"

Jack shook his head. "No," he whispered, "and I never really told you everything, either."

♦ ♦ ♦

Jack could feel the fogginess of too much drink in his head. It felt as though he had swallowed a yard of cotton batten, only to have it explode into his brain. He had found Martina's stash of aged Scotch and, as he'd made it through another half hour of Tristan's video, he had fortified himself with a few tumblers full of it. He stretched as he stood, hoping that if he moved his body in his usual, sober way, he might fool himself into reacting as though he were fully functional.

He ejected his videotape from the VCR and returned it to its envelope. He knew Martina and Blanca would be arriving soon, so he shoved the tape into his suitcase and proceeded to make a large pot of coffee for when they came down into the rehearsal space. He glanced at his watch.

Jack was about to pour out his first cup of coffee when he heard the door open and the distinct sound of Martina's voice.

"Well now, Herr Jack, where are you?"

"In the kitchen, making coffee."

"*Kaffee!* You are a god! Divine, rare, and celestial!"

"Thank you."

"Don't thank me. Thank Shakespeare. They are his words, not mine. But I do like to steal from the best!" Martina laughed.

Jack was surprised to see Martina on her own, without Blanca.

"*Sie schläft. Immer schläft.*"

"Why do you think she sleeps so much?" Jack asked her.

"Depression," Martina said, so matter-of-factly that it would seem her answer was self-evident. Martina had grown so used to Blanca's ennui that there was no longer any concern in her voice. Her darkness was simply an obvious truth.

"I have something to show you, but first I must address something that Blanca confided in me," the Punk Baroness continued.

Jack lifted an eyebrow, motioned for her to continue.

"The night we all celebrated the opening of the Berlin Wall, Blanca *was* with me that night. She was quite stoned and even more drunk, and she just passed out. I stayed awake the whole night because I was worried that she had alcohol poisoning. It was Clara who snuck into your room." Here she paused, sipped her coffee, and looked at Jack with such intensity that Jack knew that what was to come was as much performance as it was truth.

"I know. Blanca made that clear to me yesterday. Though I may have suspected it beforehand. Until Iris was three or four, though, I always thought it was Blanca."

"I think you are very wicked to think it would have been okay to have slept with either of them. Blanca and I were together even then. But it was long ago. And we were all young and reckless. *Ja?*"

Jack thought back to that night. The overwhelming joy that lasted from night to day, and then night again. They had been dancing on the wall, sharing joints with strangers, drinking champagne right out of the bottle, dancing ... and then they had eventually all crashed at the Punkarie, some in dressing rooms and some on the stage, or strewn like discarded costumes on theatre seats. Jack had found quiet in one of the dressing rooms. He already knew that the photo he had snapped would be in the paper the next day, so he lay down, feeling exhilarated and content. Then a soft knock. *"Komm rein,"* he had said in German. *Come in.* When he saw the waifish young woman, translucent skin all aglow, white hair loose in waves past her breasts, almost to her waist, he was sure it was Blanca. Why wouldn't it be? Hadn't they been teenage sweethearts, after all? By the time he questioned whether it was Blanca or Clara, it was too late. They were in the throes of passion and there was no turning back.

"But why? Why would Clara have come to me when she *always* loved Gareth?"

"You forget that Sabine was also here that night. Clara was in the washroom, and when she came out, she saw Sabine asleep beside Gareth, her head on his chest. They had just passed out that way, but Clara assumed it was much more. She was always insanely jealous of Sabine, and she acted out of spite, only to regret it the next day. She cried and cried over the mistake. Thought she fucked up her only chance at happiness."

Jack rubbed his hand over his face. His head was pounding, a dull *thump, thump, thump* resounding in his brain.

"What should I do? Tell Gareth? Talk to him?"

"I think he might know, but it doesn't matter. He loves Iris, and she is an extension of Clara, the woman he lost. Why don't you just protect her? And maybe one day she will need to know. But that time isn't now."

All the while she spoke, she was rooting through her drawers, putting envelopes into piles on her desk. But one she put aside, on its own. This one she put her hand on as though it were the chosen manila envelope. Jack noted how tapered and lovely her fingers were. And each one finished with a well-shellacked red nail that came to a point like a weapon. *Yes*, he thought, *she could do some damage with those*.

"In exactly ten minutes, the crazy Hungarian women will be here. Then we will look at the contents of the envelope and study them. We will make some sense of it all and then we will come up with a plan. Do you understand, Jack?"

"Not really," he replied, quite puzzled.

"You must swear to secrecy. Not a word to Blanca. Not till we find out the truth. And if you break your word, well … I know enough about you, don't I?"

Did she know more than that he had once slept with Clara and fathered Iris? As much as the Punk Baroness seemed a larger-than-life character at times, she also had an air of danger. At least she did when she wasn't baking cookies.

"You have my word," he told her.

Martina spat into the palm of her hand. Jack took it in his, and they shook.

◆ ◆ ◆

They arrived at the Brandenburg estate unannounced. Martina, Jack, and the two diminutive sisters, who seemed to stride with even greater purpose than their younger friends, were on a mission. Martina had the manila envelope with the opera libretto and music tucked safely away in her dark burgundy briefcase. There were clues in the composition. Of that there was no doubt; the similarities were obvious to her. Martina knew that the story of Helen was one of the most difficult of the myths to interpret. She knew that she did not know all the subtleties of the different endings, but she knew that there was one person who *would* know.

Her father, Friedrich the baron, watched from his window as they approached. He only recognized his daughter; the others were all strangers to him. He had not seen Martina for six or seven months. She had made excuses, pretended to be busy. No matter, here she was, dressed head to toe in black leather with her signature dark sunglasses perched on the top of her head. He watched as the others got out of the car, slamming the red doors of her BMW E30 convertible. But where was her lover, the beautiful albino girl, with her extraordinary voice? What a shame she wasn't there as well! Friedrich was fond of her. Fond of her canary-sweet voice.

"Papa! *Wo bist du?*" Martina's voice rang out in a sing-song way as soon as she opened the door.

Why hadn't she called ahead? He could have prepared. Had cake delivered from a lovely bakery in town.

"*Ja. Ja. Ich komme!*" he called down. Then he straightened his shirt, retucking it neatly into his grey flannel trousers, before descending the stairs.

There was the usual kiss on each cheek and requisite introductions made. Then the brief putting everyone into context, but no real discussions could take place until there was coffee. Friedrich called a neighbour, asked if they could bring over a cake. Did they happen to have an extra one?

"An emergency," he whispered on the phone. "Yes, a pound cake would be fine."

Esther and Bözsi couldn't help but be overwhelmed by the decor. There was understated, but evident, wealth on display. An Egon Schiele hung on one wall while an original Kandinsky was on another. Above the fireplace was a painting of a beautiful woman, a portrait of someone who bore an uncanny resemblance to Martina, although softer and gentler. There were other paintings and a few art nouveau bronzes, but nothing was as glorious to Bözsi and Esther as the Bechstein grand piano, which glowed with its lacquered black body, offsetting the brilliant, rich gold of the piano's inner workings. It was like a jewellery box beckoning. Although Esther had on two occasions run her fingers over a Steinway, she had never been in the presence of a Bechstein.

"It is a very beautiful Bechstein," Esther murmured.

"*Ja.* It is my greatest consolation in life. A little over the top for just one man. But it gives me great joy. Do you play?"

"A little," Esther answered modestly.

"Oh, please! She has spent her entire life teaching music and playing music. Music is everything to her!" Bözsi blurted out, and if Esther were still a young girl, she would have hit her sister just to shut her up. At seventy, one had to stop striking an older sister.

"Perhaps we will have a little musical interlude after coffee. I know Martina likes to play my piano, although she would never admit it! It is contrary to her socialist persona."

Martina loved the piano but she had not made the hour-and-a-half trip from Berlin to Brandenburg just to visit the piano; she had come with a purpose. Her father had been a professor of classical studies at the Hochschule der Künste, which was, much to her father's chagrin, renamed Universität der Künste Berlin the previous year. Why it would bother him, Martina could not understand, as he had been retired and living in Brandenburg for over three years.

"I want to talk to you about the Greeks, Papa. About Helen of Troy."

"Helen of Sparta," he corrected. "In Troy she was only a prince's wife, but in Sparta, she was the queen! All-powerful!"

"Well, not *all*-powerful. The king had more power, surely," Bözsi piped in, quite proud that she could contribute. She thought that Friedrich was quite handsome for a man his age. *Very distinguished.*

"Not at all, Sparta started out as a matriarchal society. A man became the king of Sparta by marrying the next queen. Real power was passed down from woman to woman." He paused a moment to look at the two older ladies, who both seemed transfixed by him. It was turning out to be a pleasant afternoon after all! Perhaps they could all have a stroll after coffee, and then a little music. He smiled shyly and continued, "As it should be, of course. It would probably be a gentler place if women held the power in society. Anyhow, this is likely why the old king of Sparta — Tyndareus, his name was — couldn't really make a fuss about his wife, Queen Leda, for laying those great, huge swan eggs. She was the one with the real power. Just imagine eggs big enough to hold two human-size babies in each one!"

"Who was Leda again?" Jack questioned.

"She was the queen of Sparta, the mother of Helen and Clytemnestra, and Castor and Pollux, also known as the Dioscuri. Leda had sex with Zeus, who was disguised as a swan at the time. He was always turning into animals in order to have sex with mortal women," Friedrich explained.

"Why? Did women prefer bestiality back then?" Jack laughed.

"Oh no, it was so that his wife, Hera, wouldn't catch him. You know, if he was disguised, he might be able to slip his indiscretions past her. He was a bull sometimes, sometimes raindrops. But for Leda, he was a great, powerful swan. And she laid two sets of eggs—"

"Well, it isn't true. It's just a fable," Esther interjected.

"Not a fable, a myth, Esther," her sister corrected.

"Fable, myth — no matter. A woman cannot lay eggs. Mammals don't lay eggs."

"The duck-billed platypus does." Bözsi smiled at Friedrich. "Now go on with your story. Don't mind my sister. She thinks she's a *realist!*" The word "realist" was said with such disdain that Esther crossed her arms and legs as though protecting any vulnerable points of entry. How often had Bözsi tormented her as a child, taunting her for being smaller? Well, who was the taller one now?

"Yes, but Helen? What was the true story and how did it end?" Martina asked, redirecting everyone back to the lesson in mythology. "Papa, you just need to get on with it. You always sound like you're lecturing!" Martina nudged Esther and whispered to her, "Don't mind him, he can't help it. Too many years in academia."

Friedrich glanced over at his daughter. She looked just like his departed wife, Elka. Same dark hair and eyebrows. Same pale skin and fair eyes that stood out in contrast to the dark hair. But her mind! Yes, she was entirely his daughter. His son, though. His son had looked like him, but he was lost. Lost and never to be found. Transported to the next world. Transported by the needle.

"Papa?" Martina urged, nudging him away from his darker thoughts.

"Every ending is but an interpretation. And every interpretation is different, so no one knows the true story of Helen. The most accepted ending is Homer's, that she returned to Menelaus and ruled over Sparta once again, as a much more obedient wife. Her passion for Paris being excused by the Spartans as nothing more than a ten-year infatuation! Imagine an infatuation lasting ten years! Sounds more like love to me!"

"Now, when you say *Paris*, you mean a person and not a place, right?" Bözsi questioned.

"Yes. But I suspect that the city, Paris, was named after the handsome Prince of Troy. Helen's lover." Friedrich chuckled.

For Bözsi that was enough information. The mere mention of a lover named *Paris* was a sign that Paris was her ultimate destination. The gods wanted her to go to Paris, solve the mystery like a great hero, and then spend time in the city where her great love had once lived.

"This has nothing to do with Clara!" Esther was frustrated.

"I don't agree. Clara was a beauty, just like Helen. Clara went missing, just like Helen. There must be clues in the story." Martina seemed very sure that the story of Helen and the story of Clara were linked.

Friedrich cleared his throat, as though he were a little theatre actor waiting in the wings, ready to go on. When he had lectured, all those years in various universities, he often felt like that. An actor, just pretending to be an expert. In time, though, he had convinced everyone that nobody knew the classics better than he.

> "Was this the face that launched a thousand ships
> And burned the topless towers of Ilium?
> Sweet Helen, make me immortal with a kiss:
> Her lips suck forth my soul, see where it flies.
> Come, Helen, come, give me my soul again.
> Here will I dwell, for heaven is in these lips
> And all is dross that is not Helena."

As he recited the famous Marlowe poem, Friedrich glanced at Esther and Bözsi.

"If she was intended to rule Sparta, then why didn't she try to return? Didn't you say she had a daughter?" This from Esther. She couldn't imagine that any mother would not move heaven and hell to be reunited with a child. If she had been blessed with a child ... if only she had had a child ... A child of her own flesh and blood. But could she have loved a child any more than she had loved the twins?

"Remember, she wasn't just a queen, she was also a goddess! Goddesses like their freedom. So what if Helen was married? She loved Paris. If her heart was true to Paris, was she cheating on her husband or, when she returned to Menelaus, was her heart cheating on Paris?" Friedrich continued, on a roll.

"I had a lover I once caught cheating. I was very upset, but he was such a good lover I had to forgive him." Bözsi shrugged. "It happens."

Bözsi's interjection was met with smiles and chuckles from everyone but Esther.

"What has that got to do with anything?" Esther asked with obvious frustration.

"This much I will tell you: Helen was the sort who would only be found when *she* chose to be found and, the rest of the time, she would just do as she pleased." Friedrich was emphatic, harkening back to his lecturing days.

They all listened to every word Friedrich spoke, piecing together what they understood of the music sent anonymously to Martina and the interpretation of the Helen myth as Friedrich told it. There were missing pieces and even more questions, but there was also one thing that they all finally agreed upon: Clara was still alive, her story was unfinished, and she was, after eight long years, ready to be found.

They were jolted back to reality by the banging sound of the large brass knocker. Friedrich got up from his chair to answer and then quickly returned with a decent pound cake in his hands.

"So, now we eat cake, and then a walk, and then some music! Yes?"

"Pound cake. Is that the best you can do, Papa?" Martina turned her nose up.

"For such a revolutionary socialist, you certainly are picky," Friedrich teased.

Esther stood. She walked over and took the pound cake from Friedrich.

"Do you have some whipped cream?" she asked him.

"No, but I have sour cream. I like it on my toast." Friedrich grinned at her.

"Good. And lemon?"

"Of course."

"Point me in the direction of your kitchen. Come, Jack. You must help me." She smiled at Friedrich. This she could do. She could take what was simple and make it worthy. She had done so with her least talented music students. She had done so with many of her rented homes. And certainly, she could do it with a pound cake.

◆ ◆ ◆

Esther grated lemon rind into the sour cream. It really didn't matter whose kitchen it was, nor did the size of the kitchen matter. Any kitchen, anywhere, could be hers while she worked in it. She was a woman who never felt connected to a land or a city. She always said that she could live anywhere and survive, without bonding with the geography of a place. But put her into any kitchen and she was suddenly at home. Esther often thought that she needed very little. A kitchen with a single bed in one corner and a piano in another, and she would be just fine.

She measured four tablespoons of sugar and stirred them into the zesty sour cream. Once thoroughly mixed, she took a spoonful and put it to Jack's mouth for him to taste.

"Tell me, Jack, what do you taste?"

"It is both sweet and sour at the same time. But not like a sweet-and-sour sauce. The two are together but separate. Well, more bitter than sour, really. And creamy. Smooth. Did I get that right?"

"There is no right or wrong. There's only your perception, how you sense things. For instance, we know that lemon is sour and that sugar is sweet. Losing Tristan was very sour for you. But loving him was sweet. And sometimes bittersweet is the best taste of all."

Esther found some gooseberries in the fridge and was delighted. In no time at all the simple pound cake would be quite acceptable.

"I've made so many mistakes," Jack confided. "I've hurt everyone I ever loved. I've been selfish and I have never been where I should be when those who have loved me have needed me."

"Jack, stop being so self-indulgent. Guilt is a big waste of time. Just find Clara and bring her back."

"Esther, you need to know that I searched for her. I went back and forth to Africa for years, pretending that I was reporting on AIDS or doing a piece on starvation. But all the time I was searching for Clara. What more could I do?"

"Come to Paris with me and Bözsi. We could use a strong, young man to protect us. You know that Bözsi will get us into trouble in no time! We need you ... and Clara needs you." Esther's request was forthright and simple. A request that demanded no answer. Esther held up the cake. Beneath the cream and lemon and berries there was a simple pound cake, but now it was all dressed up in its best finery.

◆ ◆ ◆

While Esther and Jack fussed with the cake and searched for plates and cutlery, music wafted into the kitchen from the living room. It was a soothing background to their conversation, as though another world, a world full of promise, was there just beyond reach.

Martina finished playing. Her music was exact, perfect, and well suited to Bach. She never strayed from her rhythm; her playing was as steady as rain. Although she loved other composers equally, she knew that when she played Bach, she could show off her virtuosity and that her quick and exact fingering gave her father the greatest joy. Always, and especially with Bach, her father would nod and smile as her fingers mapped the familiar pieces on the piano keys. Martina was suited to Bach because of the polyphonic texture so prevalent in his compositions. Bach didn't rely on one dominant melody with chords or harmonies to back the predominant voice, the way popular composers of choral music did with their homophony. Martina had the mind, and the agility, to play two or three melodies at once, all with equal balance.

"She could have been a mathematician," her father declared as she played the final notes of Bach's *Prelude and Fugue no. 1 in C Major.*

Bözsi clapped in delight. It had been decades since she'd sat comfortably in a beautiful home, enjoying salon-style music. Not since her childhood, when her family had people visiting every week, all sharing ideas, art, and music, had she so easily given herself over to music. But that Europe was gone. Stolen from her. Now, after all those years of scraping by in cheap apartments, she was experiencing déjà vu.

"Your turn now, Friedrich!" she urged.

"Yes, Papa, your turn!" Martina stood to make room for her father at the piano bench.

"Okay, okay, but I must warn you I cannot play Bach the way Martina can! Perhaps we'll start with a little Schumann."

Friedrich rubbed his hands together and began. He lacked the precision of his daughter. Some notes were slightly misplaced, but Bözsi excused that because of his age. What he lacked in exactness was more than compensated for with his lyricism and emotionality. If Martina's playing was like a well-oiled machine, a timepiece or an example of German engineering, then Friedrich's playing was a gentle breeze wafting sporadically in and out through an open window. Bözsi closed her eyes. She imagined the days when she would walk the streets of Algiers wearing a simple cotton dress, her legs bare, her hair loose, the sun beating down upon her head, and then a welcome breeze, a cool touch, brushing over her like an unexpected kiss. She sighed at the memory. How cruel is life to age the body that houses the heart of a romantic!

Friedrich seamlessly moved to another piece, as though the second offering had always been intended to follow Schumann. Something in his playing kept transporting her back to Algiers, this time to the brothel, where she rested in the arms of Henri, the music travelling up the stairs to her little room. Her lover's kisses starting at the nape of her neck, travelling down her backside. How they tickled when he reached the oysters of her back! How he lingered there. And her, anticipating, wondering when he would turn her over, cover her body in his and press his lips to her ear. "*I love you, Bözsi. I'll always love you.*"

Friedrich's playing intensified as he neared the finish. Here was heartbreak and sorrow, so unique, so profound, and so individual that Bözsi was snapped from her memories and catapulted back into the room. He held his hands above the keyboard a moment and then smiled with a shy, boyish look at Bözsi.

"I hope you do not mind. I went from Schumann to Liszt."

"Not at all. Now, let me see?" She reached out for his hands. "Oh my. Such big hands. You can span twelves!"

Friedrich laughed, "No, only tens! But Liszt had to cut the flesh between his fingers to increase his span. I have *natural* span."

"Oh, you really do!" she flirted.

Friedrich pulled away the moment Esther arrived back in the living room, a transformed pound cake looking glorious in her capable hands.

◆ ◆ ◆

After the requisite four o'clock coffee and cake time was over and plates were put away, Martina took *The Lost Queen* opus from her soft leather briefcase and placed it on the piano. It made sense to Esther that she should play some of the music, even though she was aware that her sight was not as good as the Punk Baroness's and, because of that, her playing would not be as perfect.

Esther inhaled deeply before she played the first chord, stretching her arthritic fingers across the ivory keys. There was no doubt in her mind that the music was her dear Clara's. She had been there every step of the way as Clara learned the piano, hating the note-by-note sequences, preferring an onslaught of chords. She remembered, when Clara was small, that she would stretch and exercise her fingers until they seemed like they might split from the palms of her hands, just so she could reach a higher or lower key on the piano. Many times, she saw her sitting at the table for a meal, her hands secretly underneath, secretly pulling at her fingers as hard as she could, willing them to stretch and grow. Now, as Esther played, she knew that the almost impossible span of the fingers to create the chords were Clara's hallmark. Clara was the one who was the real modern-day Liszt!

Martina began to sing one voice and, as Esther played, she joined in, as best she could, as the other voice, sometimes singing down an octave when the music climbed too high for her. She tried to keep any quiver from her voice, but it still crept in. *Is that age or emotion?* she wondered.

By the time she got to the tears of Hecuba, Esther had forgotten that there was anyone else in the room. She was lost to the music. Yes, Hecuba was crying over the body of her son Hector, the purest of all heroes, but for Esther, it was her loss of Clara. Where could she be and what might have happened to her jewel? Clara might be a woman now, but to Esther, she was still that little girl, secretly pulling at her fingers, willing them to grow.

Esther kept her eyes closed. She felt embarrassed by her own emotion, but when she opened her eyes, she saw that the small gathering had been as affected as she had been. Yes, it was Clara's work and, yes, she was alive somewhere, and yes, it was the best writing Clara had ever done.

It was at that moment that Martina knew Esther must play the role of Hecuba. She knew that Hecuba's lament would bring people to their feet. Whether Clara was found or not, the opera would go on, and Esther would have her moment in the spotlight. All Martina had to do was convince the old lady to sing before a huge paying audience in Berlin!

And Friedrich knew that whatever he was feeling, he had not felt since he was a young man, when a world of possibilities were beyond his wildest imagination.

NINE

IRIS PULLED AT THE HEM of her dress. There was a thread hanging and she knew that, if she did not fix it, nobody in the audience would be able to look at anything else. Iris knew it wasn't really an audience, but a gathering of invited guests. *A congregation.* Lots of people sitting in rows, watching the ritual. But wasn't that a performance, really? If not, then why was there a rehearsal the night before?

One last, quick tug would do the trick, but as she pulled at the thread, the hem came down in the front while it was still tacked up in the back. Iris panicked. She was the flower girl, after all. The only flower girl. People would be looking at her.

"How are you coming along in there, Iris? We're leaving in twenty minutes and I'd like to put a little rouge on your cheeks and some lip balm on your lips! Make you even more beautiful."

Sabine. Of course, *she* was ready. She'd been ready for over an hour. Her process started right after she scarfed down some dry toast to settle her constant morning sickness. After that it was tea bags on her eyes for thirty minutes to take away any puffiness, a bag of frozen peas across her neck to tighten her jawline, and then the brushing of her teeth with a homemade paste of charcoal and baking soda. Iris knew that while it may be her dad's second wedding, for Sabine this was everything. Iris suspected that she was worried she would be compared to her father's first wife, her mother, who was so much younger when she had married Gareth.

If her mother was dead, would she be watching on the other side, approving, or would she be angry that her father hadn't gone to South Africa to look for her when the abduction first happened? And if she wasn't dead, then what right did her father have to remarry? And then there was one last question. The question Iris never voiced, except in her head. A question that would cause her to put her hands over her ears to stop the voice in her head. If her mother was alive, then why hadn't she come home to her? Was she not loved enough? Not good enough?

"I hope you are ready. I am putting on my dress now!" Sabine's cheery voice breezed in from the next room.

Iris hated Sabine's dress. Hated it all the more because both she and the maid of honour, Hannah, were forced to wear empire waistlines to match the wedding dress. To Iris, all the shape of the dress did was emphasize her lack of breasts while concealing that fact that she was long-waisted and slender. Sabine clearly didn't want anyone to show off a slim waistline with hers growing by the day.

Iris found her Scotch tape, removed her dress, and set to fixing the hem herself. She pulled off a long piece, making sure that the tape didn't stick to itself, and then pressed the sticky part into the anemic, pink-coloured material. The hem appeared to hold, but the dress no longer fell in gentle folds. A stiff line of tape was evident, three-quarters of an inch thick, even though Iris had stuck it to the inside of the dress.

She could pretend to be sick. She could be having her monthly time and cramps. A few well-placed tears would do the trick. A bit of moaning. Then, to make it more believable, she would have to pretend to be upset at missing the nuptials. Yes, she could get out of the whole spectacle. And why not? All she was required to do was walk up the aisle before Sabine and her maid of honour, Hannah. She had no duties. Not like Fritz, the ring bearer, in his fancy jacket and velvet pants. He was entrusted with the golden wedding ring. He got to step forward and present it while she just had to stand there in her pastel-coloured, shapeless, taped frock.

A knock on the door. This time her father. He entered, all nervous smiles and expectation.

"How's my number-one girl doing?"

Iris threw herself onto the bed, all tears. One day she was waiting for the return of her mother, the next, it seemed, she was to sashay up an aisle, as though happy, carrying flowers for her mother's usurper. Sure, she liked Sabine, but wasn't she just a stand-in for her real mother? A mother that would someday return? And yet, ever since her father had her mother declared dead *in absentia*, Iris felt more and more alone. Nothing had changed. Sabine still made coffee in the morning. Fritz still got his mucky hands on her things. Her father still went to the oculary to make glass eyes. Nothing had *really* changed. Nothing was being taken away. Except, perhaps, hope.

"Why aren't you dressed?" Gareth asked his daughter.

Iris shrugged and then kicked the dress off the end of her bed. When Gareth picked it up, he saw his daughter's attempt to fix the hem. He pulled off the Scotch tape and down the hem fell.

"Hmmm. I guess that a home economics class would have come in handy after all."

"Only loser girls take home economics! Stupid girls!" Iris responded. And yet, she knew that she liked cooking with Hilda when she was in Canada. Hilda wasn't a loser, and she could sew and cook. But she could also make special potions. Like a *Hexe*.

"Well, there is no time to fix it now."

"I guess I will have to stay home then." Iris stared, teary-eyed, at her father.

"Is that what you would prefer? Because I really would like you there. And Sabine will be upset if you don't come."

"I have nothing to wear!" Iris shouted at him.

Gareth went to her closet. Inside were her many dresses, arranged by the season. And under each dress sat a pair of shoes to go with the outfit. He had no idea that his daughter had so many shoes. Where did they all come from?

"Do you have a favourite?"

"Shouldn't Sabine choose?" Iris turned her back to face away from him.

"The dress doesn't matter. All that matters is that you are there. And that you are happy."

Iris pointed to a Christmas dress. Rich, dark green velvet bodice with taffeta skirts. Tight to the waist and then an explosion of fabric that made a ruffling sound as she walked.

"Great! Redheads are always beautiful in green. And the green matches the leaves and stems of the roses you'll be carrying. Perfect."

"Won't Sabine be angry that I am not wearing the pink dress?"

Gareth tossed the green dress to Iris.

"She's too busy throwing up right now. Besides, it was too wishy-washy for you. You'll look far more beautiful in this one. Don't worry, I'll handle it." Gareth paused as he watched Iris. "I know it has been difficult for you. I don't want you to feel left out. Today isn't about forgetting your mother, it's about accepting what's happened and moving forward, as a family. It's what your mother would want. She'd want you to be happy."

"Okay," Iris agreed. "Now, get out so I can get dressed. I'm not a little girl anymore."

Iris sat alone in her room for a few minutes before reaching for her favourite green dress. *Moving forward*, she thought. But with a baby girl on the way and with her room being partitioned into two rooms to accommodate Fritz, it seemed that the new beginning was all about the compromises she'd have to make. Deep down, she hoped that her mother would return and take her away from it all.

Iris could now hear the voice of her grandmother coming from outside of her room. The grandmother from Canada: Grandma Elaine, her father's mother. Even she preferred Fritz! She was cooing over Fritz. Teaching him how to say his line in English.

"And now I present the ring!"

Fritz laughed back and pronounced the words in German, "*Und jetzt präsentiere ich den ring!*"

"Well, little man, you can teach me some German, and I can teach you some English, and we'll both be better for it. Maybe one day you will come and stay with us in Canada. Would you like that?"

Then laughter. Like Fritz was being tickled. A chortling sound. *Would he feel less adored when he was no longer the youngest?*

Iris slipped her green dress over her head, fastened the back, and looked at herself in the mirror.

"Ready for the circus!" she told herself. But the image that stared back did not look ready at all.

♦ ♦ ♦

It was a small church. One of the few old stone churches in the area to survive Operation Gomorrah, the British-led bombing on Hamburg in 1943. To get to the church, the wedding party had to travel past Nikolaikirche, which had been completely devastated and which stood as a memorial against war. Iris had learned to hold her breath whenever she passed, sometimes also closing her eyes, until she was sure she was beyond it. To see it and to breathe it in was to let the sadness, and possibly the spirits of the dead, inside her. She had enough sorrow in her heart, and she yearned to find a sliver of joy to carry with her into her adulthood. Perhaps one day she would be a bride and be cherished more than anyone else. Perhaps one day she would be the one in white, being fussed over and adored. But marriage would also mean allowing herself to fall in love, and she knew that would only bring sorrow. One glance at Jack, her father's best man, and she whirlwinded back in time to the sight of him by Tristan's grave. *Eventually, whoever loves you will leave you. Everyone you love abandons you. Either they will die or their affections will turn elsewhere. Perhaps they will get bored of you. Or perhaps ... they'll be taken ... stolen away.*

Her mother's doppelgänger was there, stunning in a white slip of a dress with a red cashmere cape draped lazily over her shoulders. It was the exact colour of her stained lips. Iris thought that she looked like the snow queen from Narnia. Why, she wondered, was the Snow Queen seen as so evil? Winter, to Iris, was far more beautiful than summer, with its delicate snowflakes and hanging icicles. And the queen had been generous with her Turkish delight. Iris had never tasted Turkish delight, but she was quite sure that she would like it. Yes, her aunt Blanca looked just like the Queen of Narnia, with her white-fringed eyelashes and long white hair. Would her mother have dressed like her aunt? No, because if her mother were there, there would be no wedding now.

Standing beside her aunt was Martina, the Punk Baroness, equally stunning but entirely different. She wore a hat, adorned with a feather, and her body was encased in a red bodice dress with thick black laces up the back. Her bosoms were full and round over the top. Iris wondered if her breasts would ever grow that round and full. Iris smiled and waved at them. She was old enough to know now that they were not just roommates. Not just best friends sharing a flat. Still, she couldn't quite imagine two women kissing. Not that it bothered her; she just couldn't imagine it. Sometimes, at night, as she snuggled into her pillow, she would press her mouth against the cotton pillowcase and imagine it was another face. She tried imagining the pillow as both a boy and a girl, but whenever she imagined kissing a girl, she never felt the way she did when she imagined a boy's mouth, warm and confident, on hers. And what about French kissing? She had heard the other girls at school talking about it and assumed that it wasn't just for the French. All she knew, for sure, was that tongues were involved. She had not gotten that far with her pillow.

Iris wanted to greet her aunt Blanca and Martina, but she had been instructed to stay back, not mingle, until after the ceremony. There would be plenty of time for hobnobbing afterward. In the meantime, she was to stay close to Sabine, attend to her long train flowing from her white dress and hold her flowers as needed. The bouquet was predominantly roses. Iris loved holding them. She brought them to her face, inhaled them, remembering the rose oil Hilda had sent her. She was almost through the entire bottle, although she had learned to use it more sparingly.

"Be careful, you look like you are going to snort her entire bouquet!" Jack teased her.

"Aren't you supposed to be with my dad?"

"Yes, I should probably go check on him. Make sure he doesn't have any jitters or second thoughts!" Jack smiled. Iris knew that the smile was not one of joy. It was a smile for her, to reassure her, to let her know that he understood how the day might be difficult for her.

"I'll see you on the other side! By the way, I like your dress." He winked at her.

Iris looked at the vibrant green of her dress before glancing at Hannah, Sabine's maid of honour. Her dress was supposed to look like hers, to blend and be part of a uniform party. Iris suddenly felt sick. She had wronged Sabine on her special day by putting herself and her vanity first. She closed her eyes, imagined herself in a matching shapeless, anemic dress, but still she preferred the feel of rich velvet on her skin.

Fritz was nervous. He pulled at his miniature suit, tried to loosen his bowtie. He looked like he thought he was being strangled. He put the dusty-rose velvet cushion, the ring cushion, onto the ground so that he could pull at the neckline with both of his hands.

"What are you doing? Pick that up! You could lose the ring. You should be still!" ordered the maid of honour.

Fritz ran to Iris and hid behind her as he started to cry. Iris put her arms around him, held him protectively, as Hannah picked up the cushion and the ring. Where was Sabine? Why hadn't she emerged from the car? Why was she allowing this bossy bitch to order Fritz about?

"Here, you hold the cushion," she ordered Iris. "You deal with this. I have to attend to the bride."

Iris juggled the ring and the flowers, but Fritz clung to her. She wanted to run into the church, find their father, and have him deal with it all, but she knew that was not allowed. No mingling till afterward.

"Come on, don't cry. Your face will get all red and puffy."

"Like Elmo?" Fritz asked.

"Yes. Just like Elmo. But not as furry."

"I'm scared," Fritz admitted.

"There is no need to be scared. You are the best ring bearer ever. But come on, let's rehearse one more time so you feel okay."

Fritz stopped crying. He wiped the snot from his nose on the sleeve of his velvet jacket, leaving a smear on the pink of the fabric.

"And now I present the ring!" he said loudly, in both languages. Iris clapped her hands and cheered. Fritz bowed.

"You see, it's easy. Now you won't forget, will you?"

He shook his head vigorously as though exorcising every doubt with each shake.

♦ ♦ ♦

The party queued in a line, and the traditional music, that familiar tune that announces the bride, began. Sabine stepped from the car, her cream-coloured satin shoe stepping onto the ground first. Iris noticed how the folds of her dress seemed to hide the swell of her body. She hoped that the baby would be still, that the kick of her half-sister's foot would not disturb the proceedings.

It was only when she looked at Sabine's face, with her classic makeup, and winged eyeliner, that she saw Sabine had been crying. *Why?* she wondered. Hannah took her friend's hand, directed her to her place. Perhaps she wasn't mean after all, just worried about her friend.

Sabine managed a smile at Iris and Fritz. Fritz ran to her, wanting to be carried, but Sabine shook her head. He reached out to Iris. She knew that they were supposed to be single file. They had, after all, been at rehearsal the night before. But she took his hand anyhow.

Inside, Gareth beamed at the sight of his children and his bride-to-be. This was the day that life would begin again! And his parents and his children were all there to bear witness to him making a vow, pledging his new life, to Sabine, his partner, his friend, his mate.

It all seemed to go rather well. Gareth and Sabine each had prepared their own vows, which were added to the minister's usual for-better-or-for-worse speech. Gareth sounded calm, but Sabine had a quiver to her voice. Her bluntness seemed left outside the church entry and only that part of her that was hesitant had been allowed in. A few tears from Gareth's mother. Smiling and nodding from the rest of the congregation.

But then the words came, the words that changed it all: "Should anyone present know of any reason that this couple should not be joined in holy matrimony, speak now or forever hold your peace."

It is a phrase that is only used for tradition's sake, now often omitted from the words spoken at a modern wedding. But Sabine wanted everything to be traditional. Thus, the off-white dress, the church, the little pillow for the ring. It was her insistence upon tradition that was to be her undoing.

"Should anyone present know of any reason that this couple should not be joined in holy matrimony, speak now or forever hold your peace." The minister recited, without inflection. A memorized line to be said before getting on to the exchange of rings and the anticipated kiss. When there was a clearing of a throat and a woman standing, he did not, at first, notice. He started on the next line.

"I object to this marriage," the woman said firmly.

At first, she looked unreal to the minister. A woman so pale and translucent that it seemed as though the wind might blow right through her and she would tinkle like wind chimes, soft and benign. She seemed ethereal standing there in the pew. A spectre, perhaps. The groom's dead wife, back from the grave.

"I object to this marriage," she said a second time.

And Iris saw Martina, the Punk Baroness, pull at her lover's cape, urging her to sit down.

And Iris saw her father spin on his heel so he could glare at Blanca.

And Iris saw Sabine grip at her stomach before bolting down the church aisle and out the door.

And Iris saw the congregation cover their mouths in surprised shock.

"He cannot marry her because he is already married. My sister is not dead."

Iris put her hand on Fritzi's shoulder, but he didn't understand what was happening. He thought it was a cue, so he stepped forward and faced the congregation. Lifting the pillow high over his head, he declared loudly in English, "And now I present the ring!"

♦ ♦ ♦

Gareth found Sabine kneeling in the bathroom, head up against the cool of the toilet. Her arms were wrapped about her. She didn't look at him when he came in, so he sat beside her, took her hands, then pulled her into him so that he could wrap protective arms around her quaking body.

"*Es tut mir leid.*"

That is all he could say. "I am sorry."

"Why? Why would she do such a thing?"

"We can go back in. I have Clara's death certificate; we are completely in the right. We can marry. There is no legal reason why we can't."

Sabine pulled away from him. Stared at him, eyes laser sharp, the blue-grey contrasting the red-tinged whites of her eyes.

"Gareth, there is something else."

"Yes?"

"I haven't felt the baby move for almost a day now. I was afraid to tell you. And I have been cramping, high in my stomach, for these past two hours. What if she's dead?"

Gareth remembered that the best thing to do was to drink a tall glass of orange juice. Somehow the sudden sugar would make the baby move. If the baby was alive. But where would he get orange juice?

"Just ... just stay here a minute."

Sabine shook her head. Reached for Gareth, held the edge of his suit jacket sleeve.

"Hey. You okay? Want to go back? Blanca left." Jack's voice was a port in the storm. Reasonable Jack. Logical Jack. If ever Gareth had needed his friend, it was now.

"Can you take care of my parents and the kids? I think Sabine should go to the hospital."

"Of course."

"Take them to dinner ..."

"Just go. I'll take care of everything."

Gareth took out his phone and called an ambulance.

♦ ♦ ♦

When Jack loosened his tie and undid his top button, Fritz copied him, pulling his bowtie off completely before tossing it onto the restaurant table. There was so much food, it was hard to choose where to start, but Fritz really only had eyes for the cake, three tiers of iced delight, each tier a little smaller than the one below it. He knew the rules, real food first, and then the sweeties, but it seemed to him that nothing was as it should be, so why not start with the cake? Besides, there were two people at the top of that tall cake. A mountain it was, each tier a boulder, and the two people were mountain climbers who had made it to the very top. The king and queen of the Castle! *So, who's the dirty rascal?* he wondered. Fritz looked around the table. He didn't want to be the rascal. So, who could it be?

Elaine and Mark had gone along with Jack and the children. Someone had to watch them after Gareth ran after Sabine. And they were all hungry. Jack could have brought them anywhere for a quick dinner but, since a wedding feast was already prepared and paid for, there seemed no sense in paying for another meal elsewhere. They could unwind, eat well, and then pack up some food for Gareth and Sabine, who likely hadn't eaten at all.

"Why would she do such a thing? How could she?" Elaine asked over and over again while her husband, Mark, just shook his head. "Those girls were never right. And I'm not saying that because they are albino, but because of their sad beginnings. Remember their mother. Only tragedy, right from the very start."

Elaine remembered Faye, the twins' mother. Her grief. Her breakdown. Her suicide. How she had been her nurse that day. How she hadn't stopped her from drowning in the lake.

"Some people just can't escape the darkness all around them," Elaine continued.

"Please stop," Jack requested, but Elaine looked at him blankly. It was evident that somewhere along the way, Elaine had quite forgotten that her granddaughter, Iris, was the daughter of one the twins she was openly discussing.

"You have to admit that it was awful," Elaine insisted. "Gareth should have just come back with Sabine and gone through with it. They could have asked Blanca to leave the church. I don't even know why they invited her in the first place."

It made no sense to Elaine. She knew that Blanca had lost her sister and was still experiencing grief all these years later, but hadn't they all experienced loss? Why go to a wedding if only to ruin it?

"I am just saying that it could have been so wonderful. For everyone. I can't even imagine how Sabine is feeling!"

Jack glanced at Iris. She was sitting very tall in her chair. Had she grown suddenly? Her eyes were focused on her plate, on the first course offerings: grilled zucchini, eggplant, and asparagus drizzled with a warm goat cheese dressing with a small assortment of thinly sliced cured meat on the side. Jack watched as she pushed the vegetables apart so that none were touching. Zucchini on one side, eggplant on the other, and two spears of white asparagus down the centre.

"Are you going to eat your food or play with it? I thought you were hungry," he urged her.

"You're not my father. You can't tell me what I should eat and how I should eat it," Iris snapped at Jack. But her eyes did not look up. She remained staring at her plate. Two white asparagus, long and lean, down the centre of her plate, and all that mess around them. How anemic they looked! Albino asparagus. Two of them.

"Grandma," she began, "that awful woman is my aunt." Her eyes still did not look up.

"Yes, sweetheart, I know. And I am sorry. She did a bad thing today."

Iris started to laugh, and it seemed to both Elaine and Jack that she no longer sounded like a child. Twelve is a strange age. One moment it demands autonomy and privacy and the next it demands the cuddles of childhood. An "in-between," as Judy Garland once sang. At twelve, Iris no longer had the pure bubble of a child's laughter; there was sarcasm in it now, the first little seasoning of cynicism.

"She did a bad thing!" she mimicked.

"I don't see why that is so funny." Elaine's voice was tight. She could see no way to salvage the situation.

"I will tell you what a bad thing *really* is. A bad thing is when you pretend that your wife is dead so that you can marry someone else! Now *that* is a bad thing."

The white asparagus seemed to glow on her plate. Iris stared at them. Willed herself not to cry.

Iris put her hand to her heart and felt that the hole that was once cauterized and closed had reopened, and that the rip was extending from top to bottom, dividing her heart, in equal parts. Soon there would be two hearts, and each would beat independently of the other, competing as they galloped in her chest, until one defeated the other, leaving her half-hearted.

"I just wish that someone would look for her. Maybe she needs our help," Iris whispered.

Jack put his arm around her, squeezing her shoulder.

"I don't think anyone tried hard enough. None of you have any idea what it's like to be me. I have a hole in my heart, you know." Now she lifted her gaze away from her plate. She was defiant, challenging.

Elaine had no words. Why hadn't she thought more about Iris and her loss? Was she so concerned about her own son's struggles that she overlooked her granddaughter? She looked around the table, hoping for someone, anyone, to say something that would break the tension.

"I'm going to Paris on a train later this week. There was a clue. I'm going to search for her again, Iris," Jack finally said quietly.

"Again?" Iris asked.

"Again. I looked for her before, when you were just four, but I had no luck. I spent years going back and forth to Africa, hoping to find her. And then I did lose hope. But I promise you now, Iris, I will not give up until I have some answers. I cannot promise that I will bring her back, but I will promise that I will keep looking for answers. Now come on, there is another course before dessert."

And Fritz, who had been quite bored while everyone spoke in English, broke free from the table and ran to the cake, toppling it over so that he could grab the two figures, the king and queen, from the top.

♦ ♦ ♦

The ride back to Berlin was quiet. Blanca stared at the road ahead as Martina drove, her foot heavy on the accelerator. Blanca knew that her lover was angry with her. She hadn't said a word beyond, "Get in the car. *Jetzt!*" And off they had gone, the first to leave the church once the would-be bride and groom had hurried out.

Blanca wondered if anyone might have picked up the wedding present she had brought for them: five Meissen eggcups, each hand-painted, one for each of them, including the baby on the way. And then, as something special for the couple, matching coffee cups along with two pounds of Jacobs Kronung Whole Bean Coffee. She had chosen the gift herself, actually leaving her bed to walk along Kurfürstendamm. It had been one of those perfect autumn days, a bright sun overhead, a chill in the air. Blanca breathed it all in as she browsed in the shops and peered in the windows, searching for the perfect gift.

"I don't hate Sabine at all. I did buy those egg cups especially for her. I hope she gets them," Blanca reminded Martina as they sped along the highway.

Martina looked at her with disbelief and disgust.

"If you don't hate her, then why, Blanca? Why did you do that?"

"I don't know." Blanca's shrug was weak.

Martina banged the steering wheel with the palm of her hand. *Frustration, that was all it was*, Blanca thought. But still, that look was unlike any she had seen before. Frustration she could handle; contempt was another thing.

"I really don't know. You have to believe me. I was compelled to stand up. Then people were looking at me, so I had to say that I objected. I'm not sure when, or why, I stood exactly. And I just started to talk. But I hadn't meant to. Then it was too late. It was like I was watching it, instead of doing it. It was like I was possessed."

Martina veered off and slowed to a stop in front of a coffee shop.

"I need a coffee to keep awake. Do you want anything?"

"Oh, I can come in and have a look."

"No, Blanca. I am going in there myself. I will bring you something back. Then I will walk around and calm myself before I start to drive again."

Blanca shook her head. Only when Martina was through the door and out of eyesight did she rummage through the glove compartment. Car registration, insurance papers, a brush, and sunglasses. The usual things. She reached back farther until her hand felt the cool of a metal handle. A press of her thumb and the blade popped out. *Just a few light scratches*, she thought. *Just enough to take the edge off.*

How long had it been? Eight, no, ten months since the last time she had self-harmed. Ten months and nobody even noticed how well she had coped. No one said that it was commendable. And it wasn't that the compulsion had lessened! Someone should have noticed how hard she had been trying! How far she had come in her recovery. Every day she wanted to break the surface of her skin. But she had fought against it, not for herself, but for Martina, mostly. Now, Martina was disgusted with Blanca. Why deny the urge just to please someone who only reviles you? Besides, she was feeling the exact same contempt for herself. Only one thing could relieve that. Only one thing could take away her self-hatred.

Wait for it. Wait. Imagine the sharpness of the blade, the coolness of the cut. Imagine the shock of that first cut and then the ease of those that follow. Mustn't go overboard, though, mustn't cut too many times.

By the time Martina returned, with a hot tea for Blanca even though she had declined having anything, Blanca was calm and quiet. Her hands were neatly folded in her lap. Martina didn't see the red bloodstains on Blanca's pure-white dress. She handed her the cup.

"Thank you," Blanca responded, her voice quiet and ashamed.

"It's okay."

"I'm really sorry."

"I know," Martina replied.

But Martina did not really know. And Blanca hid the utility knife as well as she did her freshly made wounds.

"I love you," Blanca said as Martina climbed into the driver's side.

Martina put the key into the ignition, turned it until she heard the click of the engine turning over. Then she took her foot off the brake and pressed down on the accelerator.

It was the first time in almost fifteen years that Martina did not say "I love you too" back to her.

✦ ✦ ✦

By the time the ambulance arrived at Asklepios Klinik Barmbek, Sabine's blood pressure had escalated to 188/120. Her hands had swollen to the point that the flesh of her fingers bulged over her engagement ring, hiding the gold of the band. Her abdominal pains had increased, and she was tired, frightened, and nauseous. All she could think about was the fact that the orange juice had not encouraged the baby to move.

Gareth didn't know why the paramedic kept checking her blood pressure but was well aware that his concern was increasing with every reading. Then, only when the car picked up speed and the siren started to wail, did he realize that the concern was severe. Sabine squeezed his hand, but even that seemed anemic and half-hearted. Her first seizure occurred even before they turned into the hospital emergency driveway.

Pre-eclampsia was the first thought, but the onslaught of the seizure implied that it had progressed quickly from pre-eclampsia to eclampsia. Sabine was immediately rushed into a private area in the ICU, given an intravenous of fluids, anti-inflammatories, and steroids, but her blood pressure remained high.

"There is only one cure for eclampsia. Only one thing we can do. Your wife needs an emergency Caesarean," the emergency doctor stated. "How far along is the pregnancy?"

"I don't know. Twenty-four, maybe twenty-five weeks," Gareth stammered.

"If anyone else asks you, say that the baby is over twenty-six weeks. Anything less and we would just abort. If you want us to try to save the baby, she has to be at least twenty-six weeks."

"I see. Yes, the baby is indeed twenty-six weeks along." Gareth was panicked. He tried counting back in his head. Was it twenty-six weeks or just twenty-four weeks?

"The baby is under stress. Her heart is barely beating. It is anyone's guess if she will even survive the birth, but if you do not choose a Caesarean birth right now, you will lose both the mother and the child. The placenta has pulled away, so if you leave the baby in there, she will die. And your wife will become toxic and possibly have kidney or liver failure. A stroke even. There is no choice and there is no time."

"What chance does the baby have?"

"I will not lie to you. She only has a ten percent chance."

Gareth swayed, reached out for support. The baby, possibly dead before she was even born. And a life without Sabine. Impossible.

"Could this have happened because of shock, perhaps?" Gareth questioned.

"There are many possible factors. The age of the mother — she is what? Almost forty, yes?"

"Yes. She's forty. Forty-one in a month."

"Also, it could be the lack of calcium. Obesity does not play a role for Sabine, clearly. She is fit. Some women are genetically predisposed. Likely there was not sufficient blood flow to the uterus, and the placenta simply did not function the way it should. Either way, if you had left it any longer at all, even an hour, it would probably have been fatal to them both. It may take a few weeks for Sabine to feel better, to heal completely after the procedure. They are readying her now."

"And the baby?"

"Every day that the baby can survive, her chances will increase; every day counts. She will need a respirator, because her lungs and heart will not be fully formed. She will not be able to suck, so she will have to be tube-fed for the first four weeks, minimum. She will likely need blood transfusions. It will be an uphill battle, *if* she survives the birth."

On a day that was to be Gareth and Sabine's wedding day, Baby Frieda was born, taken from her mother's womb, weighing a mere 468 grams. She was no bigger than the size of Gareth's hand. She was not put to her mother's breast as babies usually are. She was not held in her father's arms. She was rushed to the NICU, where she was hooked up to monitors and a respirator. Her skin was wrinkled and bright pink, almost raw looking. Her eyes clenched tightly, her fingers in fists, hiding the fact that she had not yet developed nails. There was a layer of hair all over her little body. She looked more like a kitten than a baby.

When Sabine awoke, all groggy and confused, she asked for her baby. Gareth shook his head. He had no idea if the baby would even make it through the night. Unlikely but not impossible was the consensus.

"I knew something was wrong as soon as I got to the church. I knew something was very wrong, but I thought I could just get through the ceremony and the dinner …"

"Shh, rest now."

"I should have had the sense to call it off. Thank God for Blanca."

"Blanca?" Gareth was incredulous. "Blanca ruined the whole day!"

"No! She saved the day. If she hadn't had the good sense to stop the wedding, then I, and the baby, would have died. Blanca saved the day."

"The baby has very little chance of survival. You need to know this. But we will stay positive, okay?"

Sabine closed her eyes. Her stomach was still numb where the Caesarean incision was. Tomorrow it would ache. But for now, the only thing she felt was the emptiness of her arms. Arms that should have been cuddling her daughter. She pulled herself up as much as she could.

"What are you doing?"

"I can't leave her alone. She has to know me. A baby has to smell her mother. How will she know me? How will she bond to me? And how will my milk let down without her?"

Sabine began crying. The monitor showed her heart picking up speed, galloping on its own to an unknown finish line. And with that her blood pressure also started to climb. *No. No. No. That cannot be.* Gareth balanced on the side of the hospital bed. He held her, to calm her and to keep her there, safe until morning.

"Let me go out and phone Jack. Make sure the kids are okay."

It was only when Gareth was out of the room, only when he no longer had to reassure Sabine, that he could succumb to his own emotions. He slid down the pale, cool wall, until he was squatting on the floor, head heavy in his hands. His wife would live; she would heal. Together they would heal. And yet, his little daughter, Frieda, was alone in a new world, without a mother or father to ease the transition from womb to world. It was unthinkable. And he knew that as reassuring as he may have been to Sabine, he was as lost and as helpless as his new baby.

TEN

THERE WAS A NOISE. THE sound of a door slamming. Footsteps. Hadn't Hilda locked the door? She was sure that she had. After years of not locking it at all, she had developed the habit of doing so, right before bed. Her dog had passed away a year ago, and now she wished she had gotten another.

The footsteps sounded louder. She closed her eyes and listened. They seemed casual, as though the intruder had no fear of being found out. It seemed that the intruder was in her kitchen now. The sound of boots on wood had changed to the sound of boots on tile. What could he possibly want? Surely there was nothing of worth to steal in the kitchen! There was no money hidden there. No credit cards lying about. There was only her freshly made cake. Hilda could still smell the lingering aroma of almond extract and orange peel.

She stayed as still as possible. Everything tensed in her body. *This is silly!* Sooner than later the intruder would come upstairs, looking for jewellery and valuables. Sooner or later, there would be a confrontation. Best to be the one on the offensive, be the one to surprise *him*. She pulled back her eiderdown, swung her legs quietly over the bed, and touched her bare feet to the floor. The wood was cold to the touch, but she didn't risk turning on her lights to find her slippers. Instead, she tiptoed down the hall, toward the staircase.

From the top of the stairs, Hilda could see not only her boots but also her umbrella, below in the hall vestibule. How to slip past the door into the kitchen, unseen, so that she could grab the umbrella for protection? She wasn't quite sure how she might use it. Strike him over the head, perhaps?

She had two more steps and hadn't squeaked or creaked on a stair yet. Two more steps, then a dash to the door for the umbrella. The umbrella had a metal pointy thing, didn't it? She could jab him with it. Go for the soft belly. Go for the throat. Go for the eye. *But what if the intruder was wearing glasses?* Hilda stopped her descent, paused on the last stair. The question was not what if the intruder was wearing glasses; the question was what if the intruder had a knife. Even if he hadn't come with one, there were lots of very sharp knives in the kitchen. But maybe the intruder didn't need a knife. *Maybe he had a gun.*

She was sure that the sound of her pounding heart could be heard outside her body, that it was just a question of time before *he* heard her and saw her, and then what? Hilda regrouped. Two options. She could sneak back upstairs, in the same manner in which she had snuck down, then find a safe hiding place. The other option was to continue slowly down the last two steps and then bolt out the front door and onto the street. But her feet were bare and there was snow and ice outside.

She stood frozen, afraid to make a move. She heard the sound of a chair as it was pushed back from the table. The sound of a plate being moved. She breathed and willed her heart to slow so that she could hear better what was happening in the kitchen. The fridge door opened and closed. Then she nearly jumped when the sudden noise of the whistling kettle seemed to scream out, into the silence of her fear.

The bastard! she thought. *He is bloody well eating my cake before he robs me!*

And then, before she could bolt out the door and make her way to the safety of December's fierce cold, an old familiar voice called out, "Hilda? I've made some tea. Come on, let's try this cake! It sure looks good!"

Hilda stormed into the kitchen. Sure enough, the kitchen table had two cups, a pot of tea, and her cake placed on it. Her first husband, her ex-husband, John, turned and smiled at her. He was still wearing his winter coat and scarf. That didn't alarm Hilda. What alarmed her was that on top of the pajama bottoms he was wearing a pair of underwear, hastily pulled on back-to-front.

"John?" she asked. "John, what are you doing here?"

John just looked at her, then laughed. "What do you mean, what am *I* doing here? I live here."

◆ ◆ ◆

In the morning, John's current wife, Jean, sat at the table, drinking the hot coffee. Hilda was almost out of the unpasteurized heavy cream she usually got from Karl's cows, up the road. It was the start of winter, and colder than usual, so the cows were suffering from cold stress. They had grown thick winter coats, giving them a fluffy appearance, but still the cold was affecting them. Karl had increased their food intake so that their metabolic rate didn't increase to the point of extreme weight loss, but as his herd was a dairy herd and not beef cattle, they didn't have any extra fat to begin with. If the temperatures didn't go up soon, the cows could risk frostbite to their ears and teats. Hilda remembered her days of breastfeeding her babies, her raw nipples chafing against her bra, sometimes even bleeding with the stress; she couldn't imagine the added stress of frostbite on top of that. Hilda decided to ration her cream, buy some in cartons from the grocery store, and only use a little for her own coffee every morning. So, Jean had her coffee with the usual ten percent cream and not the rich, delicious cream Hilda usually had on supply.

"He just seems to forget that he lives with me! It's like I'm a stranger!" Jean cried. "Sometimes he gets into such a rage when I won't let him go out. But how can I let him wander about the neighbourhood half-dressed?" She paused and looked at Hilda, as though sizing her up. "You know, it's not the first time."

"Not the first time?" Hilda questioned.

Jean shook her head. What did she mean not the first time? Had John been leaving the house and not returning? Had Jean gone out before, looking for him, calling his name, like one does when a cat or dog runs off? And why didn't Hilda know any of this? Her daughters hadn't alluded to any of this the last time they had visited her.

"How long has he been like this?" Hilda asked her replacement.

"Well, since the seizures. They said it could have been a series of mini-strokes."

"What seizures? How long has this been happening?"

"A little while now. The seizures, the memory loss started over six months ago …"

It was the first Hilda had heard of any mini-strokes. Surely her daughters knew *that*. Why hadn't they told her? All Hilda knew was that her ex-husband had come to her home, believing that he still lived there, believing that she was still his wife, and that Jean, his real wife, was some unknown stranger who had been holding him captive. But apparently he had been trying to leave Jean and return to his previous life for six months!

"He had no recollection of you at all last night. It's as though you never existed—" Hilda started. "I thought this was the first time. That after he had a good sleep, he'd be fine, and go home. I mean, I can't have him here …"

"He was hospitalized a month ago. The doctors warned me that there might be some confusion. But you're the only one he asked for at the hospital, you know," Jean blurted out, suddenly uncensored. She shifted in her chair, aware of how much rounder she was than when she had tempted John away from Hilda.

"He was in the hospital?" Hilda asked.

Jean nodded.

"So, what do you want me to do? What can I do?"

"Well, I am here to get him, to bring him home," Jean stated.

"Great!" Hilda agreed. "As soon as he wakes up, you can take him home. I'll tell him that he really belongs with you. In the meantime, do you want some breakfast?"

"I really shouldn't. I'm trying to stick to the South Beach diet," Jean answered, although she didn't seem too convinced.

"South Beach? Which beach is that?"

"It's just called that. It's a *diet*. Mostly just protein and vegetables. A bit of fruit. I'm trying to drop a few pounds before Christmas."

"Why, so you can put it all back on again for the holidays? Why torture yourself?"

Jean eyed Hilda. All those years older and yet still she seemed fit. And she ate cake every single day! How very unfair was that? At one time, Jean knew that she had the type of body that could drive men wild. *Dangerous curves*, they all used to say. But the curves were less defined now, and the bounty of her breasts just seemed to unite with the bounty of her hips. Why should it matter? Her husband didn't recognize her anyhow.

"Well, I am going to make some fried eggs and potatoes for John and me. He always liked potatoes with onions. Maybe things will be clearer after a good breakfast." Hilda began rooting around for her cast-iron skillet. She poured a bit of olive oil into the pan and then tossed in a dollop of butter. Soon the enticing smell of onions frying, caramelizing in butter, filled the air.

"Maybe just a small taste," Jean suggested.

The aroma filled the room and silently made its way up the stairs to where John was just awakening from his sleep. In no time, he had his shirt thrown on and he bounded down the stairs, as though it was the most natural everyday occurrence.

"Something smells good!" he called out on his way down.

Jean fussed nervously with her teaspoon. Just the night before John had accused her of keeping him against his will before bolting out the door. He called her a guard or a jailer or some such thing. How would he react to seeing her here, in his old house?

John came in, all smiles, and planted a kiss on Hilda's cheek with the casualness of someone who had done so without a pause. Hilda was as surprised as Jean, but John seemed not to notice. Then he saw Jean sitting there, head down, staring into her coffee cup.

"Oh, you have a guest!" He put his hand out for Jean to shake. "John Wagner, nice to meet you!"

Hilda witnessed John's old confidence, his old outward friendliness. Hilda had always thought he would have made a better salesman than a school supervisor. She watched as Jean readjusted herself, then reached out her hand to take John's. She hoped that the touch would reawaken his memory. But as John shook the hand of the woman who had shared his bed for twenty years in a way that suggested he was meeting her for the first time, the awful truth sucker-punched her. She had been cast as a central character in a drama that was no longer hers. And there was no way that she could read ahead in the script to know what the outcome might be.

♦ ♦ ♦

Hilda had moved herself into the guest room, the second-largest bedroom in the house, once occupied by her two daughters. She could still see the discolouration on the walls where her daughter's pin-ups and posters of teen idols and boy bands had once been. All those young men with boyish names like Bobby, Donny, and Davy, making them all the more user-friendly to adolescent girls with their raging hormones!

The house felt like a stranger because of her visitor in the next room. *Her* room. It had always been her room, with her firm queen-size mattress, her mission-style bedframe, her mahogany dresser and side tables. Sure, she had once shared it with John and then later with Siegfried, but it had always seemed that the room was hers and she had just been kind enough to give them access. Now she rested in a left-behind, soft, twin-size bed, having voluntarily vacated her domain.

The second morning after his unexpected arrival, Hilda tried to put their situation into perspective for John, but he would have nothing of it. He behaved as though there had never been an end to their marriage.

"We divorced, John. You fell in love with Jean."

"Jean?" he asked.

"Jean. The schoolteacher. And then I remarried, too, remember?"

"Oh, Hilda, stop pulling my leg!" He laughed, giving her a peck on the cheek and a hug that seemed steeped in familiarity.

There's a familiarity of gesture that stops the moment a couple decides to part company. The simple squeeze on the shoulder as one passes the other, done without thought but with tactile habit, ceases immediately. A peck on the cheek in the morning. The use of the words "sweetie" and "love." They all stop the second one or the other says that they don't want to play *married* anymore. Because of this, Hilda had an awkward full day, where all the things that were taken from her and given to Jean would be returned without warning, like library books borrowed and forgotten, only to be dropped in the repository box years later. This, she thought, was the alternative life of what could have been, had they not grown apart, had Jean not seduced him away, had he been more attentive to her, more appreciative. Hilda was at a loss. Surely, he would eventually regain some memory. Surely, he would want his second family back in his life. Surely, there would be flashes of those years apart.

Jean dropped by after dinner. She brought a few changes of clothes for John, who still didn't recognize her. Hilda hung the clothes in the closet, carefully separating his from hers. By the time John was ready for bed the second night, he believed that the clothes had always been there.

"But why are you sleeping in the girls' room?" he asked her.

Hilda made excuses about snoring and wanting to read into the night. Then she kissed his forehead and said good night. Now, as she was lying there, staring at the walls and thinking of repainting, what really bothered her was the fact that the kiss was not premeditated. That it felt as natural as waking in the morning or sleeping through the night. The fact that the kiss did not bother her bothered her greatly.

Hilda knew that sleep would not be visiting her any time soon. She got up, made her way silently to the kitchen, and warmed herself some milk. Then she added a shot of brandy to it and two healthy teaspoons of honey. If the weather had been warmer, she would have stepped out into the night, into her garden, as she waited for answers. Instead, she picked up her book, hoping that between straining her eyes with reading and the effect of milk laced with brandy, sleep would take her and give her mind some peace. Yes, sleep. There would be time for answers the next day.

♦ ♦ ♦

The following morning was bright. The sun, high in the sky, seemed to reach the snow and ice on earth, tickling it so that blinding flashes of light danced over the ground. It was deceiving and, even after more than three-quarters of a lifetime in Canada, Hilda was still not used to the deception of sunshine and light that she had always associated with warmth and the melting away of winter. It was a trick of her chosen land to sparkle with such an intense light while maintaining bitter cold. She thought of Karl's cows and how they might be suffering. She touched her own breasts, imagining how they would feel with frostbite.

It would be Christmas soon. Just three weeks away and still no plans. All the more difficult now that John had moved into the master bedroom. And yet, somewhere in the confused John there was a glimpse of the man she had fallen in love with when she had first arrived in Canada. A glimpse of what was lost and had been re-found. But how could she explain that to anyone?

After she had done her daily check-in with Jean, Hilda decided that the one to help her with her John problem was Jack. Jack was the one she could always talk to.

Hilda could hear John moving about upstairs. Sounds of drawers opening, shuffling of feet. He must be getting dressed. Dressing was one of the things that he sometimes struggled with, demanding a certain tie, fretting about what went with what, putting things on in the wrong order, then not buttoning up properly. Any minute he might call down, asking for her help. She would have to make it quick, just the barest details without cause for too many questions.

Hilda tried the number in Hamburg but there was no answer. She left a message on Jack's answering machine, asking him to call at his earliest convenience.

"He doesn't remember leaving us. He thinks he is still married to me. That he still lives here! And the girls are bullying me to sell my house! I need you to come home and sort everyone out!" She yelled at a recording, believing that it was important to speak loudly because Jack was so far away and her voice would have to travel over the miles.

When Jack finally did return the call, he spoke of the ruined wedding, of going to Paris on a wild goose chase, and of Sabine's baby fighting for her life in the NICU.

"So, now tell me, what was your message all about?" he asked her.

"Oh, nothing. Nothing at all. You go to Paris, I'll handle this."

"Mom, I'll try to make it back for Christmas. Okay?"

"That would be lovely!"

Jack didn't hang up. It seemed a shame that long distance charges applied to pauses.

"Mom? I have a strange question. If a pregnant woman breathed in your rose essence, what would happen?"

"Likely nothing. But if you breathe in a lot, it could affect things. I always caution to be careful. Always use an essential oil with a light hand."

"Affect things, like how?"

"Well, it would have to be a lot of the oil. It wouldn't cause a miscarriage, but it could be disturbing for the baby. It could either relax the baby or make the baby agitated."

"So, you don't think ..." Jack couldn't quite give voice to it. To the idea that the essential oils may have somehow exacerbated Sabine's condition. He wished he hadn't asked, because once that suspicion was given any air to breathe then how could Iris, who had bathed herself in rose essence, ever forgive herself? He wanted to put the Jack-*back*-in-the-box!

"What you describe for Sabine sounds like it was unavoidable. I don't think eclampsia can be brought on by rose oil. Please, promise me you won't mention anything about the oils to Iris. You don't want her to feel responsible."

Hilda was concerned about the whole situation. She would have offered to go to Germany, to help however she could, but she knew that Elaine and Mark were already there and that, even if she wanted to, she couldn't leave John. Still, she wasn't sure that Jack's trip to Paris was a good idea. It was opening a Pandora's box, full of spite and sorrow, even if hope might be hidden in that box as well.

"If you go to Paris and you find out that Clara is alive, then what? It will be a mess for Sabine and Gareth. Don't they have enough stress?"

"I know. But what can I do? If Clara is alive and needs our help, how can we leave her to suffer?"

After eight troubling years, it seemed that Clara had left a memory behind in her absence, while John was absent of memory. One was too important to be forgotten and the other had forgotten what was important. One dysfunction did not balance the other.

"I'm quite sure it wasn't the rose oil. Please don't upset the girl."

"Sure, Mom. Just curious, though. What is rose oil used for, anyhow? Iris was drenched in it, apparently."

"Stress, irritable bowel, sadness, loneliness. It makes you feel loved. Oh, and, of course, memory ..."

Memory. Instinctively, Hilda knew that somehow scent was the answer. What could the scent of rose really do for memory? She remembered a study where rose oil was used in the study of nerve injury in clinical worms. In moderate doses, rose oil was found to reverse nerve injury in the worms. It was an important discovery because nerve injury in worms is similar to the nerve injury in the brains of patients suffering from early onset Alzheimer's.

"I have to go! Call me from Paris, so I know you arrived safely." Hilda was excited to try out her hunch.

"Mom, I'm grown man. Middle-aged."

"*Ja, ja.* I know. Just call. *Tchuss.*"

Essential rose oil. If Hilda put rose oil into a diffuser so that a delicate fragrance would be present in the house, in an unassuming but constant way, would it possibly bring back John's memory? Hilda searched her shelf for her bottle of rose oil. Then she hesitated. John seemed content in her house. More content than he had been in years. Perfectly happy with his situation. Was bringing back his memory the best choice for John?

It was certainly the only choice for Hilda.

ELEVEN

BÖZSI WANTED TO TAKE THE train, even though it was an eight-hour trip. She preferred the train. Flying made no sense to her. It was, to her, like entering a large metal tube, only to arrive somewhere else in the world, without having the sensation, or the experience, of travelling.

"You need to see the miles passing you by. To look at the countryside you are travelling through! Only then do you get a sense of being elsewhere. When you fly, you just walk into this winged, metal tube in one city and you walk out in another city. Poof! That isn't travelling. That is witchcraft! We should book a train now."

When they had bought their tickets to Germany from New York, Bözsi had suggested that they land in Hamburg and then take the train to Berlin, even though they could have flown to the airport in Berlin. As there were no direct flights to be had, Bözsi insisted that, if they had to endure a layover in a stuffy airport, it made better sense to go from plane to train. Esther hadn't argued. After all, Bözsi was paying for the trip, but now she understood that it hadn't been about a long wait inside of an airport; it was simply that Bözsi felt that a train ride was an important part of any adventure.

"We can take the Russian train, but that is only available a few times a week and usually you have to book well in advance. But there are sleeping berths. That would be nice. I like sleeping on trains!"

"If you are going to sleep anyhow, you might as well fly. You won't be able to see the passing countryside in the dark!" Esther retorted.

"Then there is a French train and a German train. One stops in Cologne. We could have lunch there. I've never been to Cologne. It must be nice. It is like naming a city Perfume!" Bözsi laughed.

"I thought you hated waiting. We can fly straight to Paris from here and it won't cost much. Then we can take a train from the airport into town. Jack can fly from Hamburg and meet us there. He's watching Fritz and Iris for a few days." Esther only relayed that much information. No point in telling Bözsi all the gruesome details of the aborted wedding. She didn't want Bözsi to think poorly of Blanca, and so the less said, the better.

Bözsi reluctantly agreed to fly. She would have preferred an entire day of hopping on and off trains than flying, but unfortunately, Esther was sensible and, once she mentioned that they would get to Paris all the quicker by air, Bözsi acquiesced.

"Do you think that Henri ever mentioned me to his wife?"

"No. Why would he?" Esther sighed. She hated that Bözsi would not be deterred from seeking out Henri's widow.

"He might have on his deathbed. If he had died in a hospital with her at his side, he may have spoken of me then. He was interrogated and still he didn't speak. He didn't give me away, you know."

"I know," Esther said, stopping short from saying that Bözsi had told her the story many times.

"You know, he didn't even mention me to them. That is how great his love was! He died for me." Bözsi pursed her orange-smeared lips and nodded her head. "Such a great love. A man who would die for you."

Every time Bözsi told that story, the details differed slightly in each version. Sometimes he was waterboarded and killed. Sometimes he was put into a camp where he died. Sometimes he was shot after digging his own grave. But always he was questioned about her and he never did speak. Esther could not help but wonder if Bözsi could have maintained her love for Henri, over an entire lifetime, had Henri lived, had he not been the silent hero, willing to die for whatever secrets he may have had. Could she have loved him with such passion if she woke up to him every morning and watched him age, his hair thinning, his skin sagging, and his stories repeated over and over again? It was easy to love a man whom you saw only at the best of times, when he was there to spoil you with kisses and lovemaking, but how does one find the endurance to love through the everydayness of life? Esther preferred her narrative, her understanding that passion was a bright star that quickly blazed and burned and then died into nothingness. Darkness, where once there had been a blinding flame. She could understand that. She had had that in her marriage.

"People think that when you love someone you do not see all the time, that the love isn't real. Somehow the love of a mistress is thought to be less than the love of a wife. The wife is the real love and the mistress is just for fun. That is all bullshit, you know!" Bözsi was always very definite when she justified the important role of the mistress.

"I wouldn't know. I was never a mistress, and my husband never had one."

"That you know of!" Bözsi snorted.

"No, Bözsi. He never had a mistress," Esther corrected her with a firm tone.

"Well, I wouldn't judge him if he did have one. Everyone hates the mistress, but we are the glue that holds a marriage together!"

"You cannot exactly be the glue if you only have contact with one half of the marriage." Esther smiled at her sister. Then she took out her passport and put her things in order so that she could make their travel arrangements. She knew she had to do so right away or Bözsi would likely change her mind and book a train behind her back.

"Never mind. All this talk of sex with married men just upsets you. Let's change the subject. What about Friedrich? Handsome, yes?"

"He is very nice," Esther commented without conviction.

"*And* he didn't do anything nasty in the war. He was too young!"

"He was very young! Younger than us."

"Not much younger than you. A year perhaps."

"Yes. A year perhaps. Maybe two."

"*And* he plays the piano," Bözsi persisted.

"Yes. He plays pretty well. Not as well as his daughter, though."

"*And* single. *And* rich." Bözsi reached for a cigarette.

"It's a non-smoking hotel," Esther reminded her.

"Pah! I'll tell them I don't read German. I'll speak to them in Yiddish and if they charge me I'll just say, 'Really? After what you people did to my family?' It works every time!"

"You wouldn't! That is terrible, using our parents' deaths to get away with smoking in a non-smoking room!"

"Oh, Esther, of course, it doesn't make up for it, but you take what you can from life. Me? I want a cigarette in my room with my coffee. Not too much to ask, considering ..."

Bözsi seemed to have great joy when she smoked. Even when Esther told her how smoking could kill her, she seemed to suck life itself out of those cancer sticks, as Esther liked to call them. It was something to witness, the cigarette between her lips, shaking slightly. The lighter awake with a blue flame, licking the end as Bözsi inhaled deeply. She always held that first inhalation as long as she could before slowly exhaling the smoke back into the room.

"You know that second-hand smoke is just as bad, so you are killing me, too."

"If it is just as bad, then you might as well enjoy one yourself!" Bözsi offered one to Esther, and as usual, she declined. Bözsi shrugged and drew another inhalation. The second was never quite as satisfying as her first.

"I am just saying that I think he likes you. The *baron*." Bözsi emphasized the word as though it was of the greatest importance, her hand gesturing in a wave with the word. Her eyes widened. It was all a big tease to her. A way to break through her sister's prudish judgment. "You should marry him since you only like marital sex. Oh, and then you would be a *baroness*, too!" Her words seemed to finish just as she blew out her last bit of smoke.

Esther didn't know why she felt flushed. Likely, she thought, because her older sister was so infuriating.

♦ ♦ ♦

The Punk Baroness had gone to a print shop near the university to make a copy of the opera. She had decided not to trust the old Jewish Hungarian dynamic duo with the originals. It was better that Jack was entrusted with them. What was she hoping for, anyhow? Fingerprints they could trace on the envelope? A carbon dating of the ink? Saliva testing on the licked stamp? What had seemed logical enough, what had seemed feasible a couple of weeks earlier, now seemed no more than a mad caper. Two women, clearly in their seventies, going to Paris, trying to find the whereabouts of someone who had disappeared in Africa eight years ago! It was madness. Like a bad episode of an English TV mystery.

Martina hated detective shows. All those badly dubbed British mysteries that Blanca watched. She wondered if Blanca registered the bad dubbing or if she merely read the lips of the British actors instead. All the years she had been in Germany, almost twenty, and Blanca's German was still halting and cautious. It was as though she had never tried to make an effort.

Strangely, it wasn't that way when Blanca sang. When she sang, she easily went from Italian to German to French. It was as though the music unlocked language for her, and the very things she struggled with in speech were fluent and easy when she sang. It wasn't because she practised, either. She could read almost any language off the page, provided she knew the melody. But to speak, to explain herself in any language but English was a challenge for her. She could say the words in another language, but she could not think in any language but English.

Martina put the copied music into a fresh envelope. Then she ran her finger over a few bars of the original, humming the melody, imagining the harmonies. She just couldn't help herself; she sat at her piano and turned to the first page. She closed her eyes and imagined the first sound of the drums. Here is Helen, primping and unaware. She is a girl, although she has already given birth. She brushes her hair and sings of love and longing.

Stop.

The Punk Baroness remembered the day. Blanca had gone to buy wine at duty-free, leaving Clara alone in the washroom. What was Clara doing? She was brushing her hair, perhaps. She was staring at herself in the mirror. *Mirror, mirror on the wall.*

Martina continued. Helen. She sings of love and longing. Her marriage cannot hold her. She was too young when she agreed to marry Menelaus. She did what was expected. Her divine self longs for more, even though her beauty is notorious, even though she has a child she loves, even though her people adore her. What then? What does Helen want? What trouble does she conjure?

Stop.

Could Clara have been bored? Could Clara have wanted to run away? Was it possible that she had met someone and that she wasn't abducted at all? That the only way to break free from the many threads of the woven tapestry of her life was to simply walk away? Let the tapestry fall from the wall and let someone else pick up all the loose threads …

"What are you playing?"

Martina hadn't even heard her come in. But there she was, Blanca, with a prepared lunch. How unlike her! Why was she suddenly making an effort? Leaving her bed more regularly now and coming to see her, with lunch in hand! Why now, after the years when she refused to venture into the rehearsal space unless it was absolutely required?

"Just a new piece someone submitted. I am thinking of doing it."

"Oh? What about *Sleeping Beauty*? You haven't abandoned the narcoleptic princess, have you?"

Martina chuckled in spite of the difficult decision to not write and mount *Sleeping Beauty*. "I am not up to it."

Truer words could not be spoken. As much as Martina wanted to write her version of an opera based on the story of Sleeping Beauty, a feminist version, she knew that the closest she would ever get to creating was directing someone else's composition. Although putting an opera production together required vision, it wasn't the same as composing an opera. A composer leaves something on the page, and every time someone performs it or produces it, that composition comes alive again. There was an immortality to generative art. Martina knew that without someone else's music, words, and story, she was limited in her expression. As someone who could play whatever music she could read, as someone who put operas onto the stage to greater and lesser success, as someone who reworked the classics and commissioned the new great pieces, she knew that she would always be the midwife and never the one destined to give birth.

Blanca picked up the music. Martina inhaled. Now was the moment of truth. All the questions would come out. *How long has she had the music? How had it come to her? Why hadn't she told her?*

"Play it. I want to hear the melody. Who am I? Helen?"

"Yes. And Clytemnestra. They're twins."

"Ha!" Blanca snorted.

Martina placed her fingers on the keys. Played out the music, emphasizing the melody so that it was clear in Blanca's mind.

"It's in English, mostly," Blanca remarked. "Like Purcell."

"Yes."

"Play that first part, one more time."

And Martina did. Once again, emphasizing the voice of Helen.

"Okay, I'm ready."

She sang. For the first time in years, Blanca opened her mouth and a sound came out, hesitant at first and then, as she continued, stumbling through the music, she became reacquainted with the sound of her voice. She heard it rise and diminish, heard the change of tempo and rhythm.

"Again," she demanded.

She sang only the part Martina had played. Over and over again, adding more emotion each time until the song became an extension of her. Until she was the song and there was no delineation between the woman singing and the song. Then she stopped abruptly. Locked eyes with Martina, her silence demanding an explanation.

"I'm sorry," Martina said. "It arrived in the mail. I don't know who sent it."

"You don't know who sent it?"

"No."

"But you *do* know who wrote it!"

"Are you angry with me?" Martina asked.

"Yes, I am furious with you. But it doesn't matter because my anger is overridden by my intense joy!"

Martina looked at Blanca, dumbfounded.

"I should be furious, but I can't be. Don't you see? Four weeks ago, we buried my sister. Metaphorically at least. Right here, in this room! And today she is resurrected! Oh, Martina, my sister is alive!"

Blanca was crying and laughing and dancing all at once. She took Martina's face in her hands and kissed her on the mouth.

"I'm sorry I've been so difficult. I've been so sad, you know? But now, there's some hope. Now, we can go back and look for her! Oh, Martina, play some more. I want to hear my sister's music!"

Martina did not know what to do or say; she simply returned to the music, playing further into the story of *The Lost Queen: The True Abduction of Helen*.

♦ ♦ ♦

Charles de Gaulle. Yet another bone of contention between Esther and Bözsi. For Bözsi, the mere mention of his name brought a look of ecstatic reverence to her face. Although Jewish, Bözsi had, on three occasions, written a letter to the pope demanding that de Gaulle be granted sainthood. She understood that to do so there was a process, but she wanted to "get the ball rolling"; those being the exact words she wrote each time in each letter. Three letters, one written in French, one written in German, and one in her broken English. She had done her homework and knew that Pope John Paul II spoke all of those languages and, as Bözsi did not speak *his* mother language, Polish, she hadn't taken any chances and wrote to him in the three other languages she knew he also spoke. When, instead, the pope chose four priests who were executed by the Communists for spying in 1958, Bözsi was outraged. Hadn't he read her letters? Didn't he see how much more deserving de Gaulle was?

"Tell me, who saved French honour? De Gaulle. Who held France together? De Gaulle. He is the reason why France is great."

Esther rolled her eyes. Had she known that the flight would be nothing but talk about de Gaulle she would have gladly agreed to have taken the train instead.

"You know, there was a procession down the Champs-Élysées," Bözsi continued, aware of Esther's ebbing patience but inspired all the same. "And there was a sniper who was going to shoot him. Did he hide? No! Did he run away? No! He led the procession right down the street! Then, when he went inside the cathedral, there were shots being fired there, too. Many, many bullets! Everyone fell to the floor. Everyone, except de Gaulle. Now there was a real man!"

"Were you there?" Esther asked, doubting the exaggerated drama of her sister's story.

"Of course not. That was in 1944. I was still in Algeria then. I left late in 1945. That is when I went to France to look for answers about Henri. That is where it was confirmed, one hundred percent, that he had been captured and tortured to death. I haven't been back since."

Esther's opinion of de Gaulle was also extreme, though diametrically opposed. As a new immigrant to Canada, Esther had first settled in Montreal, believing that the city would feel more like Europe to her, making the adjustment less jarring. At that time, she had a small flat just off Rue Saint-Viateur, not far from a popular bagel bakery. Soon people came to know her in the neighbourhood and would nod in greeting as she passed. It was easy for her to fall in love with the city with its cafés, bakeries, and medieval vibe. It was for this reason that she went with her husband to celebrate Expo '67 in Montreal years later. It was a huge deal because Canada was also about to celebrate its one hundredth birthday. It should have been nothing but celebration, but Charles de Gaulle, then the president of France, also went to Expo '67, and decided to wreak havoc by yelling out, from the balcony of Montreal's City Hall, the very words that would fuel the FLQ, causing riots, bloodshed, and acts of terrorism. "*Vive le Québec libre!*"

On November 9, 1970, long after Esther and her husband had returned to Ontario, the news came out that de Gaulle had died. Esther bought a moderately priced bottle of Spanish sparkling wine. With a pop of a cork, she celebrated de Gaulle's death. Her only regret was that he had died of natural causes and not been hanged, publicly, in Canada, for treason.

"Innocent people were tortured and killed in Quebec because of de Gaulle. He has the blood of Pierre Laporte on his hands."

"Who?"

"Pierre Laporte! There is a bridge named after him in Montreal."

"A bridge. *Le pont!* Hah!" Bözsi roared with laughter. "A bridge, really? Not exactly like having an *airport* named after you! And not just any airport. The busiest airport in Europe!"

"He lost his life. He was killed needlessly. Garroted."

Bözsi shrugged. "What is one life, compared to a cause, a movement?"

"Then let's not hear you whine about Henri being tortured! After all, it was only one life compared to a cause. A movement!"

"Not the same at all! I loved Henri." Bözsi was hurt. Henri was a man she had known, had loved beyond reason. How could she compare some stranger, some man with a *bridge* named after him, to her greatest love?

"And Pierre Laporte had a wife and family who loved him, too!"

Because of this difference in opinion regarding de Gaulle, Bözsi referred to the airport as Aéroport de Paris-Charles-de-Gaulle, and Esther called it by its other name, Roissy Airport. Neither corrected the other for the duration of the short flight. They had decided to "agree to disagree" about de Gaulle, even though Esther hated that expression.

The airport in Roissy, Aéroport de Paris-Charles-de-Gaulle, is indeed one of the busiest hubs in Europe. The evening Bözsi and Esther arrived was no different than any other. A cacophony of different languages, voices over a speaker announcing delays, gate changes, and arrivals, and the dragging, squeaky sounds of suitcases on wheels being pulled along the floors. The extraordinary thing, though, beyond the hustle and bustle, were the extravagant shops in the airport. Then there were the bakeries with brioche, croissants, and *tartes aux pommes*. Esther thought, why bother with the train ride into Paris when everything one could possibly desire was right there in the airport?

"I will find someone and ask where to get the train into the city."

When Bözsi approached a handsome young man who was carrying a soft leather man-bag, complete with tasseled loafers to match, her tone became softer. She slipped into French as easily as one might slip into a nightgown before bed. She seemed younger, her mouth less hard, her movements sprightlier. It was as though the language was a passport back to the cancan dancer she had once been. Esther knew there was a whole life lived that she would never know. A lost part of her sister she could never meet even though she had recently been reunited with her. Coming together was like a direct flight from old-age back to childhood, without seeing the miles in between or the passing landscape. It was only then that Esther understood why train travel was so preferred by Bözsi.

"The lovely young man said that we can easily get to Paris by taking the B train. It will take about thirty minutes to get to the city centre, then we can make our way from there. He was very nice. And handsome, too. Do you think he is homoerotic?"

"Why do you ask? Because he had a purse? Lots of men carry purses now! Besides it isn't *homoerotic*. I believe the word is *homosexual*."

"Yes, but *sexual* does not sound as nice as *erotic*. It's always sex, sex, sex now. But what is sex, really? It's in the mind." Bözsi pointed to her head. "In the mind, it is not sex at all. Sex is the act but not the thought. It is eroticism that is in the imagination. It is eroticism that makes us prefer one to the other. Don't you think so, too, Esther?"

"I have never thought of the difference, Bözsi."

As if on cue, they stopped in front of a boutique that had an assortment of expensive lingerie displayed in its window. Silks and satins that seemed to barely hold on to the hangers. It was as though they could easily slide off at any moment.

"Only in a French airport!" Esther exclaimed.

"Let's go in here. I will treat you."

"Really, I have no need of lingerie." Esther dismissed her. "That sort of thing is for younger women. Not for me. Besides, who would I wear it for? No one. Now come, let's get the train to town."

Bözsi left her standing there, watching the luggage on her own. From where she stood, Esther watched Bözsi choose a mauve-coloured pajama set, lined in a thin, cream-coloured lace, and a pale peach-coloured teddy set in a sumptuous silk. Esther couldn't imagine why Bözsi would waste her money on something so useless and extravagant. Where was the woman she lived with in the Bronx, sitting in her loose house dress, surrounded by the smell of cabbage? They had barely touched down in France, and it seemed that her sister was somebody else entirely.

♦ ♦ ♦

The hotel, 34B, was moderately priced and comfortable with a clean, modern design made all the cozier by the exposed brick. There were 128 rooms at 34B Rue Bergère, many not in use because it was December, certainly not tourist season in Paris. It was close enough to everything and next to a metro station on lines 8 and 9, making it easy for them to travel around Paris as needed. And when they were not searching for clues about Clara, they could easily walk to the Folies Bergère, Opéra Garnier, and Musée Grévin. Places that held much more interest to Bözsi than to Esther.

"I think we won't get lost. Easy to remember since 34B was always my bra size and Bergère sounds just like Bözsi! I really should have changed the spelling of my name to *B-E-R-G-I-E*, which would have made it so much easier for the French and English! Nobody really likes omelets, you know. They are so confusing for most people."

"Omelets? Confusing? What are you talking about now?"

"You know, the little dots over vowels! Don't be daft. I got a name with an omelet. Be grateful you didn't."

"*Umlaut.*"

"Yes. That is what I said. Let's freshen up and then go for a walk. It's not so cold. Not like New York."

Bözsi opened the curtains, which revealed a Juliet balcony. She opened the double doors to breathe in the Paris night air and a fresh breeze overtook the room. Did the air itself smell different from one country to another? Did every city have its own scent? Esther could see, beyond the window and beyond her sister standing in the cool night air, a whole city of lights. Of course, Paris would be lit up for

Christmas. It seemed to twinkle and invite, as though something from a fairy tale Esther had never had a chance to read.

"You see, very convenient and in our budget. And breakfast is included. I usually don't like a big breakfast, but I think we should fill up so we can skip lunch and then have a substantial dinner!" Bözsi said.

"I could do with a little something now. We haven't had dinner. But something light. All this talk of omelets makes me feel like one."

"Well, the French omelet *is* superb. Unlike any other."

The great difference between a French omelet and all other omelets in the world is in the colour. Other omelets, such as a traditional Spanish omelet, may have a crispy browning on the outside, but because the French omelet is not merely folded in half but rather turned three times into a more circular roll, it must have a uniform exterior. The perfect French omelet is usually nothing but eggs and butter cooked just enough to have a soft texture and only hard enough that the inside, runny egg does not leak onto the plate. In almost all other culinary cultures, the omelet is not so much about the eggs but about what goes inside the eggs. Not so with the French omelet. Although salt and pepper, and sometimes herbs, may be added for subtle flavour, the experience of the French omelet is in the texture of the lightly cooked eggs. Esther had eaten a proper French omelet only once, with her husband two months before he died. Now, back in France, all she craved was that taste. The taste that reminded her of his cherished last days.

"We can walk and find some place that is small. The best time to experience a city is at night. The day is for tourists, for people who want to *see* things. But the night is for travellers who want to *experience* things." Bözsi sounded confident.

Esther had never thought of the difference but considered it yet another of Bözsi's strange truisms.

"You know, though, that this isn't a trip. We are here on a mission."

"Of course, Esther. Not a trip. An *adventure!*"

"Not an adventure, a *mission*. We are here to find out who sent Clara's music."

Esther took a scarf from her hand luggage. A soft, sage-green cashmere. It was just the thing for an evening stroll on an early December night in Paris. She draped it loosely over her neck. Then she ran her fingers through her fair hair. Still thick, with the slightest wave.

"Yes," Bözsi agreed. "It is very serious business we are on. But we must also take a moment to enjoy the city."

Soon they were out the door, in search of the perfect omelet.

TWELVE

HOW BLANCA HAD CONVINCED HER still baffled the Punk Baroness. One moment it was decided that only Jack would go to Paris to meet Bözsi and Esther, and the next moment they were throwing their overnight bags into the trunk of the Beemer convertible and setting out to drive from Berlin to Hamburg, where they would pick up Jack, and then on to Paris, the City of Light.

Blanca kept humming the Helen aria, bar after bar of what she had quickly memorized, believing the tune might hold a mystery to Clara's whereabouts.

"And what do we hope to find in Paris?" she asked.

"The opera was mailed from Paris. We hope to find the person who mailed it."

"Maybe *she* mailed it!" Blanca sounded like she was an eight-year-old, ready to open her birthday presents.

"Maybe, but it was not Clara's writing on the envelope, so I think it was someone else."

Even Blanca admitted that the pen was too flowery, and the lettering was cursive and so not likely Clara's hand. She reached into the back seat, grabbed Martina's burgundy briefcase, and fetched the envelope so she could study it. She held it to her face and tried smelling it. Nothing.

Even though finding Clara was a long shot, Blanca seemed to have life in her again. They had even made love the night before. Martina, used to rejection, had been surprised when Blanca rolled her slight body on top of her and began to kiss her neck and her ears, breathing words of love to Martina as she touched, kissed, and moved on top of her. Martina responded immediately. Yes, her lover was back, in her arms, in their shared bed, inviting and warm to the touch. Knowing Clara was alive seemed to breathe life back into their relationship, and as much as Martina was relieved to be loved and desired, she also feared for what would happen should Clara not be found.

"I've made a deal with God, you know."

"You have? Really? With God?"

Blanca nodded. She knew that Martina was not a great believer in God, or miracles, and that she was certainly not one to ever bargain with God. "*If God wants to make a deal, he should come out and show his face*," Martina had often scoffed.

"Do you want to know what it is?" Blanca asked.

"Of course."

"I told God that I will stop cutting while we look for her. And if we find her, I will give it up completely." She paused. "You do know that I cut after the wedding."

"I know."

"I thought I did pretty well at hiding it from you." Blanca paused. "Oh. Is that why you had the car seats reupholstered?"

Martina nodded. The reupholstering didn't matter.

"You know that I want to cut every day. Every day I have a compulsion to look for something I can cut with. I have to fight it every day. Every day I live with that compulsion. With that voice in my head, urging me to find something I can cut myself with."

Martina took her hand. "And you know that every day, when I come home, I brace myself, not knowing what I will find. Every day I worry that I might say something that will trigger you. Every day I live with terror. You cut, and I clean up the blood."

"I'm sorry, Martina. But I promise that it ends here."

Martina wanted to believe her. She wanted to believe that there would be no more cutting. That Blanca would do the opera. That a great production would be mounted in Berlin. And, mostly, that her lover desired her again. There was only one unspoken condition for it all. How hard could it be? All Martina had to do was to pull Blanca's twin out of thin air!

◆ ◆ ◆

Jack, owning a third of the apartment in Hamburg, always kept a small room there, at the back, just beyond the kitchen. It was nothing much, likely originally a pantry, no more than eight feet by eight feet with a three-quarter mates-bed, with drawers under it, and a small desk. A landing place for him whenever he was in Europe, the occasions of which seemed to occur less and less as the years went on. As he considered how cramped Gareth and Sabine were, he wondered if he should just give it up. Sell it to them, perhaps. Or give it to them as a gift. Iris could use her own room and not just a part of a room divided between her and Fritz. Not that Fritz minded; he liked his sister nearby. But Iris would be thirteen soon. She would be needing her privacy. Yes. He should just give his tiny room to Iris.

There was more to it than that. He had recently spoken to his mother, and he could tell that his sisters were pressuring Hilda to sell her house again. If he bought out his sisters' share of the house, they could have whatever inheritance was coming to them from Hilda's side, and with cash in their pockets, they might leave Hilda alone.

The world's harshness was wearing him away, eroding him bit by bit like an old piece of fabric fraying at the edges. After twenty years of chasing stories all over the world, Jack was tired. He wanted to stand in one place for a while, to plant himself somewhere. He wanted a change. Stability. All the things Tristan had wanted from him but he couldn't give to him then.

"*Bleib heir!*" Fritz yelled out, when Jack told them that he would be leaving that afternoon for Paris. Fritz had even turned his attention away from *Sesamstrasse*, the German version of *Sesame Street*.

"Yes, stay here, Uncle Jack!" Iris repeated in English.

"Your aunt Blanca and Martina have decided to drive to Paris, so we will be doing a road trip together. I was supposed to fly out yesterday, so you got me for a whole extra day."

"Is Aunt Blanca coming here? Actually?" Iris asked, unsure how she would feel seeing her so soon after the wedding incident.

"For a little bit, just for a quick coffee and a pee break. Then we'll all be on our way."

Iris wanted to tell Jack things but either didn't have the chance or didn't have the nerve. She wanted to tell him about the rose essence and how Hilda had written that it was very powerful, and that it was best not to wear it around Sabine when she was pregnant. But she had. She wanted to tell him how she had wished that Sabine wasn't pregnant and that she had hoped that it wouldn't be a girl. She wanted someone, Jack, to know that the baby was fighting for her life because of her. And she wanted him to love her anyhow. *There are no monsters under the bed or in the closet. The monster is right here.*

She had tried to make it right. She had taken out candles and made an altar to the baby. She put a few drops of mint on the altar, because mint is lively. She added some sage for protection. She called on the four directions, the four elements, and the four seasons. She whispered the name of every pagan god she had ever heard of, every god she had read about in books. Norse gods. Greek gods. Any gods she could conjure.

"*Please, please. Let the baby live. I promise to protect her. To be a good sister to her. I promise that I will love her. Just, please, make her live.*" She had prayed to them all.

Iris wanted to tell Jack about her pledge. She wanted someone to hear her confession. Now he was going to Paris and there wouldn't be a chance. The secret would be contained in the dark hole of her heart.

"Who will watch us if you go? Daddy is at the hospital every day," Iris reminded, hoping Jack might stay longer.

"Your grandparents are over here, visiting every day. Besides," he whispered to her alone, "I am on a quest to find your mother, remember? But it's our secret."

◆ ◆ ◆

When Sabine opened her eyes, Blanca was standing at the end of her hospital bed. At first, she thought she was dreaming, but then Blanca spoke and broke her sleepy spell.

"How are you feeling?" she asked.

"I've been better. Did you hear what happened?"

"Yes. I'm sorry. I'm so sorry, Sabine."

"Ah, well, not your fault. The baby, that is. I had toxemia, eclampsia. It would have happened anyhow. I should have realized. I had all the signs." Sabine paused, looked directly at Blanca. "Now, the wedding, that is another story. That *was* your fault."

Blanca didn't know how to tell her that when she stood up that day, when she objected, it was as though her body had been taken over by a force that was beyond her and that it wasn't until the words were falling from her mouth that she realized what she was doing. It sounded so false, so unbelievable. All she could do was apologize again.

"It is a strange thing to say, Blanca, but if you had not ruined my wedding, I would probably be dead now. And the baby certainly would be. Now she has a small chance. A very, very small chance. Here, help me up. You can see her."

Blanca offered her arm. Her right arm, as the left one was still sore from the cuts. Sabine grasped it and pulled herself up. It was clear that she still hurt in her lower abdomen where the C-section incision was. Another four days and the stitches would be out. She got to her feet and pulled a robe over her nightgown.

Together they walked down the hall and around the corner to the NICU. The small babies all looked uncomfortable, pulled too soon from their mothers and now hooked up to machines so that they could finish the development that should have taken place in the warmth and safety of the womb.

"There she is!" Sabine pointed.

Tiny. The smallest one there. No distinguishing features. Just a fretting, uncomfortable, pink thing, fighting for her life. Her eyes seemed fused shut, although she seemed to have only eyebrows and long lashes. The disconcerting thing for Blanca was that the baby was covered in soft hair. Her entire body and face had a fine covering. She was like a fuzzy peach and, it seemed to Blanca, not much bigger than one.

Blanca actually took Sabine's hand. How did she have the courage to walk that long hall to see her struggling baby every day? How could she bear it? Blanca had never thought of Sabine as brave. She was just the party girl. The woman who had taken her sister's place. She wasn't to be taken seriously. But now, standing there, hand in hand, Sabine was so much more than Blanca had ever imagined. To Blanca, Sabine suddenly seemed to be the bravest woman in the world.

"A week ago, she had only a ten percent chance of survival. Today it is almost twenty percent. You see? She's a fighter."

"Like her mother," Blanca reassured, squeezing Sabine's hand.

What would happen to Sabine if Clara returned? In her desire to find her twin, she had never imagined the repercussions. Never thought beyond her own desires.

◆ ◆ ◆

Gareth didn't see Blanca at the hospital. He visited late that day because he was behind with his work. Three people in need of glass-eye fittings had been put off for days, and Gareth had to fulfill his obligations, as much as he did not want to leave Sabine alone.

He worried about her. She tried so hard to express milk for the baby, but without the baby near to suckle, her milk did not let down. The emergency Caesarean did not send the clues to her body that a baby had been born and needed milk. Her breasts were fuller because of the pregnancy, they were swollen and sore, but there was no relief for her. Gareth knew that it grieved her that she would never be able to breastfeed their daughter and that she still hadn't held her.

They had been given warnings. Because the lungs and heart were not yet fully developed, the baby could likely develop asthma. But that was not the worst-case scenario. Brain function could be affected. She could have learning disabilities. Hearing and sight could be diminished or lost. And then there was the possibility of lung failure, feeding problems, and heart failure. Even as she improved daily, there were no optimistic promises. No guarantees.

The mobile was the talisman he created to give him hope. If he made each decorative glass ornament with love, blew his own strength into the glass, then the baby might know that she had

purpose and, somehow, live. There wasn't much left to do. Another two decorative glass balls and the mobile would be complete. Coloured glass orbs, from purple to red and every shade in between. Some were round balls of glass and some more oblong, but each caught the light in its own way.
That's what you have to do, little Frieda. You have to catch the light.

♦ ♦ ♦

Martina, Blanca, and Jack arrived at the small hotel, 34B, shortly after 8:00 p.m. They must have looked quite the trio with their messy windblown hair, red cheeks, and overall tired appearances. Jack attempted to make a joke about convertibles and the wonderful French climate, but the middle-aged woman at the reception desk just wanted to check them in and be done with it.

"Just the one room, for the three of you?" she asked, but her expression implied that she found the arrangement questionable.

The Punk Baroness, quite used to getting whatever she wanted without question, simply smiled at the woman, closed mouth like the Mona Lisa, and nodded her head in a very crisp manner. The woman got the keys and gestured for them to follow.

"We should check in on Esther and Bözsi," Blanca suggested. "They likely expected us a few hours ago."

Jack left the two women and went down the hall to check on them, but Esther and Bözsi were not in their room and had likely gone out for the night.

"I wonder what they've been up to these past few days?" Jack pondered when he returned to their shared room.

"I shudder to think!" Martina laughed at the thought of the two elderly troublemakers let loose in Paris.

"Maybe they've found the phantom lover!" Jack laughed.

"We'll take the big bed. Jack, you can sleep over there." Blanca pointed to a small bed, pushed off to the side, beside the small window.

The three had quite a large room with two beds, a wide and luxurious bed and a small child-size one, which obviously would be Jack's. Jack knew it would have been preferable to Martina and Blanca if he had taken his own room, but he knew that he now preferred distraction at night. When he was alone, thoughts of Tristan overwhelmed him. The thoughts would find themselves in his dreams as though the slightest open door was an invitation for despair.

◆ ◆ ◆

It was the spilling of coffee the next morning that provided the first clue. Martina had ordered up a carafe of coffee, with a side of heated milk and three *pains au chocolat*. She was a director of the theatre and in the habit of taking charge. Blanca was quite used to it and found that there was a certain freedom in not concerning herself with what she wanted to eat or drink, but for Jack, it was unnerving. He knew it was Martina's credit card that was left with the front desk for any incidentals. He knew that she would insist on paying for whatever extra charges they might incur. But he couldn't help but wonder if he would have a chance to order his own food.

Martina was fixing everyone's coffee, pouring from both the carafe and silver-plated creamer of warm and frothy milk.

"I prefer mine black," Jack mentioned.

"Nonsense, I will fix you one and it will taste wonderful. You'll see. It is better my way."

Without thinking, Jack pulled his cup away just as Martina started to pour the coffee and milk. As it spilled out on the hotel desk, neither Blanca nor Jack could grab the envelope holding the opera inside of it in time. Coffee covered half of the envelope.

"Jack! Be more careful!" Martina snapped at him.

"It's not so bad," Blanca stated, frantically wiping the bottom left side. Then she stopped suddenly, stared at the envelope. She gently moved her hand again over it. What she felt was something that had been invisible to the eye. There seemed to be a slight indentation, as though someone had been writing on another piece of paper and the firmness of the pen penetrated through to the envelope, leaving a mark without leaving an ink trail.

"There's something here! There's writing. Someone wrote something!" She exclaimed. "Look!"

"Put it on the radiator to dry," Martina commanded. "It must dry!"

The three stood, watching the envelope and the radiator as though their impatient eyes would hasten the drying process.

"How long do we have to stand here watching an envelope on a radiator?" Jack asked.

"Till it's dry, Jack." Blanca sounded sincere.

Jack poured himself a black coffee. The *pains au chocolat* were eaten. And they waited without the relief of needless talk.

"Okay, good enough, hand me my bag," Martina ordered. "I think I have a graphite pencil in it."

Martina was very careful as she rubbed the graphite over the manila envelope, keeping a steady hand to produce a uniform grey over the pen scratches. Slowly the figures and lettering came into existence.

$I = r + \pi$ but
$Y = C + I + G + NX$
replace the I with r+π

"What the fuck?" Jack stared at the symbols, confused.

"Looks like an equation of some kind," Martina suggested. "Looks like it was done in a hurry. Whoever it was might be jotting down something someone was saying, or maybe something copied off a blackboard?"

"What do you think it means?" Blanca asked.

"How should I know? I know music and opera, not equations!" Martina answered.

"That one looks like the symbol for pi, but it isn't anything I learned in high school. My guess is that this is a theory or an advanced math equation," Jack offered.

"So, it doesn't help!" Blanca threw herself down on the large bed, the duvet puffing up to embrace her disappointed body.

"Quite the contrary. Don't give up so easily. Whoever sent the envelope either understands this or is studying this. First, we find out what the equation means, then we narrow down the field of study and finally which universities teach the courses that apply to this equation! We start there." Jack was trying to console her.

"*Ja*, you see, Blanca, Jack is more than a pretty face after all. It's that investigative mind that must drive the men crazy!"

Martina sat down on the bed beside Blanca and snuggled into her.

"You see, Blanca, we are on the case, as they say. How about Jack goes off and researches in one of those cybercafés and we meet up with the old *Frauen* to form a plan? *Ja?*"

Jack knew that was a thinly disguised hint. He should leave, get to a café to research the equations, the sooner the better, so that Blanca and Martina could enjoy the luxuries of the Paris hotel room without him.

THIRTEEN

THE WIND BLEW FROM THE west, off the sea, making the air damp and fierce. Hilda had written Iris a letter telling her how cold it was in Canada, over minus twenty with the wind chill, and although Iris wasn't quite sure what a wind chill was exactly, she knew that it had something to do with how cold it felt outside when the wind was blowing hard. Hilda had written to her that there was snow and ice in Canada, but Iris couldn't imagine it being colder than Hamburg, with the chilly wind that seemed to come from far away. It wasn't freezing weather, though. The Außenalster wasn't even icy.

Lost in her thoughts, as she made her way home from school, Iris was unaware of the car slowing alongside her. A man, perhaps forty or forty-five, with dark eyes and dirty blond hair, rolled down his window and whistled to get her attention. Iris ignored him. Pretended not to hear the whistle. Then he yelled for her to come closer so he could ask her directions. Iris clutched her keys, felt the cold metal on her fingers.

"Do you speak English?" he shouted over to her.

Iris nodded.

"Then come here, I need to ask you a question." The man seemed insistent, although friendly enough.

Iris froze. It seemed that the wind chill had taken the temperature down to below freezing in that moment. She was unable to move, frozen there on the pavement.

"So lucky to find someone who speaks English! I'm so lost! You're my angel. A Christmas angel." He laughed. "You even look like an angel!"

Iris had her fingers so tight on the keys that she could feel their teeth break through her skin.

"Aw, come here. I won't bite you," the man urged.

Biting was the least of her worries. He would take her. He would do terrible things to her. But how was that even possible when she had her magical keys? How could he manifest himself against her magic?

"Okay, I get it, you're shy," he shouted over to her. "It's okay, come here. I won't hurt you!"

Iris managed to shake her head no.

"Okay. Then just point, where is the Parliament building, the Rathaus?" he asked, mispronouncing *Rathaus*.

Iris knew exactly where Der Rathaus was. The ornate, neo-classical sandstone building was impossible to miss, right in the heart of the Altstadt and on the exact route Iris took home every day. But she pointed in the opposite direction.

"That way? Damn, I was going the wrong way completely. I get so turned around in this crazy city. Thanks!" But he didn't drive off right away. He reached out his hand. Iris could see that he had a few crumpled euros he was waving at her. "Here, come get it! A little something for your help!"

"*Nein danke*," she replied, switching firmly to German.

She watched him make an illegal U-turn, and when she was sure he was far enough away, she began to run, as fast as her legs could carry her. Her boots sounded step by step as her slender legs carried her into the Altstade, past the Rathaus and beyond, to the street where the apartment stood. She unlocked the front door and darted up the stairs, two at a time.

What if he followed me? What if he knows where I live?

She slammed the door. Locked it. Then leaned against it and closed her eyes.

Maybe he meant no harm. Maybe he was just looking for the Rathaus.

Iris could hear talking in the living room. The voices of her grandma Elaine and her granddad Mark. Then she heard her father and Sabine. Sabine was home! Home from the hospital! Iris pushed all thoughts of scary men in cars from her mind. She pulled herself together. This would be her first glance of her new sister! They were home in time for Christmas vacation!

As she walked into the living room, everyone became quiet. The adults all looked at her. Only Fritz took no notice of her. He was playing with a puzzle, putting pieces together, making pretty pictures of places he had never seen.

"Come here, sweetheart," her father said. "We have some very difficult news."

Iris sat on the couch close to Gareth. She could see that he had been crying but that he was now putting on a good show.

"I'm afraid that little Frieda has some more challenges. You see, we have to make a very hard decision," he said quietly.

Iris felt his arm around her, holding her as though he was afraid he might lose her, as though she were one of those rings you toss to someone drowning. *Don't tell him. Don't ever tell him about the man in the car. Don't make him worry.*

Iris couldn't speak. Her heart raced in her chest. "What kind of decision?"

"Her lungs are still not working on their own. She has to be given a lot of oxygen every day. So much that the oxygen will probably blind her."

"How can oxygen blind her? We breathe oxygen! That doesn't make any sense," Iris questioned, her voice rising to an abrasive, high pitch.

Across the room Sabine started to cry. Elaine put her arm around her, and Iris could see Sabine's body collapse softly into the older woman.

"In very small babies, when they get too much oxygen, it affects the retina and can cause blindness." Gareth shuddered at the memory of the sight of his daughter's eyes being held open with tiny clamps so that drops could be applied. Eyes that preferred to remain tightly closed against the light. If she had lungs, if they had developed to the point of accepting breath, Gareth knew that she would have screamed out in pain, but instead she had opened her mouth and writhed in distress. All he could think was, thank God Sabine was not there at that moment, watching through the glass. Thank God she hadn't witnessed that.

"Frieda was born so early, you see. She hasn't fully developed the blood vessels in her eyes. The doctor explained to us that she has something called retinopathy of prematurity," Gareth tried to explain, not fully understanding it himself.

"What is it? Can it get better?" Iris asked, panic in her voice.

"It means that the amount of oxygen needed to help Frieda's body and brain develop is also a problem for the baby's retina. For her vision."

Gareth knew that he and Sabine would have to make a difficult choice as quickly as possible. They could lessen the oxygen given and reduce the pressure, thus still giving the baby air but lessening her chances of blindness, risking her very life and the development of her brain, or they could continue with the oxygen therapy and, with how things seemed to be proceeding, choose a life of blindness for Frieda. Either way there was no guarantee.

"Could she die?" Iris asked.

Gareth nodded. "It's very sad. I'm sorry. But we must make a decision. As a family."

"The thing is," her granddad Mark started, "the thing you have to understand is that even if the oxygen works and she gets through this, the likelihood is that she will have some brain damage."

"And so what?" Sabine yelled at her would-be father-in-law. "So what? What do you want me to do? I should just let her die, then? I should just kill her because she isn't convenient!"

"No, Sabine. No, I'm not saying that. I just want you to consider. Blind and brain-damaged? It will be very difficult. For her. And for the whole family."

"I think you should go to the hotel now. Please just go. Get out of the apartment," Sabine said quietly, pushing Elaine's arm away from her.

"Sabine," Elaine started. "We have to keep our hope. Right? Rest today. Stay strong. I have faith that you will make the right choice for baby Frieda."

Iris started to cry, soft tears at first, and then great sobs and gulps that could not be controlled. It was too horrible. It was all just too horrible.

Fritz pushed his puzzle away and ran to his sister. He tried to tickle her to make her laugh, but she just kept sobbing.

"It's nobody's fault," Gareth told her. "And even if she lives, she will have so many challenges in life. It pains her just to breathe. Breathing hurts her."

Iris pulled away and only then looked at Sabine, now silent and stoic on the sofa across from them.

"I'm tired. I think I'll go to bed. Can you make Iris and Fritz something to eat?" she asked Gareth.

But Iris wasn't hungry. She didn't want food. She wanted clarity.

"Is this Aunt Blanca's fault for ruining the wedding? You had to have the baby early because she upset you, right?"

"No, Iris. If she hadn't stopped the wedding I would have died. And the baby, also."

"If something happens to baby Frieda, you can try again, right? You can have another baby and call her Frieda all over again, right? And maybe it will be the same baby spirit. Right?" Iris blurted out.

Sabine shook her head. "No. There cannot be any more babies. It's impossible." And Sabine, who looked as though she had been through the wars, opened her arms and gestured for Iris to go over to her. She wrapped Iris in her arms and held her so close to her chest that Iris could swear that she felt the beating of Sabine's heart inside of hers. Iris felt the touch of Sabine's lips at the top of her head. She felt Sabine's love move from that spot down her whole body, filling her entirely. And she felt whatever rip she had imagined, tearing apart her heart, was drawing closed again, becoming whole.

"I have the best daughter in the whole world. Right here in my arms. You do know that, right?"

♦ ♦ ♦

Once the home had settled and everyone had gone to bed, Fritzi curled up with Sabine because he was still young and her time away had seemed an eternity to him. Iris went to bed and the apartment was quiet and so Gareth crept out of the apartment, shutting and locking the door quietly behind him.

Outside there was a light swirl of snow in the air, but because it wasn't terribly cold, the flakes landed on his cheeks and nose but were melted by the time they touched the ground. It was one thing he never got used to in Germany. Canada offered more white Christmases than not, sometimes with drifts as high as the doors. Gareth remembered the joy of snow days and freedom from school, of sledding so fast down hills that were probably too dangerous to play on that it was impossible to catch his breath, and of course endless afternoons of skating. Yes, there were decorations in the city, bright lights and tasteful baubles, and wonderful types of pastries on display in bakery windows, but the early years had reinforced the belief that Christmas required extreme cold and snow.

It was Christmas season, and what effort had he made for Fritz and Iris? No tree had been put up in the apartment. No decorations to speak of, and no presents bought. Thankfully, Jack had done the stockings on December 6 (yet another Christmas adjustment Gareth had to make once there were children in the picture) for the start of the season, the feast of St. Nicholas.

He slid his key into the lock, switched on the lights in his oculary, and entered his safe place. Hanging on a hook was the mobile, the shiny colourful planets of possibilities glowing with a mocking tease as it lazily turned from the breeze that had followed Gareth inside. Gareth reached up and lifted the mobile from its hook.

A decision had to be made. The oxygen could be ramped up, and Frieda would surely go blind and never see the mobile. They could take a risk and lower the oxygen, but then Frieda would suffer some organ and brain damage and likely never understand the mobile. Or they could lower the oxygen, save her sight, but then Frieda would likely die and never need the mobile.

Gareth put the mobile onto the floor. It seemed to look up at its creator with curiosity and skepticism. How beautiful and vulnerable the little glass ornaments were! How much light reflected off of them! That light was a gift in itself that seemed to move and dance around the room, on the ceiling and the walls. There was magic in this mobile. Magic that would never be seen, or understood, by the one it was intended for.

"I'm sorry. I'm so, so sorry," Gareth whispered.

Then, calmly and with intent, he smashed them one by one, taking the heel of his boot to every glass orb. A crack, a smash, and a shatter breaking through the silence of the night, until the mobile no longer existed. Until there was only broken glass underfoot.

♦ ♦ ♦

Iris had only pretended to be asleep. The first day of Christmas vacation had started horrifically, and any joy that the holidays could have brought was erased. She wondered if she could ever enjoy Christmas again.

"Of course, you will."

Iris squeezed her eyes closed, then reopened them, thinking that she must be dreaming, that the voice was just something she had imagined. Yes, she must have fallen asleep after all.

"Why are you here? I only see you in Hilda's garden."

"I'm visiting. You know this used to be my apartment, so it is easy for me to come here too."

"Really?"

"Really. I brought your dad here when he was very young and I trained him to be an ocularist. Then I gave him my business so I could stay with Hilda on the farm."

"Oh. I didn't know that."

Siegfried sat on the edge of her bed. Iris knew he wasn't real but she liked him all the same.

"Isn't Hilda sad without you there? At the farm."

"The old girl is fine. I may be here, but I am also in her heart."

Iris started to cry. Maybe she could tell him about the rose essence and how Sabine's baby would likely die and it was all her fault. Maybe he would still like her. But likely he already knew how terrible she was.

"Will Baby Frieda die?"

"I don't know. She is fighting for her life right now. She has slipped into my world and back to yours three times already tonight. But if she can get through tonight she might make it."

"What do you mean you don't know? You know things. You're on the other side!" Iris whispered fiercely. What was the point in having spirits visit if not to get information?

"Not everything is destined. Frieda has a strong spirit. If she lives she will need that strong spirit."

"If she lives will she be blind?" Iris persisted with the questions.

"If she lives she will likely have problems with her vision. She will see a little but will be clinically blind. But her brain is fine. Really fine."

"Clinically blind? What's that?"

"Ah, Iris. You ask too many questions. Okay, I'll tell you a secret. She will have some sight but it will worsen as she ages. At some point she will be blind, but she will have experienced the world with enough sight in the first ten years that she will function fine. Then one day your brother Fritz will create an artificial eye that can actually see. And if she does not live, then the invention your brother is destined to create will take another twenty years to make. So, if she lives it will not only be good for her, but good for the whole world."

"So is that why you are here? So I can tell them what to decide?"

"I am here to visit you because I am worried about you."

Iris put her feather pillow onto her lap, hugged it tightly.

"So you want me to tell Sabine and my Dad to make the right choice."

"Life is a blessing. Even if you do not see life fully, you still feel life fully."

Siegfried put a hand onto her heart. Iris felt his breath, or perhaps just a breeze, across the top of her head. She closed her eyes, relaxed, and let sleep take her.

FOURTEEN

BÖZSI NO LONGER OWNED A fur coat. At one time she had had a long chinchilla coat, soft fur falling off her shoulder in a creamy tan colour. It had been a gift from a male admirer, but she couldn't remember which one. Not that it mattered; the coat no longer existed. She had worn it until the lining needed replacing and the edges of the cuffs were worn down. When the shedding fur started to leave an incriminating trail every place she went, she knew it was time to part company. At that time, she took a fistful of her saved cash from inside her piano and went to the fur district, between 30th and 27th Streets and 6th and 8th Avenues in New York. She tried on red fox, coyote, mink, and sheared beaver (which was far too expensive!).

She went from shop to shop, forty-four in total, trying them on and turning as she assessed herself in the three-way mirrors. In the end, she returned home, taking the subway, empty-handed. It wasn't that some of the furs didn't suit her small frame. It wasn't that the styles were not to her taste. It was simply that no matter how many furs she tried on, she could not duplicate the feeling she had when she slipped her arms into that first fur coat.

A simple camel-coloured wool coat, knee-length, double-breasted with brass buttons and a tasteful lamb fur collar would have to do. Who was she trying to impress, after all? It was her lover's widow she was seeing, and she was no longer in competition with her. Simone — yes, that was her name, Simone. Bözsi didn't even know what she looked like; Bözsi had never seen a picture of her in her younger days. When she'd asked Henri about his wife, he refused to speak of her, wanting the two to be quite separate. He told her that it was safer that way, but now she suspected that, for him, as long as there was no talk of his wife while he was in her arms, he could pretend that his wife did not exist and imagine a world with Bözsi and him alone. The opposite was also possibly true. In the presence of his wife, Bözsi probably did not exist either.

"You look very nice. Are you sure you don't want me to go?" Esther asked her older sister.

"No, you stay here. You do not approve, and I could not bear to look at your sourpuss face."

"I was just trying to be supportive."

Bözsi sat down on the bed, undid her coat, and reached for a cigarette although it was, once again, a non-smoking hotel.

"*Kiscica*," she started, using her younger sister's pet name, "you were a child still, a favoured child, when the family turned against me and judged me. I was barely sixteen when I ran away. Later you ran away, too, but you ran away with their blessings, and it saved your life. I did not have their blessings, but running away also saved my life. I promised myself, from the day they all stopped calling me their daughter, that I would never let better judgment get in the way of anything I wanted to do. And I want to do this. Now, I am going to do my lipstick in the mirror before I go. I want to get it just right."

When Bözsi returned from the bathroom, Esther had her rather plain-looking but practical coat on, buttoned right to the top, and was just starting to zip up her boots.

"Where are you going? Out for a stroll?"

"No. I am going with you. You do not need to run away this time, just because you think I am judging you. I will support you in this crazy expedition."

"And you aren't judging me? Really?"

"Well, only a little," Esther laughed. "Come on, let's go and get this over with. The Punk Baroness has plans for this evening."

Bözsi clapped her hands in her excitement. "And with both of us going, I can justify paying for a taxi!"

♦ ♦ ♦

Jack stared at the equation on the computer screen. It was his third trip to the cybercafe, and he still had no answers. If the envelope didn't lead him to where it had originated, then the trip was useless. "*Pardon, êtes-vous un étudiant en économie?*" A man's voice asked.

"*Non. Pas du tout,*" Jack answered.

"Oh, American? I hear it in your accent."

"*Pas du tout, Canadien.*"

The man smiled. He had that carefree, dishevelled look that was only perfected through hours of preparation. His clothes all matched, one hue echoing another. But then a top button was undone, a tie loosened, and jacket sleeves were rolled up. He appeared not to be a man with a lot of extra time on his hands for hanging out in internet cafés. His clothes said that he was clearly a man with a job. His hair, too, seemed to have been perfectly done, styled into place, and then fingers must have ruffled it so that the curls were loose and free of product and placement. He was a man who knew the rules, adhered to them, and then ruffled it all up a bit for fun.

"So then, this is an economics equation?" Jack asked him.

"You don't know? You have been coming here and staring at the same equation for three days. Only an economics student would care about the Fisher equation."

"I am far too old to be a student." Jack smiled.

"And far too confused by the equation to be a professor!" The man laughed, with amusement, not malice.

Jack looked at the screen. The numbers and symbols were unmoving, remaining just as they were when he typed them in.

"The Fisher equation links the nominal interest rate, which is the i in the equation, with the real interest rate, which is r, and the rate of inflation, which is pi. If you like, I can share a little secret with you, but perhaps over dinner?" the man suggested.

"Why?" Jack asked awkwardly. "Why do you want to have dinner with me?"

"Because you are clearly not an economist. They bore me. And yet you have a mysterious interest, of some sort, in economics, and so perhaps you will not find me too boring."

Jack smiled. He had noticed the man on his previous visits to the café. He always sat, cross-legged, at a table near the back, away from the front windows. Why he went to the cybercafe Jack couldn't begin to guess. Unlike the others, he was not on the computers at all. Instead, he sat with his briefcase open, papers falling out over the table, and seemed to be reading through them, marking them with a red pen.

"Are you a professor, then?"

"I am. And I teach economics, and that is why I became curious about you. I couldn't help but wonder why you are obsessed with the Fisher equation."

"What is it exactly?"

"Ah, well, economists believe that the real interest rate is the thing that matters. It is an illusion because money really has no influence over anything long-term. Now, let's say you increase this variable by two or three percent," he explained, pointing to Jack's screen. "Then you will find that not only does that variable increase by two percent, but so does this." He pointed to the letter *r* in the equation.

"Which you said was the interest, or the rate?"

"The *real* interest. And this also changes. The pi. Which is what it is all about. The real rate of inflation and not the presumed rate. And this is the Fisher effect!" The man clapped his hands, as though proud of his explanation.

"Fascinating."

"You're lying. You do not find it fascinating at all. So, dinner tonight? When I am finished at the university?"

"Yes, please. I'm Jack, by the way."

"I'm Younis." He reached out in a very old-fashioned and formal way to shake Jack's hand. "That is Younis, not Eunice. With a *Y*, not with an *E*. It sounds the same, but different. Just like those variables."

◆ ◆ ◆

Bözsi faltered. Perhaps she should just ask for the taxi to wait. Perhaps Henri's wife would close the door in her face. Perhaps she no longer lived there. Bözsi felt in her pocket for the piece of paper with the address. How many years had she held on to it, never really believing that she would ever make it to the address? She kept it, carrying it with her, tucked in her wallet all those years as a hope. It was both a talisman and a time machine for her. And now here it was, put to use. She opened the folds of the yellowed paper. How old and wrinkled it was. *Like me*, she thought.

"Go to the door. Take a deep breath. I will pay for the taxi," Esther told her sister, aware that Bözsi was suddenly unsure, hesitant. Esther was used to her sister's bravado and confidence. Even as a child, it seemed like nothing could shake her. Perhaps that was just the vantage point of a younger sister.

"What if she doesn't invite us in?"

"It will be fine," Esther soothed, snapping her change purse closed.

Beyond the wrought-iron gates stood a classic late-Victorian house with a modest garden and two statuary lions on either side of a fine, solid wooden door. The exterior had been parged in white and the trim painted a greyish-blue, giving the house a villa-like appearance. Esther thought that at some point that may have been a trend, as they had seen other homes like it as they drove through the sixteenth arrondissement.

"The house is a bit intimidating. So big. Do you think she lived here all these years by herself? Or maybe she remarried! Maybe she doesn't live here anymore." Bözsi played for time. "Maybe we should just go. Leave sleeping dogs sleeping, as you say."

"The taxi is gone, Bözsi. Come on, let's do this. It is the real reason you came to Paris."

Because Bözsi was losing confidence by the second, Esther stepped up and banged on the door, only noticing the doorbell *after* she had banged. Esther was aware of noises inside the house. Just as she was about to press her gloved finger to the doorbell, the door suddenly swung open and a finely chiselled middle-aged man opened the door. His eyes were playful and dark, his hair waved off his head from a certain widow's peak, but his nose, although not terribly large, was sharp, slim, and very straight. Did he live here? Had he bought the house years ago?

"Come in, come in!" he exclaimed. "It is a bit noisy in there. Lots of people, you are hardly the first to arrive! The invitation did say to just come in, though."

"The invitation?" Esther asked.

"Ah, yes, we forgot it, at the hotel. I hope that is okay?" Bözsi attempted to cover.

"Don't be silly. You don't need the invitation to come in!" He opened the door wider and motioned for them to come inside. "You said a hotel. Are you staying in Paris? Where did you come from?"

"America!" Esther told him.

"Great! I will announce you and introduce you to everyone. I'm Sebastian, by the way. The middle son. And you are?"

"Introduce us as Lulu and …"

"Katja!" Esther piped in. If Bözsi could have a code name, then so could she!

"Lulu and Katja. Very good. And you came all the way from America for my parents' sixtieth anniversary! They really do have remarkable friends."

Esther quickly did the math. Sixty years ago would put the date at December 12, 1942. Either they had the wrong house or …

"May I introduce Lulu and Katja!"

The names sounded cheap and tawdry when said aloud to a room full of tastefully well-dressed party attendees — family and friends, none of whom the Hungarian sisters knew. There seemed to be generations — children, grandchildren, and in-laws. Entire families filling the room. Drinks were poured and served in one corner of the room. A buffet laid out just beyond in an adjoining room. The sound of plates and crystal glasses filled the air. Esther squirmed in her plain coat and started to undo the buttons.

Nineteen forty-two! Esther thought again. The wedding would have taken place during the war, near the start of it. If this really was the house that belonged to Henri's wife, and if this really was an anniversary party that they had crashed, that meant that Henri … no, impossible!

A very patrician older man stood from his chair. His face betrayed little, but his stance was a bit shaky. Esther looked at her sister and heard Bözsi inhale sharply. She witnessed her slight adjustment, the straightening of her shoulders, the lengthening of her back. She seemed absolutely calm. Poised. Suddenly her wool coat with its fur collar looked terribly elegant as she stepped into the middle of the living room.

"Congratulations on your anniversary! My sister and I are here on business, but your sons managed to track us down so that we could celebrate you on this most auspicious day."

She put out both hands, first going to Henri, then to his wife, taking their hands in hers in a gesture of congratulations. His wife, Simone, accepted the gesture as though Bözsi were somebody she should know but couldn't quite place.

"Please, take off your coats. Sebastian will get you some champagne. There's so much food in the next room!" the patrician man said.

A man who seemed a bit older and a bit shorter than Sebastian took Esther's coat. Esther had adopted the habit of wearing a simple black dress and a double strand of pearls whenever she went out. She believed that simplicity was the key to blending without notice. She wondered why Bözsi had not learned to adopt a more understated style. After all, wouldn't a spy not want any unneeded attention? Once the coat was in the man's hands, Esther touched her neckline. One strand. Two. Blanca. Clara. She had secretly named the strands of pearls after the twins. She tucked the shorter strand into the neckline of her dress. Hidden for now.

"I am Christian," he said to her, softly. "Now, how is it you know my parents?"

"Oh, it's my sister who knows them. I am just with her."

"I see. And how does *she* know my father?" he persisted.

Esther hesitated. She understood the switch from his use of the word *parents* to specifically *father*. How is it that they hadn't rehearsed every possible question? How is it that Bözsi had left her unprepared?

"Well," Esther started, lowering her voice and looking at the younger man with as much intensity as she could muster, "she was an operative in the French Resistance with him."

"Ah. Of course. I see. I'll just hang this up, then."

Esther stood, quite alone, watching. Her sister was chatting to people she did not know, making a great show of it. Yes, this was why she was better on the stage. She may be one to have pre-show jitters, but once she was on, once the spotlight was on her, she was in her element. Still, Esther surmised, she must be feeling something quite different to the image she was projecting. Henri, alive and well? How was that possible? And how would this change the fifty-seven-year-old narrative that had formed Bözsi's beliefs and shaped her idea of love?

Bözsi slipped out of her coat. Her deep-blue dress, silk with embroidery, looked exotic compared to the understated ones in the room. She smoothed the fabric, doing a once-over with her hands along her body. A gesture, once again, that seemed to be dragged up from the vaults of her subconscious. The dress, though an eye-catching colour, was not suggestive in the least. The gesture, however, was. Esther could only assume that Bözsi was unaware of the gesture; that it was a gesture performed many times when she was in Algeria. One that had been forgotten with marriage and only just reawakened. Esther glanced at Simone, the long-time wife. In a split second it was evident that Simone had also caught the gesture and was well aware of whom Lulu really was. Her lips, which were not ample or full to begin with, tightened slightly. Her eyes narrowed. And then, as quickly as the pursed look of realization crossed her face, it softened once again. Simone turned to a younger woman sitting next to her and smiled as though continuing a conversation. Not a ruffle, not a hair out of place on her perfectly coiffed head. Henri's wife, whom Esther assumed must be close to eighty, was the picture of composure. How was that possible?

Esther had spent her life playing it as safe as possible and had resented Bözsi for her stories and her adventures. As she watched the understated drama play out before her, she understood that she would never have had what it takes to live a life that vibrated that intensely. She could never have wrapped her being in such subterfuge. She was simply a woman with some musical talent who liked to cook and read the newspaper in the morning. A woman who knew the rules and liked good manners. She was never an enigma and, as much as this adventure had awoken her, she knew that she could not function daily with so much guile. If she closed her eyes and imagined them all in elaborate white wigs, she could be witnessing a French restoration play where the villains eventually get their comeuppance after everyone has been ridiculed, and not a sixtieth wedding anniversary. Sixty years! And with a closer look at the couple, it was clear that they would have been no more than twenty when they had wed. Mere children.

"Try the caviar before we go. It is excellent. Henri always understood the value of a good meal!" Bözsi said to Esther, her face close to her sister's as though co-conspirators.

"Are you okay?"

"Yes. I said try the caviar. Now."

Esther went to pick up a canapé from Bözsi's plate. Caviar, chopped egg, pâté de foie gras, and … a small ring. Esther lifted the ring and put it onto her pinky finger.

"Mother's ring?" Esther hadn't seen the ring since she was a child. Somewhere in her memory there was a scene, her mother yelling that *brigands* — thieves — had stolen it. But the thief had been Bözsi all along.

"I gave it to him. I said that if he ever needed me, to send me the ring and I would find him. So, he fixed me a plate of food and now here it is. Now we must leave. His son, Christian, has informed me that he has called us a taxi. But don't let all that good caviar go to waste."

It was only inside the taxi that the act disappeared and Bözsi became her older sister once again. Bözsi reached into her bag for a tissue to wipe the never-ending stream of tears cascading down her powdered face, leaving tracks in the makeup.

"Will you see him again, do you think?"

Bözsi shrugged. "Every time he left me, I imagined it was the last time I'd see him. I never really knew when or if he would ever be back. Then, one day, I was told that it really was the last time. And now, today he has resurrected. So, of course, I wonder if it will be last time all over again."

What could Esther say? Certainly not that she understood. She had had a good marriage. A solid marriage. And she missed having the contentment that marriage had brought her. But that irregularity of great passion she could not fathom.

"I think his wife knows."

Bözsi sighed. She turned away from Esther and stared out the window. Christmas lights everywhere and not a flake of snow.

"I did press the hotel card into his hand when I first greeted him. Did you catch that, *Katja*?"

"Somehow, I am not surprised, *Lulu*," Esther chuckled.

"I think we should go out for a steak tonight. Then, tomorrow, we are going to continue to search for Clara. I haven't forgotten the real reason we are here." Bözsi reached over and squeezed her sister's gloved hand. "Thank you. I owe you."

And Esther held her sister's hand for the rest of the taxi ride.

◆ ◆ ◆

After checking with the post offices and confirming that the envelope had indeed been mailed from the La Poste du Louvre, Blanca and Martina were no more ahead than they were the previous day. That particular post office was a central sorting and shipping centre where, amongst other things, parcels could be weighed and stamps and postage could be purchased from an automated machine without needing the help of a person.

"Look, we can also exchange money here," Martina told Blanca.

Blanca was discouraged. She had hoped that there might be some record of the transaction, a receipt for postage bought, a registered account of the envelope shipped on that date, anything!

"Didn't you have to sign for it when it was delivered to you?" Blanca asked Martina.

"No. It was just there with the other envelopes."

Blanca was giving up hope. They had been in Paris for eight days and had accomplished nothing in their search for Clara. The closest anyone had gotten was Jack with his economics equation.

"Now what?"

"Now we go to a bar where we drink some absinthe and eat some cold hard-boiled eggs, and we think."

Martina was well aware of the mythology of absinthe, that it caused hallucinations, madness, and creativity. She knew of the many artists who had turned to it in order to open portals to other worlds of inspiration. The drink, fondly called La Fée Absinthe Parisienne, or sometimes the Green Fairy, had been banned for almost a century and was still off-limits in America, but Europe had allowed it once again. When they had begun bottling and selling it two years earlier, there was much discussion about whether the drink was only an alcoholic beverage or whether it was a drug. Either way, Martina and Blanca would experience it properly in Paris, in a small bistro-style bar.

With their winter coats off, they hunkered down at a table near the back. It was quiet, still too early for the nighttime crowd. Martina demonstrated how to place a sugar cube on a slotted spoon over their shots of absinthe, then carefully pour ice water from their small carafes over the sugar. Blanca watched, as though under a spell, as the sugar dissolved and the absinthe changed from a light, translucent green to a milky white.

"Cheers!"

It was harsh with alcohol, even when diluted. Blanca picked up the flavours of fennel and anise, giving the drink a licorice flavour. If she could have melted down shoestring licorice from her childhood and mixed it with high-octane gasoline, this is what it would have tasted like. And she loved it. She sipped again. By the third gulp there was no sorrow, only the sensation of touch. She rubbed her fingers over the scars of her arm and imagined that she felt them receding, then vanishing completely.

Martina drank more slowly. She opened the music, ran her finger over each and every bar, listening to the notes she was reading, the sounds inside her head. Bass line. Bass line. She ignored the primary voices of the treble clef and concentrated on the bass clef. There seemed, below everything, as though a prescient voice, a low hum. A hum that was a drone supporting the rhythms and the lyrical higher notes. Martina knew that the drone of the bass is constant, never-ending. It is the foundation, the chorus voice, the driving force. Why had she ignored that in favour of the traditional voices above it?

Martina spiralled back in memory to the concert for Mandela. She saw Blanca and Clara leaving the stage, followed by the other members of the Punkarie. There was yelling and stamping of feet, demanding an encore. This time, it was only Blanca and Clara. *Bleach*, as they called themselves. And they sang *Lakmé*. While they sang, a choir entered. They were Zulu. They clapped while the picket fence, a wife and children, instead of me. Not even a card once a year. I suppose I was a passing fad. An eight-year-long passing fad!" He laughed. "So, I guess the question is, what are a Canadian boy and an Algerian man doing in a cozy restaurant in Paris?"

"Algerian?"

"Yes, I'm Algerian," Younis stated, his words coloured with defensiveness. "Do you have a problem with that?"

Jack shrugged. "No. Not at all. Why should I?"

"Some people, here in Paris, don't like Algerians. We are not always welcome. I was a controversy in Algeria and I am one here as well." Younis sighed, his defensiveness evaporating.

"Come on. Teaching economics is hardly controversial!" Jack teased.

"Oh, you have no idea!" Younis quipped back at him. "So, I am tenured. That is why I am here. Why are you here, staring at the Fisher equation in an internet café when there are far more interesting things to do in Paris?"

"It's a long story," Jack dismissed him.

"It is the weekend. I have nowhere to go until Monday." Younis signalled for the bill. "I'll make you a deal. You tell me your story and, if it's good, I might just disclose to you my very own theory of quantum easing."

♦ ♦ ♦

The bubbles had a lavender scent to them. Bözsi liked her tub filled to the brim, lots of bubbles, and for the water to be as hot as she could stand it. Soaking was one of life's great pleasures, and she tended to stay in the water until it had gone from boiling to lukewarm, until her fingertips and toes were as wrinkled as raisins. Not that she liked the wrinkles, but at least the ones on her toes and fingers were the result of a luxurious soak.

twins sang, and then, there it was, that low male voice that droned below that famous aria, joining in, turning *Lakmé* into something entirely different.

Martina shook Blanca's arm, nudging her.

"It's very nice, this drink. Very relaxing," Blanca confided. "We may need another."

"Zulu. Troy is KwaZulu-Natal," she told her lover.

♦ ♦ ♦

Jack had forgotten the cardinal rule. Do not talk about past lovers during a first date. Somehow the idea of dinner with a man brought him thoughts of Tristan, and although Tristan and Jack had never been in Paris together, every meal, every tourist site, every shop front, made him think of Tristan. It was a city he should have shared with Tristan. Why hadn't they travelled together more? Why had he gone off on his own so often?

"And what happened to your relationship? Why did it end? You still sound very much in love."

Jack took a breath. He realized that for all the talk of Tristan, he still had not mentioned to Younis that Tristan had passed away. Over two decades of deaths because of AIDS and it was still a no-go zone in conversations. The stigma surrounding it was asphyxiating.

"He died. About six months ago."

"I see. I'm sorry."

Younis didn't ask him how he died, or what the cause of his death was, and for that Jack was thankful.

"How about you? No love in your life?" Jack questioned, taking the focus off himself.

"Not anymore. I had a long relationship some time ago. He was very traditional, and so, in the end, it didn't work out. He chose a

He was alive! That was the only thought that circled her mind. Not, How was it possible? Not, Why hadn't he tried to find her? Not even, What were all those years apart for? Only that he lived. And how well he looked! At seventy-nine he still had posture and bearing. Sure, his hair was thin and had lost its dark chestnut colour, but the white hair suited him. Dignified, that was how he looked. And still so slim!

Bözsi reached for the soap. She carefully peeled the paper wrapping away from the new bar. It, too, was lavender. Bözsi loved that they matched their hotel products. She found that mixing the fragrances for her ablutions was confusing for the nose. Shampoo, body wash, and soap should all be the same so as not to compete. She created a good lather and washed under her armpits, then lathered up her pubic area. The hair was a bit coarser than when she was young. And certainly greyer. Back then, during the war years, it was all natural; there was no grooming then, just a burst of curly pubic hair that started at the Mound of Venus and wrapped around the outer labia. Later in life, as bikinis became common beachwear, getting skimpier and skimpier, razors were needed for the bikini line, removing more and more hair until every woman looked like a freshly plucked chicken. In the late sixties, Bözsi was single again, and at forty years old, found it was expected that a woman be trimmed and manicured down to what they called a racing strip. Or was it a landing strip? Bözsi no longer had any idea what was expected of her concerning the styling of her nether regions.

As she washed and soaked, she took stock of her aging body. What a betrayal it was! Her feet, once petite, with high sculpted arches, now looked tired with their unsightly bunions. Bözsi pointed her toes. She used to have the best point in the vaudeville company. Such an elegant arch that seemed to add a few inches to her leg length! Her legs were still good — slim with a bit of shape and just the slightest crepiness around the knees. She was too small for cellulite, but the muscles had relaxed over the years, giving her a softness. Back in the day, when there was scarcely enough food, she was all sharp bones and angles. And her breasts were small then. Henri used to tell her that the perfect breast could fit into a champagne glass. Not champagne flutes, but the shallow, round ones called *coupes*. Now her breasts seemed heavy, too heavy for her body. And certainly too heavy for a champagne glass. Perhaps Marie Antoinette lost her head in time, before her breasts ceased to fit in the coupes designed to fit her breasts.

"How long are you going to be in there?" Esther called from their room.

"Not much longer!"

"I thought you might have fallen down the drain! There is an envelope here. It was just delivered."

"For me?"

"Yes. Unless there is another Bözsi staying here."

Bözsi stood. The hot water made her a bit dizzy as she got up, the blood rushing to her head. She banged each foot on the side of the tub to knock the suds off, then reached for a white fluffy towel to wrap around her body. The second towel she did up around her head, turban-style. She wiped her hand down the mirror so that she could see herself through the steam's mist. There was colour in her cheeks. A flash of mischief back in her eyes. *Not bad for almost seventy-five*, she thought. *Could be worse.*

"What's in the envelope?" she wondered aloud.

She tore through the paper and shook out the contents. A simple silver key and a note.

"What is in the note?" Esther asked.

"An address. Only an address."

❖ ❖ ❖

The stairs outside the building were stone, circling up to a second-floor entranceway. Beneath the entranceway were main floor apartments, their doorways facing the street. The silver key was for an apartment on the third floor.

"It's a good thing our hips are still pretty good!" Bözsi said as she looked with trepidation at the stairway before her.

"It's not the hips for me, it's the knees. One of my knees locks sometimes," Esther answered her sister.

"You don't have to come up if it is too much for you."

"Oh no, I've come this far with you on the adventure, I'm not backing out now!"

"But what if he is up there? Naked?"

"So be it!"

Esther gripped the banister and started the climb. She imagined that at some time in the past, great exits were made down these stairs. Women with trailing skirts, men making a hasty exit, or perhaps a speech at the top of the stairs with hordes of adoring people listening.

"Almost there!"

Once inside the building, Esther and Bözsi were greeted with more stairs. Although not as intimidating, the stairs were still impressive, with curly wrought-iron banisters on either side. The wood was all dark with a rich reddish patina, the wallpaper looked handmade, with real gold leaf in the design, although Esther noticed that some parts were now faded and peeling. Everything pointed to an age of wealth that no longer existed in its opulence.

Bözsi found the apartment and slipped the key into the lock. Esther noticed that her hand shook a bit. After a quiet click, they pushed open the oak double doors and walked inside.

"Hello?" Esther called out.

Nothing.

The apartment had high ceilings, with large windows looking over the street. From where Esther stood, she could just glimpse the Musée d'Orsay and the Seine. Esther was a bit surprised at how feminine the decor was. Chintz wallpaper, sofa, and drapes. All matching in muted sage green and light blues.

"Do you think his wife decorated it?" Esther asked.

"He probably bought it fully furnished. I doubt his wife even knows about the apartment."

"Why would he have it, then?"

Bözsi looked at her sister and wondered how she could have lived such a sheltered life.

"Why would a handsome man have a secret apartment in Paris? Is that what you are asking?" Bözsi laughed.

"Oh. I see. And that doesn't bother you?"

"Please, I wasn't here for him. He would have to fill that void with someone. Likely many women were needed for him to get over the pain of losing me. Yes. It would take a lot of women to replace me. Poor Henri."

Once they entered the kitchen it was clear that Henri had high hopes. There was champagne on ice in a silver bucket and a large platter of fruit, cheese, and biscuits. Bözsi noticed a small envelope and opened it.

"My Love, I hope that you did come, even after all these years. If you are peckish, do nibble before I arrive. I will be back at eight."

Bözsi looked at her watch. It was 7:35. Henri would be there in less than half an hour.

"Oh God, Esther, he is coming. Soon. You have to go now!"

"Go now?"

"Yes!"

Esther imagined making her way back down the two staircases only to have a long evening stretch out before her. Alone.

◆ ◆ ◆

Jack awoke to the bitter smell of coffee and the sweet, yeasty aroma of freshly baked bread. He closed his eyes, trying to make sense of the previous night. It was only to be a drink, a nightcap! But who was fooling whom? Whenever anyone, be it man or woman, straight or gay, is invited into someone's home for one last drink, there is always the possibility of sex. Jack was far too experienced, and far too old, to pretend that he had no inkling that a night of meaningless sex was on offer. The question was not the sex, but rather why he chose to sleep there overnight.

Yes, it was nice to not sleep on a cot, like a child, at the end of Blanca and Martina's hotel bed. It was nice to stay warm and not have the rude slap of winter wind awaken him after being so cozy in a bed. And it was nice to experience Younis's exceptional Egyptian cotton sheets. But what was particularly nice was the warmth of another body, arms that wrapped around him and whispered stories throughout the night. Now, in the harsh light of morning, Jack wondered if it could have been anyone's arms around him, anyone's ears listening to him, and anyone's voice lulling him to sleep as they talked and talked, sharing stories. If intimacy was all that was required, all that he really needed, no matter where it came from.

God, he missed Tristan.

Jack reached for his boxers and slid them on. There was no point in remaining naked, no point in suggesting a second round. It had been great sex. And it was mutually appreciated. But still, it was a temporary Band-Aid, covering his unhealed wound.

"Well, well, Sleeping Beauty! I have breakfast ready. Some brioche that I rewarmed, and coffee. There's marmalade, too. I hope you like orange."

In the light of day, Younis seemed even more attractive. In a casual T-shirt, loose at his neck, and a pair of blue-and-white polka-dotted boxers, there was something comically adorable about him. His tousle of dark curls, almost as dark as his eyes, his square shoulders, his lean and long legs ... Jack could feel himself becoming aroused all over again, against his better judgment.

"I should get going. Blanca and the Punk Baroness likely have plans, and I don't want them to worry."

"I already left a message at the hotel for them."

"Oh."

Younis put the tray of food on the bed between them. He spread some marmalade onto a piece of brioche and handed it to Jack.

"It's not a relationship, relax. It's a weekend only. A holiday from all your worries. And judging from everything you said last night, you have a lot to worry about. So, maybe I can help."

"I don't know how you can help."

"Let's start with this crazy quest you and ... what was it again? Two insane Jewish Hungarian seniors, a Punk Baroness, and an albino opera singer are all on. Did I get that right, or did I leave anyone out? Ah, yes, and the one-eyed Jack."

"Nope. I think you got us all."

"All that is missing is a gay-Muslim-Algerian-doctor-of-economics, I guess. A mathematician who understands probabilities."

"It is *improbable* that we will find her. It is *probable* that she is dead."

"Not entirely improbable. Also not entirely probable. There is that mysterious envelope with the questionable Fisher equation, after all."

"Correct." Jack was aware of just how intently Younis had been listening the night before.

"On Monday morning we can go to the university and see who, in my department, is studying that theory. There are maybe a dozen students, I would think. It is very specific. Then we can start eliminating, and who knows? Maybe we can track down who mailed the envelope. If it isn't from my university, I know all the economics professors in Paris. We like to get together to cure each other of insomnia!" He laughed.

Jack poured himself a coffee, leaned back onto the pillows, and sighed. He knew that his late stepfather, Siegfried, would have called this "fate." Siegfried would have told him not to fight his destiny. How could randomly meeting an economics professor be anything but divine intervention? *But*, Jack thought, *I only had to meet him, I didn't have to fuck him.*

"And about last night ..." Younis started.

Jack was never comfortable with those morning-after talks. He had been with Tristan so long that, for the most part, they were not necessary with any one-night fling. He could always say that he was attached, in a serious relationship. They both understood the rules; affairs were only allowed when they were in different countries for extended periods of time. Being in a committed relationship had made the occasional one-night stand so easy to deal with, so casual. But now, single and unattached, except perhaps in his heart, it all became a bit more complicated.

"Last night was lovely. Thank you. But I do not have any hopes or expectations. Your heart is not free. I have already had that in my life. I loved a man who was in a relationship. Married to a woman. I thought I provided something different, so there was no competition with her. But eventually he chose to do the *right* thing. Or so he said."

"The right thing?"

"It is expected that you grow up, marry, and have children. Anything else is frowned upon. And being gay could mean a fine and two years in prison."

"Is this the eight-year fad you spoke of?"

Younis sighed and nodded. "Eight years is a long time. And, of course, it was very forbidden. I loved and I had my heart broken in secret and in silence. Thus, I moved to France. I got my Ph.D. in economics. I dealt with being gay, which is not a problem here. I dealt with being Algerian, which is a problem here. And I accepted everything, even my broken heart. But that took a long time. All I am saying is, take your time. I have no expectations. I made a new friend. I had great sex. It's all good, as they say."

Jack pushed aside the tray sitting between them. Pulled his new friend close and kissed his cheek.

"Thank you."

"And now, all I can hope is that I can join your group of sleuths. My life can be a bit boring at times."

Jack smiled at him. "I must warn you, they are all overwhelming. And it isn't all fun. We loved Clara in our own ways. But for Esther and Blanca, well, there is a desperation to find her. More so for Blanca, perhaps. Twins share a bond few can understand."

"Then all the more reason to break into the university records. The only thing is that many students leave town during Christmas vacation. We may not be able to follow any leads until after Christmas. You might have to stay until after the holidays."

How could Jack stay an extra ten days? His mother expected him home for Christmas. She needed his help since his father had arrived unexpectedly. Then he wanted to get back to Hamburg to check in on Gareth and Sabine. They must be overwhelmed with the baby, and besides, Iris would want to see him over Christmas, too. There were so many places to get to between then and New Year's. Jack realized that it had been that way for him for years. Here and there, travelling the world and never settling anywhere for long. He had always thought that it was because he was chasing one story after another but now, for the first time, he was only too aware that he wasn't chasing anything. He was running away from himself.

FIFTEEN

FLASHES OF MEMORY MADE NO sense to the narrative John had come to believe. The antique rectory table was triggering for him. So many times, he would look at it and a darkness would cross his face. It wasn't the table he remembered, the table that belonged there.

"Where is the pine table with the benches?" he'd ask every time he walked into the dining room.

"I told you, John. I needed a bigger table, so I got this one. It's good for when everyone comes at Christmas and other holidays."

"Oh yes. A big table is good."

"Yes, it is."

"But where is the pine table with the benches?"

The question of the table became a carousel ride. The logic, the questions, and the answers may have had an up-and-down movement, but the conversation just went round and round, covering the same territory and never breaking free.

When they had first started to date seriously, John had taken Hilda to his parents' home near Cobourg for a weekend, just so they could get to know each other. That was the weekend he surprised her with a half-hour drive north to Roseneath, a small farm community, with what seemed to be nothing more than a weekend flea market. Beside the renovated barn building that housed the flea market was a round, dome-shaped structure. When they walked inside, past the canvas wrappings, there was magic. In the middle of nowhere was one of the two oldest carousels in North America, the other one being in New York. Each horse was hand-painted, and each seemed to have a different personality. A few dollars later and they were climbing up, Hilda trying to be ladylike in her skirt and failing spectacularly, and John with a foot in a stirrup, up and over into the saddle in no time. These were not horses like the regular merry-go-round horses, the ones that tour with carnivals town to town. These were not so sad as those tired, overused plastic ponies. No, these were majestic beasts, fiercely carved of wood, with noses that seemed to snort and muscles that seemed to strain. And they were high up and only got higher and higher when the carousel started, whipping about in that circular route, faster and faster. And there was Hilda, squealing with fear and delight. And John laughing.

Now, in their retirement age, they were back on the carousel, except the years had worn away the magic, and time had silenced the laughter.

"Where's the table?" he started again.

If I give a different answer, if I do not say what is expected, then maybe we can get off the carousel, Hilda thought.

"The table?" she asked.

"The pine one. With the benches."

"Oh. It is out being repaired. One of the legs broke, but it'll be back soon. We can use this one for now." For a woman who had spent her life being bluntly honest, the little white lie needed to calm John sat uncomfortably with her.

"Oh." John seemed pensive. "Okay."

And that was it. The horses slowed, the music hushed, the carousel ride seemed to be ending.

♦ ♦ ♦

Hilda had no choice. She decided to take the chance and call Jean. Whether he remembered Jean or not, Hilda just needed some time for herself and felt that Jean could, and should, relieve her since she had other work to do. The cows at Karl's farm down the road were still chafing from the cold, and had nipple blockages, making it impossible to milk them. Hilda knew that it was more correct to call the cows' mammaries "udders" or "teats," but those terms felt too dismissive to her. Besides, it wasn't the whole udder that was chafed and blocked, it was just where the milk came out. The nipples. Hilda wanted to bring the girls relief, but she also wanted fresh cream by Christmas.

She began. She took a large bottle of aloe gel and then added thirty drops of peppermint, thirty drops of tea tree, twenty drops of oregano, and twenty drops of frankincense. She figured that she had it covered: analgesic, anti-inflammatory, anti-bacterial, anti-infectious, and anti-fungal, all in a soothing base. The cows would love her.

It was when she was counting out the oregano drops that her phone rang. A double ring, meaning that the call was long distance. Hilda wiped her hands, then ran to the kitchen phone, knowing it would be Jack.

"It is so close to Christmas! When are you arriving?" she asked him.

"That's just it, Mom. I have some new information and contacts. I want to wrap it all up by Christmas, but I don't know if I can. It doesn't make sense to fly all the way home just to fly back again."

"No, of course not. Quite right. Besides, you aren't working right now, so you have to watch your spending," Hilda answered, barely hiding her disappointment.

Hilda understood that holidays were always the most difficult the first year following the death of a partner and wondered if that was the real reason Jack was missing Christmas. Hilda remembered her first Christmas without Siegfried and how she only put his decorations on the tree that first year without him. All glass ornaments that he had either made or acquired from his hometown of Lauscha. This year, however, his decorations stayed wrapped in tissue paper in the trunk. John had no memory of Siegfried. The decorations she loved so well would only confuse her first husband. Her ex-husband.

"What news so far? I haven't heard from Elaine and Mark. Are they home yet? Maybe they'll come for Christmas. They usually do. Christmas Eve, anyhow."

"No. They've stayed on in Hamburg for a bit. They'll be with Gareth and Sabine this year." He paused.

"Will they take the baby home soon?"

Hilda heard Jack breathing. The pause held the expectation of the worst news. Hilda was about to say something, to free her son from being the messenger, but then Jack carried through with a steadied voice. "The baby is still struggling, Mom. It doesn't look good. Still on the respirator but they have lessened the pressure. It is a risk. But Sabine goes every day. Sabine is unwavering in her hope. Gareth isn't."

Hilda's chest tightened. She wiped her eye and a little bit of oregano from her fingertip burned into it. She blinked and blinked, until tears were rolling down her face, but she didn't know if it was the news or the oregano.

"You know they called her Frieda. Short for Siegfried."

Hilda blinked her eyes. They were still stinging. She knew that if she didn't rinse her eye with water the oregano would continue to burn. If Siegfried were there, he would have admonished her for not taking better care of her eyes. *You don't want me to have to make you a glass eye,* he would have said with that smile of his hovering over his words. She could almost hear him. He seemed so present in her mind that sometimes she did wonder whether his spirit was hanging around in the house. What would he think if that were the case? John pretty much living with her now! And not even his decorations on the Christmas tree.

"Jack, darling, I am so sorry but I have to go. Somehow, I got oregano in my eye and now I must wash it. I hope you get the answers you need. Let's talk soon, and if you can't be here for Christmas, at least call."

John came downstairs and into the kitchen just as Hilda had her head in the sink, water running over her face. She had to hold her eye open with her fingers to fight the urge to shut it tightly against the water. She had never liked the feeling of water in her eyes. Even with all the years she had swum in Lake Ontario, she never once swam underwater with her eyes open. The best she had ever managed was a plugging of her nose and, with eyes squeezed shut, a fast head-under dunk.

"Washing your hair?" John asked.

"No. I have something in my eye."

"Oh, you should rinse it, then."

"That's what I was doing."

"I thought you were washing your hair."

"No. I have something in my eye."

Mein Gott im Himmel! Hilda thought. *Now I am talking in circles, too! I am part of the carousel of memories lost.*

❖ ❖ ❖

The cows' teats were rough and red from the cold. Hilda remembered the pain she had with her first daughter. Her nipples had bled at the start, and every time her daughter made little sucking gestures, she had felt the milk let down and was as desirous for the relief of her breasts being emptied as she was fearful of the pain it would cause her nipples. In a note from her mother, written on flimsy blue airmail paper with a scratchy hand, there was the solution. Cabbage. Hilda began to live her lactating years with a veritable salad popping out of her bra. She wondered if a little cabbage essence would be beneficial for the cows' nipples but thought better of it. *Cabbage is too enticing a flavour for both cows and Germans*, she thought, chuckling to herself.

"Which is Elsie and which is Heather?" she asked Karl as he gently daubed Hilda's concoction onto the cow's udder.

"So, Elsie is the younger one, here." He pointed to the cow who was waiting patiently for her relief. "She's the one with the black spot near her eye. I call her the pirate cow!"

Hilda laughed. A pirate cow! She imagined the cow on a large ship saying *ooo-argh*!

"So, Heather is the older and wiser one, then!"

"You bet." Karl laughed.

"Here, let me help you."

Hilda took the tub of essence-infused aloe and began to cover Elsie's udder. Her voice was reassuring as she spoke soft words to the cow.

"You're a natural farmer!"

"Hardly. I only ever had rabbits and chickens. Small animals. And the garden."

Later, as they warmed up inside, Hilda became aware of the shake in his hands. It was a subtle movement; a tremor was all. She looked away, not wanting Karl to feel uncomfortable.

"May I help you make the tea?" she asked him.

"No, no. I am fine. I've become quite handy in the kitchen. Of course, I can't make cakes like you, but I can make a good, solid meal. Meat and potatoes, you know." He chuckled.

Hilda smiled. Of course, he could make a meal; everyone adapts when needed. Hilda had always been self-reliant, but there were small changes she had been forced to make. The biggest one was being alone in a big house without the faint sounds of other people breathing. When John first left her, she still had her children's breath within the house, and by the time they had all gone, one by one, Siegfried was well ensconced there with her. It was only after he had died that she was aware that the gentle intake and outtake of breath, quietly filling the house, had been a reassurance that she was not alone in the world. Was that why she was caring for her ex-husband? Was it only for the breathing-in and breathing-out of another being? Even in the barn, the cows all faced each other, breathing in each other's breath in the cold.

"What are you doing for Christmas?" Karl asked her.

"I'm not sure ... Jack usually comes home. Sometimes Elaine and Mark come, too. But everyone's in Europe this year. It will be quiet. The girls will come on Boxing Day. They usually do Christmas Day with their father. You know, they keep pressuring me to sell my house. They think it is too big just for me and too much work. Oh, I almost forgot. I brought some cake for the tea. Nothing special. Just a lemon pound cake. But I put some rind into it to give it some extra zest!"

"Ah, you know me too well."

Yes, she had known him for a long time. Most of those years he had spent alone, having lost his wife thirty years earlier. Like Hilda, his house no longer had the comfort of another person's breathing.

"John is staying at the house," Hilda blurted out as Karl poured out tea from a teapot that looked like a Bavarian cottage with a spout.

"John? You mean, John your *ex-husband*?"

Hilda nodded.

"Has he left his wife?"

"No, worse. He doesn't remember her. He thinks he is still married to me. That we shared all those years."

"So he doesn't know that you remarried?"

"No. And I know it's silly, but he doesn't remember and I'm the one who feels guilty. Like I'm betraying Siegfried."

"How did all this start?"

Hilda told him the story without any embellishment. She did, however, enjoy telling the part where she thought John was an intruder.

"The thing is, he hurt you terribly. Just because he doesn't remember doesn't mean it isn't so."

"I know. And he did me a favour because Siegfried will always be my great love. But I do like having a cup of coffee with someone in the morning. It isn't love. It is just company. Don't you get lonely?"

"Hell, I'm lonely every day, even with the best cows in the world to keep me company." He laughed. "I don't know what I'll do with them if I sell this place. I can't imagine sending them to a slaughterhouse to be made into dog food."

It was the first that Hilda heard that he might sell. It was unfathomable. He had always been there, as much a part of the landscape as she had become.

"And go where? Retirement housing? You would be miserable! Just like I would be."

"Look at my hands, Hilda. They shake. And I have arthritis. I am well over seventy now. Hard to believe, I know!" He winked at her. "It is just so much work, and I don't know how much longer I can do it. My boys don't want the farm. They have bigger ambitions."

Hilda thought of her own daughters and wondered if Karl's sons were pressuring him to sell as well, but Karl quickly removed that notion.

"It's not like my boys need the money. They've done well. They both have fancy jobs. It's just getting to be too much for me."

"I can help you. I can help you, and you can help me. Deal? Besides, Elsie and Heather need a home."

As though it was a business deal, Hilda held out her hand to him, and he reluctantly took it. It was only then that she knew how constant the tremor was.

♦ ♦ ♦

John was asleep upstairs, in what now seemed to be his bed. Jean was still there, reading a paperback, although she seemed too distracted to be making any progress.

"I'm sorry I'm so late," Hilda apologized. "It was a bigger job than we thought."

It was a small lie. They had finished the soothing of the cows' teats quite quickly, but tea and cake can have a way of opening up conversation, and Hilda was surprised to find that she had been at the farm for the better part of the day.

"It's okay," Jean said, but at a closer glance she could see that Jean had been crying.

"I'm sorry, Jean. I know how hard this must be for you."

"That's not why I'm crying. There was this moment, you see, a flash of memory it seemed. I was looking for something in the fridge, something I could make for lunch, and he was sitting there, reading the newspaper and making that disapproving sound he makes when he reads something he doesn't agree with. He has always made that sound as long as I have known him …"

"Yes," Hilda agreed. "He has always made that sound."

"Anyhow, I turned around with my hands full of food, and he suddenly looked up and he said, 'Oh, hello, Jean, it's you. Lovely to see you.' I mean, he was so clear for a moment. He knew who I was. Well, maybe not that I was married to him, but he really recognized me. It was a good twenty minutes before he forgot me again. Oh, now I know what women mean when they talk about becoming invisible!"

"No. It is not the same thing, Jean. When women talk about becoming invisible, it is because their husbands *refuse* to recognize who they are. In your case, your husband *can't* recognize who you are. So, you see, there's a difference. It isn't personal."

"Oh, but surely you never felt invisible? You're so strong!"

How to tell this younger woman, the very woman who had years before turned her husband's head, that she had felt very invisible at that time? But now, as she looked at Jean, she wondered if it was all just a convenient story she had been telling herself over the years. What had been her part in her own erasure? She had put her family's needs so far ahead of her own wants and desires that where she ended and their needs began was indistinguishable. She had erased herself, long before her husband had ceased to see her. Perhaps it wasn't entirely John's fault. When he looked at her, he could no longer see her as a wife, a lover, or a woman, but rather as the functions she so competently assumed.

"No, you are right. I have never, ever felt invisible," Hilda lied.

"I want John home for Christmas. He can't have it here, alone with you. I think seeing the tree and being around family might help him remember where he belongs. It's not that I don't appreciate all you've done …"

Hilda thought she heard a crack in Jean's voice. There was sadness in it, something that she had been trying to mask. The voice can be so betraying. Just one small crack let Hilda know that Jean still loved John. Yes, she had seduced John away from Hilda, but she had also put up with John for twenty years.

"Jean, what perfume do you usually wear?"

At this, Jean began crying. "I don't want perfume for Christmas, I just want my husband back!"

"Don't be silly. I'm not buying you a Christmas present! I just need to know what you wear."

Hilda could hear the muffled sniff in Jean's hesitation. Then a nose blow into a Kleenex.

"Jean?"

"Yeah, yeah, I'm fine ... Obsession. I wear Obsession. You know, Calvin Klein."

Obsession. The top notes are vanilla, basil, bergamot, mandarin orange, peach, and then a citrus — lemon, most likely. The next whiff brings the middle notes of coriander, cedar, orange blossom, jasmine, and rose. Finally, at the root, the base notes are amber, incense, civet, musk, vetiver, and then, surprisingly, another layer of vanilla, repeated. That is how Hilda would identify most of the mixture, but something wasn't quite right. Obsession's lingering last impression was almost always a powdery finish of vanilla. Jean never seemed to have about her the warmth of vanilla. Jean's base note was something else entirely. Amber mixed with sandalwood, with just a hint of musk. Something closer to the perfume Tresor. A fruity and floral top note, only to have that freshness replaced by the heavier sexiness of an earth musk.

Hilda couldn't get her head around the scent of Obsession for Jean but she rationalized that every scent becomes something quite different on each person. Body temperature, chemistry, sweat, diet, and change in hormones can all change the quality of the perfume. But then alchemy happens because of a variable, a conduit that holds the scent to the body's heat and chemistry — that variable is the skin. Skin changes from person to person in both large and subtle ways. The fattiness, the dryness, the closeness of pores, can all alter the scent of a perfume, bringing to the forefront different balances of aroma.

"Jean, I am not keeping him here. Every day I try to help him remember. He can go home to you any time," Hilda consoled her.

"Why? He'll just run away again and come back here. This last time wasn't the first, we just managed to get him back before you ever found out. He's been doing it for weeks now. The last time he really seemed to know everyone in his life was the night Jack came for dinner! And that isn't the best memory to end things with."

"What do you mean?" Hilda inquired. Jack hadn't reported back to her the events of that evening. Instead, he had hurried home just as Hilda was serving dessert and celebrated the day that Iris had stepped into womanhood. "What happened that night?"

"Well, Jack just got all snippy with everyone. He was really mean. Well, not with the kids, they all adore him. They think his impertinence is funny …"

Hilda could feel bile rising up into her throat. Of course the woman standing in front of her was distressed, but that gave her no right to disparage Jack!

"Impertinence? Really, Jean? He is thirty-eight years old." Hilda thought back to the night. Jack had been reluctant to go. It was just days after Tristan's funeral. He was putting on a good face, but inside he was ripped to shreds. Love has a way of doing that. Love is the real secret killer.

"Perhaps," Hilda suggested, "if you had all acknowledged how devastated he was with Tristan's death. Perhaps if you had shown him some support—"

"But they were just friends …"

Hilda raised an eyebrow. "Perhaps you and John and my girls would prefer to think that. *Gareth* and Jack were friends. Best friends. But *Tristan* and Jack, that was something else. Tristan was always Jack's anchor, and without him, Jack is adrift. Tristan gave Jack's life meaning. When Tristan died, Jack was lost."

Neither Jean nor Hilda saw John come into the room. They didn't know how much of the conversation he'd heard, they only knew that hearing of Tristan's death seemed new to him.

"What happened to Tristan? He died?"

John seemed broken. Tears ran down his face as though the news was new, shocking, and too much to bear.

"And Jack is lost? Why isn't someone looking for him? My son is lost? He's adrift? Were they on a boat?"

Hilda wanted to wrap her arms around John, to console him. She wanted to explain it as simply as possible and to let him know that she knew where Jack was. But she couldn't. Jean was there and Jean was John's wife.

"Do you know where Jack is? Hasn't he been to school?" he asked the woman he only knew now as Jack's first-grade teacher.

"He hasn't been in school for a long time," Jean responded, clearly wanting to drag John into the present.

John collapsed at the table, head in his hands, sobbing. "My boy. My boy. Lost."

Jean tried to calm him, putting her hand on his shoulder, but he continued to cry.

"Oh my God. Drowned? Maybe drowned?"

Hilda witnessed all the love John must have held, somewhere, for Jack, but couldn't and wouldn't express all those years. As Hilda witnessed his total collapse at her kitchen table, she finally understood that it wasn't that John wouldn't step up and help, it was that John *couldn't* step up and help. He just wasn't capable of action and grief at the same time.

"I know where Jack is. Don't worry. I'll find him," Hilda soothed. "He's okay. I'll get him. Okay, John? Okay?"

"Oh, Hilda," John replied, "Where would we be without you? You make everything right."

Jean stepped back, watched as though she were not present. Then she grabbed her purse and her coat and ran out the door.

♦ ♦ ♦

She could hear his snoring in the next room. An easy breathing. Hilda knew that the upset of the day was over now, forgotten. Tomorrow he would not ask if she had found Jack. Tomorrow, Jack might be an adult again in John's mind.

Hilda had intended for a day off, a day to relax, but as she sifted through the events of the day it seemed that at every turn there had been sadness. Jack not coming home for Christmas. Karl worried that he could not manage his farm. John being upset and inconsolable. And Jean in despair over John.

Hilda shut her eyes, willing sleep to come, but her mind raced. How to make it all right? There was only so much she could do. One thing was for certain, though. She would not attempt to make Jean's scent herself. Instead she would go to the drug store, buy a bottle of Obsession and then put three drops onto John's pillow every night before sleep. Perhaps if he could breathe in Jean's scent, she would appear in his dreams and then, hopefully, he would remember her.

SIXTEEN

ESTHER WASN'T SURE HOW SHE would spend Christmas. It was strange that even though she was Jewish, the holiday somehow held meaning. Not religious meaning. But there had always been a sense of excitement in whatever community she'd lived in. Just a few months ago, she would have assumed that she would be spending it with Bözsi at the Bainbridge Apartments in the Bronx. The thought of their sad quarters in that rundown apartment made her shudder. Still, she couldn't help but worry about the mailbox filling up with unanswered letters and unpaid bills.

"Don't worry about them!" Bözsi had said to her. "They are not going anywhere. They will be waiting for you when you get back."

Esther should have noted how she had said when *you* get back and not when *we* get back. Only now, after a week of Bözsi spending less and less time at the hotel and more and more time at Henri's apartment in town, did Esther start to consider that perhaps Bözsi was not going to return to the Bronx. Surely Henri didn't visit her that often, so why would she be staying there so much? For Esther, it made no sense at all.

Esther wondered if they'd had sex and what their conversation had been like. But the only thing Bözsi told her was that they had both spent over fifty years believing that the other had been killed and they were making up for lost time.

"His wife knew I was alive because I sent letters to her. But she let Henri believe I was dead! Poor Henri, all those years he had to rot away in contentment!"

"You make contentment sound so terrible!" Esther had exclaimed.

"No, not terrible, darling. Absolutely vile."

"Wait. You sent her letters? Really?"

"Of course." Bözsi had shrugged, then lit her cigarette.

"Don't you feel terrible being second choice?"

"What makes you think I am second?" Bözsi had questioned.

"Well, being a mistress and not a wife …"

"Oh, please. Marriage is an excremental relationship. It is the spouse that gets all the shit. But the mistress … the mistress is someone you look forward to seeing. The mistress isn't tainted by the everyday stuff. So, it is the purer, more *soulful* relationship."

Esther had heard Bözsi's mistress speech before, but still she believed that deep down Bözsi had wanted more from their relationship. For it to be legitimate somehow.

"But wouldn't you like to wake up beside the same man every day?" Esther had asked.

Bözsi had waved her hand dismissively. "Good God, no. I couldn't think of anything worse. When you wake up to the same man every single day, you let yourself slip. You take each other for granted. You fart in bed. No, no, no. A sleepover should be an event."

"So, everyone is fine with this arrangement?"

"Yes."

"His wife?"

Bözsi had paused.

"Not so much," she had finally admitted.

"Not so much?" Esther had pressed.

"Not so much. After the party that day, and you know she looked calm and collected, but apparently, she smashed every dish in all the cupboards. Poor Henri not only had to clean it up but had to buy new ones!"

"Yes, poor Henri." Esther had laughed, trying, unsuccessfully, to keep any sarcasm from her voice. "And you feel no remorse for stealing her husband?"

"Stealing!" It was Bözsi's turn to laugh. "I am not stealing him! I am only *borrowing* him. And I always return him just a little better than when I got him! Besides, *I* was his great love. And she knew that! And when she knew I was alive, she kept us apart for all those years. He probably would have left her for me a lifetime ago. She hoarded him, and so now, in these last few years we all have, she has to learn to share. A little late, but there we are."

After that, Bözsi was not as forthcoming with information. Esther regretted how she had reacted. She longed to hear the latest story and truthfully, she knew that beyond her criticism she had been living vicariously through her sister's escapades.

Esther went to the bar fridge and helped herself to a small single-serve bottle of white wine. It was not in her character to drink alone, but it was almost Christmas and she was alone in Paris, alienating her only sister and failing desperately at finding her surrogate daughter.

The bang on the door startled her. She assumed it must be Bözsi. Likely she had forgotten her keys again.

"Coming," Esther called out.

Outside her hotel room door Blanca and Martina were laughing. If nothing else, the adventure had seemed to pull Blanca out of the abyss of her depression. How much of that was buoyed up by hope and how much deeper she might fall if hope was pulled out from under her feet like a trick evil clowns might play for laughs?

Esther opened the door to the two women standing before her. All dressed up as though ready to go out for a festive evening. Beyond their heads she could see that someone was crouching, trying to hide, but a cheap red fuzzy Santa hat kept coming in and out of view. Esther assumed it was Jack just acting silly. Only when the head popped up, like a premature pop of a jack-in-the-box, did Esther startle with surprise. Not a jack-in-the-box at all, but a Friedrich-in-the-box, all smiles as he looked at her.

"Friedrich! What are you doing here?"

"It's Christmas, and I never spend Christmas without my daughter. So, when she said she was going to be in Paris, I thought, why not go there for a change!"

Esther fumbled. "But where is Jack?"

"Oh, he is gathering intel!" Blanca stated. "With his *statistician*."

"Economist," Martina corrected.

"And we are all going there for Christmas dinner tomorrow, so you will meet the mystery man then," Blanca continued.

"Ach, Blanca. They are just friends. Jack is using him to crack the code. I don't think it's romantic." Esther sounded quite sure of herself.

Blanca and Martina laughed at her naïveté.

"And tonight, I am taking everyone for dinner! I know the perfect place!" Friedrich announced. "It is very popular, so we should go early to ensure a good table."

Martina gave Esther a quick up and down.

"Papa, let's leave Esther to dress for tonight. It really wasn't fair of us to surprise her like this."

Esther was surprised when Blanca sauntered into the room with excuses that Martina and Friedrich likely needed a bit of father-daughter time. As soon as the door closed, she was flipping through the closet, looking at Esther's clothes.

"These won't do at all. Don't you have anything more festive?" "I expected that we would be back home by now." Blanca's hand landed on something soft to the touch. A fine knit. She pulled it out and smiled, thinking that the rich plum would complement the hazel-green of Esther's eyes.

"That is Bözsi's—"

"Try it on!"

She shook the hanger at Esther with such determination that Esther had no choice.

"Oh, and these as well …"

Blanca had found the silk cami-teddy set Bözsi had picked up at the airport.

"And don't tell me these belong to Bözsi because, trust me, she *is* getting laid, so either she doesn't need this sexy little number or they are actually *yours*."

Esther started to object but Blanca put her finger to her lips.

"We deserve a little break. It's Christmas, Esther. We are not going to find her tonight. So, let's eat and drink and then we can resume our battles after Christmas."

Maybe there would be news of Clara after Christmas, or worse, maybe there would be nothing. Either way, as soon as the holidays were over, they would continue. But for tonight, Blanca deserved a ceasefire. Esther put on the silk undergarments then slid the soft knit of Bözsi's dress over her body. It was a little tighter on her, but it looked rich and elegant even as it hugged her wider hips.

"Oh, Esther, you look beautiful!" Blanca exclaimed. "I know I haven't told you this, but I am so happy that you came looking for us."

A year ago, she had neither of the twins; she had lost them both. Now she had Blanca back in her life. Somehow, she was determined to keep her in her life and doubly determined that she would find Clara as well.

♦ ♦ ♦

"The thing is that we tend to look at the big picture, not at the variables. It is all about probabilities, my friend. Other factors. Take that equation, for instance ..."

"The Fisher equation?" Jack asked, knowing full well that was what he meant.

Younis pointed to a head of garlic, and Jack tossed it over to him. He pulled off three cloves, placed them onto a wooden cutting board and then placed the wide blade of his cleaver over the top of them. With his fist, he banged down on the cleaver's blade. The cloves were split, busting through their skins, practically peeled and ready to go. How was it that he had gotten through life without ever learning that trick?

"I think my mother always just peeled them, but that is so much faster. More efficient."

"I'm an efficient man," Younis replied, a huge smile on his face.

"Tristan had a garlic press. He liked, you know, gadgets."

Younis pushed the garlic aside and leaned against the counter.

"The first holidays are the hardest."

"It would have been harder if I had gone home to Canada. I feel guilty that I didn't, because of my mother. But I also feel relieved." Jack paused. "So, you were saying? The Fisher equation?"

"It is all about the i variable, which we've already discussed. It is that variable that Fisher attempted to locate in his equation. Now, here is the thing. You are trying to locate a missing woman based on the information you have. A market-trend kind of thinking. You know she was in South Africa, somewhere. You know that the envelope was mailed from Paris. You find the Fisher equation and it all leads, in your mind, to the belief that *if* she is alive, someone studying economics must have mailed this opera she wrote. And all the while, you wonder why the opera was even mailed and why Clara didn't just go home to Germany."

"Yes," Jack agreed, "but now we are at a standstill. Where do we go from here? You seem to think that you do not have any students from South Africa at the university."

"You see!" Younis exclaimed. "This is why you need me!"

"What am I missing?"

"The variable! You see, you have been misled. Like two plus two equals four."

"Doesn't it?" Jack asked, confused.

"Usually, but not always. If you mix two millilitres of two liquid elements together to make a compound element, it is unlikely that the compound will be four millilitres. Usually, it will add up to a little less."

"I thought you were a math guy, not a science guy."

"I have hobbies, you know!" Younis laughed. "Anyhow, your mistake is your presumption. You use progressive logic to your detriment. Although it is a very attractive trait in you. But, in this case, your logic has put you into a stalemate. You see, it doesn't have to be a student with an interest in the Fisher equation who mailed the opera. It only has to be a person with access to the envelope. And *that* opens up possibilities."

"That makes it so much harder when you cannot narrow it down."

"Oh, but it does narrow it down! Immensely. But it does so without excluding possibilities. Now we go through all the possibilities, until we nail down the probabilities."

Jack had never met anyone who thought the way Younis did. He had always surrounded himself with the company of artists. The twins were musicians and opera singers, Gareth was a visual artist, and Tristan was a filmmaker, an auteur. As a photojournalist, he was likely the most logical of the bunch, and yet his progressive logic had, evidently, gotten in the way of considering *probabilities* and *variables*. The truth was, Jack had never considered either in his entire life.

♦ ♦ ♦

Friedrich was right, the restaurant was popular even on Christmas Eve. There was a din that seemed to reverberate off the walls and high ceilings as waiters with domed plates rushed in and out of the kitchen. Martina requested a table away from the speakers so that the only competition to their conversation would be the sounds of plates, voices of other patrons, and the hustle and bustle of a crazy-busy kitchen.

"Why is this place so popular?" Esther asked.

"Because it has just received a Michelin star and so everyone wants to try it to see why."

"That means it must be very expensive." Esther secretly calculated what money she still had in her purse and what she might have left on her one credit card, but she knew that even with it all combined, she was dining out of her league.

"It is not for you to worry about," Friedrich assured her, taking her elbow as he led her to the table.

"I think Bözsi will be coming a bit later, but we can have drinks and starters," Martina informed.

Esther wondered how Martina would be better aware of Bözsi's affairs than she. Had Bözsi been informed that Friedrich was coming, as well? Why was she the last to find out anything?

"What about your son? What will he do for Christmas if you are here in Paris?" Esther asked.

It seemed that the entire restaurant stilled, slowed, and paused. Of course, it hadn't. Indeed, the waiters were still moving at a ridiculously quick pace, but the table seemed to freeze, and Friedrich visibly paled.

"I'm sorry," Esther continued. "Was I mistaken? I am sure you said that you have a son as well."

"My brother overdosed six years ago. On Christmas. It is why we always spend Christmas together," Martina said sadly.

"I'm so sorry," Esther started, struck with sadness and shame. "I assumed because you said you *have* a son, not that you *had* a son …"

"He does not cease to be my son because he is dead," Friedrich said softly. So soft that Esther only knew what he had said by reading his lips.

"I have ruined the evening, perhaps I should go. I am so sorry."

"You will only ruin the evening if you *do* go. Please, it is a holiday of mixed emotions, but I have so looked forward to sharing this experience with you. With all of you. My beautiful daughter and her lovely partner. And with you, as well."

At that moment Bözsi burst into the restaurant. She seemed to have been at a beauty parlour, her hair newly styled, her nails polished to a high shine, and her makeup freshly applied.

"Oh, Friedrich," she called across the room, though she could barely be heard, "How absolutely marvellous!"

Friedrich stood and then kissed Esther's sister on each cheek. Esther marked how easy the gesture seemed, and how he had not done the same for her.

"I have news for all of you!" Bözsi announced. "Perhaps champagne is needed!"

Martina gestured toward a waiter, one who seemed to hover around the table, his eyes watching as though he might have to predict their next need.

"*Oui, madame?*"

"Champagne, *s'il vous plait.*"

He handed Martina a list but, as he did so, his eyes fell upon Blanca. He smiled shyly, then looked away as he waited for Martina to make her choice.

As she seated herself, Bözsi's eyes rested on her sister. She noted the plum knit dress with just a hint of the peach camisole showing at the décolletage. Esther shifted uncomfortably in her chair. Would Bözsi say something about the borrowed dress?

"Esther, darling! You do look wonderful tonight! Doesn't she look radiant, Friedrich?" She asked the man sitting across from her but didn't wait for an answer. "Now, where is that champagne? Never mind, I cannot wait. I will tell you all now and then we can clink when it gets here." She paused for dramatic effect. "Henri has asked me to stay in Paris! To live in his apartment full-time so we can be together as much as possible. Of course, there *are* strings attached!"

"Well, of course there are—" Esther started.

"Yes! He told me I can come and go as I please, but I will have to water the plants!" Bözsi laughed loudly.

Esther listened to the congratulations and the happy murmurs of approval and wondered if she had missed something. Her sister was agreeing to be *what*, exactly? A kept woman? And they all seemed fine, even happy, about it. Hadn't there been women's liberation? It seemed to Esther like her sister was agreeing to an arrangement that had been made in a previous century.

"And what about our apartment in the Bronx?" Esther asked.

"Oh, God, I hate it. You can have it if you want — the rent is paid through May."

"But your things?"

"I only care about the pictures. They can be sent."

"But I only lived there because you lived there! I went there to be with you ..." But before she could finish, Friedrich put his hand on hers, and the unexpected touch stopped her mid-sentence.

"Ah, the champagne!" Martina announced.

"May I?" the waiter asked before popping the cork. Again, he looked at Blanca.

"You would think he had never seen an albino before," Blanca whispered to Martina.

"Perhaps he has never seen a *lesbian* one before!" Martina joked back.

"Let me propose a toast. To Bözsi and Henri, even though Henri is not here," Esther began as she stood, glass in hand. "And so, Bözsi, I will say this to you, I know you think I do not approve of this, but please believe me when I say that what I *do* approve of is your happiness. And since I finally found you after all these years, I have never seen you as happy as you are right now."

Esther hadn't had champagne since de Gaulle had fanned the flames of the FLQ, but she was, after all, in Paris, and her sister seemed happy!

The waiter was there the moment their glasses reached half empty, topping them up. When he got to Blanca, he could no longer remain silent. He looked around to make sure that none of his co-workers could see him engaging in conversation with her.

"*Excusez-moi, mais n'êtes-vous pas dans le groupe* Bleach?" he inquired.

"I am half of Bleach," Blanca responded to him in English.

"I love your music!" he told her, his English heavily affected by his Parisian accent. "Are you here for a concert? Are you still performing?"

"No, I am just visiting."

"Oh, that is too bad. I thought that you and your sister might be performing. It's been such a long time."

At that moment, the maître d' looked over to the table and nodded, not in an approving manner, at the young waiter. The waiter bowed slightly to the table and then backed off.

Blanca imagined performing again, singing with her sister, being in front of an audience. Yes, she would find Clara and she would return to the stage, with her sister. And as the first course arrived, Blanca felt a hunger she had not experienced in a very long time.

"To good friends, new and old!" Bözsi toasted.

As they all raised their glasses again, they knew that the time of enjoyment would soon be over and they would all be frantically searching for Clara once again.

◆ ◆ ◆

Esther shut the lights in the hotel room so that only the light of the streets illuminated her surroundings. She could see the gold and red and blue of Christmas lights shining beyond the window. Usually, they would be turned off by 2:00 a.m., but not on Christmas. Esther was sure they would be left on all night.

They had missed the first peals of the bells for mass. Mass would have begun at ten thirty, and at that time, they were just finishing up their Christmas Eve dinner: oysters set into spinach purée as though floating in a green sea, aspic with crab and cilantro and red berries, quail, simply seared, atop an Asian-inspired salad. Esther had prided herself in being quite sophisticated in her palate, a *foodie* as the young would say, but she had never experienced such an explosion of tastes.

The menu did not do anything as gauche as to list the prices. She could only imagine! But she had looked at Friedrich when the bill was presented, and there was no reaction to the sum. Now, as she reconsidered the night, she couldn't be sure that he had even looked at the bill. Perhaps he had just discreetly placed his credit card down without so much as a glance.

Then he had suggested a walk, saying it would be good for them after such a big meal. Blanca and Martina wanted to go back to the hotel, feigning exhaustion. Esther had hoped that Bözsi would come back to the hotel so that they could wake up on Christmas morning together. Esther had even found her a small gift, a lovely silver bracelet, which she had wrapped and put onto the bedside table on Bözsi's side of the bed. But Bözsi said no, she wanted to get used to her new home right away, and then she winked. Esther could only presume that perhaps Bözsi held out a hope that Henri would slip away for a quick late-night visit.

It was, awkwardly, just Esther and Friedrich.

"We can stroll down the Champs-Élysées, see all the lights. I hear that there are literally a million of them."

"Surely not!"

"Oh yes, and that is just between Place de la Concorde and the Arc de Triomphe. Perhaps there will be some Christmas bells from a church. When I taught in Frankfurt, there was always a celebration on Christmas Eve. We would all go out and hear the bells, and people would be selling food and drink on the street. I miss those days," he said, and Esther knew that in missing those days he also missed a life now gone. A child and a wife both lost.

"Come on," he said, brightening. "If you aren't too cold, we can line up and have a Christmas Eve Ferris wheel ride!"

"Oh no! Really?"

"Of course, dear Esther. We are only young once!" he teased.

Once they returned to the little hotel and buzzed to get in, Friedrich walked her to her door and then he bowed in a formal and comical way.

"I guess it really is Christmas now. So, Merry Christmas. Sweet dreams."

Esther never dreamed. Dreaming was something that she had given up when she was in hiding and trying to survive. Dreams were not sweet for Esther, they were nightmares. She had chosen not to dream in any way whatsoever. Without dreams there would be no fear.

She knew that Bözsi had no problems with dreams. She lived in her dreams and seemed to be able to make them become a reality. Esther wondered if Henri had shown up at the apartment, in the middle of the night. She knew that Jack and the economics professor were likely having a romantic tryst, after all, they had barely seen him in three days. Even Blanca and Martina appeared to have rekindled their passion. Everyone was having sex in Paris! Everyone but Esther.

What did it matter anyhow? It was just foolishness and muckiness. Besides, she was about to reach another decade of life soon. Almost seventy! Who in their right mind pursues sex at seventy? Apart from her older sister, of course. Her sister who always felt free to do what she wanted, when she wanted. A sister who was never burdened by the approval of her parents, nor age, it would seem.

Esther could feel the cool of the silk camisole against her skin. Why hadn't she taken it off and changed into her more sensible nightie? Oh, but it was silky and soft. It felt nice. It felt so *very* nice on her skin. So flimsy and sweet. And *slippery*.

◆ ◆ ◆

After they made love, Martina fell asleep, filled with good food and sexual satisfaction. But Blanca was very much awake. She got out of bed.

Blanca knew that Jack had left his shaving kit in the bathroom. She knew that there would be a fresh razor there. How easy it would be, while Martina slept, to go into the bathroom, open his kit, disassemble the disposable plastic razor and remove the stainless-steel blades. She could almost feel the cold, sharp edge, cutting through her lower arm, between the wrist and the elbow. The top of the arm, not the underbelly. Rarely did she cut the underbelly. This was not a cry for help. It was not a suicide attempt. It was not an act of performance to make Martina or even Jack worry about her. This was a secret. Just a few slices to take the pressure off. Twenty, she reasoned. Twenty wasn't a lot. And it was winter, so she could wear long sleeves. No one would notice.

Blanca unzipped his shaving kit. There it was. Baby blue, with its clear plastic protective shield over its blade. Blanca held it. She hadn't been alone with a razor in such a long time. For years now, Martina had made her shave her legs in front of her. Sure, it was kind of sexy, but it was also so demeaning. Why couldn't she be trusted to shave her legs?

Blanca removed the plastic. Such a small thing, a razor. But those blades could work quickly. Blanca's hand trembled slightly as she held the razor close to her face, studying it. She saw the refection of both her desire and the instrument of her desire in the vanity mirror. If she closed her eyes, she wouldn't see it. *Fuck!* She did see it, though. Now she couldn't erase her image from her mind. An image no longer of pure desire, because now what she saw was guile, and guile weakened her longing.

She knew she would be breaking a promise. Not the promise she had made to Martina. Of course, she would be breaking *that* promise, too. And she did want Martina to love her the way she had before, and to forgive her for the sorrow the cutting had caused her. But she also knew that she could fool Martina — pretend that she hadn't cut. No, it was those other eyes that might be watching. Eyes that never slept and never looked away. She had promised God, the terrible God of her youth, that if He somehow returned Clara to her, she would never cut again. But there was more; she had promised that until they knew her whereabouts, she would not cut. It was foolproof. The only way she would allow herself to cut would be if she found out that her sister was, indeed, dead. She made that promise believing that if the stakes were high enough, she would not want to go on cutting. And that Clara would be found.

Blanca put the clear plastic back onto the razor head. She put the razor into Jack's shaving kit and zipped it closed. Then she ran cold water over her wrists.

When she returned to the bedroom Martina was still fast asleep, content. Blanca went to the window and looked out. It was quiet, except for a few merry revellers passing, drunk in the street below. But Blanca didn't look into the street. She fixed her gaze upward, toward the moon. There, just beside the moon, she saw it, as it always was, wherever she went in the world. She knew that it was the planet Venus, but she preferred to think of it as the brightest star in the sky. Then, she whispered quietly, so as not to disturb Martina, the story she had been told so many times.

"I fell asleep with my mouth open and I swallowed a star. The star broke into two, and when you are together, that star becomes whole again."

SEVENTEEN

ONCE SABINE AND THE CHILDREN were in bed, Gareth slipped away and went to the oculary. There were still shards of glass on the floor; they snapped and cracked the way ice does underfoot. Did he miss that cold? The below-zero frigidity of Ontario at Christmas, where a sharp inhalation would freeze the nostrils and send sharp pangs deep into the lungs. Gareth planned to make a necklace for Sabine, melting the broken glass of Frieda's mobile, refashioning what was meant for their baby as a gift for Sabine. It would be easier if he knew her fate, but Baby Frieda was still in the intensive care unit, still needing oxygen, though the pressure had been turned down. Her chances of survival had risen to almost sixty percent. Sabine was hopeful, sure Frieda would make it, and she visited her every day. But still, Gareth was quietly worried.

And so Gareth lit a blue flame, stared into contained fire, and willed Frieda to both live and have sight.

♦ ♦ ♦

"Isn't Uncle Jack coming for Christmas? I made him a special present. Want to know what it is?"

"What is it?" Gareth asked.

"Now don't get angry."

"Okay."

"I took one of the eyes from that drawer," Iris pointed to the cabinet that had once been Siegfried's. "Then I took apart a digital camera and put the camera lens into the eye. It is a prototype."

Gareth stared at his daughter. He knew she was on to something but that it wasn't yet time for her creation. But there was the internet now, and the magical exchange of information, data, images. Could there be an artificial eye that could one day send images from a lens to the brain?

"Iris, this is very exciting! Can I see it?"

"No! It's not for you, it's for Uncle Jack! I thought he would be back from Paris by now," Iris replied.

"Paris?" Sabine asked. "I thought he went home to Canada to be with Hilda."

"No, he went to Paris to look for my mother."

It was too late, Iris realized. She had said too much, opened a Pandora's box, and there was no way to put all the troubles she had accidentally released back into the box.

"Why would he think she was in Paris?" Gareth asked.

"Because of the envelope." Iris managed a tight, apologetic smile. "Never mind. Maybe I misspoke."

"Who exactly has gone to Paris?" Sabine asked.

"The strange old ladies — you haven't met them — and Auntie Blanca, Martina, and Uncle Jack …"

Sabine started picking up the paper wrappings, folding the ones that weren't badly torn while throwing away the rest.

"I don't know what they expect to find. If she hasn't come back in over eight years, it is unlikely she will!" She hurried into the kitchen.

Gareth followed; he came up beside her, tried to hush her. *Please, please,* he thought. *Let's not ruin Christmas.*

"It's just madness, you know that. Jack feels guilty, and it's just gotten worse since Tristan died," he whispered.

"Really? What envelope, Gareth? What is that about? There must be some reason they *all* went! And what if they do bring her back? What then? What happens to us? Have you thought of that? What happens for Fritz and Frieda? For me?"

Suddenly Fritz ran in, his hands and face covered in chocolate. "*Schmutzig! Schmutzig!*" he cried out, wanting it to be washed off. The chocolate mess was of no consequence while he was taking the chocolates off the tree and cramming them into his mouth, but now that he was finished, he needed the chocolate washed off right away.

Gareth picked up his son. He seemed a bit heavier, more solid.

"Okay, okay, I'll wash you. Then we can choose some nice clothes for Christmas."

Sabine followed, her eyes blinking hotly. *Don't cry. Don't cry.* But always, always, the ghost of Clara haunted their relationship. And now, it seemed, that ghost was believed to be alive. There was proof. An envelope!

"What would you do, Gareth?" she asked him in English so as not to upset Fritz. "You have one healthy child with each of us. And a baby in the hospital, still fighting for her life. So, who would you choose if she *did* come back?"

It was preposterous. Clara simply could *not* be alive. The game of choosing one over the other was a game Gareth did not want to play. He finished wiping around Fritz's mouth and put him down.

"Jack might seem like he is okay, but he isn't. Ever since Tristan died, he has been at a loss. He stopped working, and you know he lived to work! He needs a distraction, and Clara is just that. And the others are all going along with it because, well, they are all *mad*! That is why! Haven't you noticed how insane Blanca and Martina are?"

"But why? Why would he choose Clara as his distraction? *You* were married to her, not him!"

"Oh, please don't make me say what I think, Sabine."

"Say it! You must!"

"No. I can't."

"Say it, Gareth. You must tell me!"

"Because he is Iris's biological father. Come on. You must have seen it in the eyes. They have the exact same eyes! And so does Hilda. Iris is Jack through and through."

"I don't understand. What are you saying?" Sabine asked, completely confused. Hadn't Gareth married Clara all those years ago *because* she was pregnant? Hadn't he been with her in the delivery room? He had cut the cord. He was the first to hold Iris.

"I'm not Iris's biological father. Jack is. You must have noticed the similarities."

When they heard her voice from just beyond the kitchen door, it seemed surreal, impossible. Each hoped that they had imagined it, but Iris's voice was clear. They heard her words. And if they were not sure, she repeated them with a slow yet wavering breath.

"You're not my dad?" Iris asked for the second time.

Sabine reached her arms out. Took Fritz from Gareth.

"Go on. You'd better deal with that now," she said. And as she exited the door she added, her voice dripping with sarcasm, "And Merry Christmas."

◆ ◆ ◆

She was the problem. It was clear that everyone would be happier if she just didn't exist. If her mother hadn't gotten pregnant with her, then her father wouldn't have married her mother, and he could have been with Sabine this whole time instead. Jack would probably have worked in Canada and not come to Germany so much to see her, and then Tristan wouldn't have had other boyfriends and he wouldn't have died of AIDS. Baby Frieda wouldn't have been born early because of the rose scent, so she would have been fine, too. And, most importantly, her mother would never have been stolen that day in an airport! She would have continued with the Punk Opera company and been happy there, with her sister. The world would have been a better place if she had *never* been born.

And then the sadness seemed to lift; she knew what she must do, how she could make everything all right again. She crept from her room and went into the bathroom. She opened the medicine cabinet. There they were. The painkillers Sabine had been given when she was in the hospital. How many were there? She dumped them into her hand, counted them out. Twelve. Only twelve. One for every year of her life. She filled her glass, the one with the smiling shark and the words BRUSH YOUR TEETH written underneath. She crammed them all into her mouth and tried to gulp them down. Some of the pills stuck in her throat, and she coughed up water, but she persisted until they were all washed down. "Down the hatch," as her uncle Jack would say. Well, actually, as her father would say.

She felt nothing at first. *How long will it take?* Iris went to her room. Arranged her pillows all around her in what she thought a fashionable manner. Here she would just wait. Here she would remain, waiting to sleep. Sleep forever, like Sleeping Beauty.

♦ ♦ ♦

Gareth's mother, Elaine, listened to the morning events with horror. She had hoped that Christmas would bring some family unity, some healing and hope, into the home. There had been nothing but sorrow and tears since Tristan had gotten ill. And now this.

"I know, I shouldn't have said it out loud. It was a mistake. I made a mistake," Gareth moaned over and over again.

"But why? Why would you say such a thing?"

"Come on, Mom! You knew already. It's why you find it so easy to love Fritz and why you never bonded with Iris. You never did, but Hilda loved her the second she saw her. It's so obvious!" Gareth accused, his voice hushed. Too easy for little ears to hear things.

"That's not true. I love Iris. It's just that she reminds me so much of Faye. You know, Clara's mother was in my charge that dreadful day. Iris looks exactly like her. I look at her, and it is as though poor Faye were still alive. It's as though I hadn't looked away and she hadn't drowned."

"Really?"

"Yes, really."

Then suddenly Elaine was on her feet, hurrying to the bedroom door. She tried to open it without knocking, but it was locked. She banged with the flat of her hand against the wood.

"Iris? Iris, honey?" she called out.

Nothing.

"Iris! Answer me!" she called out again.

"She said she needed some private time to think things through," Sabine said. "We are respecting her privacy now that she is almost a teen."

But Elaine didn't listen to Sabine. Years of being a psychiatric nurse, and then her later career as a therapist, alerted her to the signs of potential danger.

"Iris!" One last shout before the sixty-seven-year-old woman backed up and charged the door, shoulder-first into the wood, with all her might.

"Mom?" Gareth called, but by now he was pumped with adrenaline, ready to finish the door off. She charged at the door, again and again, until the wood finally gave in to her.

Iris lay there, quite still, as though asleep. When Elaine moved her into a lateral position, Iris began to gag and vomit all over the sheets and pillows. Elaine kept her hand on the child's back, feeling the swell and fall as she breathed.

"Call an ambulance. She is probably okay, she threw everything up, but she has to go to emergency, just in case."

Gareth made the call. Sabine was grabbing her coat and her boots.

"Maybe you should just stay here and relax, Sabine. You still haven't healed. It's too much for you. Stay with Fritzi," Elaine suggested. "You and Mark stay here. Gareth and I will go."

"*Bist du verrückt?*" Sabine yelled at her. "Are you crazy? I'm not letting my daughter go to the hospital without me. I was the one who was with her when she woke up after her heart surgery! I was the one who stayed by her, whispering stories in her ear! She's my girl!"

"Of course," Elaine agreed. "You should go with your daughter."

♦ ♦ ♦

To Iris, the woman with the long red hair seemed very angry. Iris had never seen her angry before. She kept shaking her head and pointing at Iris, as though she were disappointed in her. Iris tried to reach out to her, but the woman crossed her arms and shook her head no. Then a giant wave came and washed her red-haired grandmother away. Iris could taste the lake in her mouth. It felt like she had swallowed the entire lake. Then all she could remember was retching and heaving. And the lake receding far, far away.

♦ ♦ ♦

Elaine and Mark played games with Fritz while they waited. He couldn't understand why there was no Christmas dinner ready. And where was everyone?

"Come on up here, big boy, let's have another horsey ride," Mark tried to cheer Fritz.

"It doesn't matter how many times I look at the phone, it won't make it ring." Elaine sounded agitated.

"Elaine ... something you said. That Iris looks like her other grandmother. Why did you say that?"

"Because it's true. She is so much like that poor woman. Faye was so young when she had Blanca and Clara. Sixteen only. Not much older than Iris. A child-mother. What did she know? And it all ended so badly."

"But even if she does look like Faye, that doesn't mean that Iris isn't Jack's child. They are a lot alike, too."

"What do you think being a father really means, Mark?"

Mark looked at his wife. So many years together, so many shared moments and the marking of life's most usual experiences, and yet sometimes he had no idea of what might be in her head. Mark shrugged and encouraged her with an anemic half smile.

"Well, I think it is a bit more than just sticking a penis in and then walking away. Not that Jack walked away, exactly. He adores Iris. But Jack is a big-picture person. That's why he flies here and there. He needs to see the whole world, to be part of the big picture. It's why his relationship with our Tristan wasn't exactly perfect. Tristan wanted him home, and Jack wanted to be everywhere all at once. But our Gareth has always been a details man. He frets over the smallest details. And *that* is what being a father is. Day in and day out. Even when the world seems mundane, even when you are bored to tears, you focus on all those little details."

"More horsey!" Fritz yelled, climbing back onto his grandfather's lap. "Giddy up!"

"You see, he's speaking English, Mark!" Elaine clapped her hands to encourage Fritz.

The phone finally rang just as Mark's legs were tiring from too much horsey. He watched as Elaine spoke. He watched her nod. He watched as tears of relief poured over her cheeks.

"She's fine. Just fine. And there's more news, Mark. Good news."

Mark just waited for her words.

"Baby Frieda is strong enough to come off the respirator. She'll be put onto a mask now. She's out of the woods. They saw Sabine in the hospital and just told her. Now Sabine, Gareth, and Iris will be home in a couple of hours. I'd better make a Christmas dinner!"

"How long will they keep her?"

"Usually they are kept till they reach what would have been the due date. Frieda was barely twenty-six weeks, so it'll be a while yet. Another three months. But she'll be home for Easter."

"And her sight? Can she see?"

"It's too soon to tell."

Mark wanted to wrap his arms around his wife. He always thought of her as more practical than intuitive, but today he had discovered a new aspect of the woman he had known for decades.

"Merry Christmas, Grandma."

"Merry Christmas, Grandpa!"

"More horsey! More horsey! Giddy-up, Opa!"

Mark scooped up Fritz.

"You know, I'll never get used to being called Opa."

Elaine took her husband's hand and squeezed it. "You were something today. You saved Iris's life."

But somewhere Elaine imagined a woman, not even thirty, turning away from the lake to thank her. Her long red hair tangled with seaweed as it caught the wind, before she returned to the cold waters of Lake Ontario.

EIGHTEEN

LAKE ONTARIO WAS GREY, STEEL-GREY, with a green tinge below the surface. It seemed that the water was quite far away because, beyond the sand, there were a few feet of ice before the water started. Hilda had walked down, a bowlful of apple-and-raisin stuffing in her hands for feeding the birds. Those beautiful Canada geese who no longer flew south, but like her, courageously faced the winter, would be waiting for her. The sun was bright on her face, and she wished that she had worn sunglasses because the reflection off the snow made the light doubly bright.

This was something she had always done on Christmas morning. After the crazy opening frenzy was over, she would go down to the water alone. It was an escape for her before she had more cooking to do. And when her daughters were teens, they would say, "Yesterday you were cooking the goose, and today you are feeding them. She's probably fattening them up for next year already!"

Different geese. She cooked and ate farmed goose. That was their purpose. There was no point in being sentimental about it.

But these were a different breed. Born to be wild, to fly overhead in a beautiful V-formation. To fend for themselves, as she had done for herself.

"Come on, come on. You know you want the treats," she called out to them.

Hilda took her time, tossing out the apples to the geese. She had no reason to hurry. The house was quiet, empty. She considered bringing some of the desserts over to Karl. If his sons were there, they could all enjoy them. If they hadn't arrived, perhaps she could share a quick coffee with him. If he had gone to Toronto to be with them in one of their homes, she could let herself in. (His key was always just under the welcome mat. Not really a good hiding place!) She could leave a note and a lovely plate of sweets and baked goods to cheer him after a long drive back.

Her stainless-steel bowl now empty, she tilted it to show the geese it was all gone, but they honked greedily, demanding more.

"Maybe a bit more later," she told them.

She headed uphill to the house, imagining a plateful of leftovers. As much as she had always fussed over the big Christmas Eve feast, Hilda was always happiest the next day, picking at cold leftovers.

She was surprised to see John there when she returned. Back early from Jean's, where she had dropped him the night before, after the two of them ate what they could of the huge Christmas goose dinner.

"I walked," he said. "I didn't want to trouble you. I know how you are always so busy on Christmas."

"But you didn't stay there for dinner? Did you see the girls?"

"Oh yes. They're fine. Not sure why they are doing Christmas there and not here, but you know, they're adults."

"They didn't drive you?"

"No, no. I walked." He paused, a look of confusion crossing his face. "You know, sometimes things don't make sense, Hilda. I don't know why I was there. I woke up there. Maybe I drank too much? Are you angry?"

In the years she was with him, he seemed to do as he pleased, rarely asking how his behaviour might affect her. Now there was concern as he tried to make sense of things.

"It's okay," she reassured him. "I was just out feeding the geese."

"Ha! Yesterday you were cooking goose and today you're feeding them!" He laughed. Yes, he remembered that tired, yearly joke.

"I got you a present," he blurted out, as though he had just remembered. He reached into his deep coat pocket and handed her a smallish box wrapped in shiny green paper.

"Oh, John. That is very sweet," she said.

Stuck to the paper was a gift tag reading, TO OUR OTHER MOTHER! LOVE MARGIE AND BETH. *Margie and Beth?* God how she hated nicknames! Hilda gave John a reassuring smile. He looked like an excited kid, hoping she would like the present. It was clear that he had just stolen it from under their tree. Did he have any idea what was inside the box?

She carefully loosened the paper, revealing the pinkish-beige box with the words DUNE BY DIOR.

"Do you like it?"

Hilda opened the circle-shaped bottle and sniffed. Amber, peony, sandalwood were the first notes to jump out at her. There was no powdery finish. No vanilla lingering in the air. If Obsession felt like the autumn, then Dune was a summer's day. Jean was a summer spirit, full of adventure and activity; there was no contemplation, no acceptance of change in her at all. Hilda closed the bottle.

"I have a small gift for you, as well." Hilda got up and went to the tree. She thought now that it was a silly gift, too nostalgic, perhaps, but at the time that she had bought it, she thought it was perfect. "Here. Open it."

John tore off the paper with great excitement, as though he were a boy who had gotten a gift when he least expected to.

"What is it?"

"It's a kaleidoscope! Hold it to your eye the turn it. It makes pretty pictures."

Hilda had gone into a small toy shop in town, seen it in the window, and when she noticed that a carousel pony was engraved into the wood, she impulsively bought it.

"Oh, it's wonderful!" he told her as he shifted the beads within its glass.

♦ ♦ ♦

Hilda's daughter arrived late Christmas morning. Hilda was surprised to see Margaret with her son and daughter in tow. Where was her husband? Likely at Jean's, polishing off his first drink of the day, joking with Elizabeth's husband.

"He's here, right? You should have called," Margaret accused before even taking off her coat.

"I'm sorry, I thought you would have assumed—"

"I don't pretend to assume anything! You don't get it, do you? He is degenerating. He will not get better. He will lose more and more memory, and then he will die. Why are you keeping him here?" Margaret's voice climbed higher in frustration.

"Come in, come in, out of the cold. Do you want something to eat? I have goose."

The teenagers slipped by them and settled in the living room, in front of the tree. The daughter was a clone of her mother, but the boy was a bit like Jack, with an impish grin and curiosity. Hilda imagined that if Jack hadn't fallen from the tree, he would have been even more like her grandson. Percy. *Rhymes with mercy,* Hilda thought.

"What I don't understand is all this bitching you're doing. I don't see Jean coming to get him every day," Hilda stated. "Besides, I am sure that he will start remembering her very soon and everything will be fine."

"Why? Because of your aromatherapy, Mom? Even if it worked a little, he is way past that point now. He needs constant care. *Professional* care."

It was at that moment that Margaret saw the bottle of Dune on the counter. She picked it up. Saw the wrapping paper, the card.

"Oh, I don't believe this!" she shouted at her mother.

"Me neither. She told me she wore Obsession. It's nothing like Dune."

"She just said that because she thought you wanted to wear the same perfume so you could seduce Dad!" Even to Margaret the idea was rather ludicrous.

Hilda started to laugh. The jealousies between two women can last a lifetime, long after the best-before date has expired. Margaret picked up the bottle, but before she could pop it into her purse, Hilda reached for it.

"No, I'm sorry, that was a Christmas gift," Hilda told her.

"Yes," Margaret corrected. "It was a gift, but not for *you*!"

"Tell your father that. You can always get another one. Maybe a Boxing Day sale! But your father would be very sad if the bottle was gone. It would confuse him."

Then it all slowed down. The reaching for the bottle, the other set of hands intercepting, the knocking of the bottle from anyone's grasp, the bottle flying across the room, then the smashing onto the floor, a crashing sound, and the overpowering smell of too much perfume in too small a place.

Everyone ran into the kitchen. The kids saw the puddle of perfume on the floor and all the broken glass. But John wasn't alarmed by the sight. It was the overpowering smell that reached his nose that caused him to shake. He retreated until his back was up against the wall. He seemed terrified.

"No! No! No!" He was crying.

"It's okay. It's okay," Hilda reassured.

"I don't want to be locked up!" he yelled at them all.

"No one is going to lock you up, Dad," Margaret tried to soothe. She knew that her father had what Jean called "episodes," but she hadn't yet witnessed one.

John stared at her as though he didn't know her. Then he saw Percy and tried to appeal to him. "You tell her, Jack. You tell her that I don't want to go."

"Jack isn't here, Dad," Margaret reminded. "That is Percy, my son. Your grandson."

"Don't correct him. It doesn't help. It only upsets him more," Hilda cautioned.

John pleaded to Percy. "Help me, Jack."

"Stay out of this, Percy," his mother suggested. "Maybe just go into the other room. The both of you."

But Percy stayed, adamant to be a part of it all.

"It is okay, John," Hilda started, but John was spiralling out of control in his confusion and fear.

"Tell me what you want, Dad," Percy said to his grandfather. "Tell *Jack*, and we will see what we can do."

"Stop it, Percy!" Margaret was losing any control she had.

It was clear to everyone that John was sure that Percy was Jack. He was back in time and Jack was a teenager once again. The delicate paper of their life had been folded and twenty-odd years were caught in its crease. There was only then and now, joined together with the slightest of seams.

"I just want to be home." John sounded pathetic.

"And where is home?" Percy asked him.

John waved his arms, indicating the space around him.

"Okay. Let's see what *Jack* can do. Okay?" Percy emphasized the presumed name.

"I said stop it, Percy." Margaret tried one more time. "You aren't Jack!"

"Oh, fuck off, Mom!"

"Don't you start!"

There was something Hilda was missing. She had assumed that Jean wanted John home with her, and yet she seemed to have tried to put him into a home but couldn't. Why? She was his wife. She could force him into any situation because, at present, he wasn't of sound mind. What rights did John still have?

"Tell her, Mom. Just tell her."

Margaret glared at her son.

"Fine, I will, then!" Percy looked directly at his grandmother. "Jean wants to sell the house, put Grandpa into a home in Toronto, and move there. But she can't because she doesn't have power of care. Uncle Jack does. So now Jean wants to change that in his living will."

"That is *Grandma* Jean to you," Margaret reminded him.

"Oh, Jean's *not* my grandmother. *She* is!" He pointed to Hilda.

"What do you mean Jack has power of care? What does that even mean?" Hilda was completely confused.

"It means, Oma, that if someone has to make a decision to pull the plug, it's going to be Jack," Percy explained. "If Grandpa is put in a home, if he is put into long term care, all those decisions fall to Jack."

"Because Jack has always been both the most fair and the most logical. Does Jack know any of this? Surely he can't have power of anything without being told."

"It was a long time ago. Jack's probably forgotten," Margaret mumbled, seething. "Jack the most logical. Please. Always running around chasing his stories! He was always your favourite."

Hilda tried to get her head around it all. Jack, who had always seemed to be John's least favourite, was the one he ultimately chose to trust in the end. John was clearly afraid of being locked away, and yet her daughters were pushing to get him out of her care. Why?

There would be time to sort it out later when they would have to talk to lawyers to make sense of it all. But the immediate concern was to calm John. Hilda took his hand.

"Let's go into the living room, away from this perfume smell, and watch the kids open some presents, *ja*? Wouldn't that be better?"

"Just Jack and his sister. Not her!" he said, pointing at Margaret.

"You see, Mom? Do you really think you can manage him? He thinks my daughter is me, my son is Jack, and he doesn't even know who I am!"

"Why don't you have some leftovers in the kitchen, *Margie*? You must be hungry. Trust me, tomorrow he won't remember how upset he was today. There's just the memories of long ago and whatever is in the present. No yesterday, no tomorrow. It's not so bad."

It bothered Hilda that they wanted to put him into a home and that they also wanted to put her into a retirement residence. It seemed as though they were all to be locked up, jailed, for the crime of their failed marriage. Or perhaps it was for the crime of aging? The crime of going from being the caretakers to needing care. The crime of becoming inconvenient.

The phone rang a double ring, and Hilda knew it would be Jack with Christmas wishes for her. It was the one thing she had looked forward to all day.

"Merry Christmas, Mom!" Jack's voice rang out over the phone.

"Merry Christmas, sweetheart. Come home!"

NINETEEN

JACK HUNG UP THE PHONE, a wave a regret washing over him. He would have to go home. The situation with his father, fuelled by the pressure from his sisters, had only worsened. Why had he really stayed? He didn't really think they'd find Clara in Paris. He looked at the home Younis had opened up to him. A home, but not his home. Would he ever mark time somewhere, would he ever become part of a landscape the way his mother had? Even his mother's loss and sorrow seemed to dilute in the landscape she loved so well. Suddenly a wave of nostalgia washed over him. He imagined the feasts his mother always prepared, her big dining-room table that was open to anyone who showed up at her door, and the shared glances he would sometimes catch between his mother and Siegfried. He longed for the smell of roast goose, and the anticipation of his mother's homemade cakes: *Apfelkuchen. Pflaumenkuchen.*

"What is that? That isn't a turkey. Not even a goose!" He knew he sounded snippy the moment the words left his mouth.

"It's couscous. I've never made a turkey in my life! But if you want goose, I did get some goose liver pâté," Younis replied.

"They'll all be here soon. Do you think you have enough?" Jack asked.

"Enough to feed an army. Go look at the table! It's heaped with food."

Jack knew the effort was more for him than the guests. He wanted to apologize, to explain, but what was there to say?

The guests began to arrive as they were putting the last few dishes onto the table. Festive but casual was the theme. Bözsi entered first in what looked like a stage costume, all ruffles and bright colours. Blanca in tight white jeans, topped with a slouchy white cashmere sweater that fell off her pale, white shoulders. Then there was the Punk Baroness in her usual black leathers and bodice outfit; Esther, tasteful in her simple black dress with her double strand of pearls, and finally Friedrich, a man they did not know was coming, wearing typical Eurotrash chic — a black turtleneck sweater, a camel jacket, and dark red corduroy trousers, which he wore because he thought it looked festive *and* casual.

"Come in, come in!" Younis told them, taking their coats. "I hope everyone is hungry!"

The apartment smelled of Moroccan spice and savoury meat. Bözsi knew the aroma well. It catapulted her back to the night she crossed into North Africa. To a meal she had shared with Henri. The smell alone signalled new beginnings and new adventures for her.

"Where did you learn to cook couscous like that? I haven't tasted such good couscous since I was in Algiers!"

"I'm from Algiers! I left in 1991. Just before the civil war started."

"No!" Bözsi gasped. "I danced the cancan there for years! In the forties!"

"Oh, I don't believe you!" Younis goaded her. "The cancan? Really? Do you still know how?"

Bözsi got up and walked across the room. In no time, her skirts were lifted, not up to her knickers, but well above her bony knees, and her legs were kicking as high as she could. Younis clapped with delight. The others had all seen it before.

"Now special for you. A song!" And with that Bözsi surprised everyone by singing a love song, a song of yearning and lost love, love beyond the grave, and the hope of being reunited after death, in perfect Arabic. She kept glancing at Younis, just to be sure that she was impressing him. Esther stared at her sister, surprised once again. How many languages had she mastered? How many dances could she do? How many songs were in her head? And how many lovers had she really experienced? She couldn't help herself. She glanced at Friedrich. He caught her eye and smiled.

"Ah, Bözsi, you make me less homesick! That was beautiful. You can come here and sing any time!" Younis told her.

"Good," she agreed. "Now that I am moving to Paris, I will need a friend. Every mistress should have a best *homoerotic* friend to share her secrets with!"

"A mistress? You are having an affair with a married man? Well, I did that once, too. I hope yours will turn out better than mine did!" Younis grinned at her.

"Oh, we are so alike! We'll be best of friends!"

She was a clever cat, Esther thought, always landing on her feet. Able to create a new life without missing a beat and never cleaning up after herself. And what was Esther to do? Go back to the Bainbridge Avenue apartments, reeking of cabbage and rice and beans, alone? Live on her meagre old-age pension, making do, while her sister made new friends, ate out, and had a handsome, rich lover doting on her?

I did what was expected of me and lived a shadow of a life.

"Merry Christmas, everyone!" Jack called out, raising a glass. Maybe it wasn't his usual tradition. Maybe it was a change. Maybe it was exactly what he needed.

"Merry Christmas," they all responded back to him.

"May this be the last Christmas without my twin!" Blanca added.

TWENTY

ON THE DRIVE BACK TO Berlin, Martina drove a bit more reasonably, her foot not quite as heavy on the pedal. She knew that while her father did break the rules from time to time, he believed one should only do so when absolutely necessary. To him, getting home by nightfall was not absolutely necessary.

"I don't know why you didn't stay a bit longer," her father started. It was the second time he had brought it up.

"It was getting expensive. Besides, I have a business to run. The opera won't run itself!" Martina replied.

"Are you starting rehearsals soon?"

"At the end of the month. But there are pre-production things to consider. Casting, paperwork, hiring stagehands, set design. So much to do."

Friedrich leaned back in the bucket seat. He had turned on the seat warmers when they started the trip and now his bottom and back were well toasty. The warmth made him sleepy.

"And Jack flew to Canada and abandoned the cause?"

"He went back to help with his father. Alzheimer's, maybe. Or a stroke. It's not clear."

Martina stared at the road ahead, seeming to concentrate on her driving. All she really wanted was to race through the passing scenery.

"And how about you? Any New Year resolutions? Goals?" Martina asked him, redirecting the conversation.

Yes! He had goals, but the goals were those suited to a much younger man, a man whose days stretched out before him like the long highway they were on. A highway where there were unexpected turns, and the destination was always a bit further and never, in the end, quite what was imagined. He had started a new journey of sorts. A private journey. It began New Year's Eve, at the stroke of twelve. He had said, "Happy New Year, Esther," and then he took a risk and had kissed her, lightly, quickly, and benevolently. On her lips.

"Goals. No. I'm too old for such. I just live each day as it comes. At my age, that is all one can do. Goals are for you! For the young."

"I'm hardly young anymore, Papa." Martina laughed.

"Ach! You're a baby still!"

Martina smiled at her father. Nothing escaped her. She had caught him that night! They were at a restaurant for New Year's. A cozy place with great food, although not nearly as brilliant as the one they had tried on Christmas Eve. It was getting later and later, nearing the New Year moment. The countdown started. Ten-nine-eight-seven ... Younis and Jack reached out to hold hands. Six-five-four ... Martina reached for Blanca's hand. Three-two-one ... and as the Happy New Year cry went up, as Martina leaned over to kiss Blanca, she saw it happen. She saw her father lean over and kiss Esther. And then she looked away and kissed her own partner.

"You know the deal I made, right?" she asked him.

"No, what deal?"

"I told Blanca and Esther that they could stay in Paris, that I would pick up the hotel bill, provided that they return at the end of the month for rehearsals. Both of them. Whether they find Clara or not, that is the deal. They come home and sing."

Friedrich knew his daughter too well. Of course, she suspected that he was secretly smitten with Esther, that he had been since she played the piano at his house, but to insist that she do something with her opera company to keep her near him was something he would never have expected.

"Oh, and don't think I'm doing it for you. I saw that kiss on New Year's, Papa, but I had already asked Esther to sing before that. Nobody could sing the role of Hecuba like her. So much pent-up emotion. So much regret. You heard her."

"Indeed, I did."

Friedrich closed his eyes and relaxed into the warmth of the seats. The moment Martina thought he had drifted off, she pressed down hard on the gas to make up for lost time.

◆ ◆ ◆

The Fisher equation was written across the board. Younis usually didn't teach the Fisher equation, but he put it up there, in big chalk letters, hoping that any discussion may lead to clues.

"Let's talk about the i variable and the replacement value, should the i become changeable."

He looked at his class. Was there a face there, somewhere, with a look of recognition? Someone who had, perhaps, written it down before, on a piece of paper, the heavy-handed writing indenting on the envelope below a sheet of paper?

A young woman with short, dark hair, fringes falling into her kohl-rimmed eyes, shot her hand into the air with the gracelessness of a duck. *Ducks are not graceful*, he thought. *They are just greedy birds with their quacking, and comical with their waddling. Certainly not like swans. Long-necked swans, with their elegant wings. Swans who mate for life.* He thought of Jack. Hoped he would return to Paris soon. Tried to push any expectations from his mind.

"Yes?" he asked, pointing to her.

"Are we covering the Fisher equation in this class as well? Professor Forêt also touched upon it."

"We are covering variables and their use in probabilities. But tell me, what is your take on it? I'm sorry, what is your name?"

"Agathe," she replied. "Yes, well, I think it is most important for banking and finance. The markets are constantly misread and certainly cannot be predicted, but the Fisher equation is an equalizing …"

But Younis stopped listening because, from the corner of his eye, he saw a young man, a teenager only, pass by. The boy had that startling look of black features on unworldly chalk-white skin, and hair that seemed a bleached light red-blond. The boy glanced at him and Younis saw that his eyes were also pale, though not with the pinkish-purple quality that Blanca sometimes had. His eyes, though Younis only caught a brief glimpse of them, popped out with an intensity that could only be compared to the waters of Plage Kadous Heraoua where he swam as a child before everything changed. Clearly, the boy could be no more than sixteen. He was too young to be studying at the university, so why was he there?

Younis ran out of the class. There he was: the missing variable! The variable they were all looking for! Of course! And he had even said it to Jack, it didn't have to be someone studying the equation; it just had to be someone with access to the envelope. But why had he never noticed the albino boy before?

Younis yelled after him, but the boy didn't turn around. He quickened his pace. Younis also quickened his, following.

"Hey, hey! *Attends, attends!*" he called out.

The boy turned a corner. Younis hurried to catch up, but once he got to the end of that hall, the mystery boy was gone. He had vanished into thin air. Into the music department.

❖ ❖ ❖

Esther called down to room service and asked for a fresh pot of coffee with a side of croissants. They had only a week to ten days left. That was all Martina had agreed to pay. Ten days to find Clara.

"You know, Esther, I was surprised that you agreed to do the opera. I mean, if Bözsi had been asked, I could totally see her jumping at the opportunity. But you always seem to step back, to let her perform instead. You're a bit like Clara. She always preferred creating to performing."

"Well, I never had the chance to perform. I survived because I hid. Bözsi survived because she could do the cancan. Same circumstances, different survival techniques." Esther ran her fingers through her hair. A cut, a wash, a set was long overdue. She smiled at Blanca.

"Do you regret it?"

"What's to regret? I'm alive. But strangely, the hiding and the cancan worked equally well." She laughed.

"But after it was all over. You never thought about performing. I mean all those —"

"No. I never did," Esther cut her off.

"So, why now?"

"Because I made a deal with Martina. I could not afford to stay here longer, especially as Bözsi is now out of the picture, along with her generous purse. So, I agreed to her terms, which were for me to sing. You see, I, too, am determined to find Clara."

Blanca knew that Esther had always watched out for them. A fairy godmother who was present when their own mother was not. Even before their mother had walked into the lake to drown herself, Esther was there giving advice, instructing them and loving them. Without Esther, there would have been no music, no manners, and no escape from their past.

When there was a knock on the door, the women both assumed it was room service. Blanca answered, padding quietly across the floor in her bare feet.

"Come in," she said even before the door was open.

It was not coffee and croissants, but rather Younis, out of breath and very excited.

"I have news. There is a boy, about fifteen or sixteen, who has been sneaking into the music lectures at the university. He is from South Africa and he has albinism! I think he may be the glue that holds it all together!"

"A boy from Africa?" Blanca repeated, confused. There had never been a boy in any of her dreams.

"Yes! And I think his father might work as a janitor at the university!"

"I don't understand," Esther stated. "What has this to do with Clara?"

"Well, there is the fact that Clara went missing in South Africa, right?" Younis's voice was full of hope.

"Just because the boy has albinism doesn't mean he is connected to Clara," Esther added with hesitation. Mustn't get her hopes too high. Be wary.

"Don't you see? He is the missing variable! Why was the envelope mailed from here and not South Africa? Why an economics equation? Why a non-registered student in the music department? Get all the variables right and you solve the equation! God, I wish Jack were here!"

Blanca and Esther glanced at each other, knowing that his last sentence had slipped out, unguarded.

"Well, Mr. Sleuth, what is our next move?" Esther asked, feeling that the ticking of time may have slowed just a little.

♦ ♦ ♦

"I'm not going to turn him in, so don't even ask me. I know that it's against university policy, but what chance does he have in life? He has a gift. A gift of music! So, I turn a blind eye." Madame Arcand was very resolute. She would neither give up the boy's name nor allude to anything more than the fact that his father was a janitor.

"How long has his father worked here? You might as well tell me as it's something I can easily find out," Younis pressed.

"His uncle, not his father," Madame Arcand corrected. "He began last term. At least, that is when I started to see the boy and that's when I became aware of his uncle, so he might have worked here longer. Look, I cannot tell you anything else. Please do not bother them." Madame Arcand stood in order to let Younis know that the conversation had ended. "*Bon*, I have a class in twenty minutes, so I must prepare."

"One more thing. Do you think he has a natural talent, or is it something he has learned?"

Madame Arcand laughed. It was only then that Younis noticed that her front teeth crossed a little, an imperfection which only added charm to her bright and curious face. *Yes*, he thought, *there is no guile and no deception here. Only the face of a woman attempting to do the right thing with whatever information she might have.*

"He was trained. He has basic music theory, nothing too advanced. He does have an understanding of composition and drama. Whoever taught him focused on harmony and colour, if that makes sense. He was given a natural voice, although I suppose that he comes from a culture that sings. With Africans, music imbues every part of their lives, from morning to night, from birth until death. Most of us in the West think of music as something to listen to, to see, and for those few, to perform. We *learn* music, we do not *live* music — not in the same way. Oh, I am going on too much." She stopped herself and fidgeted. Why was she telling him about African music? He was from Africa; she wasn't. She knew there was nothing more irritating than someone explaining a person's culture to him. Younis came from Africa, but from the north. He was an economics professor. Tenured. Her knowledge of him began and ended there.

"No, please, continue. I am fascinated. One cannot think of numbers all day long, although, you know, there is a relationship between music and numbers."

Madame Arcand felt a flush in her face. Surely, he wasn't flirting. She had heard rumours. No, he couldn't be flirting with her. Charm, that's all it was.

"I think of the South Africans the way I think of the Corsicans. Have you ever noticed how all the Corsicans can sing? Although I should be careful. Even giving a compliment to a group of people can get you into trouble these days. But, between you and me, some cultures appreciate a musical life more than others. It's part of their everyday. Their workday, if you will. Like the Welsh, you know? Every mining town in Wales seems to have a great choir." She paused, regarded Younis. Was he following her drift? "Well, he came from that type of culture. A musical culture. But whoever taught him was likely Eurocentric."

"Eurocentric? Why would you say that?"

"I saw something he wrote. It was very interesting because the one culture in this opera — it's about the Greeks and Spartans — all emphasize the downbeat when they sing, which is predominantly favoured in European and Western music. The Trojans, on the other hand, sing their arias with an emphasis on the upbeat, which is more African. The other interesting thing is that there's a constant rhythm throughout. It is solid, but not like Eastern Africans. The rhythms he uses are like waves in an ocean. That is very Zulu." Madame Arcand smiled as she finished her sentence. Did the curious man in front of her know the extent of what it meant to be a musicologist? To have a Ph.D. in music with a minor in cultural studies? Too often, she thought, the music department was not taken as seriously as the math and science departments.

"Your knowledge is immense, Madame. Please continue. You were mentioning an opera he wrote?" Younis encouraged her. He had heard much about the opera from Esther, Blanca, and Martina, but he felt that an outside perspective would be illuminating. Besides, Madame Arcand seemed to contradict the belief that Clara had written the opera and seemed to think that it was the work of the unregistered student. "The Trojans sing upbeat and the Greeks downbeat, you were saying?"

"Yes. With one exception. The main character, Helen. Hers is the only voice that straddles both styles. Well, that makes sense, doesn't it? She's between two worlds, isn't she? So she sings as both a Spartan and a Trojan. This tells me that even if she is in one place her soul is in another. Perhaps like you? You are here in Paris, you have a life here, but you are still Algerian in your soul. Am I right in my presumption?"

Madame Arcand paused as though assessing him, watching for a reaction. When none came, she glanced at her watch, although she didn't really look at the time. It was a gesture to indicate that Younis should leave. "Please, promise to leave the boy alone. I hope I can trust you."

Younis nodded in agreement. He would not be the one to approach the boy. He could promise that much.

"By the way, I met someone who runs a company called the Punkarie in Berlin. Have you heard of them?"

Madame Arcand looked at Younis with doubt and suspicion.

"I think it is time for you to go." She crossed her arms, then turned away to look at the chalkboard.

Now it was Younis's turn to laugh.

"You did it. You mailed the envelope. You sent them the opera. Didn't you?"

◆ ◆ ◆

It was a simple enough plan. And possibly all they could do. Blanca and Esther would go to the university and wait outside the music department daily. Eventually, the boy would show up.

"This is the sort of thing that Bözsi would do so well. You know I now believe she really was a spy after all!"

"Oh, I don't know, Esther. I think you have been discovering new talents in yourself since you got here!" Blanca began to apply her signature red lipstick. Esther watched, wondering if she would keep the shade into her twilight years, reapplying it the way Bözsi did with her orange shade of lipstick. She remembered when the twins started to wear lipstick. How they shocked, at fourteen, with that bright-red smear across their lips, while all the rest remained bleach-white — no blush, no mascara, no eyeliner.

"What if it is all unrelated? How will you behave toward the boy then?" Esther asked Blanca.

"Well, the music professor said that he is talented and that music is his only hope in life. I remember being that age and music was my only hope. So, either way, it's good that we meet him. Perhaps I can do for him what you did for us."

Esther put her arms around Blanca. "Have I ever told you how proud I am of you?"

Blanca laughed. "Once or twice!"

◆ ◆ ◆

While Esther and Blanca waited at the doors of the music department, Younis went to the administration office to ask for a janitor to come to clean his lecture room.

"It is quite awful," he complained. "Someone in the previous class must have been ill or hungover. The smell is extreme. I need to have the vomit cleaned right away. It is causing a huge stench."

Then he waited. He knew that there was a possibility that someone else from the staff could come to clean it up, but he was willing to wager that the newest man, and likely a foreigner, would be sent because the worst jobs are given to the newest workers.

"*Excusez-moi*, monsieur," a rich voice spoke loudly from the back of the lecture room. Younis heard the accent and the tone and knew that he had played it well.

"Ah, yes. You took so long that I cleaned it myself," Younis addressed him in English.

"I am very sorry, sir. I came as soon as I was told. I did not dilly-dally."

"I suppose then that you best stay here for a little while so you don't get into trouble. How long would it usually take to clean it all up? Fifteen or twenty minutes? Perfect! I don't have a class for half an hour. Come sit down. Do you drink tea?"

The man looked confused, but his face hinted that he was afraid of losing his job. He came forward, nodded, and sat.

"Milk and sugar?" Younis inquired.

"Yes, please. If I could partake in three spoonfuls of sugar."

"Three!" Younis exclaimed.

He poured out two teas from his Thermos and placed them in front of him.

"We only have about twenty minutes, so let's be frank. I will tell you what I know and you fill in the gaps. Okay?"

The man nodded. Younis noticed how tired he looked for someone not yet forty. It seemed that life had taken a bite out of him and then swallowed what it took with a great gulp.

"I know your nephew has albinism. I also know that he has musical ability. He has been sneaking into class, but he is not registered at the university."

The man became agitated. He shook his head as if denying it, but not a word came from his mouth.

"I think that is fine. I will not get him into trouble. But he had an opera that was written down. Did he write the opera?"

He didn't speak. He shook his head no. His eyes were filled with tears and fear.

"Who wrote it, and how did you get it?"

"I know nothing about an opera. My boy just likes music, and he is bored staying home!"

"You best come with me."

By the time they got to the music department, neither Blanca nor Esther were where they were told to sit and wait. It seemed that the plan had changed. *Ah yes, there is always the hidden variable to consider.* In this case it was that the musical African boy did not come to the university that day. So while Esther and Blanca sat waiting for him, Madame Arcand had turned the corner and seen the pair of them. By the time Younis and the janitor got to the music department, Blanca and Esther were in a rehearsal room with Madame Arcand, performing.

"I am Younis, by the way. Your name is?" he inquired.

"Musa."

Younis and Musa watched from the door. Esther was playing "Dido's Lament" by Purcell, an aria that Esther and Blanca had often worked on when the twins were young and yearning for lyrics in English. Neither Younis nor Musa were familiar with the aria. They stood frozen, listening. Musa put his hands to his face. He was crying.

"What is wrong?" Younis asked him.

"It is a ghost of what could have been, if only. You have bent time! You are not a teacher. You are a magic user. A *sangoma*!" He blurted out.

"Why? Why do you say that?"

"Because there stands my wife. She sounds like her. She looks like her. She is well. She is whole. My wife, I do love her. I love her to the heavens and the stars, but she is broken!" he cried. "She was broken when I found her. I did not break her! I didn't do it! I love her. What have you done? What magic is this?"

Blanca finished the last lines, closing her eyes with the final words: "Remember me." Silence. Then there was just the sound of Esther closing the piano and Musa's footsteps as he ran away, down the hall.

◆ ◆ ◆

Madame Arcand was a collector of secrets. Her bright and open face seemed to urge even strangers to reveal their most intimate of details, which she held on to as though they were valuable pieces each in themselves, and all the more valuable as a collection. She knew who was sleeping with whom at the university, who had not bothered to properly grade papers, and who was struggling with personal matters, like troubled offspring and unavoidable divorces. She was told secrets without anyone ever asking her about her personal life, so she could travel the university corridors as an enigma. The only person she knew little about was Younis. Only Younis seemed more secretive than she. So it was with some irony that she proceeded to share what she knew.

"Musa had run from South Africa. The boy, Themba is his name, is his nephew but he thinks of him as his son. Themba's real father was the headman of the village, like a chief in a way. Now, he was under pressure to cast him out due to his albinism. You know that albinism is much more common in Africa, right?" Here she glanced at Blanca.

"Yes. I know. Go on." Blanca didn't look at her as she answered. She was far, far away, imagining the village, the everyday life there, and her sister's place somewhere that seemed so very different to everything she knew.

"Well, from what I know, Musa agreed to take him, as an infant, into his home and to raise him, even though he was a single man at the time. The boy was Musa's son in deed and in act, but not in any official or legal way. When it became clear that it was becoming more and more dangerous for albinos in Africa, Musa's brother sold half of his cattle in order to send both his brother and son away. Musa left the world he knew and his place in the village for the sake of the boy. And he took this menial job here."

"But why Paris?" Esther's asked. "Surely another town or village ..."

"No. He needed to go far. There was a cousin, or a second cousin, in Paris, so they came here illegally. Musa now lives in this city, but it wears him down. He is a rural man. But what can he do? He comes to the university, he cleans, and he goes home. This is his life. But he does that to protect the boy. It is horrible what happens to albinos in some places. Unspeakable." Madame Arcand finished the story. Relaying just the facts, as Madame Arcand understood them.

Blanca stared off. What horrendous things had her sister endured? What torture had she survived? Pieces of her chopped off and sold for the purposes of potions and magical balms. She started to gag. She could feel the bitter taste of her morning coffee raising into her throat.

"Why would anyone hurt people just because of their albinism?" Esther whispered.

Madame Arcand shrugged. "There is a lot of money to be made. Anyone who puts money above human life is capable of horrendous acts. I am sorry to say that albinos are seen as spirits, like genies by some. Some people think they are already the walking dead, zombies. Or that they don't have souls, and don't really feel pain. Look at movies and literature! Albinos are almost always seen as villains and evil-doers. Sadly, they are not considered human by some people."

Nor were Jews considered human, Esther thought to herself. And so, you ran, you hid, you tried to fit in.

Hated for being gay in Algeria, hated for being Algerian in France, Younis thought to himself. He could have been imprisoned, fined for being different. And so, you ran, you hid, you tried to fit in.

"You sent the opera, though ..." Blanca urged.

"Themba gave it to me. I just assumed it was his. I asked him to sing some of it. He was magical. Then he asked if I knew of a company in Germany. He wanted to know if there was one that ever had an albino opera singer. In Berlin. He was very specific. So, I did what I could. I went on to the internet and found the Punkarie. I showed it to him, and when he saw the photo of you, Blanca, he got all excited. So, I agreed to mail it for him. I asked if he had an envelope. He said no. I didn't have one the right size, so I sent him off to find one."

"Did he find one?" Younis asked.

"Sure! Someone in the math department had an extra one. A student. A punk-looking girl. Although now I think they call themselves emos or goths."

It was a small variable he had missed. His own student, studying the Fisher equation in another class, bored in his class because she had already learned about it. Agathe, she was the one who had provided the envelope. Wasn't she always jotting things down? Always mounds of paper about her. A young woman who was seemingly scattered but in possession of an analytical mind. How did he miss that?

"And did he or Musa ever mention a woman? An albino woman?" Esther asked.

"They never did. I knew nothing about a wife until Musa had that meltdown." She looked at Blanca. "He seemed to think you were her."

"Obviously you were never a fan of Der Oper Punkarie. If you had been, you would have known that I have an identical twin. One that has been missing. One that was stolen in an airport in South Africa and never seen again."

Madame Arcand stared in disbelief. There was the very story, validated in the opera her student had given to her. Twin girls. One abducted and missing. Helen and Clytemnestra. Clara and Blanca. Not a work of the boy's imagination after all. The opera was a creative memoir of sorts, and the boy, Themba, was merely the sweet-voiced messenger. Hermes in myth.

"What does his name mean? In Zulu, that is," Blanca asked. "Any idea?"

"Themba? I believe it means 'hope' in Zulu. It means to be in the possession of hope."

"Themba," Blanca whispered, knowing that *themba* was all she possessed at that moment.

TWENTY-ONE

ALTHOUGH JACK WAS, IN MANY ways, just like his mother, the comparison ended when it came to his relationship with animals. Whereas Hilda would go in close to the large beasts, sometimes even blowing into the nostrils of a cow or a horse, Jack always gave a wide berth. Now he wondered if that caution, like so many, was a result of the eye he had lost in his childhood. But hadn't he overcome that? Hadn't he put himself into war zones just for a story?

"You see that? Their udders are all healed from my concoction. Their nipples are as good as new now!"

"Oh, if I had only brought my camera. I'm sure that could make the front page of a national paper!" he teased his mother.

"So, what will we do about your father? I thought it was a good time to talk here in the barn. I told Karl to make us tea, so we have some privacy."

"He sure does trust you with his livestock."

"*Ja*, well. We are all old girls together." She patted the black-and-white cow on her backside. "Isn't that right, Elsie? Honestly, Jack, I would come and help Karl every day, but I have to watch your father."

"Mom," Jack sighed, "you always take care of everyone else. Maybe we should talk about what *you* want."

"Well, I want to help your sisters. You know, with some money put away for their kids to go to university. I want you to be settled. To find love again. And your father, I want him …"

Jack shook his head.

"No, no, no!" He held up his hand. "What do *you* want for *yourself*?"

It was such a strange question. She knew that to be free of her many worries would be the thing she wanted most, but how to say that without stating all the concerns she had for other people?

"I don't know, Jack. I don't know what I want beyond a nice garden, a walk by the lake, and a good cup of coffee with a piece of cake. With fresh cream!" She laughed. "And maybe to share those things with someone again."

She felt her heart constrict. Those were her best days. The days where the worry was shared and diluted with someone she loved, when moment to moment the smallest of things held the greatest importance. Those days had unfurled as they would, without expectation and only gentle surprises. The days when the old and the familiar seemed new every day, simply because they were shared.

"And do you want Dad there with you because you want someone to share your life with?" Jack asked.

"No. As lovely as it is to share some of my day with someone else, the truth is that he just isn't Siegfried." Hilda realized her words were true. She did like the shared moments, but they were also lacking because of all the missing pieces.

"I just know that your father is happy — well, happier — there at my farmhouse. And I think that maybe he doesn't have a lot of time left to be happy. Keep that in mind when you talk to the lawyer tomorrow."

Hilda gave the cows a final pat.

♦ ♦ ♦

It was all written down and very clear. Jack had been named both John's power of care in the living will and the executor of John's will. How the rest was to be divvied up was not divulged because John was still alive, although the lawyer offered to mail him a copy, as he was also named the executor.

"But he is not of sound mind, so surely naming Jack as power of care should have no relevance," Jean refuted, keeping a calm and friendly tone.

"Quite the contrary," the lawyer replied. She was a plain-speaking, salt-of-the-earth older woman, the sort who likely wore pantsuits before anyone else had even heard of them. A no-makeup, hair-dye-is-for-flakes, and why-wear-anything-but-comfortable-shoes sort of woman. Her tone and manner of explanation were as straightforward and simple as her appearance.

"But surely in his condition ... he has a brain tumour, and it is causing symptoms similar to Alzheimer's. He was probably confused when he made that will!" Jean continued.

It was the first that Jack had heard of a brain tumour. All he had heard were the words *forgetful, dementia, Alzheimer's, stroke*. Was Jean lying?

"You see," the lawyer, Ms. Webber, continued, "your husband made these wills shortly after you married. He was quite well then. Completely of the right mind. They have been adjusted with the births of your children. While you have power of attorney now, Jack has been granted power of care. This has been constant throughout the past ten years. However, he is also the executor of the will, which will give him power over John's share of the estate once John dies. Although you will be inheriting the house as his spouse."

"What am I supposed to do, then?" Jean questioned, her voice small and overwhelmed.

"Nothing. You don't have to worry. It isn't up to you, so don't fret. You really do not have a say. Of course, if you cannot afford the house without him contributing, you could file a request to sell it ..."

"The thing is," Jack began, "it is difficult for me to be his power of *anything* because I travel so much. My work, you see ..."

"I'm his wife. It should be me!"

"Well, of course, you feel that way. But what do you think, Jack?" The sensible lawyer looked squarely at Jack.

Jack hated the responsibility; it tied him down. It was clear that although his father had preferred his sisters from start to finish, he did not trust them. They could pull the plug too early. They could put him into a home.

"I don't mind him moving back in with Jean. But I will not allow him to be put into a care facility. Nor will I allow a forced sale as long as my father is alive. So I'll stay and see this through."

Ms. Webber gulped at her cold coffee, a Tim Hortons large, likely a double-double, Jack guessed. Jack glanced over at Jean. He felt for her. She had clearly loved his father over the years and yet something had told his father not to trust her. She was weak. Too easily influenced by his sisters. *They are Regan and Goneril*, he thought. *And I am the misaligned Cordelia.* If there was any chance of them getting their hands on a part of his estate, they would rally together and bully Jean into having him committed to a care facility, and then they would suggest that she sell the house.

Jean stood up and pulled her sweater over her body, smoothing it over her girth.

"I think I'll go now," she said. "And for your information, he should *already* be in a home. He needs proper care. If properly trained people looked after him, then we could all visit him without the stress of caring for him. It would be better for him and better for all of us. We could be family instead of caretakers. Think about that!"

Jack said nothing. He stared at the bad, fake wood panelling, the cheap bookcases filled with leather-bound law books, the seventies brownish-orange shag carpeting, and the one good piece of furniture, an Arts-and-Crafts-style coffee table that was covered in papers but also had a sculpture of the lady with the scales of justice in her hand. Ms. Webber caught him looking at the sculpture, a wry grin on his face. The scales were completely uneven.

"I try to correct them daily, but they always slip. It's probably more truthful that way."

"It probably is," Jack agreed. He liked her.

"Now, my suggestion is that you go and catch up to her. Smooth things over. It's always a good idea to make it better before the loved one actually dies, because then all hell breaks loose. Always does." Ms. Webber got up and adjusted the scales, but as soon as she turned her back, they slipped again.

Jack got to the door and turned back with one last question.

"Did you know anything about a tumour?" he asked her.

"I'm his lawyer, not his doctor. But do you want some off-the-record advice?"

Jack nodded.

"It sounds to me like there isn't a lot of time. You seem to want to make everyone happy, but as the power of care, that's not your job. Your job is to look after your dad's interests only in his final days. So where does your father want to be? On his good days, when he's lucid, what does he want then? Do you know?"

"I believe I do."

"Then do exactly that. You don't control the situation, Jack. You're supposed to facilitate his wishes only."

Jack sighed. He knew that neither his father's current wife nor his father's ex-wife would be happy with his decision.

◆ ◆ ◆

It was early evening when Jack returned from meetings with John's lawyer and his doctor, but because the days were still shortened, it felt much later. The sun was barely skimming the earth, and already the moon was making its ascent into the cold sky. There was a crispness all around him. The clarity of cold.

No matter how many times Jack turned over the information he had collected that day, he could clearly see the only path to follow. His father's memory would not be restored. His dementia was caused by his brain tumours, fast-growing gliomas in the sticky cells surrounding his nerve cells. They were prone to bleeding; his father already had had one hemorrhagic stroke three months earlier. The bitter fact remained that once a person with a brain tumour suffered a first major stroke, a sudden second stroke was probable. And fatal. His father was a ticking bomb.

Jack knew that the easiest choice for everyone would be to have his father placed in a home. That round-the-clock care in a facility would be preferable because his needs would intensify day by day. The amount of extra work Hilda had to do was already an unfair burden on her. Jean and his sisters were only being practical in their desires to settle him somewhere where his needs could be met daily. But Jack knew that wasn't the right path. The only time his father seemed at ease was when he was sitting in the kitchen, looking out the window, a cup of coffee in his hands. Being named power of care was a burden. But Jack also knew that it was a privilege, and that he was named because his father knew he was the only one who would not choose convenience over humanity.

Jack looked at the old farmhouse, with the lights from the living room and kitchen shining through the windows. He saw the shape of his mother as she moved from the stove to the sink. She would just be putting out an evening meal. She understood routine and the comfort it held to a man slowly losing his mind.

Before he made the move to go inside, he took out his flip phone. What time would it be in France now? Eleven, no, midnight. And a school night. He hesitated, then dialled.

"*Oui?*"

To Jack, the voice seemed a lifetime and a world away. How was it that just a week ago he was in Paris, having an affair, searching for a lost friend, and celebrating Christmas? It seemed as though it had been a hallucination, and the sound of Younis's voice only underlined how strange it all was. How could he ever describe any of it? The farmer's cows with their chapped teats, the intense cold of a real winter, and mostly his father's slipping memory.

"Hi. It's me, Jack."

"I know. You will be very proud of me. We have located Clara. She is here, in Paris, after all! And tomorrow Blanca will see her for the first time. Oh, I wish you were here, Jack!"

Jack took a sharp breath, and because the car had already started to cool, he could feel the stab of cold in his lungs. Clara. Found. After all these years. He wanted to know everything, but as he watched his mother helping his father to his feet, he suppressed his curiosity.

"I'm needed here. I won't be back for a while."

Younis said nothing. The phone was quiet as they racked up their long-distance charges.

"But ... I found Clara," he repeated. "We found Clara!"

"Thank you. That is fantastic. I have to go."

TWENTY-TWO

IT WAS NOT A LONG journey from Paris to Nanterre. Even by metro or bus, it was not that far. A mere eleven minutes, but that ride brought you from one world into another. Apartment buildings, built as machines for living, without decoration or continuity for architecture of the past, rose up, incongruous with the architecture of downtown Paris. Blanca stood in front of one such building, concrete, functional, and ugly. But it was the shape of the windows that bothered her. Circles, small in contrast to the cold exterior walls, looked uninviting. Blanca wondered how anyone could put plants or knick-knacks onto round window ledges.

Inside one of the apartments was her sister. Her twin. Blanca had come alone for the first visit. They had decided not to surprise Clara. She was vulnerable, unsure of her memories, and confused as to her whereabouts. Musa had said so. Now, as Blanca stood there, she wondered if it was Clara who needed to be prepared or if she was the one in need of preparation.

Blanca found the intercom, pressed the button, and waited. She felt herself shivering but wasn't sure if it was the chill in the air or her excitement. She was hesitant, wishing that she hadn't agreed to come alone. She thought that having Jack or Esther with her would have been better. Or Martina. Martina would be nudging her now, telling her to go on, go in, go upstairs. *This is what you wanted.*

The buzzer sounded, and she pulled at the door. Inside, the hallway was functional. There was a lack of walls, in favour of pillars. She took the elevator to the third floor.

Blanca ran through her head how she would walk to the door, bravely knock, and then walk in without expectation. As the elevator doors opened, as she stepped out, she heard an apartment door open and then the sound of running feet. She expected that it would be Clara, arms open, but instead it was a tall boy of about sixteen. Pale skin, African features, and hair in tight curls, cut close to his head. Pale eyes — pond-greenish-blue and see-through. Blanca assumed it was Musa's nephew.

"Come, come!" he said to her, hand out. "You are the angel, the *ingelosi*, I have prayed for. You are the well half of my *umama*."

"*Umama*?" Blanca asked.

"My spiritual mother. The mother who came from the heavens to save me."

"Will you take me to her?"

Blanca tried to remember his name, but there had been so many developments and so much confusion that it slipped from her memory. He was handsome, and confident, that much she could see. And albino.

The young man led the way down the hall into the apartment. There appeared to be only one bedroom, where Themba slept, while Musa and Clara slept in the small living room. It was clean but utilitarian. A place to sleep and eat, but nothing about it said *home*. If it was a machine for living, Blanca wondered who would want to live there.

"She is in the wash closet," Musa informed her. "She will be out in a minute. She just wants to adjust her eye patch."

Eye patch. Why an eye patch? Surely her sister had not lost an eye.

"What else? What else has been taken? I need to know."

"Two fingers on one hand. One on the other. She still has her thumbs," Musa informed her.

"Then she can't play the piano anymore!" Blanca realized how foolish that sounded the moment she spoke the words; how trivial it was when her sister's life had been entirely in jeopardy.

"Oh, she can!" Themba exclaimed. "It is quite something to see!"

"She has adjusted," Musa said, speaking over Themba.

Blanca sat on a simple chair. There was no sofa. To the modern functional movement, chairs were architecture and sofas were bourgeois.

And then she remembered.

"Themba, that is your name, right?"

The boy nodded. He was innocent, although he had lived his life hiding in shadows.

"Themba, I hear you can sing."

"Yes, but *Umama* taught me all your songs."

"My songs?" she asked.

"Opera! She taught me opera!"

Blanca fidgeted. What was taking Clara so long? She had waited eight years, she had managed to count the seconds, the minutes, the days, but this final waiting was too much.

"I love opera. That is why I took her manuscript and sent it to you."

"How did you know where to send it?" Blanca asked him.

"*Umama* used to tell me stories about another life. A magical life that she thought she had dreamed. But she always described the same place. Always said Berlin. So, I told Madame Arcand, and she figured it out on the internet."

"I see. So, you went behind my sister's back?" Blanca questioned him.

"Forgive me. I had to know if her stories were true. And I just wanted so badly to be part of that magical world."

"What do you mean, a magical world?" Clearly there was no benign magic in a world where a woman could be taken away. Stolen. But weren't there stories about fairies stealing human children? Perhaps the magical world was a world to be feared.

"The world of music, on a stage, where stories become real!" Themba answered.

"Well, maybe you could sing for me now. To help pass the time," Blanca suggested.

"Okay I know one I can sing."

Blanca nodded and encouraged him with a smile but expected nothing. When Themba started with those only too familiar first notes of "Nessun Dorma," Blanca was taken aback. She was not prepared for the force of his voice. She assumed there might be some musicality and a pleasant sound, but the power of his voice astounded her. He was not a boy of girth. He looked frail, though tall. And in no way a powerhouse. As his voice moved through the room, filling every corner, Blanca could feel the notes, the vibration of voice, wrapping around her. And it was in the atmosphere of his music that Clara entered the room. Bone thin. Tired. Nervous. And slightly pregnant, perhaps. Blanca went to her, took her face in her hands, looked at the scars that ran from her cheekbone to her lip.

"It's frightful, I know," Clara said, her voice shaking. "*I'm* frightful."

All Blanca could think was, *What have they done to you?* She wanted to scream and swear. She wanted to hurt someone the way her sister had been hurt, but instead, she said, "Oh, Clara, you are still as beautiful as ever. Still my beautiful sister."

Themba stopped singing mid-phrase. He and Musa watched in amazement as a reflection of what seemed to be the same woman embraced tightly. Two of the same woman, one who had been distorted on the other side of the looking glass.

♦ ♦ ♦

By the time Blanca returned to the hotel, Esther was sound asleep. She tiptoed quietly around the room, leaving the lights off. She was sure that the excitement in her heart would wake the entire city, and yet the world slept on. Only when she was alone in the bathroom did she turn on the light, her eyes blinking with the sudden brightness. Once they adjusted, she looked in the mirror. How many times had she done that, looked at her own reflection and imagined it was her sister, that she could speak to her through the looking glass?

Oh, but today, she had spoken to her sister, had embraced her, had listened to the snapshots of the missing eight years. She needed to share her news. It was far too late to call Gareth, but she was bursting inside to talk to Iris, to tell her. Even Martina, the night owl, would be asleep now. If she could stay awake, then it would only be another few hours till they were all up and ready to start a brand-new day. A brand-new day! That is what it was.

Jack! He was the perfect person to call! It was five or six hours earlier in Ontario. Blanca could never remember which it was. That fall-back, spring-ahead custom always made it confusing for her. Blanca dragged the hotel telephone into the bathroom. She didn't have Hilda's home line number anywhere, so she called Jack's cellphone. She assumed it must be between eight and nine there, still early enough not to disturb.

"Hello?"

"Jack! It's Blanca. I've just come back from seeing Clara. Oh, Jack, I hugged her!"

"Oh my God. It's real. It's true. She's alive."

"She is! Oh Jack, she is alive. And I feel whole again!"

"And what about Iris?"

The phone was quiet. Jack wasn't sure if it was Blanca who was quiet or if it was the connection.

"Iris," he repeated. "She will need answers. Like why did her mother stay away from her? Why didn't she come back?"

"We all need answers, Jack. I tried to find out what I could, but some questions seemed to put her into a state of shock. PTSD, I guess."

"Of course. But Iris needs those answers. Her mental health is also at issue. Tell me what you know."

"Well, she was held prisoner for years. Tortured …"

"… tortured?"

Blanca spoke quickly (aware of long-distance charges) and quietly (so as to not wake Esther), which made it difficult for Jack to understand her entirely. What he did learn was that Gareth would have to make Clara an artificial eye as hers had been cut from her head; they would need to speak to Gareth about them divorcing so that Musa and Clara could properly marry, as quickly as possible, so that the union would be acknowledged by European and Canadian law; that the boy, Themba, could sing like Pavarotti, and that they would have to figure out how to best help him as well.

"And Clara? Does she want to return to the opera company? Try to resume the life she once had?"

"It is hard to know. She is so self-conscious about her injuries. I mean, once she has a new eye maybe it will be better. But she is very skittish and nervous. Her husband is a farmer. That's what he loves most. It would be great if he could get some work on a farm, but where in Germany?"

"Perhaps not in Germany."

"Where, then?" Blanca asked sleepily. The day's excitement was wearing off, and fatigue was finally taking over her body.

"I may have a solution. Let's talk tomorrow."

Jack shut off his phone and went into the kitchen where his parents were enjoying a last cup of chamomile tea before bedtime.

"Mom?" Jack started. "They found Clara."

"Really? They did?

"They did."

"Where was she?"

"They found her in Paris."

"What was she doing in Paris?" Hilda questioned.

"I don't know. Hiding, perhaps. Blanca said she was tortured and disfigured. I suspect that she didn't know what she was doing in Paris, either."

"Why didn't she reach out?" asked Hilda, astonished. "Why didn't she come back for her daughter?"

"I don't know yet. It's odd. Maybe she couldn't. We found her and it is still a complete mystery." Jack smiled at his mother. "Oh, and I think Karl might be able to keep his farm."

◆ ◆ ◆

It was still very early. Martina hadn't yet heard from Blanca, so she busied herself with the needed preparations for the upcoming casting for the supporting roles. Work had always been her antidote to worry. By 8:00 a.m., Martina had yellow sticky notes all over the music manuscript. Some were just marked places that proved more challenging in the staging, others suggested casting, and some were ideas about the sets and costuming. The opera might be *The Lost Queen: The True Abduction of Helen*, but Martina could see no reason why the visuals had to only reflect Ancient Greece. Her production would be more universal, modern. It would, as usual, have elements of the present state of the world, reflected in the story of the ancient world. It would be an opera of endings, of war, and of change. One society destroyed, heroes dead for no good reason, and then, from the ashes of Troy, Rome is born when Aeneas, the only Trojan hero to escape the fires and destruction, leaves with the sacred statues of Troy. Aeneas represents the hope for the future. He is the phoenix rising from the ashes of destruction, destined to create a new version of Troy, in a new land. Why hadn't she paid closer attention to that detail? And who would possibly play the role of Aeneas?

Martina called her father to pick his brains about the opera yet again. He told her that Aeneas's character is often described as brave and pious, but his physical attributes, beyond being strong and tall, have always been a mystery.

"Perhaps this is because he was a demigod, like Helen. But in his case, his divine parent was Aphrodite, goddess of love. He would have to be beautiful. All children of gods are beautiful!"

"Really, Papa? I guess that Mama was a goddess, then, and you forgot to tell me!" she teased.

"Of course your mother was a goddess. I thought you already knew that. And you look just like her."

"Do you miss her?"

"Yes, you know I do. But the dog barks, and the caravan moves on. Perhaps it is time for me to come out of isolation. Anyhow, you didn't call to talk about me." Friedrich sighed. He imagined that he could hear the sigh echo in the emptiness of his large house.

"So, now, about Aeneas," he continued. "Virgil suggests that he is very pale — bone-white — with light eyes and light-reddish or auburn hair," Friedrich informed her.

"His physicality is of no importance. What is important is that this minor character in the opera must be charismatic enough that the audience knows he is the promise of new hope. Someone capable of believing there is a great future even though he has nothing left. Someone young and brave enough to go to the strange new land, not knowing what is in store for him. Where will I find that performer? Oh, and he must be a tenor." Martina replied.

Martina needed a young man with a big voice. A huge talent who would agree to play a small role. As Martina sorted through it all, organizing her thoughts and ideas, she became more and more convinced that her father would have to come aboard as a consultant. He understood every detail of classical mythology. She would just have to remind him, from time to time, that it was still her company and she was the boss!

"Oh, Papa, that is someone beeping in. I have to get the other line. Talk soon. *Tschuss!*"

She knew it had to be Blanca. She couldn't answer quick enough.

"Have you called Gareth and Iris yet?" Martina asked.

"No. I'm a little afraid to. It'll be so disruptive. On the other hand, Iris will have her mother back. That might be harder than not having her, though."

"And how is our Clara? What happened to her? How does she look?"

"Well, she looks destroyed, like she's been through a war. She wouldn't go into all the grim details with me, though. When I asked for specifics, she went quiet. Like she froze. But talking with her for hours made me realize that she isn't completely defeated. The spirit of Clara is still there. Buried, maybe. But I caught glimpses of the old Clara. She has such resilience."

"Tell me everything you found out!"

Blanca told her everything she had learned, from the abduction to Musa saving her from the man who held her captive and tortured her.

"How did Clara get away?"

"That is where Musa comes into it. Musa had decided to rob the man. He was going to steal just one expensive item to pay some of his bills — something that the man might not miss right away. He knew that the man was evil, but he had no idea just *how* evil, until he found Clara tied up in the dark." Blanca chose not to tell Martina about Clara's missing eye and fingers. She would see for herself soon enough.

"And did the abductor ever come after her? Didn't he look for her?"

"No. His house burned to the ground shortly after. He was inside. He burned to death. He had lots of enemies. They found the body."

"But all those years. Why didn't she let us know she was alive?" Martina questioned.

"It's complicated. And she lost her mind for a while. She forgot who she was, where she came from. Forgot Iris. Forgot me. But now she's back, and that's all that matters."

"She lost her mind for a while? But she must have got it back and then still the silence. Clearly she had all her wits when she wrote that opera."

"Martina, we might be twins, but that doesn't mean that I know everything that goes through her head. If I did, I'd be the composer."

"True. But still, Blanca. Eight years!"

"Shame. I think it was shame. She wanted to be remembered for what she was and not what she's become. All I know is that I would have made a different choice. But I can't judge her. I made some bad choices, too. The cutting …"

Then Blanca tried to explain how *she* felt. How it was no longer a question of Clara and her completing each other. They had grown individually, and separately, but not apart.

"Does that make sense? Can you understand that?"

"Only if I put myself in your shoes and imagine what it means to be a twin." Martina thought of the twins Helen and Clytemnestra. Blanca was set to play both roles as the two characters were never on stage together, until the end. At the end of this opera, Troy is rebuilt as Rome, the twins are reunited, and Clytemnestra lives on. How would she possibly do the final scene with only one opera diva? Who could be the second voice in the shared duet, an aria that rivalled the "Flower Duet" from *Lakmé*? Somehow, Clara had to do one more opera and come back to the stage, if only to play Helen after the ravages of Troy have left her burned and disfigured. Blanca could do all the rest. The beautiful Helen, the angry Clytemnestra, until Troy burns and the twins are free to reunite. Clara would only really be needed at the end, after she runs from the fires of a sacked Troy.

"And this boy? Themba, is it?"

"Yes. I'm so worried he'll be sent back. Clara loves him. He's like a son to her. She feels responsible for him. But you know, it isn't safe for albinos in South Africa. Although I hear Tanzania is even worse."

"That's it. I'm never going to buy coffee from Tanzania again." Martina paused, then asked, "So he sings, you say?"

"Themba? Yes, I told you, like Pavarotti. You don't expect it because he's so young and thin."

"Okay. Leave it to me. We can get him a student visa to study music at the Universität der Künste Berlin, where my father taught. Then I will have him apprentice with the Punkarie, and by then, we can apply for citizenship. Him, at least, I can take care of. The rest I'll leave up to my father. He's better with political red tape and paperwork."

"It helps that your father's a baron!"

"It helps that he is rich. *And* that he was a much-loved professor." She paused. "So, this boy, he can really sing like Pavarotti?"

"Trust me. He could be a star."

Aeneas was cast!

♦ ♦ ♦

Gareth held the phone to his ear, not quite believing what Blanca was saying. Clara found? After all these years.

"I don't think that Iris should be surprised, Blanca. I do think she has to be prepared for this. She hates surprises and change."

Gareth was sure about that. All through her years, until now, the very worst thing that could happen on Iris's birthday was for her to be surprised with a party. She wanted to know what flavour the cake would be, who would be attending, whether the gifts would be opened before or after cake. Gareth suspected that she would have preferred that the birthday presents were labelled so that there would be no surprises when she opened them. If a birthday could stress his daughter out that much, he could not imagine what a surprise call or visit from her missing mother might do.

"Whatever you think is best," Blanca agreed.

"All those years and she didn't try to find her daughter. Why didn't she try to contact me? How did she explain that?"

"Gareth, she's broken. She thought she'd be rejected by all of us."

"Oh, come on! Did she think that her family only loved her because of how she looks? She left her daughter without a mother!"

"She wasn't just broken physically. Her abductor broke her spirit, her soul. In some parts of Africa, they believe that albinos don't have souls, and by the time she was rescued, she thought that maybe she really didn't have one anymore. Mostly she was worried that she'd frighten Iris. She wanted her daughter to remember her as a beautiful mother and not as a hideous monster."

"How bad is it?" Gareth asked. He could feel that his breath was uneven. He tried to exhale slowly, the way he did when he was blowing the orb for a glass eye, to keep his voice steady and even.

"It's bad. She … she doesn't look the way you remember her at all. They cut off pieces of her. Entire fingers. She has scars. Her appearance will disturb you. And Iris."

"Email me a picture of her first. No surprises. Understand?"

Blanca waited for more, but Gareth seemed distant and cut off. His curtness indicated that he was finished with the conversation. Blanca was well aware that Gareth had doubted that Clara would ever be found. The news must have been shocking to the man who had recently declared his wife dead *in absentia*.

"And how are *you* with all of this?"

"Blanca, it has been a difficult time, to say the least. My wedding was ruined, my baby is probably clinically blind, my daughter tried to kill herself … and all of this right after my brother's funeral! I haven't even properly mourned Tristan because it's been a constant whirlwind of destruction all around me. So yeah, something that should give me immense joy just brings me more stress," he said impulsively. Then he quickly added, "I am really, really sorry to say that. I am happy and relieved that Clara's been found." He paused. "And did you tell her about Sabine?"

"No. Not really. Sort of."

"Sort of?"

"Only that she was wonderful with Iris."

"You didn't mention Fritzi? Or the new baby? Why, Blanca, why?"

"It wasn't time yet."

Even though Clara had asked Blanca not to tell Gareth about Musa, Blanca knew that Gareth needed to know. She hoped that in breaking her word to her sister, she might bring Gareth a little ease. She crossed her fingers behind her back, a practice she had started as a young girl. The need for survival in a world that was so often cruel allowed for superstitious loopholes in Blanca's mind.

"Gareth, there is something else. She loves another man. I mean, I think she always loved you. But now, you need to know that there is another man."

"Oh. Okay." His voice sounded flat. "Of course."

"She married him."

It was a strange and uncontrollable laugh that escaped Gareth. Not a laugh of joy or relief. It was the laugh of someone who found something unbearably funny and ironic at the same time. A laugh of incredulity.

"Oh God, that is rich. You know, we aren't divorced, so I'm not sure how that could even happen!"

"He's Zulu. The culture is polygamous, although Clara is *his* only wife. His brother already had three wives."

"Is that why he married her, then? To try to catch up to his brother?" Gareth's voice held a sneer, the kind of tone one employs to cover a pain one no longer has a right to claim.

"No. It was decided amongst the community. In order to keep Clara safe, it was best that she married into the family. That way she could stay in the *kraal* safely."

"The *kraal*?" Gareth asked. "What the fuck is a *kraal*?"

"It's like a communal farm. A contained community. At least that's what I'm guessing. Children, wives, all together."

"I see. So, Clara chose to say at this *kraal* instead of insisting that she come home to her child and her husband? God, Blanca, she didn't even try to contact us!"

"She was in shock, Gareth. What don't you get? She didn't know who the fuck she was!"

"I see. But eventually she did know, didn't she?" Gareth persisted.

"Yes, but by then she had married Musa. And he came to love her very much."

"So, then, he didn't love her when they first got married?"

"God, I don't know," Blanca sighed. Keeping calm, validating Gareth's feelings, and manoeuvring through the verbal minefield was getting exhausting. "Look, it was agreed that she would be protected within the *kraal* as long as she stayed there and cared for the headman's son. Themba, his name is Themba, and he's lovely."

"Why didn't this *headman* raise his own son?" Gareth questioned. For him the story seemed more and more implausible.

"Because Themba's an albino and his mother rejected him. He could have been abducted, killed, or mutilated at any moment. Or his mother could choose to leave him on a hill to be eaten by hyenas. Why can't you understand this, Gareth? We are just not liked! There are places in this world where we are hunted! It was stupid that we sang there years ago. And Clara suffered for it. She suffered for being who and what we are. She was kept there to protect her. Marriage was the only way. And then after they were married, they grew to love each other."

By now Blanca was yelling her explanations. It was an onslaught that was fired at Gareth with many sharp arrows of information attacking him. He felt the prick of truth pierce his body, strike at his heart. Gareth was finding it harder and harder to swallow his pain, let alone swallow the saliva building in his mouth. The only way to combat pain was to be on the attack.

"I waited for her. For a long time. Do you know how hard it was to have her declared dead *in absentia*? Any idea? And now she's married? Wow, just wow! Maybe she disappeared, but she erased me. And our daughter."

"Stop it right now. I will not have you steal away my joy of finding my sister!" Blanca yelled at him. "You don't get to do that!"

"That's not my intent. But you do need to understand just how fucking hard this will be for Iris. Let alone Sabine. And you more than anyone should be empathetic to her, considering ..."

Blanca knew she needed to ask. She felt a strange responsibility to the new baby. She thought about how red and helpless it had looked. She should have asked about the baby at the start of the conversation; she realized this after the fact.

"And little Frieda? She's home?"

"No. Not yet. Soon. I didn't think she'd live, but she's got more determination than anyone I've met. The kids have seen her at the hospital. Iris loves her desperately. Max thinks she's a toy. And she seems to react to our shadows when we approach, so we know she has some sight. You know, Sabine always believed she would live. She has twice the belief I've ever had."

Yes, Sabine. How would she react to the news? Gareth did not look forward to telling her. Of course no one wanted Clara dead, but it was going to be a shock to Sabine.

"And do you still want to be with Sabine, now that Clara is back?"

"What the fuck, Blanca! I think it's time to hang up now!"

Blanca had wanted to broach the subject of the eye. She thought her moment to ask might have passed. She should have asked him about it when Gareth still sounded cold and aloof. Now, in his distress, it seemed less than the optimal moment.

"She was tortured, Gareth. Terribly. The man who tortured her stole her to make money; told everyone she was worth more because she was a *foreign* albino. She's missing three fingers, in total. Her eye was cut out of her face. She wears an eye patch to cover it. Just try to imagine what she has gone through. It took her three or four years to even remember who she was. I suspect she had a kind of dissociative amnesia caused by the trauma. By the time she started to remember fragments of her past, she was someone else."

"Do you know what he did to her? Exactly? How he kept her? How he treated her?"

"No. Just vaguely. She tries to talk then goes silent, as though she's still in shock."

Gareth felt his eyes watering. Poor Clara. If he hadn't encouraged her to go on the concert tour in the first place ...

"Tell her ... tell her that she needs to come here. I will make the most perfect glass eye for her, here in her old home." Here he paused for what seemed an infinity all wrapped up in a few seconds. "Tell her that it will be the most beautiful eye I have ever made. Tell her that."

He hung up. He couldn't move, couldn't think, could barely breathe. Only the sound of the door opening brought him back to his present world.

"You were on the phone a long time. You'll be late for work! Who were you talking to?" Sabine asked, calling out from the bedroom.

But when she came into the living room, when she saw his face, she knew.

"They found her. *Richtig? Mein Gott!* They found Clara."

♦ ♦ ♦

Esther sat between her girls, Blanca to the left, Clara to the right. *Her girls.* She felt her double strand of pearls at her neck, believing that as long as she wore them, the girls would always be safe and that she would never lose them again.

It was to be their last dinner in Paris before heading back to Berlin, where plans for the future were already in the works. Musa, Themba, Clara, and Esther would stay in Friedrich's apartment in Berlin for the time being. Rehearsals for *The Lost Queen: The True Abduction of Helen* would commence, and during that time, they would get through the waiting period for Gareth and Clara's divorce. Musa and Clara would properly wed in order to legitimize their marriage. Once that was done, Musa and Clara would eventually go to Ontario, where they would live with Hilda so Musa could work on Karl's farm. Musa would surely save Karl a fortune on vet bills and in return have the thing most Zulu men prized — the company of cattle.

"I do not want the company of cattle! What about me? Will I have to go and work on a farm, too?" Themba asked.

Blanca was very aware that Themba had set destiny on its course when he first stole Clara's opera. There was more to it than a desire for them to be found. Themba was sending up a flare, wanting to be rescued and delivered into the world of music.

Blanca suggested to him, "If you feel you are old enough, and if you feel you would like this, then you can live in Berlin. You can go to university to study music. And you can think of me as a replacement for Clara when she is away. I can step in as your *umama*. And your first *umama*, Miss Clara, will be back every year to do one opera."

Esther smiled at the boy. How young, yet capable, he seemed! She remembered how eager Clara and Blanca were to learn at his age. How she had helped to shape and form their voices, their unique sound. And she remembered being his age and being separated from her own family.

"I promise, I will be back every year with either a new opera, or to sing, or just to visit you. And you can come to Canada, too, to visit. You can come for the summers, when you aren't at school or working for the opera company," Clara soothed the boy, speaking to him partly in his native Zulu. "It is the only way," she continued in English. "Even though we think of you as our son, the authorities do not, and so, if you want to stay someplace safe, this is the best option."

Bözsi and Henri arrived late for the farewell party. Esther was aware of the little gestures shared between them, indicating their private intimacy. *Well*, she thought, *they all got what they wanted in the end.* She had her girls back, and Bözsi had her great love returned.

"Can he still … you know?" Esther asked Bözsi quietly, in private.

"Yes. The apparatus appears to be working. You know, sometimes with some help from a little blue pill."

"Was it all worth it, Bözsi? He's almost eighty. What if he only lasts a year or two?" Esther questioned.

"If it was only for one day, Esther, it would be more than worth it! Even if it was only for one hour."

Esther wanted to believe that love was still possible, that her sister knew what she was doing, and that sorrow would not find her too soon.

"That is very romantic. But perhaps you should keep the Bainbridge Avenue apartment just in case? As insurance."

"When you go to the circus, isn't it more exciting to see a trapeze artist or a tightrope-walker who doesn't have a net to catch him? Besides, I already called them at the Bainbridge Apartments. They are shipping my personal items and getting rid of the rest, so there is no need for you to go back there, either." Bözsi clapped her hands twice. "You see? All done. I have taken care of everything!"

"But where will I go after we do the opera? I won't have a home! And what about my things?"

"I have arranged for them to be shipped to Martina."

"But I don't live there!"

"Oh, don't be a silly goose! How can you go back to the Bronx after you've been to Gay Pareeeeee!" Bözsi laughed. "I think, little sister, that your adventure is not over. Not yet."

Younis looked at the gathering. People he hadn't even known three weeks earlier were now gathered in his apartment, sharing as though they were family. Some would be leaving, others would be staying. And some were newly found. He knew that he was an unexpected stranger who had come into their lives to change their destinies. But did the experience change his life in any way?

"We should call Jack!" Bözsi called out. "He should be a part of this! Let's open champagne, call him, and then have a toast to finding Clara! Henri, where is the champagne?"

"It is here, my darling," Henri responded to her. He had brought a fine bottle of Dom and was ready to pop the cork on the champagne.

"Oh, I don't know," Younis stalled. "Jack hasn't talked to me since the night he called to say he was staying in Canada."

"Oh, go on! You know you want to!" Bözsi encouraged.

Younis let himself be persuaded. After all, it had been Jack with his obsession over the Fisher equation that had brought him into all their lives. He should be called since he was a big part of finding Clara. Besides, Younis could always say it was their idea and not his.

"Hello?"

"Jack, we are all here. Esther, Bözsi, Blanca, Clara ..."

"Oh, Younis. Thank you for calling. How did you know that my father just died?"

"I didn't know, Jack. I just wanted to hear your voice, that's why I called. Oh, Jack, I'm so, so sorry."

TWENTY-THREE

"JUST LOOK AT THAT FAT BIRD!"

Hilda had thought how strange it was that the last dying words in movies and in books always held some importance. Words of love, wisdom, or forgiveness are whispered from a fictional character's mouth as he struggles to pass a final message, brimming with meaning, to a loved one. For John, any words of love or forgiveness, any apologies were mumbled before his end, spoken to Hilda only when forgetfulness had taken over and John couldn't remember how important it once had been to be right.

It had been a sunny morning, that last day. One that held the winter's false promise of an early spring. The cold had abated, and from the kitchen, an uneven dripping sound of melting icicles could be heard coming from the roof outside. Hilda cracked the window, just a little, to let in some fresh air. The kitchen soon filled with the smell of thawing earth and brewing coffee. Hilda knew that the false spring was just a tease, but still she inhaled it.

Once John was settled with his morning paper and coffee, she slipped on her boots and jacket and went outside to refill the bird feeder. She put some grease on the pole to stop the squirrels from getting into the feeder. When she looked back at the house, she saw John watching her. She waved at him, and he waved back. It was at that moment that Hilda thought, *Yes, why not get a new dog. A puppy might bring some life and joy into the house. A puppy is what we need.*

Back inside, Hilda poured herself a coffee and spooned a little unpasteurized cream on top.

She was about to tell John that they should look into getting a puppy and that Karl, *remember the farmer down the road?* had a bitch about to have litter, when he interrupted her thoughts by saying, "Hilda, just look at that fat bird!"

Hilda put down her coffee and looked out the window. Indeed, there was a fat bird at the feeder, feasting away on the fresh seeds. Its feathers were a brilliant red against the blue-sky background. It was possibly the fattest cardinal Hilda had ever seen.

"Oh, he is a fat one, John!" She had laughed.

But John didn't answer, and when Hilda turned from the window, John was still there, at the table, head down, arms loose at his side, his coffee cup, still half full and warm, just beyond his reach.

"John?" she repeated.

But she knew. She had been warned that his next stroke would kill him.

♦ ♦ ♦

When Jack got off the phone with Younis, he found his mother sitting in the dark of her study. She had taken out the seldom-drunk Scotch, poured herself a small serving, and stared ahead at all her little brown bottles.

"Mom? Are you okay?"

Hilda gave her son a reassuring nod and gestured for him to sit. There was already a second glass out, just in case he wanted to join her.

"He liked to read the paper and have his coffee in the kitchen. I suppose that there couldn't be a better death for him."

"Much better than dying in a hospital bed with tubes and needles jabbing into him," Jack agreed. It was clear that the reality hadn't settled in yet, that mourning had not yet gripped Jack.

Hilda lifted her glass. "Here's to your dad. To John. Safe travels."

Jack lifted his glass, and they clinked.

"And here's to us for doing what was right by him."

Hilda knew, for her, that would be it. She would not attend a memorial or funeral service. Those arrangements would be in Jean's hands, and she would not step on her grief.

"Now, what is left for you to do?" she asked her son.

"Well, it's no secret that Jean will want to sell the house, so likely that part will be cleared up quickly." Jack laughed in spite himself. "The girls will do okay with half the house, so I guess they'll stop pestering you to sell yours. Who would have thought that, by leaving me out of the will, Dad would inadvertently save your house!"

Hilda raised her glass in a second toast.

"What are we toasting to now?"

"To the house! And to you having this house one day. You and Iris. Why not? The girls and their children have been taken care of by your father. So, I'll take care of you and your daughter."

There, she said it. It was out in the open.

"She may well be my biological daughter, and God knows I do love her, but she is Gareth's daughter, through and through."

"*Ja*, of course. And you are an important godfather. But I am still her grandmother."

They clinked their glasses, then sat in quiet for a while, until Hilda interrupted any sad or regretful memory with a change of subject.

"Now Jack, perhaps you can tell me who you really spent Christmas with, and who that was you just called."

"Just a friend. He called earlier, and I told him I'd call him back because, you know, we had to deal with the body first."

"Poor Jean. It has all been very hard for her."

"Yes, but we did the right thing, Mom."

"We did. In life there are always second chances, for everything, even love." Hilda paused and looked at Jack as though she were making a point. "The exception is how you are born and how you die. We have no say over how we are born, but we only get one shot at dying. And no one has the right to fuck that up because we can only die once."

Hilda sipped again. The alcohol burned down her throat. "So? I can't imagine that you would talk to someone today, with everything going on, unless he was very, very important."

Jack put down his glass and looked directly at his mother with that okay-you're-right expression. "Okay, he wants to come here. To be supportive. But I hardly know him, and I think it's just too much, too soon."

Hilda took a big last sip. Emptied the glass in a gulp.

"Love is like having a baby. There is never a convenient time."

"I didn't say I loved him. He's a friend. A *new* friend, at that. He's the one who helped find Clara."

"Oh! *Ja!* The professor! That guy? So he's not old and dusty, with a great gnarly beard?"

Jack chuckled. "No, Mom. Not at all."

Hilda got up. Her body felt stiff suddenly. *My knees sound like the door hinges of a rusty car,* she thought.

"I'm going to bed. You have a lot on your plate between your father's estate, dealing with Jean, and then also worrying about how Iris will respond to Clara. You keep so many secrets, but it is always good to have *one* person in the world you can talk to. You know, I won't be around forever."

"Oh, please, Mom. Dad only just died today, let's not start fantasizing about your death!"

"I'm just saying ... it doesn't have to be love. But if he is someone you can talk to, call him back." She kissed the top of his head. "Good night, sweetheart."

"Mom?"

"*Ja?*"

"I love you, Mom."

Once Hilda was upstairs, Jack went into his travel bag and pulled out Tristan's video diary. He hadn't watched it for over a month. It had sat, ignored but not forgotten, in his bag.

"Hey, Jack, I think this going to be my last entry. I'm getting too thin and I'd rather you remember me at my prettiest! I just wanted to say that I think you may have loved me most, but maybe I was not your grand passion. Not your soulmate. God, you hated that term! Ha ha. But I want you to have that. A grand love. Go and have your adventures and travel, but maybe stop just long enough to have love. Maybe find someone who can deal with your absences better than I could." Tristan paused here. Jack wasn't sure if he was trying to find the strength to continue or if he was mentally struggling for his next words. "I'll be going into Casey House soon. You know, Casey House is like a roach motel — you check in, but you never check out." And then there was a long pause. "And thank you for all the time we had. You made my life worth it. Now, go and live. Live for us both. I love you."

"I love you too, Trist. And thank you."

Jack put the bottle of single malt back into his mom's drawer in her study. He locked the front door and turned off the lights in the hallway. Then he picked up the phone. It would be four in the morning in Paris. But somehow Jack knew that Younis wouldn't mind.

"*Oui?*"

"Okay."

"Okay?" Younis questioned, his voice thick with sleep. "Okay what?"

"Okay, come to Canada. Just for the funeral."

"Okay," Younis agreed.

TWENTY-FOUR

WHEN IRIS AND GARETH FINALLY arrived at the loft in Berlin, it was Martina who answered the door. She seemed full of life, brimming with enthusiasm. Gareth had been in her company enough times to know that her newly found *esprit* probably had more to do with the fact that she was in rehearsals and less to do with the reacquainting of Clara with Iris.

"Your mother has taken back to the stage like she was riding a bicycle! Nothing too strenuous, though, don't worry," Martina announced to Iris.

"She can't ride a bike, Martina. She could never see well enough to learn," Gareth corrected.

Iris could hear that her father sounded as nervous as she felt. What must it be like to see someone you were in love with after all these years? And did he feel betrayed that she had met another man and fallen in love? Of course, her father had fallen in love with Sabine, but Iris had always held on to the hope that, if ever her mother were found, her parents would realize the love that they had always shared and together they would live happily ever after.

But that was just a dream. *Wake up, Sleeping Beauty, the whole world changed while you were dreaming!*

"Iris."

Her mother's voice was soft, a breeze reaching her from what seemed a far-off place. Iris saw how much smaller she seemed than her twin, who stood beside her, holding her hand. Iris stared, saying nothing. The black eye patch stood out in contrast to her mother's bleached skin. It looked too large for her mother's face. Iris noted the long scar running from her mother's browbone to her chin. Then, she couldn't help herself, she saw the missing fingers — stumps where tapered digits must have been. It was hard to imagine that she was ever beautiful. Hard to imagine that she was *identical* to her aunt who always seemed like some magical, otherworldly spirit. A white queen, a fairy, a sprite. Her aunt was Ariel from *The Tempest*. She was studying Shakespeare in school, but her mother wouldn't know that. Her mother knew nothing about her.

"Go on, give your mother a big hug!" Martina encouraged.

"It's fine, Martina. In her own time," Gareth cautioned.

It was only then that Clara refocused the gaze of her one eye and looked at Gareth. Here stood the man she had loved, even when they were children. The man who knew secrets that weren't even shared with Musa.

"Gareth," she whispered.

"I think it is time for coffee and cake. The others will join us later." Martina fell back on her usual custom of providing food whenever there was any moment of discomfort. A bad review meant a Bundt pound cake, whereas a good review meant a layered cake. A breakup called for a plain cheesecake, while a new love meant something with custard and fruit. Today's fallback dessert was a thin chocolate hazelnut cake, not iced but rather dusted with powdered sugar and a few raspberries on the side. Chocolate and hazelnuts, Iris's favourites, because the Punk Baroness knew it might be a difficult day for Iris. No, she wasn't as fierce as she looked.

"Please take off your eye patch?" Iris asked.

"Oh, no. No, I can't do that." Clara answered her daughter, her voice not more than a raspy whisper.

"Take it off! Now! Please!" Iris repeated, demanding. "What are you hiding?"

"It is too terrible. Really. It's better with the patch. It really is."

It wasn't curiosity. Iris needed to know how awful it was so that she could understand why her mother hadn't found her way back to her; so she could understand why her mother had abandoned her. She needed to see the worst just so that she could excuse her.

Iris walked toward her mother, the woman who had not held her, not touched her, not spoken to her, since she was four. Clara opened hers arms to her, defenceless. Iris hesitated, staring at her mother's face, looking for what she had remembered from childhood. It was then that Iris reached up, pulled the patch until the elastic snapped and broke, leaving Clara's flesh-healed wound exposed. Lash-less lids, fused together and sunken into a violent, pink abyss where her eye had once been. But it was only a flash because Clara quickly crumpled, as though she were the Wicked Witch of the West, doused with water. Her hands covered her eyes as she fell, in panicked tears, to the floor. Blanca squatted beside her, tried to comfort her twin.

"No! No! No!" Clara cried out.

Iris looked down to where the twins held hands. It was only then that she noticed that the scars on Blanca's arms were the echoed markings of the scars on her mother's arms.

"*Umama! Umama!*" a voice called out from behind them.

A beautiful young man, slightly older than Iris, ran in and rushed to Clara. He lifted her up, held her.

"Who are you?" Iris asked.

"I am her son, Themba."

Her son? How was that possible? He was older than she was! Who was he, really? An easy replacement, that's who he was! Iris hated him on sight. Yes, he was attractive but Iris knew that the Devil could assume a pleasing shape.

Clara seemed to relax into Themba's strong arms. Iris noted how tall he was. How he looked more like a statue than a person. He was perfect. Handsome, caring, well behaved. Of course her mother stayed. Of course she picked him over her. He was the better, easier child.

"I want to go home. Now!" Iris demanded.

Within ten minutes they were back on the Autobahn, making good time.

"What happened?" Musa asked. "Why did they leave?"

"Don't ask," Blanca replied. "It wasn't good."

"Not her fault. Not her fault," Clara repeated over and again. "Not her fault. My fault. My fault. My fault."

Martina put the cake and coffee out anyhow. No matter that there was upset, people still had to eat.

"The children here don't have respect. In my home, a child would never—" Musa began.

"You're not in your home now," Themba reminded Musa. It was perhaps the first time he had ever contradicted his uncle. "You will have to adapt. I felt as sad for Iris as I did for *Umama*. It is very difficult. She was full of pain."

Martina smiled at the boy. He was like no one she had ever met. So gentle, so polite, so wise. She had always believed that she didn't have a maternal bone in her body, but now she felt that she could, perhaps, love this boy. Be both a mother and a mentor to him. She thought that, if Blanca was willing, she would like to ask him to live with them once Musa and Clara went to Canada. They could move into the big apartment together, take over Friedrich's place, and Esther could live in their smaller loft above the Punkarie.

"Where is Esther? I told her to come, too," Martina inquired.

"Oh, she went for coffee with a handsome man," Musa informed. "She seemed very pleased to see him."

"An *older* man," Themba added.

"Oh. I see," Martina replied. She hadn't been informed that her father was coming into town.

♦ ♦ ♦

Sabine snuggled into Gareth, secretly relieved that he hadn't stayed overnight in Berlin, that he had made the long drive home. She had tortured herself all night, playing and replaying scenarios in her head. A vulnerable woman was always more attractive to men. Clara he could heal and save. Then together they could imagine what their life would have been if she hadn't been abducted. And that would lead to what, exactly? How would she cope as a single mother of two because surely Clara would take Iris away from her. By the time Gareth returned, she was spiralling, clearly agitated by her own imaginings.

Once Iris went to bed, they poured a brandy and curled into each other.

"How bad was it?"

"Iris was very upset. It will take time for her to forgive Clara. And I was numb. It was like I didn't recognize her. As if the Clara I once knew was taken off in bits and pieces and someone was made to fit her body. Like a blackboard was erased and new writing was put on top."

"Will you make her an eye?"

"Yes. It's the one thing I can give her."

"But you didn't talk to her? Didn't make plans?"

"No. I'll make the eye here in my oculary. So, she will have to come here."

Gareth didn't tell Sabine that he thought Clara was pregnant. Instead, he took a handful of Sabine's long hair, brought it to his face, and breathed it in.

"Marry me, Sabine. Please marry me."

"Gareth, every time we try this, it's a fiasco."

"I love you, Sabine."

"I love you, too. But I prefer that you come home to me because you want to, not because you are contractually obligated to."

"We have two children together."

Gareth reached for the brandy, had a sip, and then kissed her so that the brandy touched her lips.

"You would be the children's father whether we married or not."

"Yes, but you know, if you marry me, then our kids won't be bastards!"

Sabine started to laugh, throaty and unexpected.

"It makes sense for the long term, really," said Gareth. "You know, not to have bastards for children!"

"*Ach*, so now you are thinking long term?"

"Yes. And my long term includes you. So, Sabine, I'll ask you again. Will you marry me?"

"*Ja, ja.* Okay. If you put it that way. Now let's fuck to seal the deal!"

"It's okay? Not too soon after the hospital?"

"It's been eight weeks!"

As she moved over him, her body on top of his, leading the way, her skin warm on his, his breath in her ear, she knew for the first time that the ghost of Clara was no longer in the room.

♦ ♦ ♦

Sabine jumped at the sound of a knock at the door. It was a delivery. Something for the oculary. When the second knock came,

Sabine moved to the door, assuming it was the delivery person, back for a needed signature.

"*Ja, ja! Ich komme*," she called out.

Beside the Punk Baroness stood Clara, her white woollen coat in stark contrast to Martina's black leather trench coat. Sabine saw the scar down her face, the eye patch over one eye, and the fear in the other.

"Clara," Sabine whispered, unprepared for the sight of her.

"Gareth is expecting us," Martina informed. "But Clara wanted to see you first, and I thought perhaps you and I could have coffee and wait together until he has had a look at the eye."

Sabine's mouth went dry. Here was the woman who never returned for Iris. Here was the woman who broke Gareth's heart. Here was the woman who always breezed back and caused a disturbance in Sabine's life. It had happened once before, and that time it was Clara who had won while Sabine was recast as a friend. Now, with two babies she shared with Gareth, here was Clara, returned like a phantom from the past. And yet, here was a broken woman. A shade, it seemed. A shadow of her former self. Thin, shaky, and timid.

"Come in. Come in. Gareth is down in his workspace. Well, I guess you know better than anyone where that is."

Clara's one good eye took in the apartment. This was the last home she had known before she was taken. This was the place she would have returned to, if she had returned. Sabine hadn't changed the apartment much, but still it wasn't as she had left it. There were changes. Small changes. The kind of changes a woman makes in an attempt to erase the previous woman.

When Clara took off her coat, Sabine saw the slight swell of her belly, a curve that was more prominent than it should have been because of the sharp angles of Clara's protruding hipbones. Sabine instinctively placed her hand on her own belly. In a perfect world, her baby would still be there, resting and growing inside of her. In a perfect world, she would be feeling the baby's movements as she turned and made adjustments. In a perfect world, she would be awoken in the night by her baby's kicks. Instead, her baby hardly knew her. She was cared for by a team of nurses and doctors around the clock. And although Sabine went to the hospital daily and could now feed the baby formula from a bottle, it was very different to the experience she'd had with Fritz. How he had seemed like a physical extension of her. His chubby face crying for the breast. His sleepy beauty as he became milk-drunk. Even though she had held Frieda, bare flesh to bare flesh, just a week ago, her connection still felt removed. Frieda had made sounds of annoyance as she was lifted and disturbed from her sleep. Sabine had held her tightly to her chest, reminding herself, *Yes, this is my baby. I have a baby. A baby girl. With Gareth.*

"I should go down," Clara stated.

"Yes. Gareth has gone ahead to prepare for you," Sabine replied. Why hadn't anyone told her that Clara was pregnant? Pregnant with someone other than Gareth. Sabine slowly exhaled. Yes, she would go to the hospital again today. She would hold her baby. Maybe today she would settle into her, know her smell, feel her warmth. Maybe today would be different.

Martina let go of Clara's arm and nodded to her, encouraging.

"I wanted to see you, too, Sabine. After."

Sabine stared at her. Clara didn't seem like a rival. She no longer seemed like a threat. Clara was a having a baby. Her own baby.

"Why do you want to see me?"

"To thank you. You did what I couldn't. For Iris. You were a good mother to her."

"Were?" Sabine asked. "What do you mean, were? Do you think I was just filling in for you and now I am to just go away? Do you think you can just take her?"

Clara wrapped her arms around her body, as though those bony limbs would protect her from Sabine's words.

"No. No. I didn't mean."

The Punk Baroness put a protective arm around Clara. How she wished Blanca had come. Blanca could be abrasive at times, but she also could smooth things over.

"Well, what do you mean? What are your intentions now that you're finally back?" Sabine persisted. "I've done my job, but ta-da! Here you are back! No, Clara, I am not a stand-in waiting for the leading actress to return. It doesn't work like that in the real world."

"Please, Sabine," Martina interjected.

"It's not like you didn't raise a boy while you were away. It's not like you aren't pregnant now!" Sabine's anger made way for frightened tears. She loved Iris as her daughter and could only hope to love Baby Frieda equally one day.

"Please. You are a wonderful mother. And you will always be. I just hope to get to know her. That one day … one day she will allow me to love her, too."

Sabine knew how Iris had behaved when she saw Clara. She knew that she had rejected Clara. It must have ripped Clara apart.

"You do have another baby coming. Don't you?"

"Yes, but that doesn't change how I feel about Iris."

"No. And I have another daughter, but that doesn't change how I feel about her either. Please don't take Iris away from me."

Sabine squared off, stared down at the shorter woman. Perhaps Iris didn't have her DNA, perhaps Iris never called her Mom, or Mama, or Mutti and perhaps Iris had always longed for Clara instead. But Sabine would never have abandoned her as Clara had. Never.

Martina smiled approvingly at Clara. "I think Gareth is waiting. Go on."

"Is Iris here?" Clara asked, straining to peer down the hall, hoping to catch a glimpse of her.

"No. She's at school."

And then small footsteps approached. Run, run, hop. Run, run, run, hop. The afternoon nap over, Fritz bounded into the living room, pausing hesitantly when he saw the company.

"Tante Blanca?" he asked his mother as he regarded the new visitor.

"*Nein*, Tante Clara!"

Fritz ran to Clara and hugged her. He didn't see her injuries or her trauma. She was his new *tante*, his aunt, and that was good enough for him!

"Oh my God! He looks just like Gareth!" Clara exclaimed.

"Yes. He is Gareth's mini clone!" Sabine paused before adding, "Unlike Iris, who doesn't look like him at all."

"No. She looks exactly like my mother. Same hair. Same cheeks and lips. She's just like my mother."

Once Clara was gone, Sabine shook her head in sadness and disbelief.

"What can I say, Martina? It is all too much. And you must know that Gareth isn't ..."

Martina put her finger to her lips. "Hush, Sabine. There is nothing you can say. Fate has been cruel." The Punk Baroness looked at Fritz. "But sometimes without the incomprehensible twists of fate, there is no spark for the future."

"My baby probably will be partially blind. Fated to live a life in shadows only."

"Your baby is alive. *Ja*? Against all odds."

"*Ja*." Sabine kissed the top Fritzi's head.

"Now, the great question is, do you have cake?"

"*Kuchen! Kuchen!*" Fritzi chanted, dancing all around the Punk Baroness.

♦ ♦ ♦

It was awkward. Silence where there had once been chatter, sadness where there had once been laughter, and wariness where there had once been familiarity.

Gareth wanted to lift her eye patch, as though it were a veil concealing the truth of a bride's expectant face. There would be such sacredness in the act, born of history and trust, betrayal and forgiveness. But for now he just looked into her good eye. Her untouched eye seemed to hold her hope, her sorrow, and all her experiences, unshared and secret. Gareth thought that if he could look deeply enough into her eye, he might know what had happened, might feel what she had felt, then he could understand her absence.

"It was good of Martina to drive you here. She must be busy with rehearsals now."

"Yes. She thought it was important. It *is* important."

"And how are the rehearsals? Is it strange to be performing again?"

"I thought so. It's not. It's strange. I thought singing ... on stage ... would be ... I don't know ... distant? It's not. You know?"

Clara fidgeted. Nothing seemed to have changed in Gareth's oculary. Same Bunsen burners, same tubes of glass, same instruments laid out in the same order. She had forgotten his workroom, his precise habits, his rituals of work, but now, seated as his patient, it all rushed back to her as though there had been no passage of time, no nightmare. It was all the same. The only thing that had changed was her.

"The stage. The only place I'm safe. When I'm on stage, I fold time. The bad part doesn't exist. It's outside the fold."

"That is how I feel when I am working, creating the perfect eye. Or painting. Though I haven't painted at all since you were taken.

Ah, Clara, only an artist can fully understand another artist. I do miss that." He smiled at her, a look of soft regret. "I miss our talks. I miss talking about creating, Clara."

"I know."

"And you are okay coming here? It must feel awkward."

"I was hoping to see Iris. To put things right. To try," Clara deflected.

"That will take time. It was very hard for her when you were away. And meeting Themba made it even worse for her. You were the longed-for mother and you were the mother to someone else. She is very hurt and betrayed." Gareth knew it was a harsh truth, but one he had to say in defence of Iris.

Clara folded her hands together, one covering the other, hiding the missing fingers. She had suffered, yes. She had also caused suffering.

"Tell me, Clara. Tell me what really happened to you. I am the one person who needs to know," Gareth urged her,

"I can't explain it. To anyone. Not even Musa knows everything."

"Then tell me. Tell me, Clara. Let me be the one person you trust. You know the process of making a glass eye. You were with me long enough. Everything you experience must be reflected in the eye. That is what makes it authentic. I learned from the best."

"Yes, Siegfried. And your daughter? She's named after him?" she replied, her voice soft as morning.

"She is. Her full name is Siegfried-Elaine, but we call her Frieda." He paused, stared hard at her face. How much older it seemed. How haggard. "Now, you tell me your story, and I will make you an eye that will keep your secrets safe. Forever."

Clara touched the space where her eye once was. She knew that the flesh had melded together in a hideous closing of the eye. When she put her fingers up to her missing eye, she could still feel the pain of when it was removed. She could only hope that Gareth's new eye would alleviate the memory. That her replacement eye would take away the psychic pain.

"When they do it ... when they remove a body part ... it is believed the more pain it causes us, the more powerful the magic. It's the worst during election years. They need a lot of albino magic."

"The magic?" Gareth asked her. It seemed unbelievable. His heart pounded loudly with anxiety. There was a woman he had once loved more than anything. A woman who had been his world. But she went missing. She was tortured.

"They think different body parts have different magic. For healing. For power. For wealth." She shook her head, felt her memories and thoughts shift in her brain. "A new country. Apartheid is over. All the talk of equality. But albinos disappear. They vanish from beds. They vanish at night. Nobody cares. Only sometimes the bodies are found. Sometimes dead. Sometimes mutilated. Usually discarded. Gone. The call us *veros*. They think we don't have souls."

"But who does this?"

"Whoever needs money. Our parts are worth a lot of money. As much as a hundred thousand U.S. dollars. If someone can harvest an albino, they convince people that they need our body parts. Our eyes can heal cataracts. Our hearts can heal heart failure. And our blood can bring power." Clara remembered the hushed whispers, the stories, the gossip. "They dig up fresh graves, too."

"And the man who took you? He used your fingers and eye for magic? He did what? Make potions or something?"

"Oh, no. He was just a supplier. The man who took me had been an interrogator. Before." She laughed wryly. "Well, that's just a nice word for torturer. Right? He'd worked for the C1 unit."

"The C1 unit?"

"An interrogation unit."

Gareth took one of Clara's hands in his. He ran a finger along where hers had once been. He didn't — he couldn't — protect her, but he could do this. He could listen.

"What was their purpose?"

"They'd kidnap people during apartheid. Anyone against apartheid. Anyone vocal. They tortured them till they changed their minds. If they didn't, they made them disappear."

Clara looked confused and tired. Gareth knew that he couldn't push her much further, but there were still unanswered questions, still parts that made no sense. Why would someone who had worked for the police start dealing in body parts?

"When apartheid ended, he didn't have a job. He went to the Truth and Reconciliation Commission. Confessed. Was pardoned. But still, you know ... he needed to make a living. He didn't like torturing me. He didn't hate it, either. It was just a job. A job. That's all. Supply and demand. And he had the stomach for it."

"That's horrific."

"Sometimes I heard him. On the phone. Convincing someone they needed my blood. Or something more. At first I listened as hard as I could. To prepare myself ... then I learned not to listen."

"And where did he keep you all this time?" Gareth's voice was barely a whisper; his words were becoming smaller and smaller.

"He kept me tied up. In the dark. A basement. Like a cold cellar. When he came downstairs, I never knew if he was going to feed me or hurt me." Clara rolled up her sleeves, exposing her many scars. "But that's not the worst part."

"What could possibly be worse?" Gareth stared in horror and disbelief.

Clara paused. She knew that it was overwhelming Gareth, and yet, she could feel the weight of secrecy lifting from her.

"He videotaped it." Her voice became monotone. "He had to prove how much pain I had when he, um, harvested me. The more pain, the more he could charge. The more pain, the more magic, he said. He said if I cried and showed the pain, it would be better. The fingers were bad, but the eye was unbearable. I screamed, but there was no one to hear my screams."

"How long did he keep you there?"

"Two years. Maybe more. I prayed to die. And then Musa broke in and saved me."

"He broke in to save you?"

"No." Clara smiled for the first time. "He broke in to rob him. He was going to take his money. His electronics. Anything he could quickly sell. He needed money. But he found me. So he took me. He took the man's most valuable possession."

Gareth could cry, but he knew that it would make a mockery of her suffering. He wanted to find a magic amulet in his workroom — a shard of glass, a perfect glass orb, perhaps — so they could go back in time just so he could say to her, *"Don't go, don't go, stay here, stay safe."*

"Then I met Themba. He didn't have a mother. He was so young. Only six or seven. I think he brought me back to life. And then I heard music. Singing. Every day outside Musa's home. So I started to sing back. And that was nice. Then memories started to come back. I remembered I could sing. I remembered a little girl."

"Iris? You remembered Iris?"

"I didn't know who she was. I just knew there was little girl. That maybe I loved her."

"So, you didn't remember anything, really. You didn't remember Iris. You didn't remember me? Our life together?"

"When parts of my body were taken from me, my memories were taken from me. Until I was empty. Then the only thing I remembered was fear."

Gareth could see all her memories in flashes and shadows reflected in her one good eye. He could not imagine how she had suffered. How lost she must have been. But now, she was found. She was home. And somehow, he would keep her safe.

"What was his name?"

"Whose name?" Clara asked.

"The man who tortured you. What was his name?"

"It doesn't matter. He's dead now." Clara shook her head. She knew his name but wouldn't say it. To give voice to his name would give him power. To remember his name would give him an existence in the afterlife. Only in silence does the monster sleep.

"And Musa? He treats you well? He's a good man?" Gareth asked.

"He's a good man. Without him I would have died. Without him, I would never have made the journey back home. Musa took me from darkness and brought me to light."

"And he loves you?"

"Yes, he loves me."

"And you love him?"

Clara's face betrayed her regret for only a moment.

"I understand," Gareth told her, squeezing her hand.

"You can't understand. You could never imagine it. That basement was dark. So dark. Too dark for even the angels to visit. Musa saved me. He loves me. I owe him my life."

Gareth stood, lifted her up into his arms, and held her closely. His eyes were red and irritated with burning sorrow.

"Forgive me," she said, her voice barely audible.

Gareth kissed the top of her head.

"No, forgive me. Forgive me for believing you were dead, forgive me for not finding you, forgive me for not holding on to you tightly enough."

He knew he could not be her husband now. Tragedy had changed their shared path. But he *could* make her the most perfect replacement eye. He would start creating it even before the eye surgeon opened her eye socket. He would put her story into her eye and there it would rest, alongside her courage, her love, and her soul.

"You understand that your eye will have to undergo surgery? The wound will have to be reopened. The flesh will have to be raw again. That you will need a conformer first before I can replace your eye. But for now, I can get started with the colours, choosing the glass. You should leave the operation until after you have your child."

"I know. It's okay. I trust you." She paused. "I am wearing a patch for the performance. It works. In context with the sacking of Troy."

"Of course it does." Gareth smiled at her. Here was a tortured woman, a wife, a mother, but mostly an artist.

She reached up and caught his teardrop on the tips of her remaining fingers, then, without thinking, touched her mouth, tasting the salt of his sadness.

"There is one more thing I never told you. About Iris," Clara said softly.

"It's okay. I know. But still, she's my daughter. I sang to your belly throughout the pregnancy, I caught her when she was born, and I was the one who handed her to you. I cut the umbilical cord, remember? I changed diapers and read bedtime stories. And I told her that her nightmares couldn't hurt her. Told her not to be afraid. She's my daughter and always will be. Just as Themba will always be your son."

"Yes. Thank you."

"Now, you have to take off your patch. Just for me. And I will start my measurements."

Clara froze. She couldn't bear to be seen without the patch. She shook her head.

"Clara, it has to be."

She nodded.

Clara and Gareth both understood that lifting her patch would be the most intimate moment the two would now ever share.

TWENTY-FIVE

HILDA COULD SMELL SPRING IN the air and, with that, the whiff of change. Soon she would be alone again, Younis and Jack were planning to return to Europe so that they could see the production of *The Lost Queen: The True Abduction of Helen* before it closed. The walls, the rooms, the stairs, and even the floorboards would hold their secrets in silence.

"I wish you could stay a while longer," Hilda suggested. "It has been so lovely having you here, even if you came for difficult circumstances."

"We really must get back before the opera closes. It's sad we won't be there for opening night, though."

"When is opening night?" Hilda asked.

"Tomorrow. Thursday. It's okay, the show is up for three weeks."

"Oh, everybody goes opening night! And then they go again for closing night. Going midway through the run is when the audience is needed most!" Younis contradicted Jack, but to Hilda, it seemed that the contradiction was meant to cajole.

Three weeks of having Younis as a guest and it seemed as though he had been there for much longer. He was at home in the kitchen, making dishes Hilda had never imagined, cleaning up as he went along. He would often bring her a cup of tea, aromatic with spice, and place it beside her without a word. And, Hilda noted, he always made his bed. His thoughtfulness was quiet, constant, without any showiness. *Easy to miss*, Hilda thought, hoping that Jack was aware of the small gestures Younis made daily.

"Before you go, I'd like you to come with me to Karl's to help me pick out a puppy. They are newborns, so I can't take it home for eight weeks. But since you are determined to leave, I would like to do this with you."

"Hilda, it's not only the opera we have to get back for. I also must get back to work. The university has been very accommodating," Younis reminded Hilda.

"Oh, don't worry about my mom. I'm sure Karl will keep her company!" Jack teased.

"We are only friends. I keep telling you this. Again and again. Do you have potatoes in your ears? We are friends only! And I like the cream!"

Younis was laughing. He liked the farm. He liked Hilda. And when Jack took him to Toronto for a few days, he liked it there, too. He thought that Canadians were strangely accepting of him. No one seemed to care that he was gay. No one even asked if he was Algerian. And now, to top it all off, they were going to go and choose a puppy!

"What will you call him?" Younis asked.

"Hundi. I call all my dogs Hundi."

"God, Mom. That is just so German. Why don't you wait till Iris gets here and let her name the dog?"

"I'm so happy she's spending time with me! But she's not coming till the summer!"

"In eight weeks! And you don't take the dog home for eight weeks!" Jack reminded.

"And what will I call him in the meantime, before I take him home?" Hilda inquired.

"Hmm ... how about, Hundi?" Younis joked. But it wasn't his laugh that caught Hilda's attention. It was the way Jack looked at him, and the ease that settled on his face.

Please, Jack, please. Stop punishing yourself. It is time to bite into life and taste a little bit of joy.

"Come on. Stop your goofing around. Hundi awaits us!" Hilda urged.

"She's just impatient to see the old farmer!" Jack said in a forced stage whisper.

TWENTY-SIX

IT WAS ALWAYS MARTINA'S FAVOURITE moment when the house was full of excited chatter and people checked their stubs to make sure that they had the right seats. Then, as curtain time approached, the sounds of the orchestra warming up and the tuning of the instruments. Martina loved the chaotic sounds the strings section made as violinists and cellists adjusted to one another. And the sounds of the woodwind and brass — noises that seemed to her to be between the sounds of lonely animals and musicians. She imagined that loons might sound like that, although Martina, the Punk Baroness, had never heard the call of a loon.

She was nervous. She hadn't mounted an original opera in years. Since Clara went missing, it had all been reimagined operas. *Carmen* with a man in the title role dressed like Sid Vicious. *Lakmé* with an Indian cast, the lyrics translated from French to Hindi. *Eugene Onegin*, but instead of a broken-hearted Tatiana finding contentment with a marriage to someone other than her beloved Onegin, she falls in love with a woman instead. All moderate successes, but nothing that stood out. Nothing that made headlines the way the production of *Antigone* had right after the Berlin Wall came down. Clara had been pregnant then, too, but barely showing. Martina shuddered with an overwhelming sense of déjà vu.

Musa wasn't entirely comfortable with his pregnant wife being on stage with her rounding belly for so many people to see, but Themba had once again urged him to adapt. *Themba.* How Musa loved him, as though he had always been his own son. Musa wished that Themba would have had similar interests to him; that he didn't have to strike out on his own in a field that seemed so foreign to him. Sometimes Themba seemed more like Clara than like his Zulu family. But there was much for Musa to look forward to. A new child on the way. A new life with the woman he loved. And a farm to manage somewhere in Canada.

Themba also knew that he was changing, becoming someone whom Musa would never fully understand. It saddened him, but when he turned his eyes from the sadness of change, all he could see was a golden path before him. Unimagined and attainable. *How a few short months can change a whole life*, he thought. As Themba applied his stage makeup, he regarded his reflection in the mirror. He was about to be a man, carving a destiny for himself, creating a new world just like his character, Aeneas. Themba started his vocal warmups, knowing he would only have to do them again after the intermission. He didn't appear at all until the very end.

To Esther, it all seemed surreal. A dream from which she would awaken, shaken by the harsh slap of reality. How foolish, knowing that she did not dream, and yet if she did dream, it would be exactly this: a stepping into the shoes of great and tragic Hecuba, into a world that extended only as far as the edge of the stage. But if she were to step past the edge, if she lost her balance, she would find Bözsi and Friedrich on the other side. Waiting. Listening. Expectant. Esther took a deep, sharp inhale and started her vocal warmups.

Blanca. Ready for her double role. Clytemnestra, the twin left behind, ruling without a husband, betrayed by the Greeks as much as the Trojans had been. Lonely, abandoned, judged and misaligned. Living in the shadow of her demigoddess sister. And then, her second role, as the abducted and desired Helen. Between acts, her makeup would change, making her more beautiful. Adding glamour so that the simple beauty of Clytemnestra would become the bewitching and manipulative beauty of Helen. And of the two twins, only Helen would wear that signature red lipstick of hers! Blanca started her vocal warmup.

Clara wasn't bothering to warm her voice. She knew that by the time Troy was burning, the opera would almost be over. Only then would she make her entrance, through a fog created from smoke machines, as though emerging from the fires themselves. She would be the Helen who had survived the flames, the one to return to Sparta to resume a life that seemed far away and foreign. That last entrance would be announced by that impossibly high note, which, Clara knew, only she could sing in that echoing and haunting way of hers. She would sing that note with all the pain, and all the hurt, and all the confusion she had endured when she had stepped from the fires of Hell to emerge as a damaged and mutilated woman, hoping for a second chance. That one note was for one person only. It was her only chance to appeal to her lost daughter.

As soon as the audience hushed and the lights dimmed, the first players took their places.

♦ ♦ ♦

Act One. Paris, a handsome German tenor with piercing blue eyes and dark hair, did not abduct Helen in this production. A hooded man carried her off instead. He was big, oafish, and because he never sang in this opera, was played by someone Martina had found in a boxing club. A heavyweight who could easily pick up Blanca and toss her over his shoulder.

With the abduction, the audience seemed spellbound, waiting for the retribution of Menelaus and Agamemnon.

Onstage, there was dancing, the stomping of feet, followed by choral music. Helen was still on the abductor's shoulder as the dancers encircled her. Was it a hallucination or a threat? But then Paris entered, and a choreographed fight ensued. Paris challenged a man almost double his size. He won and reached a hand out to Helen. They shared a ballad of love. Helen seemed under his spell, unable to remember her past.

The moment Hermione and Clytemnestra started to sing about the lost Helen, Iris sat up in her seat. Hermione was Helen's daughter; left behind in Sparta. Like Iris, Hermione felt motherless, but unlike Iris, Hermione had a voice and could sing her abandonment.

Clytemnestra sang along with her because she, too, had been abandoned. They were abandoned women alone, without even the distraction of men, who had all gone in search of Helen. Hermione was angry. A daughter who sang to Clytemnestra that she hated, hated, hated her mother. But, when Clytemnestra left the stage, Hermione, staring out to the audience, sang out her longing with the words, "Did I grow so heavy in your arms, you had to put me down? And now I am all alone, alone upon the ground. While memories of you soar above me. So far above they're out of reach ..."

Iris reached for Gareth's hand and squeezed it as hard as she could. She knew that it was really her up there. It was Iris, not Hermione, and that song was her song. She was Hermione. She was the weight that was suddenly too much for her mother to bear. And this singer, this young woman, this stranger, understood exactly how she felt!

◆ ◆ ◆

Act two. Helen was trapped, by fate, the gods, and love itself. She couldn't return to Sparta where she knew she belonged. Troy was losing ground, and because of her, the heroes were dying, one by one. Esther-as-Hecuba wept, her favourite sons, Paris and Hector, both dead now. Her song was syncopated, as though the music were racked with the gasps of a mother mourning. It was raspy and despairing. Hecuba asked for Death to take her, to be with those she has lost. For Esther, it was everyone from her past — her family, her way of life, her history, and even herself. For Esther, it was her memory of hiding from the Nazis as her family all died. It was Esther seeing her loves taken, her dreams stripped away.

Bözsi wept as she watched her sister sing. It was totally worth the train trip to Berlin, even if Henri had prior engagements and could not join her. She sat beside Friedrich, afraid he would see her tears. When the aria concluded, she saw that he, too, was crying. She leaned in and whispered, "You better marry her. She's not like me. She's not mistress material, you know."

Friedrich touched his breast pocket. "If she will have me."

Blanca was holding up through the demanding and gruelling performance. Playing two leads was a challenge, and she hadn't been before an audience in years. *Pace yourself,* she told herself. *Pace yourself. This is a marathon, not a sprint.*

◆ ◆ ◆

Act three. There was now a huge wooden horse on stage. The Greeks ran out of it and set Troy on fire. The stage was aflame from red backlights behind the scrim and moved with the rustling of red silks.

Where was Helen and why wasn't she in the arms of Menelaus? There, when she could get away, she didn't. She chose not to. In a moment's madness, she broke free of the Greeks and ran straight into the flames of Troy. It seemed that the fire consumed her. The stage lights flickered in orange and red. The smoke machine coughed up a wall of smoke. The stage silks wrapped around Blanca. She was now finished with the role of Helen; there was only the role of Clytemnestra for her to perform.

Finally, all the Trojans were dead or enslaved, except Themba-as-Aeneas. He was on what was the tower of Troy, but was now lit to be the prow of a boat on an ocean. The flames, red and orange strobe lights, were below him. He sailed above the destruction in order to create a new world. Rome! The gods entrusted him with the statues of Troy, and, for this, he was the only Trojan spared. His voice was pure, unwavering, sure. He was beautiful and looked like hope itself. The blue lights dimmed so all that was seen was the strobe of the fires. The sounds, the music, and the singing, even the footsteps, stilled until there was complete quiet.

The audience hesitated, unsure if it was over, if they should clap. And all Iris thought was that Themba was the most handsome boy she had ever seen.

Then there it was, seemingly out of nowhere. A sound like a wailing siren, breaking through the chaos. A reverberation that cut through everything. The orchestra was absolutely silent, and the note continued in purity and fierce defiance. It was music and scream combined! It pierced through the fire, cut through the dark. And there she was, dressed like a spring bride whose clothes had lost their sweetness in the flame. Clara-as-ravaged-Helen emerged from the fire itself. A goddess, immortal and alive. She had survived war. She had survived fire. She had survived love. She had scars, missing fingers, and an eye patch. Under the fitted patch, the wound cried out to Clara-as-Helen. She suddenly felt the phantom pain of when the eye was torn from its socket. She touched the patch hesitantly, pausing before she was to sing about love and sacrifice.

"Sacrifice is the currency of love," she sang, "You measure love by what you give away. And if they cannot love you in return, then love them till your last breath fades away."

And then Clara-as-Helen did something that was not rehearsed. Something so impetuous and inspired that it frightened even her. She stepped forward, found her light. Pause. Pause. Pause. Then she reached up and ripped off her eye patch, exposing the cave that was once an eye. She stared with defiance at the audience, at her past, at the whole world. No longer would she lie. No longer would she hide her story. She would not hide her pain. She was abducted. She was tortured. She was treated as though not human at all. She was kept in fear, in darkness. But fuck them all! Here she was now, unashamed and unapologetic! Silence. Silence. More silence. The orchestra had stopped playing. The audience sat frozen. And Clara stood, the broken demigoddess, the lost queen, re-found, before everyone.

"I lived. I lived! I walked through Hell. But you burned. You burned! Here, look at me! Look at me! Look! Here is the truth!"

She thought the words were only in her head, that there was only silence. But no! It was the cry of the banshees, the scream of the Valkyrie, the curse of the burning witches reverberating through the whole opera house.

The light seemed to hit her good eye and her vacant socket equally, until it seemed that all was in darkness but the eye that could see, and the place where an eye had once been. Clara winced in the brightening light. But she stayed there, the red and scarred evidence of her trauma unabashedly on display.

The lighting changed, became softer, more benign. Then Hermione and Clytemnestra returned to join Helen in what seemed to be a new world. Were they real or a dream? Was this the last vision Helen had before she died? But then the three joined hands. Hermione did a recitative about a mother returned as the lead-up to the finale — a duet where two equal and strong voices, sopranos who were not ingenues or love interests, but who were both strong queens, sang their victory of survival and reunion.

The cast was not prepared for the eruption from the audience. Every audience member was standing, feet stomping, hands clapping, voices shouting *Zugabe* and *encore*. What to sing? Which song to reprise? The cast tried to just bow and make an exit, but the audience would not allow them to do so. The demands intensified. White roses were tossed onto the stage. Berlin had their twins back; Bleach had returned and they could not love them enough! Martina knew that she had a hit once again.

Nobody noticed Esther as she walked to the piano and sat down in her unassuming way. Compared to the return of the twins, she was invisible, and that was just fine for her. Her arthritic fingers started with the first few notes of the song she had once taught the twins when they were young girls, wanting to sing an opera in English for a change. As soon as the music from *Dido and Aeneas* could be heard over the audience's demand for more, Blanca began and Clara soon joined in, their voices in unison sounding as one as they sang out "Dido's Lament."

When the repeated chorus of "Remember me" played through a second time, the entire cast joined them until the words were no longer a wish, no longer a request, but a resounding demand.

But Iris saw much more than the cast. She saw every woman who was ever lost. Centuries of women were there, all standing behind her mother. The music had found them.

And Iris understood that she was never forgotten.

ACKNOWLEDGEMENTS

MY DEEPEST THANKS TO MY acquisitions editor and publisher, Meghan Macdonald, and to the wonderful team at Dundurn for bringing this book into the world with such care. I am also grateful to Laura Boyle for creating a cover that so perfectly captures the spirit of the novel and to Eden Boudreau for marketing and publicity.

Heartfelt thanks go to my agent, Rob Firing, and the team at Transatlantic Literary Agency for their belief in this book. And gratitude to Jason Martin for championing this book.

This book has been fortunate in its editors. Rachel Spence, who first acquired *Two White Queens and the One-Eyed Jack*, provided the earliest overview and evaluation. Aaron Brown offered a proofread before submission. I was especially fortunate to have Shannon Whibbs as my editor once again. Shannon guided both novels, *Two White Queens and the One-Eyed Jack* and *The Lost Queen*, with precision and brilliance, and I am deeply grateful for her continued support, insight, and genius in shaping this novel, too. And a thank-you to my final editor and point person at Dundurn, Janna Green, who oversaw the production of the book.

I owe much to my first readers — John Ramsbottom, Ragini Kalil, Mark Kaczmarczyk, Gwynyth Walsh, Daniel Matmor, Peter Horton, Hal Eisen, and Matt Zimbel — who all gave their time to read and respond to an earlier, much longer draft. To Rod Carley, who encouraged me and believed in this book even in times of uncertainty, my heartfelt thanks. And to Craig Sheffer for taking every discouraged phone call, for believing in my talent all these many years, and for always having my back. Literally.

For cultural sensitivity, I am especially grateful to Karlie O'Donohoe (Thamsanqa) and Kati (Ruder) Preston, whose perspectives ensured authenticity and respect. And to my steadfast and wise cousin, Frauke Palleske: Thank you for reading with such care, ensuring that every German reference rang true. Your notes were simply incomparable.

To my readers, who wrote to me again and again asking when — or if — there would be a second book: Without your love for *Two White Queens and the One-Eyed Jack*, this book would never have come about.

Finally, to my daughter, Cavanagh Matmor — who always believes in me — my deepest love and gratitude.

POSTSCRIPT

I WOULD LIKE TO ENCOURAGE readers to learn about and support the Canadian not-for-profit Under the Same Sun, founded by Peter Ash, which advocates for and educates about those who are persecuted due to their albinism.

ABOUT THE AUTHOR

Photo by C.L. Matmor

HEIDI VON PALLESKE is a Toronto-based novelist, actress, poet, and screenwriter. Her novel *Two White Queens and the One-Eyed Jack* was a finalist for the Foreword INDIES Award for Best Literary Fiction. She is also the author of *They Don't Run Red Trains Anymore*, winner of the H.R. Percy Award. Best known to film audiences for her breakout role in David Cronenberg's *Dead Ringers*, Heidi has appeared in numerous film and television projects over her lengthy acting career. She divides her time between the shores of Lake Ontario and Nova Scotia's Northumberland Strait.